Delightful
Finds

Katherine McLellan

For my friend J.D.

Never once, during our long and loving friendship did I consider death to be part of it. It seems so final now; that you must lay and I must stand and carry the burden of being left behind for it all seems my fault. With fondest memories, this story is for you.

CONTENTS

CHAPTER 1

Washington, D.C.

Violent crimes gave no man rest. He drove the brand new Chevy truck into the swampy area just to the east of downtown Washington Saturday afternoon in the middle of a good SEC game. He set his DVR to record it so he could watch later. The dark gray truck had been his gift to himself for the promotion. New truck and an office with a locking door, it couldn't get any better. Or in the case of the woman who lay face down in the marsh, it couldn't get any worse.

He shut the door of the truck and stepped into mud. He was glad he'd thought ahead and wore some old walking boots. He ducked under the traditional yellow tape which marked off the crime scene area and walked to a group of officers who were milling about. As he walked he removed his badge and ID from a pocket of his dark cargo pants and held it up as he said, "Special Agent Lowery, who's in charge?"

"That would be you, Special Agent," Martinez said as he joined the group. Martinez was a man of small stature, solidly built with the deceiving ability to outrun anyone when chasing down a perp. His Latino heritage gave him light brown skin and dark hair that was kept short at all times. Smith nodded to them, a grim line on his mouth as he walked with his friend further into the swamp.

"What'd you think of Miss Laughlin?" Martinez asked as they walked.

"Better than expected," Smith said with a smile for the lecturer. His mind wandered to the previous day. Delilah Laughlin, a self-made billionaire had straight, nearly black hair which fell almost to her waist with the loveliest nose he'd ever seen but it was her eyes that made him stop breathing. Emerald eyes, the shades of green he'd only seen once before on a trip to springtime Ireland. His grandparents who wanted to show him the old country where they had been born and raised before moving to the Florida/Alabama line. He wondered what possessed a beautiful, obviously intelligent young woman to become the leading producer, distributor and retail source for sexual implements and toys. She'd definitely made it an interesting Friday.

They stopped at the murky water's edge. The smell of decay was all around and Smith suppressed the urge to rub his nose.

"This absolutely qualifies for a violent crime, boss."

From his vantage point Smith watched a plane getting ready to land at National Airport. Off to his right in the distance were the monuments and skyline Washington was famous for.

"You are going to hate this," Martinez said seriously.

Smith looked back and asked, "How so?"

"We've tentatively ID'd her."

Smith watched the forensics guys wearing black waders push the body closer to shore and turned her around. The victim's blonde hair floated in the water. Smith exhaled deeply not realizing he'd been holding his breath.

"It's Senator Travis from the great state of Tennessee," Martinez continued.

"Aw shit," Smith grumbled, taking in the information. Her body was brought to shore and immediately placed into a body bag to help preserve evidence she now contained. "Wait a minute," he said, motioning for the men to stop. He stepped close as he Googled the senator on his smartphone and came up with a few pictures. He squatted down to compare.

Martinez crouched beside and pointed to the neck wound with a pen. "That's ugly."

"Yeah…that's her," Smith said remorsefully. She hadn't spent enough time in the water to make her unrecognizable. "It is ugly and personal." Smith nodded to the forensics guys giving silent permission for them to move her and stood. "To get that close to her, inflict that kind of wound. She probably knew him. We'll have to wait for the autopsy to find out what other kind of damage was done." He knew from experience that there was a good chance of sexual trauma.

"Hey, what did I miss?" Jenkins asked as she picked her way through the mud. Smith's eyes fell to her shoes. Flats were a mistake.

"Jenkins, didn't you get the text that the crime scene was in a fucking swamp?" Smith asked. Her blonde ponytail swung back and forth as she ignored him but only to a certain point since he was now the boss. She walked normally the remainder of the way sacrificing her shoes to avoid damage to her ego. "What you missed," Smith said when she got closer, "is the opportunity to meet Senator Mildred Travis."

"I'm from Tennessee! I voted for her!" She looked temporary incapable of speech which only pissed him off further. Even senators got offed occasionally. "Okay that explains why we're here," Jenkins said.

"We're here," he explained, "because this lovely piece of property is federal land which makes this our jurisdiction." He shook his head and ordered, "Start interviewing anyone who witnessed anything. Find me some video of this area too. It's fucking D.C., there's got to be a camera somewhere close by." He watched his people walk away before he began barking out orders, directives, giving everyone he came into contact with something to do that would hopefully help the death investigation. His iPhone rang and he cursed at the number before answering it, "Sir." Assistant directors of the FBI didn't like the phone to ring more than once when they called.

"I heard you have someone important with you, Lowery," Assistant Director Patten said.

"'Fraid so, Sir. The coroner will have to confirm but the vic, in my opinion, is Senator Travis."

"Has her family been notified?"

"No, Sir, not that I'm aware of but we'll coordinate it and make sure it happens as soon as ID's been confirmed."

"What's it look like?" he asked.

"It was violent, personal, Sir. We'll need to interview her husband."

"I don't want you just supervising on this one, Lowery. It's too important, too high profile. I want you investigating."

"Yes, Sir. Give me a little time and we'll figure out who did this to her."

"Let me know before you talk with her family. I'll keep the boss apprised. He might want to go with you. I know Director Stanton was friendly with her."

"Yes, Sir." Smith cursed silently as the assistant director hung up. First case and it's a friend of the fucking Director of the Federal Bureau of Investigations. This was going to kill his career if he couldn't figure it out soon. No cold case on this one.

Smith leaned back in his chair exhausted and pissed, never a good combination for a man who carried a weapon. The desk lamp was the only light on in his office creating a single stream of light to the middle of his desk. His computer was off, the building empty. He ran a frustrated hand through his short sandy brown hair. He just needed time to think and a quiet place to do so.

The coroner had moved Senator Travis to the top of the pile, so to speak, and confirmed within hours it was the senator. That bit of information led to a crappy afternoon with him, Assistant Director Patten and Director Stanton at the Travis household. He'd never liked the DuPont area with that damn circle but now he'd remember it for a crying kid and a husband who looked like he'd been punched repeatedly. Worse off, when he had little to no information to give the family the directors kept assuring the widower they would find his wife's killer. That justice would be done. Smith could make no promises. Shit happened. Bad things to good people and some criminals could just get away with it.

He leaned forward and pressed the on button for his computer, sliding his badge into the reader for permission. He needed to do some research. His smartphone rang and he lifted it absently, answering the unknown number on the second ring. "Lowery," he said.

"Smith," her raspy voice was almost panicked, "I mean, Special Agent Lowery."

The chair squeaked as he sat up straight. "Delilah?"

"Yes." She was upset, her voice stressed.

"What's wrong?"

"I heard about Millie."

There was something off. She was shouting over music and he asked, "Where are you?"

"I'm in Amsterdam. At a club."

"Isn't it like," he checked his watch, doing the mental calculations and asked, "three am there?"

"Yes, I'm at a meeting but I just heard. I had to call. Smith, I had dinner with her last night! I mean Friday night, ah, the fucking time zones are screwing me up." The background sound around the phone call suddenly silenced. "That's better. Freaking loud music," she complained. He heard her step onto gravel, he assumed, away from the club, the meeting and the music.

"You had dinner with Senator Mildred Travis?" he asked to confirm now that he could hear her better.

"Yes. We had dinner with Senator Carter too. Both are on the Finance Committee. We ate at the Horseshoe Club. Do you know it?"

Yes, he knew it. He'd never been there but he'd heard of it. He needed time to process but knew he didn't have it. She had been with the senator just hours, maybe minutes before the killing. He made a choice, putting the most important thing first and asked, "Delilah, do you feel safe? Are your guards with you?"

There was momentary silence. "Yes, Brody and Armstrong are here with me. Why do you ask?"

"You had dinner with the victim of a violent crime. I need to make sure you're safe." He exhaled and said, "Tell me about the dinner."

"Um, it was fine. I had the salmon."

He almost smiled and said, "Not that I don't care what you ate but don't worry about that part. Start with what time you met."

"We met about eight. Talked business, personal things. You know she has a son. He's about five, I think," her voice was emotional. "Senator Carter left about nine-thirty, almost ten. I don't know. I wasn't paying attention."

"That's okay. You're doing fine," he offered, trying to calm her a continent away.

"She and I had drinks for a little while then I had to leave to catch my plane for New York."

"Which flight were you on?"

"I don't understand."

"Which airline did you fly? It'll make things easier to verify."

"Oh, I have my own plane. It was a private flight. It left about midnight."

He shook his head. He should have realized. "Then what?"

"We got to New York and I left immediately for Amsterdam. I have the store opening in a few days."

"Delilah, you're a material witness. You may be the last person to see and talk with the victim, I mean Senator Travis. You're going to need to give a formal statement."

She was silent for a moment then asked, "Do I need to come back right away to do that? I'm here until the end of the week."

"Sooner rather than later is best." He thought for a moment. Could she go into the Europol office and give a statement there? Would that be acceptable to the rules he was required to follow concerning witnesses? Would it be admissible? He assured himself it would be as his mind flashed through the rules. "OK, this is what I want you to do," and he told her. She agreed before he said, "Stay safe, Miss Laughlin." He thought he heard her smile before she hung up.

He took a second to absorb what she'd just told him. She was with the victim hours, moments before the killer struck. It unnerved him. He scrolled through his contacts and pressed Martinez's number. Three rings, given the time of day, it was fine.

"Martinez," Smith said when his friend answered. "I've just gotten a call from a material witness to the Travis murder." He breathed, "You'll never believe who."

"Tell me, man. I'm waiting," Martinez said.

"Delilah Laughlin."

Martinez's laughter trailed off. "Oh shit! You're serious. OK, she's coming in to talk?"

"No, not yet. She's in Amsterdam." Smith typed a name into the system as he said, "In the morning we're going to knock on Senator Carter's door. He joined them at dinner Friday night."

"You know that'll be Sunday morning and he's a senator."

"Thank you for reminding me but he's our witness as well. We need to know what he knows. We'll go out there for nine?"

"Sure, I love waking up people who can ruin my career."

"You're my number two on this investigation, Martinez."

"Appreciate that, boss. See you in the morning."

CHAPTER 2

They stood in front of a big, beautiful white house with a wraparound porch which reminded Smith of old fashioned southern mansions like the ones that lined the old avenues in Alabama. He jogged the few steps to the porch with Martinez trudging behind. Martinez grimaced as Smith knocked loudly breaking the Sunday morning tranquility.

The door pulled open and Senator Carter stood looking at the men. Smith and Martinez pulled their identifications out as confirmation. Senator Carter was in his early seventies but only his snow white hair gave his age away. The rest of him could have belonged to a man fifteen years younger. "Gentlemen, I appreciate the heads up," he said sarcastically.

"My apologies, Senator," Smith said. "We only learned late last night of your dining with Senator Travis. It seemed too late to call and give notice."

"Yes, of course. I heard on the news."

"Our condolences, Sir," Smith offered trying to smooth over the early morning house call.

"Thank you. I've been expecting you, or at least someone from the Bureau to call." He stepped aside and gestured for them to enter. "Please come in." He led them to a study along the first floor hall and closed the door behind them. He walked around a large carved desk that expressed the power of his station in life. "What would you like to know?"

Smith began, "Tell us about the dinner. About what time you left." The senator talked them through dinner and advised he left about nine thirty. "Did you come home directly?" Smith asked.

The senator smiled and answered, "No."

Smith looked up from his notes. "Where did you go, senator?"

"To see my mistress."

"Oh my," Martinez mumbled.

The senator smiled brightly. "Thank you, Viagra."

Martinez complained after they arrived back in Smith's office, "That was the biggest waste of time I've ever managed." He slumped down into the visitor's chair sulking. Smith stared at him in commiseration and agreed it was a waste. Nothing valuable could be discerned from the senator; at least the formal statement was taken care of. Martinez mocked, "Dear Diary, what I learned today," and continued, "Is that the food is great at the Horseshoe and Senator Carter is a whore."

"We knew about the food already."

Martinez sighed in frustration and said resolutely, "I'm taking Maria there for our anniversary."

"She'll love it," Smith smiled and leaned back in his chair just as his phone rang. He rocked forward and grabbed his cell. "Special Agent Lowery," he said in anticipation.

"Special Agent, my name is Detective Vandersloot of Europol."

Smith sat up straight and mouthed a curse to Martinez. "Yes, Sir. What can I do for you?"

"If I may explain my call." There was a heavy sigh. "We have a murder who has struck three times in the last six months. He cuts the throats of his female victims then dumps them in the canals." He paused then added, "There were two victims approximately six months ago. Another just weeks later."

"I'm sorry to hear this," Smith said. "But I'm not sure how our agency can assist. The FBI works within American domain."

"Yes, well, I'm sorry to say we've had another victim." There was a pause. Smith heard paperwork being shuffled. "We've identified her as an American. Monica Lambert, eighteen, from her passport I see she's from Dallas, Texas."

Smith's hand went to his hair. An American citizen's murder

was a game changer. He could see the potential negative headlines splashed across papers if he didn't offer assistance. Smith had no choice. He inhaled and said, "I'll be on the next available flight, Detective."

CHAPTER 3

Amsterdam, the Netherlands

Delilah pushed up the long sleeves of her stone colored, cowl-neck sweater dress and proceeded to get down to work. The new teak shelving units arrived with lots of time before the store opening. The construction workers had manhandled them leaving them grimy and dirty but nicely installed in the new store. She had abandoned the old store and knew in her gut it was the right decision. It had been in a bad part of the red light district. It was what she could afford at the time she opened that store, her second one, a little over nine years ago. A lot had changed in nine years but Amsterdam hadn't.

Amsterdam exuded old world charm, appeal and sexual independence Delilah wanted to capture in the modernization of the new store. Gleaming bay windows hid nothing. It was in the best part of the district. Her employees would be unafraid to come to work at the new store's location even after the red neon glow broke the darkness of the district. The artful sign with her company's logo on it, a biblical reference: the waist-up, line-drawn image of a naked, dangerous seductress with immense dark hair holding a knife to the side was already hung above the main entrance. Her biblical namesake had cut off Samson's hair, ensuring his weakness and seemingly guaranteeing her future.

Delilah smiled to herself as she carefully lowered onto her knees on the marble tile. She started wiping down the shelves so the merchandise could be put out. She had not just survived in the man's world of sex. She had taken over the industry and cut out its weaknesses with a vengeance. Revenge was best served cold, on a gilded platter she thought as she cleaned.

"Sir, the store is not yet open," Delilah heard one of her employees say in Dutch. The little redhead with the feminine voice and the nice rack Delilah mused. The young woman looked about fifteen but was going on twenty-one. Delilah listened as she worked. The young woman switched to English and repeated. Some misplaced tourist or hopeful perv wanting in before the grand opening. The construction workers had left the front doors unlocked again as they moved their equipment in and out of the store. She'd have to speak with them about that. Delilah leaned back on her heels and observed her progress. She'd missed a bit of grime in the back corner and reached in to wipe, also wiping away her view of the aisle.

There was a sharp intake of air beside her then a husky Southern voice joked charmingly, "While you're down there."

Delilah leaned back on her heels and looked up. She discovered Smith grinning wildly down at her. She'd only met him once and he was tasty then in khakis and black polo shirt, even more so now. She'd always loved a man in a suit, a natural weakness of hers and found him mouthwatering as her eyes raked up him. Her eyes met his, warm and brown and she smiled subtly. He wore a navy blue suit with a good cut displaying his fit build and broad shoulders. She knew from the khakis he had a lean waist. A crisp white shirt showed off the cool ice blue tie he paired with the suit. His dark, sandy blonde hair was just a touch longer than when they had first met. Images flashed through her mind of what he'd look like in Tom Ford or Valentino, or for that matter, what he'd look like out of it.

The thought made her smile wickedly as she declared, "In your dreams." She deliberately pulled the long sleeves back in place covering deep, ugly scars which began on the base of her wrists. She set the cleaning rag aside and lifted her hand as she said, "Help an old lady up."

He shifted his cell and folder to an empty shelf and bent for her, grasping the sides of her chest. He lifted her easily and affirmed, "You're not old."

She slid up the length of his muscular body with help. "No," she replied, "but I have the knees of a seventy year-old."

"Why's that?" he asked, holding her in front of him. His warmth and virility radiated off of him in waves.

"I got my knees bro...ken...," she slowed to a stop when she realized she'd offered something personal, something important. Hastily, she added, "When I was younger," and placed her hands on his muscular chest to balance herself in the heels.

"What?" He joked, "Like the mafia?"

She took a step back and dropped her hands ignoring his inquisitive look as he silently asked for more information. She didn't give it.

He bent low in front of her. She gasped in reaction to his sudden movements and close proximity as he gently wiped off each of her knees then stood straight. She was sure he had to have noticed the ugly surgical scars. At least he was gracious enough not to say anything.

His intense gaze shifted from personal to professional as he asked, "Do you have a moment for me, Delilah?"

She almost blushed, almost lost the control she craved like a drug as she thought of giving him more than a just moment of her time. She locked it away with her secrets, returning to her cool, professional air and said, "Of course, Smith. What brings you to Amsterdam?" She led him away from the aisle. He grabbed his cell, folder and followed. In passing, she told her assistant Shannon to continue where she'd left off and to start putting out the merchandise. "Arrange the vibrators by size. Make the display look good." Her eyes flicked to his chocolate ones and said, "Presentation matters." She continued towards the back of the store as he followed.

"I'm in the city working with my Europol counterpart on a case of theirs," he said, answering her question.

He stepped ahead of her reaching for the closed door she was intent on passing through. He placed his hand on her lower back, gently guiding her. The warmth of his touch radiated completely through her body causing her heart to race. Liquid warmth suddenly filled her lower belly and she struggled for control before his hand fell away and he followed her once more. It wasn't the race of panic and fear she normally felt with another's touch. It surprised her how much she'd enjoyed it.

"I thought I'd track you down and get your statement for Senator Travis' investigation."

"Oh," she exhaled heavily, trying to calm herself from his touch. "Of course." She was disappointed, she admitted to herself but not surprised. He certainly hadn't flown to another continent just for her, or her statement. She gestured to another closed door and he opened it.

A small office was revealed but unlike the store it was completed. Everything had its place. An antique-looking leather couch hugged the wall to the side of the office. An armoire filled the space between two closed doors on the far side of the room. She moved around the dark wooden desk with a fluidity that defied her previous injuries and pulled her cell phone from the pocket of her sweater dress.

"Please sit," she said with a gesture, offering him a seat on the other side of her large desk.

She pressed a number on her contact list. Lifting it to her ear she waited two rings before a male voice answered, "Law offices of Ellington and Fitch, John Stearns speaking. How may I assist you today?"

"John, this is Delilah Laughlin. Is Mr. Ellington available?"

"Ms. Laughlin, may I place you on hold for a moment?"

"Certainly." She looked up when the music began and found Smith's eyes on her.

Predator versus prey, which one was she?

The music clicked off and a deep male voice boomed, "Ms. Laughlin, how are you?"

"I'm well, Eric. I hope I'm not interrupting."

"No, of course not. What can I do for you?"

"I'm in Amsterdam and I have Special Agent Lowery of the FBI with me. He would like to take my formal statement concerning my dinner Friday night with Senator Travis. The one we discussed." He murmured something about inopportune time and that he wished he could be there with her in person. "May I place you on speaker while we discuss the statement?"

"I prefer it since I can't be with you."

She nodded and pressed the button laying the phone on the desk. "You're on speaker now, Eric." She proceeded with introductions, "I have Special Agent Lowery of the Violent Crimes Unit, Special Agent, my attorney Eric Ellington."

"Thank you for your time, Mr. Ellington," Smith said as he opened his folder, spreading his information and documentation in front of him on her desk.

"I want this on record, Special Agent that I'm very unhappy about your sudden desire to question my client without me present. We could have easily set a date for Ms. Laughlin on her return to the country."

"Yes, Sir. I'm aware but as I'm here assisting on another investigation and the death investigation for the senator is a priority matter I thought it best to get this small portion of the investigation completed." She watched Smith brace his forearms on the desk opposite her as he leaned forward. "Your client is a material witness as I'm sure you're aware. Her statement is imperative."

Delilah leaned back in the soft leather chair and smirked with pleasure as the two men bickered about timing and law. Finally she had enough and leaned forward saying, "Eric, I'll give my statement and the matter will be done." Her intense stare fell to Smith and asked, "What would you like to know?"

He passed over a notepad and a pen then said, "Please note, Mr. Ellington your client is providing a voluntary statement." He looked back to Delilah, his expression and voice softened, "Please write down the events of Friday night starting with what happened approximately thirty minutes before you met at the restaurant. Include as many details as you can remember." He shifted slightly. "I do have a few questions once you're finished."

"Ms. Laughlin, I'd like you to read me your statement before you sign," boomed the disembodied voice.

It took her a few minutes to complete the paperwork while both men waited patiently. She took a moment to reread what she'd written then said, "Eric, if you're ready I'll read my statement."

"Go ahead. I'm recording it so we will have a record of it as well."

She nodded and looked up to Smith. She read it to him, "On Friday night, October thirteenth, I met with Senators Travis and Carter of the Finance Committee at The Horseshoe Club in Washington D.C. at eight for dinner." She breathed then continued, "During this visit to D.C. I stayed at the Four Seasons hotel. My security team and I left the hotel approximately twenty minutes before eight to arrive on time." She looked at Smith and said, "If you think I need to add something, please let me know."

"Of course, Ms. Laughlin, I will," Eric said through the phone.

Smith and Delilah smiled at each other.

She looked back to the statement and continued, "Dinner lasted until approximately nine forty-five when Senator Carter left. After that Millie and I moved from the restaurant area to the bar of the Horseshoe Club. I had a glass of wine and Millie had two mixed drinks. She told me she wasn't driving."

Smith interrupted, looking up from his own notes, "Did she say how she was getting home, if she wasn't driving?"

Delilah shook her head. "No, I didn't think to ask at the time." Smith began to scribble notes furiously before he finished and looked to her. Her eyes caught his before she looked back at the paperwork. "I left the bar about ten fifteen and was driven to the National Airport where I boarded my plane for the trip back to New York."

"What time did the flight depart Reagan?" Smith asked, his eyes back on his notes.

"I really can't tell you. Before midnight, if I had to guess."

"Why the time difference? Why not leave right away?"

"I realized I'd been rude. Not offering Millie a ride home after she'd had a few drinks. I sent my security back to the restaurant to provide a ride. Plus, we were waiting for Shannon to get back from her appointment."

His eyebrows lifted in surprise as he asked, "Did your security give the senator a ride home?"

"No. Brody told me she was gone by the time he got there."

"I'll need to speak with Brody as well."

"Sure, he's in town with me." She gestured to the phone and said, "Eric can listen to Brody's statement as well, if you don't mind."

"No, I don't mind, Ms. Laughlin, I'd be happy to. Do you have any more questions of my client, Special Agent Lowery?"

"A few." He paused then said, "If that's all you can recall, please sign and date the paperwork." He glanced at his watch. "It's the seventeenth." She signed as he said, "The formal statement has been completed, Mr. Ellington, if you need to go."

"No. I'll listen to your other questions."

She watched Smith shift nervously before he said, "Okay." He lifted his gaze and asked, "Can you think of any reason someone might target the senator?"

"No," Delilah lied determinedly.

"Do you know if she was involved in extra…curricular…activities," his eyes caressed her, "extramarital? Something her husband wouldn't know about?"

"She's not my friend, Special Agent," she misstated. "But I didn't get that vibe from her."

"I thought you were," he said. Her brows furrowed not understanding so he clarified, "I thought you were friends."

"No, I don't have any female friends." She said it so casually she could see his surprise. She tried to explain, "The Finance Committee is vitally important to the smooth operation of my business within the United States. We are, were, good acquaintances but I wouldn't say friends."

"Is that what you two talked about at the bar? Business?"

"Business and other things." She waited a moment then continued, "On occasion I take people to dinner who can, for whatever reason, help my business." She smiled subtly and saw him visibly move closer. "I can be friendly without being friends."

"What about you?" he asked, shifting again, "Are you involved with anyone currently?"

"What does that have to do with the investigation, Special Agent?" Mr. Ellington asked.

Smith glanced irritably at the cell phone and explained, "I have to view the motives for murder from all angles, Mr. Ellington. If Ms. Laughlin was the target and the senator was in the wrong place, wrong time sort of situation then its best I know more details about Ms. Laughlin." He looked up from the cell phone and asked, "So, are you?"

She grinned and answered, "No, I'm not in a relationship."

"Any death threats? Threats against your company?"

"I get a few during the year. I can't do what I do without someone thinking the worst of me. As far as company threats I haven't heard of any recently but you can always confirm with Brody." She glanced at her watch then said, "Eric, I'm going to end this meeting. I have an appointment I need to leave for. I appreciate your time."

"Your time is my time, Ms. Laughlin. Enjoy the rest of your day." The attorney hung up.

She leaned back in her chair and let her eyes appreciate the man before her. He was amazing to look at she admitted with a jawline angels fought over to kiss, and chocolate brown eyes which reminded her of melting warmth. It was nearly indecent how she looked at him as her lower belly pooled with desire. "Did you get everything you came for?" she asked, wondering if he understood her question fully.

"I think so," he said but didn't move from the chair. "I've got your number if I think of anything else."

They sat staring at each other for a long moment, evaluating, devouring the other with their eyes. Delilah liked the line of his nose, how his sculptured lips parted to accommodate his breathing. Images of his rushed breath against her skin intensified the yearning between her legs. She liked how his hair was short as she expected from law enforcement but it was still disheveled, just a little too long. She wondered what it would feel like to run her fingers through it. She found him very male, very pleasurable to study and admire. How would he look naked, she wondered? She knew him to be fit. She briefly wondered if he was well-hung and did he know how to use it? The air began to spark between them, so charged with sexual tension.

He broke the stare and began to gather the documents and his cell. "I won't keep you from your appointment."

"I misrepresented," he stopped and looked up. His eyebrows rose in surprise. "My next appointment to my attorney," she admitted.

Smith relaxed and grinned, "Now, why'd ya do that?"

"Because, I'd very much like you to be my next appointment. My attorney's a little tight in the ass. I don't think he'd appreciate my question." She waited, holding his attention before she asked, "Would you like to go to dinner with me?"

□

CHAPTER 4

"Everyone has to eat," Smith said with a charming, crooked smile. "Sure, Delilah. I'd like to go to dinner with you."

She exhaled silently, not realizing she had been holding her breath. "Great." She smiled and rose from the chair. "We can go to Oli's. It's close and the food's great. I'll just get my things." She removed her purse in the desk drawer setting it on the desk before she moved to the closet and took removed her beige cashmere coat from it.

Smith offered a hand for the coat. Their fingers touched as she passed it over, warming her again. He shook it open and held it out for her. She shifted into it as he leaned to her from behind and said, "A beautiful coat for a beautiful woman."

Delilah smiled over her shoulder as his hand slide along her back. She adjusted a colorful silk scarf around her neck and left it hanging. He reached over and took up his paperwork and cell.

Brody held the rear door of the sleek black Mercedes open for Delilah. She shifted across allowing room for Smith to follow.

Smith stopped at the door and spoke with Brody, "I'll need to talk with you later about last Friday night."

"Whatever you need, Special Agent Lowery."

"My parents used to bring my sister, Rachel and I to Oli's when we were kids," Delilah said, once the vehicle started moving.

"You lived here?" he asked, surprised by her admission.

She nodded and said, "I grew up in Europe. My dad was in the Army when I was born in Germany. We lived there for eight years before he was transferred to Rotterdam for another four." She glanced at the passing scenery watching buildings and people pass quickly. She murmured to herself, "Maybe that's why I had so much trouble."

Her body shocked as his thumb caressed her hand and he asked, "Trouble with what?"

They both knew her smile was insincere as she said, "Nothing." Her smile brightened into a real one, caressing her eyes as she squeezed his hand, reveling in the warmth and strength of it. "The restaurant's in a five hundred year old windmill."

His thumb graced the back of her hand again sending liquid warmth rushing into her lower belly. "Very cool. I've never been in a windmill, let alone an old one. This will be new for me."

She was sure if he entered her world there would be many new experiences.

Armstrong dropped them off just steps from the front entrance of the old place. Delilah craned her neck as she looked up the side of the massive old windmill. It sat directly next to one of the many canals, lit up with decorative lights. It was barely six but the world turned dark quickly, bringing in the North Sea wind that stole her breath.

Smith squeezed her hand, gaining her attention. As her eyes fell to him again he smiled for her almost lovingly. The effect was devastating. She felt her heart crush against the kindness she didn't deserve.

He gave her a little tug and said, "Come on. I'm hungry."

The restaurant remained as charming as she remembered. Huge, old oak beams were exposed above their heads. The wood floor was uneven and she had to tread carefully in her heels.

"It's been too long!" Oli exclaimed when he saw her. He grasped her hands in a friendly manner, kissing both of her cheeks before greeting Smith. "Ah, the gorgeous woman," he leaned to Smith, "but I remember the lovely girl. Please come."

He made a gesture to climb the stairs to the second floor and Smith asked, "Do you have a table on the first floor?" She gushed with pleasure, his taking into account her aching knees.

"Of course, a table with a stunning view of the canal. Very romantic," Oli said as he shifted to the side of the staircase and walked them to a private table.

A delicate linen lay across the small table tucked beside a large bay window was the table Oli had chosen for them. The twinkle of a strand of decorative lights danced across the tabletop providing light in the dimly lit room as it hung crossed over the window. Delilah was seated first then Smith slid in across from her.

"Come here often?" he joked.

She smiled. "Not as often as I'd like."

"What do you like?" he asked, reviewing the menu.

"The appetizers are all good. The stuffed mushrooms are fantastic."

He closed the menu and grinned. "Then let's do that." She looked inquisitive so he continued, "Let's order all the appetizers and share, family style." She agreed with a smile.

After the order was taken she refocused on Smith, giving him all of her consideration. Curiosity got the better of her and she asked, "So you asked me if I have a significant other." He looked directly into her eyes. "What about you? Someone you love? Someone you fuck on a regular basis?"

His grin widened. "You have the most attractive mouth that curse words come out of," he paused as she smiled, "No. I don't have a girlfriend."

She nodded, pleasantly happy he was available.

"Tell me how you got your business started," he said, bracing his arms on the table, leaning his body towards hers. "Not many teenagers have access to start up money."

"You're right. My family's not from money." A manicured nail circled the rim of her wine glass once then she looked up into his warm eyes. "I went to my grandparents and borrowed ten thousand dollars." He looked at her, toying with his beer bottle. "Then I went to my parents and borrowed another ten. It was all they had, all of their savings and they willingly gave it to me."

"They must have had a lot of faith in you."

"Things weren't the best at that time. I think they would've given me anything, mortgaged the house if I had asked for more than they had in savings." She sighed, not wanting to say too much.

"Parents, grandparents are like that," he offered.

"They were so angry at me." She slapped herself mentally. Why would she tell him that?

"How so?" he asked as plates of food were delivered. "This looks wonderful," he said, scanning the plates. He thanked the waiter then started dishing out a few of the appetizers onto her plate.

She let him, holding back on being controlling which, she thought amusingly, was a form of control. Wonderful aromas of baked cheeses and spices taunted her senses. He looked up and gave her an expression which reminded her he was waiting for an answer as he set a loaded plate in front of her.

"I told them I wasn't going to college. I think they were expecting that. Plus, I had to tell them about the business for them to make the initial investment."

He chuckled. "I bet that was a great conversation."

"Yeah, I'm sure it's tough enough as a parent to admit your kid's sexuality but another to have them be adamant about going into the business. I couldn't have shocked them more if I had told them I was going to be a prostitute or going into the movies." Delilah shook her head. "I think my dad had a heart attack!" She half-heartedly laughed at the memory. She raised her fork to her mouth, her whole body relaxed around a stuffed mushroom.

"I'm sure they're over it by now," he said, sliding a forkful into his mouth.

She smiled, not wanting to talk about her parents and sipped a crystal glass of white wine. She said casually, "I took your advice from when we met." His brows lifted in curiosity. "I treated myself to something."

"What's that?" he asked, leaning forward, bracing his muscular forearms on the table.

"In celebration," she almost grinned, "Of my personal wealth milestone I've had my attorneys set up a scholarship fund."

"That's great! Tell me about it," he said, taking up a brown bottle of Palm beer.

She hid a smile behind the glass of wine and sipped then said, "It's based," she set the glass down, "on merit and need. I wanted something to be available for kids whose grades aren't quite perfect but who show resiliency and determination. The accountants and lawyers are still figuring out the details. It should be set in a few months."

"That's very generous."

"Don't tell anyone," she grinned sheepishly, "I'd hate for anyone to think I'm a nice person."

Smith was very close and smelled deliciously wonderful. They stood together in the brightly lit gravel parking lot of the restaurant. She wondered briefly what was taking Armstrong so long in retrieving the car. Though she had on her luxurious coat the wind still gave her a chill. "You didn't have to do that," she said with a pout as the Mercedes drove up.

Smith rubbed her arms lazily. "You're a girl. Of course I'm going to pay." An arched eyebrow shot up in disbelief. "Don't give me that look," he said with a laugh. "Pops would kill me if I'd let you pay."

She hadn't been called a girl for a very long time. Bitch, yes. High maintenance, of course but not girl.

"Listen, Delilah," Smith stepped even closer, drawing her into his arms to protect her from the vicious wind. She felt the tension in her body melt away as he held her. She exhaled heavily not realizing there was such comfort in his arms. "You're a witness. I can't be with you romantically but I'd like to. God, everything about you turns me on." He pressed a soft kiss to her dark hair. "After the investigation's complete when everything's done I want to be with you. I can come to New York. We can go to a show or fuck all day long, whatever you want but it has to be later, okay?"

Brody opened the Mercedes door as Delilah stepped from the embrace and said quietly, "I'd like that too." She enjoyed his honesty about his desires. It didn't shock her that he wanted to fuck her since that's exactly what she wanted to do to him. She shifted in her seat to face him when he got in. He told Armstrong which hotel he was staying then moved so he could see her, face to face.

"How long will you be in Amsterdam?" she asked.

"For a while, until we can get a handle on the Dutch investigation."

"Then back to D.C.?"

"Yes, ma'am," he said. She grinned. "I need to check in with my number two, get Senator Travis' case wrapped up. Bring some justice to her family."

CHAPTER 5

Techno music pounded around her, lights keeping time as Delilah finished her martini and set the shapely glass down on the little table in front of her. Fucking meetings at one in the morning, she wondered if other captains of industry had to put up with the same shit.

The impressive man, built like a bull with long, black hair and dark, eagle-eyes sat opposite her. He wanted to fuck her. She was sure about it, reading the cues his body gave. Porn was her business and she wasn't illiterate. If anything, she was a fucking genius. Delilah sighed and leaned back into the cushioned half-moon seat, drawing herself away. The internet allowed her to sell to anyone with computer access but she wanted to open stores in Russia. To do that she had to chat-up the man. A means to an end. Bribes weren't uncommon just part of doing business in some countries but her time was precious and he was taking too much of it. The waitress set another round of drinks between them on the little glass table.

"Darius," Delilah said curtly, "I am not a patient woman. I need your decision," she paused, "when I get back." She stood, needing to separate herself from the Russian bear. He offered her a hand when she wobbled on her sky-high heels. Delilah ignored the gesture, balancing herself and walked off.

The VIP ladies room had just been remodeled. She knew from the checks that had been written. She'd gotten a deal on the marble buying in bulk from the Italian mine directly. She'd gotten enough of the beautiful stone with tones of brown and flecks of reds to finish the entire new store and the club's bathrooms. Dark hardwood doors closed off the individual stalls and several giant mirrors framed the room. She took care of business then stood examining herself in the mirror above the sinks. Her green eyes were rimmed in black kohl which was smudged slightly from hours of wear. She took a cloth hand towel and tried to fix the makeup.

"Ah, I love your shoes!" the young woman beside her gushed.

Delilah glanced at her in the mirror and said, "Thank you. I love them too." Too high, in a nude color which was supposed to create the optical illusion of longer legs on her petite frame. She kept the short black dress relatively modest, having taken into account the company she was keeping for the business meeting. She glanced back at the young woman and thought of her as an Amazon. In heels the young woman had to be a foot taller than her with tremendous blonde hair down to her waist. The sapphire blue dress showed off her svelte body. Standing next to a woman like that left her a little depressed. At least I have curves, Delilah thought as a way of cheering herself up. "Are you having fun?" Delilah asked, setting the towel down and reexamining her makeup.

"Lots." The young woman leaned in as if to tell a secret, "This really hot guy bought me a drink so I think my fun's going to last!" She giggled in delight.

Happy with the fix, Delilah leaned back from her reflection. Her eyes fell on the young woman. "Stay safe. You can buy condoms from the hostesses, if you don't have any."

"How do you know?"

"Because it's my club." She gave a brief smile and walked away from the blonde. Delilah wondered what Smith was doing then realized he was probably sleeping. Alone, she hoped. She smirked as she pulled open the door. "Back to the bear," she muttered quietly.

CHAPTER 6

Delilah knew by the next morning she needed to reign in her emotions when it came to Special Agent Lowery. She hadn't been the least bit interested in a bribe-fuck when the Russian asked, or demanded depending on the perspective, for one. Fortunately, Darius was as willing to take her money as he was to take her body. In the end, she got what she wanted. Two stores would open the following year in the Russia and more the year after.

Her emotions were becoming a liability. She found herself reconsidering her no relationship policy. She needed to stay focused but damn Smith was taking that away too. Taking away the control she needed so desperately. She needed to refocus, stay focused. Senator Travis' murder had triggered something, something Smith didn't know. It was something she wasn't going to tell him.

Brody pulled the sleek, black Mercedes close to the main entrance of the store. Two more days then the opening and she could run for home. Once more she could cocoon herself in spreadsheets and research and development and twenty-four hour work days. Emotional disconnection was the best protection. Work was like a balm to a sensitive wound. It always made her feel better. She'd put in a good ten hours of hard work. She moved boxes, stocked shelves and cleaned, all in high heels and a willowy, green dress. She made last minute decisions and enjoyed every minute of it. She was so physically exhausted as she tugged on her coat she considered falling asleep on the ride home.

"Ready, ma'am?" Brody questioned, stepping to the open office door.

"Yes," she said, and picked up her bag. Her legs felt like

weights, barely moving as they crossed the expansive store. She followed Brody out the door and took a step off the sidewalk towards the waiting Mercedes. Armstrong stood beside the open door as she stopped and tossed her purse in then looked up. There was too much activity, too many people. It was nearly dusk but the lights from the police cars slashed through the darkness like the techno lights at the club. Police were keeping people away from the canal and the small stone bridge which lay directly in front of the store before the road split into two directions, running parallel with the store.

A face in the crowd stood out amidst the chaos, staring at her with a worried look. Delilah tilted her head in recognition of two navy blue jackets with FBI imprinted like a logo. His attractive face had haunted her dreams for days. Her stomach fell. FBI, Smith, police, Europol agents; her eyes swept over the lot of them. She came to one conclusion, and it wasn't good. She stepped away from the door and slid around the backside of the Mercedes. She walked across the cobblestones towards the canal and towards Smith.

He stepped close and immediately began talking, "Delilah, I'm sorry. I know it's too close for comfort but this doesn't have anything to do with you."

"The assistance you mentioned?"

"Yes," he breathed. "We've found another body."

A young woman with a bouncing blonde ponytail, wearing the other FBI jacket stepped close to Smith. Delilah immediately recognized her from the Quantico lecture. She was the catty one. The one who was envious and thought she was better than Delilah because of how she made her money. Delilah was suddenly pissed. She didn't want to the young woman near her, or her store, or Smith.

Smith's eyes flashed from the young woman to Delilah then back again, "What's up, Jenkins?" He watched the women eviscerate each other with their stares. "Delilah, you remember Agent Jenkins from the lecture?"

A scorching look raked over the young agent. "The jealous one."

Jenkins face hardened. "Bitch, the strip club's across the street if you're lost."

It was like a lid on a very angry box slid open. Delilah inhaled sharply at the verbal smack and exhaled expletives, "God damn motherfucking cock-stained bitch..."

"Whoa!" Smith shot out as Delilah took a step forward.

"Just because your dad had to blow the admin office to get you into that Ivy League school..." Delilah started but didn't get to finish.

Smith wrapped an arm around Delilah as the women got closer. His bicep strained just beneath her breasts pulling tightly on the green dress she wore. She was still cursing as he walked away with her, carrying her with one arm.

He walked about ten steps, enough to separate the women as Brody called out, "Sir, you need to put Ms. Laughlin down." Brody's hand rested on his gun holster. Armstrong had his gun out and a third man had come up behind them.

"Shit, Brody," Smith said, setting Delilah down. "You know I'm not going to hurt her."

"No, Sir. I don't know that."

When his arm had completely released her, Delilah pushed back a step and turned her fury on him, "What the fuck was that?"

"I could ask you the same thing, Delilah. What the fuck?" He ran a hand through his hair. "Shit, I had to separate you two before you took my agent down Jersey style."

Delilah hiccupped a laugh and asked, "Jersey style?"

"Yeah, you know, bitch slapping, hair pulling. You were going to start pounding her head into the street. Shit! Delilah I can't have you kicking my agent's ass especially in public."

Delilah glanced around. She'd forgotten where she was. She'd been so angry. Two of the three bodyguards now stood by the Mercedes, watching her and Smith like hawks. She tugged on her dress and coat, straightening out her appearance. "I'm sorry," she said sheepishly.

He stepped beside her and looked back at the canal as shouts interrupted them. The victim had been pulled out of the water.

They were scrambling up the bank with her. Delilah gasped in recognition. She clamped her hand over her mouth as the body was lifted into view. Her stomach ached as if she'd been punched. She bent awkwardly, suddenly needing to vomit.

Smith placed a firm hand on her back. "Hey, it's alright. The ones in the water are the worst."

Flashes of the huge gash across the victim's neck, the bloodless open wound made her gasp again. She grabbed Smith's arm to steady herself. "I met her. I know her." The Amazon from the bathroom. She still wore the beautiful blue dress. Delilah swallowed hard and steadied herself.

Smith looked shocked then pissed. "How? Where do you know her from?"

Delilah took an unsteady step away from Smith, away from the canal.

"Don't forget your change for the ones," Jenkins yelled out.

Smith snapped, "Shut it, Jenkins!"

Delilah made it to the Mercedes. The intense desire to escape was overwhelming making her heart race. She needed to get away from the brutal carnage.

Smith grabbed her upper arm when she leaned into the car. "Wait! Fuck it, Delilah, wait!" He let her go based on the look Brody gave him.

Delilah settled into the beige leather seat as Armstrong and Brody crowded the door space. Brody nodded, silently instructing the other. Armstrong stepped away walking purposely around the sedan to the driver's seat. Brody took a step away but hovered nearby.

"Shit," Smith cursed, squatting beside the open door. "You know the deal, Delilah. Two murders within a few days. You're my fucking witness again."

Her eyes rimmed with tears as she stared at him. Her immense stare broke and shifted to Brody, giving instructions, "Give him the house address."

Smith stood and Brody closed the door once he moved out of the way. She heard them though the silence of the car as Brody told Smith the house address then said, "Come over later."

A minute later the black sedan was flying along the narrow streets and Delilah said, "Gentlemen," both men shifted slightly in the front so she knew she had their attention, "I want to thank you for doing your jobs today." They murmured something about her unwarranted appreciation. She continued, "But, if you ever let another man pick me up and walk more than two steps you're fired." She leaned back into the sumptuous leather and closed her eyes.

A thousand questions ran through her mind, keeping her heart racing. She'd briefly met the dead woman. She knew what the young woman had talked about. How the woman had wanted to spend the remainder of her night. Delilah didn't know with whom. No name and no real memories of the companion's face she could remember. She'd seen him though. She'd have to tell Smith that. The club had surveillance video of the exterior. Smith would want that as well, she was sure. He'd want to go to the club talk with her employees. It wasn't really the kind of place to do police interviews. Maybe she could bring in the employees during the day when it wasn't so busy. Or maybe she should just take him there later when it would be crowded and noisy.

Let Smith see for himself.

The guy she'd seen might come back. Isn't that what criminals did? She wondered, do they really return to the scene of the crime? She swallowed hard at the prospect of her club being a crime scene. She briefly wondered if she could pick out the stranger. She'd seen him from an odd angle in the club leaning against the VIP bar with the blonde wrapped around him. Of course, she'd seen more of him in the basement. More of the girl too, lots more. That presented another problem: The basement.

Brody opened the car door and she stepped into the crisp evening air. Her home was beautiful in every way. She looked over the structure. The soft brown of the brick exterior flowed naturally with the browns and greens of the century-old trees and decorative gardens which surrounded the sides of the massive home. Nestled beside a canal on the back side, the home sat in an exclusive neighborhood of Amsterdam. She paused as she walked and heard the gurgling of the canal current close by. She always liked that sound.

Brody pushed open the heavy wood and crystal front door and stepped in then aside for her. Wide-planked polished hardwood floors lined the entire home. Huge, nearly floor to ceiling windows gave the house a modern atmosphere in the living and reception rooms. The exposed ceiling beams made it feel warm and comfortable throughout.

From the reception room Delilah walked purposely through the house, past the staircase which led to the staff and guest rooms on the upper floors. She took a few steps down into the ultramodern and sleek kitchen, glancing quickly out the bay windows to the nighttime view of the city just beyond the dining room area.

She knew Brody was behind her though she didn't hear him following. She announced over her shoulder as she entered the hall to her personal rooms, "I'll be swimming. Tell Shannon to order me some food. Have Trina text me and let me know when Special Agent Lowery arrives."

"Yes, ma'am," he said, turning from her path.

She closed the door to her side of the house and finally relaxed. What a shitty day. She exhaled a heavy sigh. The urge to run had brought her to this room, to her home. She peeled off her coat and tossed it and her purse haphazardly onto an overstuffed chair that sat near the doorway. Her phone pinged from the depths of her purse and she mused with a smile over Brody's efficiency as she dug for it. She took it and quickly texted Trina back with the details of what she wanted then tossed the phone back.

She stepped further into her quarters. A massive, ornate wrought iron bed filled the initial space of her private quarters. A comforter in spruce green, made of woven gold threads, wool and hand-spun silk with vanilla colored bedding lay folded back and waiting for her, tempting her. Built-in bookcases and their colorful texts lined one wall while a fireplace sat directly opposite the bed. A flat screen hung dark over the mantel for those rare moments when she had a chance to watch. The sprawling room led in four directions, one way was to a massive closet filled by her personal shopper, Trina. The Parisian was very good at her job, very good at finding Delilah's small size in the most beautiful fashions and charging them to her accounts.

The far wall, beyond the bed and the small office, was one smooth sheet of glass - save the glass double doors in the middle which opened up into the back gardens. More overstuffed chairs and a crafted leather ottoman filled the remaining space in that area. In the spring when the flowers were in bloom she would purposely leave the double doors open simply for the fragrance. Compared to the apartment in New York, the personal space in this house was small. She liked it though. It made her feel comfortable and safe.

She stepped into the bathroom and began to undress with a sigh of relief as she stepped from the heels. She tossed her clothes onto the floor of the closet through a connecting door. Removing her beautiful Patek Philippe watch she set it carefully on the marble countertop along with her emerald drop earrings. She walked naked through another arched door on the opposite side of the luxurious bathroom taking a snow-white bath towel from a neatly folded stack. She stepped down onto Italian tiles which lined the floor of the smaller room triggering the motion sensitive soft lighting.

Setting the towel on a cushioned bench Delilah pressed a button on a small control panel above the bench. The water in the swimming pool began to move. The air smelled faintly of gardenias. Small rectangular windows framed the rim of the domed ceiling but only darkness showed through the glass as she slid into the warm water.

The warmth of the water surrounded her aching, tired body soothing her. She dunked under completely submerging herself. The pool was deep enough her feet didn't touch the bottom. She pushed off the wall and swam against the current of the small pool. She stayed in one place as it rushed against her. When her stroke slipped a little she was forced to swim harder to keep her place.

Finally, she rolled and stopped, allowing the water to push her to the smooth concrete edge of the pool. Her feet pressed against the side and she floated, held in place by the current which surrounded and rushed against her. She flexed her manicured toes and stared at the painted ceiling of the dome. She had paid an artist good money to paint angels and fat little cherub babies in the style and coloring of Leonardo. She didn't like the excessive pastels of the impressionists or the dazzling abilities of the modernists. She liked the dark, earthy tones of the sixteenth century Italian art of Leo and Raphael. There was something realistic about the gritty yet ethereal beauty. Her hand ran over her face, pushing away water and dark hair. She closed her eyes on the painting and sighed, relaxing for just a moment before she pushed off the side and began her backstrokes.

Unexpectedly, sobs racked her chest and she stopped swimming allowing the current to sweep her poolside. It pushed against her back, keeping her in place as she braced her arms over the side. Delilah pressed her hands into her face and sobbed. Seeing that girl, gray and bloodless, pulled from the water triggered the stored emotions. Deep down she knew that's what Millie looked like. What fear she must have had to endure during the last moments of her life? Delilah dreaded the prospects.

She laid her face on the cool tile and wrapped her arms around her head protectively as the tears continued. Poor Millie. It wasn't supposed to be like this. Millie had been her ally in vengeance. There was a plan. It was set but now, without her, Delilah didn't know if she could continue. Or even if she should. She pulled her arms from her head and looked at the ugly scars that lined the soft skin of her forearms. At times, she could still feel the knife delving into her silky skin. Subconsciously, she ran a fingertip between her breasts to another smaller scar the knife had left those many years ago. Perhaps it was time to let it go, to turn from vengeance and seek a cosmetic surgeon to help her rid of her body of the ugly reminders.

With every effort she pulled herself from the water and squeezed the excess water from her long hair. She walked to the wall and pushed a silver square knob. Instantly hot water washed over her, rinsing the pool water. She pushed the knob again and the water stopped. She took a lined waffle-knit, powder-puff blue robe from a hook near the arched doorway and wrapped it around herself. Drying her hair with the snow white towel Delilah left the apse. She tossed the towel on the floor beside the bed as she sat on the edge. She barely remembered lying down before her eyes closed.

"Ms. Laughlin, ma'am," Armstrong said as he tried to rouse her.

Delilah bolted upright at his touch. "What? What's wrong?" she demanded.

"We couldn't get you by intercom, ma'am. Shannon's already gone to the club. I knocked. Everything's fine." Delilah breathed heavily. "Special Agent Lowery is here," he said.

"Oh, okay. Give me a minute," Delilah said, pushing her hair from her face. Armstrong walked out of her room and closed the door behind him. She glanced at the clock on her nightstand and realized she'd gotten about three hours of sleep. She felt pretty good considering how tired she had been when they arrived home. She stood, shifting the bathrobe back in place and padded barefoot into the kitchen finding everyone there, waiting for her.

Her eyes immediately went with hatred to Jenkins and said to Smith, "I want her out of my house now."

"That's not fair!" Jenkins complained.

She continued past the long hardwood table and chairs in the dining room as Smith nodded to Jenkins, and she left in a huff.

Delilah smiled briefly in victory as she walked into the kitchen. She immediately began searching for the food she'd told Shannon to get. She found a cream colored Villeroy and Boch plate in the fridge and pulled it out.

"Delilah," Smith implored, "I can't believe this. Two deaths on two continents."

She ignored him and popped the plate into the microwave. She maneuvered her way around the kitchen gathering a fork and her pill box. She took the plate from the microwave when it pinged and walked back to one of the empty bar stools.

"I'm not giving you a statement," she said defiantly, scooting up into the seat. She set her plate, fork and the pill box on the counter. She looked up into Smith's chocolate brown eyes and ordered, "Make yourself useful, Special Agent and get me a glass of water."

"Don't be a bitch, 'cause I know you're not, Delilah," he said as he stepped into the kitchen. She pointed to a frosted glass-door cabinet above the immense granite countertop. He pulled a tall glass from it and stepped to the ice/water dispenser in the fridge door.

"I don't want any ice," she said. He glared at her as she continued, "I'm about to take some serious medications so don't give me any shit about ice. I like my water room temperature." She shoveled a ravioli into her mouth. She was greeted with an explosion of the wonderful flavors of mushroom and lobster. She glanced over to Brody. "This is fantastic, thank you for telling Shannon." He smiled before she looked back at Smith.

Smith set the glass of temperate water beside her plate and sat on the bar stool next to her. "So why won't you give me a statement this time?" She swallowed another ravioli and set her fork down. She popped open the pill box and found the ones for the day. "What are those for?" Smith asked.

"None of your business," she said, taking four from the box. Mentally she reviewed the meds: one for depression, one for anxiety, one for the bitch of a headache she felt coming on and her birth control pill. "I whole heartedly believe at this time it's in my best interest if my attorney is present while I give a statement." She gathered the pills and popped them into her mouth at one time then held up a finger as he started to speak cutting him off. She drank half the glass of water before she continued; "Now I know you can subpoena me but again my attorney would need to be present for questioning. Plus, I don't like the fact you brought that bitch into my house after what happened."

"Just tell me where you met the victim," he asked too sternly.

She looked him over; he was much too handsome with those melted chocolate eyes and muscular frame. She could tell he'd had a long day too. "No," she said rebelliously. "You'll have to go through the process of getting court orders for me and for the club I was at. A very long proposition since I don't think the FBI has much weight in a foreign country. I can't imagine you waking up a judge at this time of night who'd be happy or obligated to give you anything you'd like."

"Shit, Delilah, why are you making this so difficult?"

She shrugged and finished off the ravioli. "I don't like Agent Jenkins."

"Really?" He smiled charmingly. "Why's that, other than the cattiness?"

"She's a bitch. And she hates everything about me. She thinks I'm guilty of something. Not that I am," she said, throwing it out there for clarification.

"So, what do you want?" Her insides turned to goo from his smooth voice.

She pushed the empty plate to the side. "I want her away from the investigation. On the next flight back to the States is preferable."

"And, if I send a perfectly capable agent home, what will you do for me?"

"I'll let you bypass all the court orders for myself and the club."

"And, give me the information I need?"

"Yes," she said.

"It's your club, isn't it? You own it?" he asked.

"I own several clubs around the world. Yes, this is one of them."

He shook his head in resignation. "I'll tell Jenkins she's going home in the morning."

"Send her back to the hotel now. You can handle it from here." She looked him up and down and frowned. "You look like law enforcement."

"I am law enforcement."

"But, you need to look different for the club."

"What? We're going now?" he asked, surprised.

"Yes, as soon as I can change. You'll need to change too." She looked to Brody. "Did you get what I asked for?"

"Yes, Trina dropped it off earlier." Brody walked into the

living room then back with a white shopping bag in his hand. He held it out for Smith, who accepted it with some uncertainty. "That's for you. Think of it as a disguise," he said with a smile and walked away.

CHAPTER 7

Delilah stood for a long moment staring at herself in the huge, gilded full length mirror which lay propped against one of the walls in her closet. She almost didn't recognize herself as the vixen who stared back. She silently worried the dress might be too over the top. She asked for sexy. Trina gave her heart-racing, car-accident-causing sexy. The piece of fire engine red silk that tied delicately at the nape of her neck and draped over her front couldn't have been more than eight inches across at most. It exposed the sides of her full, round breasts baring the flawless skin of her back before it hugged her hips like a jilted lover who screamed, "Fuck Me!"

To make the matter more devilish she pulled her air-dried long hair into a high ponytail with the knot almost on the top of her head. She debated earrings for a while and finally went without. Her only jewelry were the platinum bracelets that twisted around her wrists and forearms like silvery snakes crawling over her pale skin.

Smokey eyes played up the vixen look. It was a show, she reminded herself. A show for the paparazzi who would be outside the club. A show for the patrons who stared at her in the VIP section, longing for her lifestyle. And a show for Smith. She groaned again thinking it was all a bit too much. She had to admit, she really did want to show off for Smith. He'd only seen her in work clothes. This was her chance at blatant sex appeal.

She took a deep breath trying to steady her anxieties. The medicine would help, she knew. It always did. She grabbed a pair of sky high red ballet sandals, and sat on the chair in the corner of the closet, quickly tying on the heels. A hasty recheck in the mirror and she knew she was good. A fuck-me dress for the guy she wanted as if he were her next breath of air. She hated herself for the emotions but they were there.

Delilah found Smith sitting on one of the leather couches in the large living room as he waited for her. He was leaning forward, elbows braced on his knees, scowling. His face relaxed to the point of a droopy hound dog as he took her in. Finally, a smile settled on his handsome face before he stood and said, "Now, that's a dress." It brought a smile to her face.

"You look great," she said, taking in her clothing choices for him.

He moved fluidly, efficiently across the room to stand before her. "Like what you see?" he joked. "I have to admit, I was a little worried you'd picked out some kind of bondage outfit for me. Leather and chains," his charming smile brightened, "But this is good."

What she had chosen was a pair of good jeans, dark leather casual shoes for his big feet, and a white button up shirt with really short sleeves to show off his biceps. It was all very fashionable, top of the line and with his tall, muscular frame he wore it well.

She smoothed the collar of his shirt, enjoying the soft feel of the fabric and her brief touch on his skin. She looked at Brody and dropped her hand. "We'll take the Aston. Meet us at the club."

"Yes, ma'am," Brody said.

Delilah led Smith out of the living room into a long hall, past the main staircase to the garage. He followed her in and stopped. "Holy Shit!" he exclaimed. She turned and saw adoration and pure lust on his face. "What is that?"

"It's an Aston Martin One-77."

"Besides you, it's the most beautiful thing I've ever seen." He was ogling a bit as he stepped close to the dark silver sports car. His hand glided over its lustrous body. "Ah, God, I want to fuck you on it, in it and all over it. I have a hard on just looking at it."

She smiled but didn't say anything as she delicately grabbed the passenger door handle and it unlocked for her.

"I'm driving?" he asked, completely surprised.

She opened her door and slid carefully into the sports car at the same time Smith did. He pushed the button to adjust the driver's seat to accommodate for his long legs. She let him take a moment to adjust things. She set her high heels on the dash in front of her and gained his attention.

"Your dress is really short to be sitting like that," he said, leaning close. He ran a firm hand over her thigh then beneath it.

Delilah's breath hitched as the strong but gentle hand glided over her delicate skin. He got very close, close enough to kiss her if he wanted as his hand slowly became familiar with her legs, one then the other. Startled by the warm rush of her body, Delilah leaned past him and pressed a button above the rearview mirror.

A disembodied voice immediately filled the car and Smith leaned away. "Good evening, Ms. Laughlin. My name is Jody. It's my pleasure to serve you this evening. How may I be of assistance?"

"Jody," Delilah said, "I have with me Special Agent Smith Lowery of the FBI. Say hi," she told him.

"Hi, Jody," he said happily.

"Hello, Special Agent. How may I serve you?"

He looked back to Delilah for guidance so she continued, "I'd like to give permission for Special Agent Lowery to drive all my vehicles."

"Worldwide permission?"

"Yes."

Smith looked at her and whispered, "How many vehicles do you have?"

Delilah smiled and shifted in her seat, setting her feet on the car floor, intentionally ignoring his question.

"Certainly," Jody said. "Could you please place your thumb on the ignition button, Special Agent? Keep it there while it's lit. This will take a scan of your thumbprint and place it within our database." Smith did as directed. "Sir, have the mirrors and seat been adjusted to your liking?"

"Yes."

"These will also preset for any vehicle you drive. Also, as you listen to the audio system it will remember and recall your favorite genres." The light went out, and he removed his thumb. "Special Agent, Ms. Laughlin, you're all set. Is there anything else I may assist you with this evening?"

"No, I think we're good," Delilah said with a wry smile. "Thank you." She reached over and pressed the button again to disconnect the call. She pressed another and the garage door opened smoothly. Delilah leaned back in her seat, trying to escape the heavenly smell of his body wash. It didn't work. She damned her fucking horniness. Maybe all she needed was a good fuck then she'd be back to normal, plotting revenge and world domination. "Press the button to start the car and tell the Nav system where you want to go," she ordered.

He leaned to her, well within her personal space. "I love when you're a bitch." He kissed her quickly on her forehead and leaned back. She huffed at his endearment. He pressed the button and the engine roared. The car came alive, waiting for his slightest movement or instruction, "Oh yeah!" he said enjoying himself. He grinned. "Where are we going, Delilah?"

"We're going to the Temple of Dagon," she answered. He told the navigation system then tentatively drove the vehicle out of the garage. Once in the street he left his caution behind and drove like a man enjoying himself and Delilah delighted in it.

Delilah thought Smith looked almost disappointed when they arrived at the club. "You can park in front," she said, viewing the line of people that extended around the corner of the old brick building. Good crowd for a weekday. A valet opened her door and she very carefully, very coordinately got out of the sports car.

Smith met her and took her hand. "Awesome! That was awesome! I feel like freaking Bond, James Bond."

She laughed at his amusement as they walked past the crowd of potential patrons and paparazzi. Flashes of cameras momentarily left stars in her eyes but she kept moving forward. Security let them in immediately and she caught sight of Brody and Armstrong following a few, discreet steps behind. She led Smith into the building and leaned to him. "Remember, you're not in America anymore."

The loud, pulsing music overwhelmed her. It was pounding into her body. The flashing lights blinded her as they stepped from the hall into the club. It was almost sensory overload, almost too much which is what made the club so popular. An immense, polished steel bar was immediately to her left, lit up with neon lights that danced on the bottles of alcohol. Further to the left was a wide staircase to the second floor terrace of the VIP section. Acrobats, high in the air, tangled in red satin rolled towards the floor.

Shannon stepped through the crowd. She was wearing a short, sparkly gray dress and dazzling high heels. She went directly to Delilah and nodded to Smith, "Special Agent." She leaned slightly down and her voice rose over the music, "Ms. Laughlin, everything's set. The club's fine tonight so please feel free to have fun."

"Next meeting?" Delilah asked.

"It's an Adobe call to Tokyo at five. It's set up for here or at home whichever you prefer."

Delilah nodded and Shannon stepped away, stopping only briefly to say something to Brody. He smiled quickly at her unknown comment before Delilah glanced away. Smith started moving, entering the mass of heated, swaying bodies. She placed her hand on his chest to get him to stop. He was heading into the mobbed dance floor, where she didn't want to go. She wanted to move upstairs, where they could have a better view and be away from the crowd.

"Stripper poles?" he asked, over the music as he leaned in. She nodded, and glanced to the stage where he was looking. There were currently two men and two women working the poles. She cringed slightly as she saw Smith watch the sex show. A very attractive, very naked couple was going at each other like wild animals on the center stage. The S&M set was raised in the middle of the dance floor about five feet off the mirrored floor. Surrounded by thumping, swaying bodies, the young couple was putting on a good show.

Delilah stood tall in her heels and leaned into Smith's

muscular chest pressing her breasts smoothly against him. "This is legal here." His eyes left the couple, and his hands found the side of her bare chest. His thumbs caressed the outer curves of her breasts. She kept talking as he held her close, "It's not love. It's just sex." Her hands found his muscular arms. "He wears a condom. They keep the same partners." She worried of what he might think of them, of her. She looked away, back to one set of strippers. They were upside down, straddling the poles, making out. She appreciated the physical aspect of the trick.

Smith leaned close, his breath tickling her ear as he reassured her, "I'm fine, Delilah." He nuzzled her neck briefly and whispered in her ear, "I like the mirrored floor. Red is my new favorite color." She looked down to see the red lace of her panties was visible. "I want to clarify, you own a sex club?"

She nodded. "It's a hybrid, dance and sex." She took his hand and led him away from the center of the dance floor. They walked back towards the bar and away from the reflection of the mirrored floor.

Brody was leaning against the metal railing of the staircase as they walked past. Another staircase led down. It was roped off and a massive bodyguard stood to the side. He was bald and heavily tattooed, holding an iPad. He looked at odds with it. As she neared, he stepped to the elevator and pressed the call button. "Ms. Laughlin," he acknowledged.

She didn't let go of Smith's hand until they were in the elevator for the short ride up to the terrace.

"What's downstairs?" Smith asked.

"I'll tell you later," she said as the elevator chimed and the doors opened. She again took his hand, reveling in its warmth and strength. She led him past a smaller bar and dropped his hand as she reached out for the second floor polished railing.

He stood beside her, his hand on her bare lower back. The connection was so casual yet so intimate, she found herself leaning closer. They stood looking over the dancing crowd. She surveyed the acrobats, dangling from the satin fabric just a little higher than the second story. Her eyes fell to the floor below and watched the sex show continue. The strippers worked their magic. A hostess walked to them and passed over an apple martini for her and a bottle of Palm beer for him.

"I can't drink this, Delilah," he whispered in her ear. "Something about drinking while working."

She smiled and sipped her cocktail mentally calculating the time since her meds. "I can't drink this either. Something about alcohol and my medications," but she did, and enjoyed it.

"Hey," he called out to the waitress. When she turned back, he said, "We'll take two glasses of water. Room temperature and no straws. We're not five." The hostess smiled and walked off. Smith took the cocktail from her as Delilah got in one last sip. He set it and his beer down on a small glass table. He turned back for her and firmly grasped her hands within his. He led her away from the railing to the cushioned half-moon sofa. They sat together and he faced her, tucking a long leg under so he could comfortably lay his arm over the back of the small sofa. Delilah looked at him, mesmerized by his charm and striking good looks until the hostess brought the glasses of water, distracting her.

Smith reached out and took her ponytail in his hand. He toyed with her hair, pulling her silken locks slowly through his fingers before he let it fall back in place. "Delilah," he said, "Don't be nervous."

"I'm not nervous," she snapped defensively.

"Yes, you are. I can tell." He leaned in giving her all of his attention. A finger traced the line of her face. "When you're nervous you get extra bossy. You nibble on your bottom lip which makes it red and puffy." His finger traced her bottom lip. Adrenaline shot through her. "I'd love to do that." Her heart rate spiked. He paused then continued, "I didn't get to be a Special Agent without being observant."

"A very special Special Agent," she said quietly.

He laughed, his voice masculine and rich, making her flush with pleasure. She felt as if he were blocking out the world, making her the center of it. "So this is what you're going to do." Her eyes met his. "Just look around. Look at the bar. Look at the people, no rush, no fuss. Think of one thing that stood out about the guy. Just talk with me and look for that one thing." Her eyes fell to his after she quickly scanned the VIP section.

"He's not here," she said with a huff.

"Try again. Take your time." When she looked away he asked, "So, what reasons does a seventeen year old girl have to start a business in the sex industry?"

The piercing emeralds flashed back to him. There was nothing accusatory in his tone or the way he looked at her. He just wanted to know. She looked away as he had told her to do and said, "I grew up here, in Europe. Sex is no big deal. Just part of the human nature."

"And," he asked.

Her eyes briefly met his before she glanced away again. She didn't like talking about her past but said, "I always seen the world a little differently. I was able to see things which could bring pleasure." She stopped and returned her focus to him, and shared, "I was fourteen when I went to a party with my sister. Just a house party with lots of kids and alcohol. The normal thing. Someone started a porn on the TV. I was standing off to the side, trying not to be seen," she admitted, "and everyone's attention went to the TV. They were mesmerized for a few minutes. Completely awestruck. Of course, everyone started joking around about it but those few minutes were a revelation." Her eyes fell back to his. He wasn't passing judgment on the kid she used to be. "I knew right then what I wanted to do. That there were people who wanted what I could provide." Her eyes fell to her hands. There was more, so much more than just that night. She looked up when his hand caressed hers. "He's not in the VIP section."

"OK," Smith said, rising from the couch. His hand tightened around hers and he pulled her up. Their fingers intertwined as he led her towards the terrace dance floor. Smaller, private and without the mirrored floor, it was well hidden in shadows from the VIP area. The music was pounding rhythmically around them. Smith took Delilah in his arms, ignoring the rhythm and gently swayed with her.

His warmth radiated through her body. She melted into his arms as his hands lay gently on her back, holding her against his muscular chest. Her hands caressed his back feeling his strength beneath the soft fabric. She tensed feeling a metallic hardness. She pushed her fingers beneath the hem of his shirt and felt the shape of a holster and gun. She almost panicked before she remembered his job. "You brought your gun?"

He kissed her temple. "Yes, I always carry." He lifted her hand away from the gun and kissed her fingers before releasing them. "Don't touch my gun until I know you can handle yourself." It was a gentle order. Her fingers ran freely along his back once again. After a long moment, he leaned closer and whispered in her ear, "I'm awestruck by you, Delilah."

"You shouldn't be," she said with a heavy sigh. Her hands slid under his shirt once more, touching his skin before resting on the edge of his jeans. "I made several mistakes when I was younger," she claimed quietly.

"We all do when we're kids," he said as he nuzzled her neck.

Her breathing halted at the soft, exciting touch. She whispered in his ear, "Mine were...life altering." She exhaled heavily and scanned the main dance floor beneath them. She leaned her head on his chest seeking comfort. It had been so long since she talked about her teen years. Finally, she said, "When my dad got out of the Army he moved us to a small community in Connecticut. My sister fit in so easily. She was smart and beautiful and funny. Everything came so easily to her. But I couldn't adjust. I was like a round peg trying to fit into a square hole. My English wasn't good. I had an accent from all of my years in foreign schools. I had no friends and couldn't make any, plus I was fourteen which is just awful anyway." She felt a kiss press against her head.

Delilah scanned the crowd below as they gently swayed together, caught up in each other's arms. "I, unknowingly, set myself up as a target." She felt his muscles tense beneath her touch. "I was bullied but that doesn't really describe what happened." She took a deep breath, "It started off with just mean kids but it escalated. My freshman and sophomore years were a living Hell. I was assaulted nearly every day at school, beaten and kicked in the halls, in the locker-room." She hiccupped a laugh and said, "I wouldn't go into the school bathrooms. I made that slip-up one day and some girls cut my hair off with a knife." Her whole body relaxed against his. She wanted the comfort he offered in his arms desperately. She liked it. She liked him. "I made three very big mistakes. I've spent every day of my life trying to make up for them." She leaned away slightly from him and looked across the mob below. His hands pressed against her lower back, his thumb tracing the low edge of the red material.

"What are those?" he asked with sincerity ringing through his voice.

She caught movement of a man below. His physical stature: tall, bulky with long blonde hair stood out as he moved through the crowd, close to the bar.

Absently, Delilah answered Smith's question, "I let them get to me so when I fell in love for the first time, well, what I thought was love, it was so much worse because he was part of their crowd. A teenager and in love, it was awful." Her eyes shifted from the man below back to Smith as she said, "I was depressed. I lived in fear. On the worst days, right before it happened I was getting about twelve-hundred text messages a day telling me I was a waste that I should kill myself. I agreed. I could see only one way out of the pain. I couldn't see a future. I tried to kill myself." Her eyes locked with Smith's, not finding any surprise by her admission. "I recognize the man. He went into the basement with a pretty blonde." She tried to step away but he wouldn't release her.

"What's the third mistake, Delilah?"

She stepped back as he released her and said, so low she was sure he couldn't hear, "I got my sister killed."

She stood staring at him for a long moment. Those around them danced, and partied, and enjoyed themselves while she revealed a secret which would end any hope of his wanting her. She stared, watching, waiting for some indication of what he was thinking, of what he was going to do. She expected him to walk away, but he didn't.

Instead, Smith reached his hand for hers and said, "I assume the basement is below us."

She took his hand, and they walked away from the terrace dance floor. She walked straight past Brody, who was stationed near the seating area and said, "We're going to the basement."

He nodded and followed. Armstrong moved to join them before they reached the elevator.

The elevator doors opened with a ping and its light flooded the shadowy basement hall. Small LED track lighting barely brightened the circular hallway. Delilah stepped into the hall and everyone followed. The odd shape of the hall ran away from her in both directions. Numerous closed doors lined the hallway on the innermost side of the basement. A solid brick wall which had been painted white years ago, ringed the exterior of the hall. The paint was chipped and peeling in places to reveal the dark beneath.

To her left was the staircase to the upper levels. Dancing lights and loud music filtered down. She led the group of men forward to a closed door. Unlike the others, this door had a frosted glass center. Delilah opened it with a code entry and crossed into an anterior room. Armstrong stopped and remained outside while the others entered.

It was the continuation of a hall that ran perpendicular to the circular hallway. Delilah was directing them to the interior of the basement. She considered the room she was taking Smith to as the center of her universe like the sun and the rooms like stars were strategically placed around it. She was nervous, almost shaking. He hadn't said a word about her admissions. It's not like she talked about her suicide attempt or her sister's death with anyone, ever. She didn't know what to expect, and waiting for his judgment was physically painful. She'd also never brought anyone into the room. The closest were Shannon and Brody, but they never entered any deeper into the basement than the anterior room. Brody was a second layer of protection beyond Armstrong, who remained out in the hall for however long she needed. Delilah walked directly to a second, solidly built door. At the doorway she glanced over her shoulder to Brody and said, "We'll be a while." She turned back for the door and leaned forward to the security reader.

"Is that optical security?" Smith asked.

She held very still as the computer read her iris. "Yes, it's a biometric iris reader." She leaned away when it pinged and unlocked the door automatically. "Much better than a thumbprint," she mocked, thinking of her Aston. She grasped the door handle and said seriously, "No one gets in here without me." She opened the door nervously and walked inside. She stepped to the side, and watched Smith enter. Once he was in she closed the door, and it locked automatically. Soft LED motion lighting came on, outlining the edges of the room near the floor. The room was kept in heavy shadows purposely, and she said, "Just give it a minute for your eyes to adjust." She stood nervously near the door, her arms wrapped across her chest defensively. She needed to find out what he was thinking. "You haven't said anything, Smith."

He turned to her and ran a hand through his hair. "The only thing I can think, Delilah, is Holy Fuck."

CHAPTER 8

He shook his head and turned from her as he said, "I don't even know what to say."

She took a hesitant step towards him. "This is my R and D room. Research and Development," she clarified. To explain the presence of a low-set mattress resting on a bare metal frame that kept it about a foot off the floor, she said, "I sleep here sometimes." The bedding was still rumpled from her last visit. The dark cream colored comforter lay wrinkled; pillows jumbled and out of place. She felt the intense urge to tidy the room; she hadn't expected to bring anyone here.

The very low LED lighting showed the room as a hexagon shape. The floors were solid polished hardwood but the walls and ceiling were glass. Smith looked up at the dancers above, to where they had been an hour ago. Bodies jumped and danced to music on the mirrored glass ceiling. Delilah could hear the musical vibrations through the flooring and walls.

Smith pointed to the walls and asked, "Is this one-way glass?"

She heaved a sigh of relief and relaxed slightly. She crossed to him. "Yes, it's also bullet proof and sound proof. A charging bull elephant couldn't break it, I was told. They can't hear you."

"That explains the lighting," he murmured. She nodded and watched him glance around. He pointed to the opposite side of the room. There was a slender door, hinged on a track. "What's in there?"

"The bathroom. You just have to be careful to completely close the door before you turn on the light." There was only one solid wall, the one they had entered. Beyond that glass surrounded them.

He shook his head and moved to stand in front of one of the glass walls. "They can't see you but do they know you're here? Watching?"

Her gaze fell over the multiple rooms she could view at any one time. So many people in various degree of contact. She watched them taking their clothes off their partners as if they couldn't wait another second, fucking against the walls, against the mirrors of her room, countless degrees of pain and pleasure being delivered at any one moment.

"There's a release that's signed when they pay for the rooms. I only provide rooms." She pressed her fingertips to the cool glass and watched the couple on the other side. "I made that," she said absentmindedly, trying to figure out his mood. He hadn't run away calling her a monster but he hadn't told her what he thought either. She pointed to a swing which was hooked to the ceiling of the room they were watching. "I got the idea from a tree swing in my cousin's backyard. It was made from an old tire. I used the tire material, straightened it out a bit and hooked it to the ceiling with heavy chains." She pointed again at the apparatus. "I added leather shackles for the knees and feet."

"For people with bad knees?" he asked with a half-smile.

"Actually, yes." She looked again into the room, almost ignoring the fucking couple. "You see if the person is very flexible then their partner can hook them in any way that pleases them. But if you have bad knees, or just need more support it can be adjusted to just above the knees or lower, depending on comfort. The foot straps are really just for keeping your balance." He chuckled, and it gave her pleasure in explaining something she had created.

She took him by the hand and pulled him to the next room that came into view. "Okay don't laugh," she prefaced. "See the cushion." Again, she ignored the couple. It was just a basic red square with two cut-outs. "If you have bad knees and can't kneel down for long periods of time while giving head…," Smith broke out laughing. She smiled and mock complained, "I said don't laugh!"

"OK, OK, you created a blow job pillow for bad knees."

"Yes, it's very popular."

"I can imagine." He was still chuckling.

Her hand fell to his shoulder with a light touch. Her smile brightened the dark. "It's had another benefit too. If a large-chested woman gets tired of lying on her breasts she can slide the pillow beneath her."

Smith was laughing again. "I think I like this room."

She smiled again and relaxed a little more.

CHAPTER 9

"Delilah," Smith said, with a heavy groan like a plea. "I don't know how you do it." His palms pressed flat to glass. He watched the couple fuck. Live-action porn. She watched him look up to the panties of women dancing. He looked away and leaned forward, pressing his forehead against the cool glass. His eyes closed as if in pain.

Delilah knew his frustration; hours of arousal, unadulterated sexual intensity with no release. She shouldn't have expected to keep him in the small room with no hope of relief when he wasn't used to it. She crossed to him, her hand tightening around his bicep as she swung under his arm and stood within his shadow. She molded herself to his chest as he leaned against the glass. Her other hand caressed the nape of his neck as she leaned in for a kiss. Her soft lips nuzzled against his neck trying to ease whatever pain he was feeling. A thrill ran through her body like a bolt of lightning as she touched him. She held herself close to his body, making sure he felt every curve as her hand slid south along his stomach then lower. She exhaled in pleasure as her fingers found his erection pressing against his jeans.

She smiled to herself at his considerable size and kissed his neck again, tasting the saltiness of his warm skin. Her fingers moved against him coaching his erection to full firmness through the denim. She whispered in his ear as she nibbled and licked his lobe, "I want you to masturbate. I want you to put on that condom in your wallet and masturbate for me." He leaned back from her with a what-the-fuck look. She raised a shapely brow. "Don't give me any shit about this. I know best, when it comes to sex." She moved closer as her hand slid across his athletic body to his back pocket and pulled his wallet out. She couldn't resist a squeeze of his firm, muscular backside. Without looking she opened the wallet and took the condom from it then dropped the wallet to the floor. It sounded through the quiet of their room. She remained intimately close as she pressed another kiss to the base of his neck, swirling her tongue lavishly over his skin.

"Every human is hard-wired for arousal," Delilah whispered as her fingers found his erection again. She gently unzipped his jeans and slid her hand inside his black boxer briefs. She exhaled in pleasure, feeling him from his thick root up his impressive length to the tip of his cock. She massaged the crown with her thumb, causing him to groan in pleasure. "Every human is predisposed for mating. It's in our genetics from the dawn of mankind." She managed the condom down his substantial length with both hands as she nuzzled and suckled his neck. Her hands left his erection and she clutched his hips.

She startled as he grabbed her wrists and spun her around. He pushed her hands to the glass forcing her to step forward. He spread her hands wide and quickly kicked a shoe between her heels. She was sure he was going to frisk her next which was really unnecessary considering the dress she was wearing. It's not like she could hide anything.

"I didn't mean to make you mad," she said meekly.

Smith kicked in each direction pushing her legs further apart. She tried to keep her balance in the high heels. He forced her hand to the other and held them tightly in one of his. His free hand ran the length of her spine, making her skin tingle with anticipation and excitement. He cupped her ass and almost growled, finally answering, "You didn't make me angry." Pressing his chest into her back as his hand found the curve of her backside at the junction of her thigh. He pushed her lacy panties aside. Sliding two fingers between the moist folds of her sex, swirling them about he asked with a heavy exhale, "Is this for me, Delilah? Or is this just human nature, watching these people fuck like its nothing?"

She leaned her head back on his shoulder and closed her eyes in pleasure as his fingers fucked her. His rhythmic thrusts in and out of her body heated her desires. She felt frustrated as his fingers left her. He placed the tips of his fingers on her lips; moistening them with her own arousal. She flicked her tongue across his fingertips before he drew them away.

He leaned over her shoulder and licked his fingers clean, murmuring, "God, you taste so good." She watched, almost with jealousy as his tongue and lips cleaned her from his fingers.

His clean fingers moved to her hip and he grabbed her roughly. His other hand left her wrists but she kept them on the glass. His hand moved beneath the thin red silk and splayed across her taut stomach. Her head lolled forward and her eyes fluttered closed as his hand dragged greedily up her stomach finally finding her plump, full breast. He rolled and tugged at her nipple, playing with it, teasing her. He grabbed hold of her; tightening his grip on her fleshy mound as he took a step closer.

She felt his massive erection against her thigh and the curve of her backside. He circled her wet folds with the tip of his erection. She braced herself, pulling her hands further apart just a moment before he slammed into her behind. She cried out as he filled her in one move. He tightened his grip on her breast and hip. Her face reddened with painful desire as his erection slid from her body and slammed back in. The heat radiating off of him was intense almost burning her with pleasure as he took her roughly.

She found herself pushing back on him. Her body yearning for his fullness. His hand released her hip and pressed against the glass as he tried to take some of his weight off of her. Her hips tilted, rocking against him offering him more as he continued fucking her against the glass wall. She felt him thicken inside of her as he crashed into her over and over. He cursed as he came, milking his body into hers.

He finally slowed to a stop panting heavily against her bare shoulder. She leaned back against him, putting an arm up over her head to his hair, holding him in place as their world quieted. He breathed and slid from her body. He leaned his forehead to her shoulder and said, "Ah, shit, Delilah. I'm so sorry. I didn't even ask you. I didn't even kiss you."

She turned slowly to face him. Her fingertips caressed his face. "If I didn't want it to happen it wouldn't have."

She wanted to steal the agony she saw in his eyes. It was almost too much to bear before he leaned forward and pressed a tentative kiss to her lips. Tenderness turned to restrained lust as he moved closer, his hands shifting to take her body as his mouth took hers. He licked her bottom lip leisurely as if enjoying every inch of her. Her hands fell to his chest and she began unbuttoning the shirt as the kiss intensified and he devoured her lips. She pushed the shirt from his shoulders and he let it fall to the ground.

Her breathing hitched. Her already inflamed cheeks blushed at the sight of his body. He was spectacular to look at. Tall and muscular but not bulky, he was a man who kept himself in shape. A splattering of chest hair led south to the evidence of his virility.

Delilah leaned into him, her arms wrapping around his shoulders. She wanted to consume every inch of him. He was delicious. He was a fantastic kisser as her lips became puffy with craving. His dexterous fingers untied the little strap of the dress at the nape of her neck. Her dress fell forward and his lips followed its descent. He leaned to her breasts and she gasped as he suckled hard on the nipple of one and massaged the other. Her manicured nails massaged his muscular shoulders, running through his hair as she held him close.

He rolled her hard nipple between his thumb and fingers, pinching and pulling as his tongue flicked the other. Hot liquid desire pooled deep in her belly as he played with her breasts, moving between one and the other, heightening her arousal. She held his head in place as she gasped for air. She could feel her body tighten with penetrating yearning. His hands glided expertly beneath the silky material around her hips and pushed the dress and her panties from her body in one move.

He pushed his boxer briefs and jeans from his body as he suckled her. The gun fell to the floor with a heavy thud. It distracted her for just a moment before he stood. His fingertips ran slowly over her stomach and breasts caressing her as he murmured, "You are so beautiful."

She blushed at his kind words. He leaned forward and kissed her again as her hands fell to his stomach. She moved them expertly as she removed the used condom from his still rock-hard erection. She let it fall to the floor as he maneuvered her onto the bed. He pushed the comforter out of the way as he knelt between her legs when she sat.

He took a knee and untied her heels, lifting her feet from them, up and away. She scooted back on the bed and he grabbed her ankles. He pressed a deep, lingering kiss to each of the scars on her knees. He followed her onto to the bed for another lush kiss as his amazing body hovered over hers.

Smith braced himself on his forearm and started to untie her hair as he whispered, "I want nothing between us, Delilah. I want to feel your hair fall around me." He kissed her again with such passion she felt as if he couldn't live another moment without the feel of her lips on his.

He pulled her hair getting the band out. She lifted her hands above her head with an, "Ow!" and playfully smacked his hands away. "I'll do it," she said, her voice husky with desire. His lips and tongue fell to her breasts as she worked the band distracting her. Finally, her hair freed and she dropped the band over the edge of the mattress.

"And these things," he said, a luscious smile on his face. He braced himself on his forearm and pulled her arm close. "How do these come off?" he asked like a kid trying to figure out a new toy.

"Smith, no, please," she demanded as he tried to pull the bracelet off of her wrist.

"Got it," he said triumphantly pulling it off and dropping it over the mattress before turning his attention to the other. He wiggled the second off and said, "Nothing, Delilah. I meant it when I said I want nothing between us." She gasped as he pulled her wrists, one at a time, to his lips and pressed lingering kisses to her scars.

Tears trickled from her eyes, over her temples as she whispered, "Don't...please don't. They still hurt."

"Let me make them better," he offered with another kiss. He kissed the small scar between her breasts. She didn't want him to know about the knife that had punctured her skin there. He pulled back from her. "Delilah, I don't have another condom." She hesitated; she had several available in the bathroom but was desperate to feel him. "I'm good," he offered quietly.

She knew what he meant. Shannon had given her a very detailed informational report on Special Agent Smith Lowery when she asked for one. Shannon had included his last physical and test results even though those were supposed to be confidential. Anything could be purchased from the right person, at the right price. Delilah knew he was perfect in every way.

She had never had sex, not once, without a condom but as she stared into his beautiful chocolate eyes she knew she wanted nothing between them either. She wrapped her arm around his neck and said, "I'm good too." She stretched up for a kiss and relaxed back into the mattress as he followed.

Smith gazed down at her and asked, "This is your safe room, isn't it?" She nodded, unsure why she couldn't stop the tears that dripped steadily over her temples. He leaned in for another long, soul-touching kiss then whispered, "I'll keep you safe." His lips moved to her neck as he whispered again promising, "When others fail you, Delilah I will keep you safe." She nodded, knowing he would. He shifted and her legs parted.

Her body rushed with excitement as the crown of his heavy cock notched between her wet folds. Her breath caught as he shoved the silky hardness of his erection forward to the thick root. His lips caught hers again as his hips rolled back and he glided forward. He growled, "Such a tight, wet little body." Her body rushed another time as his hips thrust again and again. He slid his hands beneath her thin shoulders and flexed his fingers, grabbing her. "So beautiful," he said as his grip tightened. The impressive length of his wet cock slid slowly from her before he crashed back into her over and over again.

She gasped at the assault. Her nails dug into his sweaty back dragging them slowly along his spine caressing the flexing, working muscles of his backside further. She wanted him inside of her. She cried out as he gave her what she desired. She was sure he couldn't get any deeper as her primal instincts swept over her. Her hips tilted to meet his and he inched deeper. Pent up emotions rushed her. She wanted him as she had never wanted anyone. "Come in me," she gasped, "I want you!" Gasping again, she nearly begged, "I want to feel you in me."

Her body washed with liquid heat. Her core tightened in response to his measured pace. Her legs drew up, her toes curling as her orgasm exploded. Her back arched as she cried out, swept away in pleasure and pain as he drummed against her rhythmically, answering her plea. She felt him harden, thicken again within her body. He came with a growl as his hot liquid spurting deep inside her.

For a long moment they lay tangled in each other's arms. She held his head to her shoulder feeling his warmth, rushed breath against her glistening skin. Her fingers slowly traced his spine sliding through the sweat that dampened his skin.

He kissed her shoulder and pushed himself up onto his forearms. His eyes searched hers, before he whispered, "Wow," and she nodded in agreement.

In the back of her mind was the whisper of longing and adoration for him. Smith leaned in, pressing his lips to hers for a long, lazy kiss. He answered her silent plea as his hips began to move once more.

Her words were unintelligible as he caressed her body. He rolled onto his back, forcing her over and on top of him. He sat up, taking her breath. She wrapped her arms around his shoulders as his hands touched every inch of her glistening skin. Her dark hair fell about them creating a curtain of privacy as she began to rock her hips against his. His cock was so thick and so long she lifted herself to get a better position to their connection. He smiled and the world she had known was lost. She was pleased knowing she was delighting him as much as he was her. She rode him as if nothing existed except them, just as she wanted. There was no world outside of the bed they shared.

She felt her body warm and constrict. Her core tightened again with the coming orgasm. She gasped and blinked her eyes open. His hands fell to her hips as he pushed her violently down upon his cock. He was staring into her eyes, lust and desire and something else was there. He yanked her hips forward, all of him filling her as her body responded to his movements and she cried out as her body spasm and orgasm against his immediately. He rolled over with her and slammed his body into her, crying out her name as his cock released its thick hot liquid into her again and again. He milked his body into hers as her orgasm continued around his. Her body tightening, squeezing every last drop of liquid from him before Smith collapsed onto her chest.

Delilah slipped from Smith's arm that draped over her as he slept. He was beautiful to look at. She propped herself up on one arm. He was masterful in bed. She couldn't remember the last time, if ever, her body had responded like that to another's. Looking at him she felt her desire take over again. She was surprised her body felt empty without his. She longed for contact. She would take whatever she could get: the brush of his fingertips against her skin; the pounding of his cock into her cunt. She wanted it all from him.

She glanced again at him with wanton lust. Viewing the sinuous muscles of his ripped stomach, the oh-so-happy trail of dark hair beckoned her to follow it but she pulled herself away and slung her legs over the edge of the bed. She padded to the bathroom and closed the door completely before turning on the light. She caught her reflection in the mirror. He repeatedly told her she was beautiful but her self-esteem just couldn't get there. She would never see what he saw.

She stood staring at herself. Her face was blushed, her cheeks rosy. Even her chest was flushed. Her hair was tousled and sexy. Overall, she had a nice just-fucked look going on. She smiled brightly. She liked how her body responded to his. Liked the just-fucked look he gave her. She came to the stark realization, he made her happy and her smile faded. No one had ever made her happy like how she felt at the moment. "Ah, fuck," she whispered in realization.

His big bare feet were just lying there, exposed by the sheet that had been tugged higher to cover his midriff as he slept. Delilah balanced on one high heeled shoe and kicked him playfully on the bottom of his foot. Smith shot straight to sitting then rubbed the palms of his hands into his face. When he pulled them away he smiled at her, devastating her to the core.

"Hey, beautiful," he said, scooting to the edge of the mattress.

He reached out and grabbed her thighs, pulling her between his legs. "You're dressed," he observed disappointingly. He leaned forward and pressed his nose between her thighs.

"Yes, I have a meeting and you have to catch the bad guy," she said, but now he was awake she didn't feel any rush from the outside world. She caressed the back of his head, running her fingers through his soft hair as he pressed forward. His persistent nose stirred the desire she had been trying to calm.

"Ah," he sighed with serenity, "You smell like me." It was the sexiest thing anyone had ever said to her. Smith pushed her dress up a little and her panties to the side. His hand slipped behind her and he pulled the curves of her backside closer to his face. His other hand massaged her thigh then lifted her leg and pushed it over his shoulder. She grabbed at his shoulders and his head to help her balance. His tongue delved between her moist flesh and she panted. Her core tightened deliciously. He licked and murmured, "You taste like me. I can taste my cum all over you."

His tongue flicked at her clit and she tilted her hips, rubbing herself shamelessly against his face as he ate her with gleeful delight. He moved two fingers around her sex and she almost fainted with craving. "I can't stand up much longer," she whispered, grinding against his eager tongue.

He stopped just long enough to say, "I'll catch you, babe." He returned to her with a vengeance. His eager, delving tongue and fingers made her whimper as her pleasure heightened. Her body quaked, squeezing his fingers tightly as she came.

She nearly fell into his lap, exhausted and overcome by pleasure. He kissed her. The wetness of her arousal shared by their lips. She tugged on the sheet removing it from between them. Her hands found his erection, long and hard between her legs. She lifted herself and manhandled his cock roughly into her. She pushed him into her cunt with one hand and held him around the shoulders with the other.

"You're so fucking warm and tight," he growled into her lips as they sat connected on the very edge of the mattress. She wanted him to come as violently as he had before. She wanted his cum in her, all over her. She barely had him inside of her when she began moving, rolling her hips. "I can't get enough of you," he said into her neck, as she rode him hard.

Her arms curled around his muscular shoulders keeping him close. The delicious tingle ran throughout her body again and she moaned with delight. Delilah could feel him thicken and harden within her. He began pushing and pulling her hips, screwing his cock deep into her as her body quickened.

"I can feel you coming again. Come on, come for me," he ordered. He pulled her hard, pressing her down, forcing her body to take all of his as he came. The feel of his body spurting hotly into hers overwhelmed her, making her come with a cry. It rolled through her in a wave overwhelming her as her core tightened. Her body squeezed everything from him and she shook in pleasure.

She breathed raggedly into his shoulder, trying to catch her breath before she leaned away slightly and pressed a kiss to his skin. She looked into his eyes. She couldn't even think of the words to express how she felt. His fingers traced her jaw before he leaned forward and kissed her softly, passionately expressing all of the words she couldn't think of to share with him.

He gently lifted her off of him and pressed a kiss to the end of her nose. "I know you have a meeting." She shifted to the bed and sat watching him move around the room to gather his clothes. Her body relaxed as she enjoyed watching him dress. Surprise raked through her as a gush of liquid left her body. She moved and looked down to see what she'd felt. A huge wet spot marked the sheets and craned her neck as he stood above her.

"It has to come out one way or the other," he said with a huge smile and a shrug of his shoulders. Her nose wrinkled in distaste before he laughed and bent down for her. He lifted her easily, helped her get her balance. She even thought it gentlemanly when he reached between her legs and set her panties and dress right.

Her hands stayed on his shirt as she asked, "What's the other way?"

"For someone who knows everything about sex, you don't know much about sex, Delilah," his smile brightened and he pressed a quick, hard kiss to her lips. His fingers toyed with her ponytail briefly before he walked away and slipped on his leather shoes.

Her fingers intertwined nervously. "I have to tell you something, Smith." He stepped close. "You're not going to like that I didn't tell you earlier."

His hand took hers, his face turned serious and asked, "What's that?"

She pointed over her shoulder at one of the rooms. "The guy fucking the blonde in number four is the guy from the other night." She shrugged. "I thought you'd be mad I took advantage of you before telling you."

His smile warmed her heart and he pressed another quick, hard kiss to her lips. "Take advantage of me like that anytime. I thought you were going to tell me you weren't on the pill or something." His eyes flicked to the room with the same predatory look she had previously seen in her office.

"Use the Aston and take Brody. I don't want you going in alone," she said. "Armstrong will take me home."

He kissed her again and left.

CHAPTER 10

Delilah glanced at the illuminated clock in the Mercedes as Armstrong started the vehicle: three twenty-five. Plenty of time to get home and get ready for the meeting. She needed a shower and to change into work clothes. She reclined onto the leather and let the movement of the car take over her senses.

She was sure Hell was breaking loose in the club's basement. Brody was to tell Shannon he and Smith needed the code for the lock of room four. Better than breaking down the door. Shannon would provide it and call Europol if any kind of backup was needed by the men. The tall blonde would be taken into custody, interrogated to see where it led. She was sure of it; she just was so unsure of herself at the moment.

Delilah felt fragile, breakable. It wasn't a feeling she was used to. Sex had always been just that, sex. A way to release pressure and stress. It never involved emotions and now she was drowning in them. She rolled to her side and put her feet on the seat beside her. Lying there watching out the window she saw the stars in the clear night sky fly by as Armstrong drove home. She didn't feel used and that was a good thing but rather her feelings were the opposite, she felt overwhelmed.

She felt loved. She was dumbstruck by the idea. Her hand pressed against her lower belly. Her insides felt tingly. She ached where Smith had been. Where he had left himself deep within her. Sex had been about her and her needs up until the point they had met. Now, she was confused. She didn't know what she wanted. She'd never thought about marriage or children but when he made love to her which she realized was exactly what he had done she saw the future in his eyes.

She shook her head with silent regret as the tears began once more. Her business was her baby, she clearly recognized that. It was her ten year old child. She wouldn't turn her back on her creation. She had nurtured it, loved it, protected it, and watched it grow. Wasn't that what mothers did? Could she do both? Have a future with Smith, and run her business in the same intense way she ran it now?

"Ma'am, we're home," Armstrong said, turning the car off.

As he opened his door and exited the car she wiped the tears from her eyes with the back of her hands. She sat up as he opened her door. Accepting his hand to assist her out of the car, Delilah felt the chill of the mid-October night. She steeled herself against the wind and cold as she followed the path to her house. She hardened herself yet again when she realized the future would never happen with Smith. Not when she was deceiving him, keeping secrets of vengeance and hate from him.

There was a buzz over her shoulder that distracted her from the meeting. She hated interruptions. The staff knew not to bother her during the internet meetings. The meeting was being conducted in English but some of the men were spouting off in Japanese and she needed to concentrate on what they were saying. Japanese was her newest language and, therefore, her weakest.

There was a quick knock on the door so she yelled, "Come in," but stayed focused on the monitor. She glanced at the time on the computer; it was going on five hours. She still had the accounting to do, another meeting at three. She sensed his presence before she glanced over her shoulder. A smile instantly brightened her face. "Hi, Smith," she said as warmth radiated through her body at the sight of him. She waved her hand gesturing for just another moment. "I think we've covered everything," she said to the group in Japanese. She switched to English, "Send me the figures within a week and we'll revisit when I'm done with them." She said goodbye and ended the call. When her screen turned dark she swiveled in her leather office chair to face him. He was looking around her room, poking through things. It would have been invasive if anyone else was doing it. "Finding anything you like?" she asked as he opened the nightstand drawer.

"Huh? Oh, sorry, professional habit," he said with a charming smile and closed the drawer. "You speak Japanese?" he asked.

"I speak four languages though I'm still learning Japanese."

"I'm so out of your league, Delilah," he said, taking a seat by the glass wall.

She stood from the office chair and crossed the room to sit on the ottoman in front of him. He looked stressed so she reached out. Her palm pressed to his cheek and he leaned into it as he closed his eyes. "What's wrong?" she asked.

He kissed her palm and leaned back. "I couldn't understand the fucking interrogation. It pissed me off. I have to wait for the transcripts."

She leaned into him, her hands bracing against his legs, massaging his muscular thighs. "You should've called me. I could've translated for you."

"Meeting," he said, pointing to the computer. He smiled and leaned forward for a quick, passionate kiss. He sighed and flopped back into the leather chair. "I can't kiss you again."

His words were a shock to her system, almost like the feel of a cold knife to her chest again. She inhaled sharply and crawled into his lap. Her legs straddled his and she asked, "Why not?"

His hands massaged her backside, plumping the cheeks through her black slacks. "Because I'm a fucking federal officer and you're a witness."

"But you like me?" she asked as her hips began to grind and push against his.

"I like you very much, Delilah," he said warmly.

She could feel his erection grow beneath her. He wasn't immune, just torn. She popped open a button on her cranberry colored silk blouse. "Oops! Officer, please help me!" she teased seductively. He tried not to smile. She popped another then another watching as his eyes caressed her skin. She stood on her knees and leaned against him, pressing her breasts into his face.

He was laughing as he said, "Delilah! Stop, you're going to suffocate me!"

"Hold still," she managed sternly, leaning awkwardly past him. She pressed a button just to the side of the glass and it frosted instantly so no one could see in or out.

"Death by boobs. I can't imagine a better way to go," he chuckled.

She leaned back and relaxed against him, rolling her hips. "No one will know, Smith," she said seductively. "I won't talk about us. I know you won't. My staff, my security have all signed NDA's. We can keep this a secret." She nuzzled his neck, ran her fingers down his chest. She was used to getting what she wanted, and she wanted him. She'd never wanted anything more.

"Delilah," he complained weakly as she kissed and suckled his neck. He grabbed her and pushed her back. Her lips were puffy with desire. Her body yearned for his. "I'm supposed to have fucking morals, a code of conduct I live by, Delilah but," he pulled her close so his erection rubbed against her through their clothes. "I can't deny you, how I feel about you. Like isn't a strong enough word for what I feel."

His lips pressed furiously to hers. His hand fisting her hair as he lifted her and pushed the ottoman aside taking her to the floor. The buttons scattered as he ripped her shirt apart. She yanked his shirt up and over his head. Clothes were torn in the race to get naked. He shredded her slacks and panties off of her legs, leaving them where they fell. He pushed her legs apart and climbed her body as she reached behind her back for her bra hook. He pressed her down, pinning her arm as he shoved his cock deep inside.

"You're so fucking wet," he said in awe as he kissed her bare skin.

"My arm," she gasped in pain. He rolled his hips and propped himself up on an elbow to get his weight off of her. Her breasts released as she tugged on the purple lacy bra. Smith took it from her and tossed it aside.

He nuzzled her breasts. "You have the most beautiful tits."

"I'm very impressed with your cock as well," she said with a sly smile.

"Are you now?" he asked, pushing a strand of hair from her face. He tilted his hips, rolling them against her, grinding into her and she groaned still tender from their early morning together. "You're sore, aren't you?" he asked, smiling.

She grimaced slightly. "Yes," she breathed.

"I'll make you feel better," he said as he leaned in for a long, passionate kiss. He moved his heavy cock in and out of her with gentle ease. A slow, rhythmic pace ravaged her body as he lavished kisses and caresses.

Her hands stroked his body, running along the sinuous muscles of his shoulders down his spine to his flexing powerful backside. She forgot about the soreness, about the tingles she'd had previously and let herself be absorbed by the carnal pleasure he was giving. A moan escaped her parted lips as her hips lifted, wanting him deeper. Her hesitancy slipped away within his passion as he rocked her back and forth on the bedroom floor. Her body tautened and quickened with the coming bliss, and she gasped at its intensity. Her body shuddered in pleasure and she cried out, arching her back and her hips as his powerful strokes pushed against her. He thrust into her once more before he released, draining himself into her wet folds.

"Ah, Delilah," he panted into her shoulder. She held him close trying to reign in her own racing heart. "What are we going to do?"

She pressed a kiss to his ear and whispered, "Welcome to the clandestine services." He smiled into her neck as she added, "We're going to keep a secret."

Delilah briefly thought having all of her electronics near the pool was a bad idea. Water and electronics never mixed well. The laptop lay open with spreadsheets filling the screen while she texted on her iPhone a quick question to the head accountant a continent away. Her arms were propped over the tile edge keeping her above the water level her naked body suspended in the warm pool water. Beside the laptop were a dinner plate of angel hair pasta in Alfredo sauce and a bottle of wine. She finished the text and set the phone aside to pick up the crystal glass of red wine. She took a long sip of the fruity liquid before setting the glass back on the titled floor.

She looked again at the spreadsheets and did the math in her head. She knew it made her something of an oddity, the ability to do high level calculations without having to put the figures into a computer or calculator. She had always considered herself abnormal with a past to prove it. Her math skills were something she appreciated, something of a touchstone for her over the years. Delilah treasured the fact she wasn't dependent on anyone else to take care of her business financially. She shoveled a forkful of pasta into her mouth and drank some more wine, popping the nightly pills from the container. She saved the spreadsheets and finished off the pasta. The phone pinged and she read the reply from the accountant. The answer was what she expected as she drank the remainder of the wine. She set the empty glass down and pushed away from the wall.

The current wasn't running so the pool room was silent as she quieted her mind and took a long slow breath. She didn't release it but pushed herself under and drifted to the bottom of the pool. She leaned against the wall and closed her eyes. Silence enveloped her, infiltrated her body. She always felt more relaxed when she was able to calm her mind and her body. Her psychiatrist had encouraged her to find something relaxing to do, to somehow mitigate her stress and anxiety though Delilah was sure he wouldn't have suggested hiding under water as a choice.

Her eyes flashed open as the pool filled with a person. Bubbles and an air vortex surrounded Smith as he swam fully dressed to her. She shook her head, silently thinking he was ridiculous. She pushed away from the wall and headed for the surface. He grabbed her arm and pulled her up. They broke the surface together.

"What are you doing?" she asked, pushing a clump of wet, dark hair from her face.

"I'm saving you?" he asked, treading water in his clothes.

"I'm an excellent swimmer," she said, treading water in front of him. She smiled and asked, "You thought I was drowning?"

"I came in and you were at the bottom of the pool."

She swam the short distance between them. "My hero," she flattered and wrapped her arms around his neck, forcing him to hold both of their weights as he treaded water. Delilah leaned forward and planted a big, sloppy smack to his cheek.

He kicked the water and swam the short distance to the pool's edge. Delilah took a look at her computer and dinner area. It was soaked, sitting in puddles of water. "You jumped in? For me?" she asked, releasing him.

"I thought you were hurt or drowning."

She pulled herself up and out of the pool. She walked to the bench and grabbed the towel that sat on its cushion. "I wasn't drowning! I was meditating," she snapped. She walked back and carefully knelt down to the electronics. "Shit," she grumbled. She picked up the laptop and let the water drain from it. She gave it a shake to get the last drops off and moved it to a dry area. She took the iPhone in the towel next. She looked scornfully back to Smith. He was floating on his back in the pool looking at the mural on the ceiling. She caressed the phone with the towel trying to save it. She grumbled again and set it gently on the bench beside the other occupants. Somehow in his rush he'd managed to save his own phone, badge and his gun from the water.

She glanced over her shoulder and he was leaning against the pool's edge, refilling the glass from the dark bottle. She caught his eyes and her anger dissipated. She turned back and he said, "I'm sorry about your computer and phone."

He took a sip of the dark liquid as she stepped back. She walked right off the pool's edge and fell into the water with a little squeak of joy. She popped up and swam to meet him at the edge. "Don't worry about it," she said, taking the glass of wine from his hand. She sipped then said, "My computer automatically backs up to the mainframe at headquarters." She sipped again and clarified, "Back in New York." She set the glass down. "The iPhone's different. Maybe my techies can save it."

His hand reached through the water for her naked side. "If not, let me know. I'll buy you another one." She didn't want to tell him her phone was a business expense therefore the company provided it. He pulled her close, enfolding her within his strong arms and the pool's edge. He leaned in for a kiss, covering her mouth with his as an apology. He pulled away and pushed a wet strand from her face. "How was your day at work, dear?"

She smiled at the endearment. "Just fine. How was yours, honey?"

He smiled and leaned to her once more for a kiss. "It was fine. They're still working on the guy. I finally got the transcription of the first interview. That took a while to read through." He nodded towards the powered off computer and asked, "What were you working on?"

Her arms folded around his neck. "The fiscal year finished at the beginning of the month. I was just doing the accounting. It's not very interesting."

"Everything you do interests me." He smiled and kissed her again. His brows furrowed. "Don't you have a team of accountants?"

"I have an entire department of accountants."

"Then why the math?"

"Quis custodiet ipsos custodies?" she said with a shrug.

He leaned back, surprise overcoming his handsome features. "What was that?"

"Latin." He didn't say anything so she explained, "From the Satires of Juvenal. He was a Roman. It's better known as 'Who watches the watchmen'."

"I know the comic. So, you trust no one, Mulder would be proud."

She chuckled and commented, "I trust you." She instantly recognized she meant what she had said. For someone she had only recently met, she trusted him unquestionably. She pouted as her eyes raked over him then broke into a smile. "I think you're overdressed," she observed then leaned in for a long, passionate kiss, giving him enough tongue to make things interesting as she began to unbuttoned his shirt. He was still wearing his clothes from the previous night.

"I can help with that." He leaned away and disappeared under the water. He broke the surface with two shoes in his hand. He dumped water out of them then tossed them to the floor. She pushed herself up and out of the pool again and turned back for him. She stretched a hand back for him. He took it, pushing and pulling at the same time to get himself out of the pool. She stepped back as he stripped, dropping the soaked clothes to the floor.

"You're gawking," he said with a sly smile, before her eyes rose to meet his.

"Sorry," she said, not really meaning it. Her hand took his and she led him to the wall shower. She turned the silver knob and water sprayed on them as she pulled him close. She rinsed under the warm water as she said, "Your cock is just so huge. I can't be blamed. I can't drag my eyes away. Really," she said sarcastically, "the FAA should put out warnings when you're in the area."

Smith's laughter broke the room's silence as his fingers traced her lips. "Such nasty talk, what else is your mouth good at? Besides kissing and cursing?"

She adjusted the knob again, shutting off the water. "Let's see if we can find out." He leaned and picked up the two iPhones and his gun off the bench as they passed.

Delilah dragged him back into the bedroom, leaving a trail of water behind them as they touched and tangled their way to the bed. She pushed him down and smiled with pleasure as she stared down at him. He set the cell phones and his gun on the nightstand and watched with a knowing smile as she crept up onto the mattress before he reached out for her.

She lowered her body onto his as their lips met. He sighed with pleasure at their physical connection and rolled, taking her with him. She laughed and reveled in his weight as he lowered himself onto her fully. "You're so beautiful," he whispered. He shook his head and said, "I'm so out of your league, Delilah. What can I possibly give you?"

"You've said that twice today. Isn't it for me to decide?" she asked with a kiss lifted to meet the sculptured curve of his lips.

"I can't provide for you. Not the way you're used to. I'll never make the kind of money you do."

Her hand caressed his face. "This," she said as she pressed the palm of her hand to his heart, "isn't about money. It never will be and you're only going to piss me off talking like that. I don't need you to provide for me." Her eyes searched his and she whispered hesitantly, "I need you to be with me for all the right reasons."

He leaned in for a kiss. "What are those? Tell me how you feel, Delilah. Tell me what you need from me. I need you to reassure me, convince me." His hand caressed her inner thigh, massaging her delicate skin before his fingers circled her most intimate parts. Her body flexed and rocked against his hand. Her body shuddered as she came quickly. "Wow," he whispered. "Does that mean I'm getting to know your body?"

Her fingers ran through his soft, wet hair, she closed her eyes. Her emotions overwhelmed her. His fingers brought her pleasure while he continued to work her over. She whispered them, the ones he wanted to hear as her breathing hitched, "I'm in love with you." He shifted, taking her body with gentle force and she gasped. His lips met hers, pressing passion and desire into them.

His body rocked against her as he whispered, "I'm in love with you too, Delilah."

Her eyes flashed open, unsure if she had imagined what she needed to hear from him. She saw it in his eyes implicitly. Love was there and he smiled subtly. She reached out and touched his beautiful face with her fingertips. "Do you? Really?" she asked, as her breathing hitched with his strong, rhythmic thrusts.

He rolled over taking her with him. He sat up as she straddled him. He pressed a soft, warm kiss to her nose. Her body immediately took over from his rocking against his hips. Her body was suffocating in the pleasure his fat cock was giving her. Her fingertips ran across his shoulder muscles and she said it with more certainty, "I'm in love with you, Smith."

He leaned in quickly and took a kiss from her. "Good." He slapped her ass and she jerked forward, "Now, fuck me like you love me."

Delilah smiled and pushed him down. She outlined the flat circle of his nipple with the tip of her tongue before she leaned back, changing the position of their cherished connection. She pressed the palms of her hands against his thigh for support. She lifted her body, tilting her hips then slid back down the length of his shaft. She reached behind her with one hand and rubbed the inside of his leg. She delicately massaged his heavy balls with her hand.

He moaned in pleasure as she took control of his body. His fingers ran over her flat stomach as she continued to play with his balls and rock against him. Her thumb and fingers circled him, cinching where his sac attached to his body before she squeezed and pulled his sac down and away from his body.

"Gawd, Delilah," he growled. "What're ya doin' to me?" his drawl turned heavy and thick as she rode him furiously.

She gasped trying to catch her breath from the fucking she was giving him. "You want the technical answer or just the basics?"

His fingers gripped her hips tightly. "Ah, fuck, the basics."

She rode him, flexing and squeezing with her body. "By pulling here," she panted and tugged, "I'm holding your orgasm back." She fucked him and flexed her fingers, firmly tugged his sac again where it connected beneath his erection. "I won't hurt you."

"I know," he reassured her, tilting his hips to meet her greedily.

"I'll let go right before you come." She rocked against him.

"I'm going to come," he gasped, his fingers digging into her hips.

"I can feel it," she said, panting. She felt his body harden inside of her. She grinded into him then released her grip.

He poured into her with stunning power as he called out her name. He pulled her down onto his chest and rolled over with her, crushing them together. He held her close as his hips crashed into her, milking himself into her tight body with powerful thrusts. He pressed a deep, passionate kiss into her lips as he held his hips against hers.

She bit her bottom lip nervously, trying to calm her racing heart and asked, "Do you trust me, Smith?"

He nodded and whispered, "Yes, I do."

A grin broke across her face. "Good, get offa me."

He immediately rolled from her, sliding his fat, wet cock from her body. She instantly missed their intimate connection as she scooted to the edge of the bed and walked away. She padded into the closet and found her bag of tricks contained in a navy blue overnight duffel bag she hadn't used in a while. Its nondescript design held many of her favorite toys from the store. She found two things in the bag and left it unzipped on the closet floor. Feeling nervous and a bit giddy, she sauntered back into the bedroom with two things in her hands. She hid them behind her back as her eyes found his. She didn't break the stare as she walked to the edge of the bed. She held out her left hand and let a silky emerald green bathrobe tie fall casually onto his chest.

He picked it up, letting it drag up over his muscular chest. He murmured, "I like it." She took her right hand from behind her back. She watched his eyes stare at the crop in her hand. He pointed with his index finger and admitted, "That makes me nervous."

She smiled and crawled onto the bed. She knelt beside him and leaned over for a kiss as she said, "You don't have to be." She set the crop on the nightstand next to his gun. She briefly thought of those as the tools of their varying trades. His just seeing the crop, knowing it existed in her world of pleasure was enough for tonight.

Delilah continued to kiss him, licking his lips, shoving her tongue down his throat as he groaned with pleasure. She lifted his arms, one at a time, over his head. "Hold the metal," she ordered. He took the wrought iron in his hands and flexed, showing off his arm muscles before she made a good knot around his wrists and tied him to the bedframe.

He stretched up and nipped her breast as it hung above his face. She gave the smooth material a tug to check her knots. He was in there tight. "You've been asking a lot of questions," she nibbled on his neck, "making a lot of inquiries," then moved to his chest as she dragged herself slowly down his body, "about how good my mouth can be." She bit his side lovingly and he laughed. She looked up at him with a raised eyebrow. "Hold still."

"I'm ticklish there."

She went back to teasing him.

He tried and failed to restrain his laughter.

Her voice was husky and dominate, "If you continue to disobey me I will have to punish you."

"Yes, ma'am," he said with an unrestrained smile.

She nibbled and bit her way across his lower stomach, dragged her tongue up the cut lines of his stomach muscles as he tried to control his laughter. "So naughty," she said coolly, before she smiled. Her phone buzzed and she sat back from him, staring down with a smug smile. She reached out and answered it on speaker with the slide of a button, "Laughlin."

"Um, I'm trying to reach Special Agent Lowery." Delilah clamped her hands over her mouth, her eyes wide with fear. She looked at the phone and realized it wasn't hers that had rung. They looked so freaking similar! Even their ringtones were the same! She cursed in her mind, trying to remain completely silent.

"Yeah," Smith said with a grimace. "I'm here." He pulled at his bindings but gave up quickly. She mouthed 'I'm sorry' and looked back at the phone.

"This is Detective Vandersloot. I wanted to let you know the suspect hasn't confessed. He keeps insisting he was with the victim but nothing more. I'll need you to bring in Miss Laughlin for her official statement. Perhaps we can get something useful from it to work with."

"That won't be a problem," Smith smirked, looking at her.

"I wouldn't think so considering she answered your phone," the detective said critically.

"We'll be there shortly." Smith nodded for her to end the call so she slid a finger across the phone's screen.

"I'm so sorry," she laughed. "Would it help if I shove my breasts in your face?"

"Special Agent," the disembodied voice said. Delilah jumped in surprise. "You and I will need to talk when you and Miss Laughlin arrive." The line went dead.

"Delilah," Smith said his voice lethally calm. She looked up, her face, racked with pain and worry. Tears dripped down her cheeks. "Untie me, Delilah…one thing at a time." She nodded and leaned across him. She tugged on the material and his hands instantly freed. He sat up and took her in his arms.

"I'm so sorry," she said again, leaning heavily onto his chest.

He took his phone up and checked to make sure the call had actually ended. She leaned back and caught his eyes. He was pissed and she jumped from his arms, from the bed.

"I'm sorry! I thought I'd hung up!"

He ran his hands through his hair and said desperately, "We're supposed to be a secret! I can get in a lot of shit for this. Delilah, I can get suspended or fired!"

She stood in front of him. "Punish me," she shrugged, "for my slight indiscretion."

"Slight?" he half-heartedly laughed then said seriously, "I'm not going to punish you."

She reached across him and pulled two pillows closer to the edge of the bed. She yanked him up and dropped the pillows at his feet when he finally stood. "Then fuck my mouth, or let my mouth fuck you, either way, we'll both get something we want."

"Delilah," he said with a half-smile, "I'm not going to punish fuck you. Shit happens." He shrugged and added, "The Dutch are laid back people. Maybe he won't care." She fell to her knees, her mouth watered as she placed her hands on his thighs. She nuzzled his fat cock with her face as he groaned. "Delilah, you don't have to."

She wrapped both hands around his root and squeezed, rubbing him hard along his significant length to bring him back to a full erection. She leaned forward and pressed a kiss to the tip of his cock. Her mouth watered and she flicked her tongue over his crown. She slid him into her mouth, and he groaned again. She smiled, very pleased with herself as his hands fell to her head, caressing her hair. His hands fisted into her dark hair and he moaned as she took more of him into her mouth. She slid his thick shaft along her tongue to the back of her throat then out. He tasted a sweet mixture of their arousal. Her hands fisted his length as she massaged him. She hollowed her cheeks as she took his erection in her mouth again.

He helped her along as he tilted his hips and pushed himself further into her saturated mouth. She gasped as his cock hit the back of her throat. He withdrew and she looked up at him. A dark, ominous gaze was in his eyes before she broke the stare and filled her mouth once more with him. She hollowed her cheeks again, sucking as hard as she could causing him to groan with carnal desire. His fingers tightened in her hair as he let go of his caution. His hips began to move faster as he plunged deep into her mouth over and over.

Her hands dropped from his cock and she dug her manicured nails into his muscular ass, pulling him deeper into her mouth. She reached for the nightstand and took the crop in her hand. She almost gagged as he thrust against the back of her throat. She whacked his backside with the crop. The snap of the crop against his skin echoed through the room. She swallowed reflexively as the first spurt of cum filled the tip of his thick cock. She dug her nails into his skin and sucked harder as his cock move in and out.

"Ah, fuck it," he said in a husky voice, crashing against her mouth.

She hit him again with the crop, enjoying the sound of leather on skin. She hit him once more and dropped the crop as he came in her mouth. She grabbed his cock and squeezed as the hot liquid hit the back of her throat. She gulped hard and kept swallowing as he poured into her. She gasped as his fingers fisted into her hair, hurting her as he held her into place, fucking the last little bit of cum from his body. She sucked and licked and massaged him. Cum and saliva mixed and slipped from her mouth as she exhaled heavily.

His grip instantly released her hair and he steadied himself against the mattress, bending over as if physically exhausted. He pushed her shoulders, forcing her away from his spent cock. He ran his hand through his hair and inhaled heavily as he stared down at her. He reached down and pulled her up from the pillows. He pulled her closer before he licked the liquid from her chin. He turned with her and pushed her onto the bed. She scooted back, expecting him to follow but he didn't.

Smith reached down and grabbed the pillows from the floor, tossing one to the top of the bed. He shoved his hand under her hips and lifted, thrusting the second pillow beneath her hips. He knelt between her legs and pushed her knees wide apart. He ran a gentle hand over her sex, and her breathing hitched in anticipation.

His fingers ran through her groomed hair as he said affectionately, "Look how wet you are." His chocolate eyes looked up and found hers. The menacing look had been replaced by one of awe and wonder. "You love giving head. It turns you on," he said, his fingers toyed with the wet folds. Two fingers dipped inside and pulled slowly out causing her to moan with delight. Her body clinched around his fingers as he pushed them in and out. He put his fingers to his mouth and sucked them clean as she watched, completely turned on by his touch.

He was the sexiest thing as his head lowered between her legs. She groaned at the intimate touch. He pulled her hips up, tilting them to give him easier access as she laid spread across the pillow. She moaned again as he ate her, sucking and licking her clit while his fingers fucked her. Her hips rocked against his face. Her nails dug into the sheets as he drove her crazy with his tongue. He blew on her clit, the warm air spending shivers through her and she writhed in pleasure. He swirled his tongue and she rubbed herself brazenly against him. He pushed her to the brink with his lips and tongue. He sucked her clit hard and Delilah cried out with a hoarse voice as her entire body tightened in carnal pleasure.

He was on her in a second, feeding his heavy cock into her in a rush. He pressed her down into the mattress, kneeling between her stretched legs, pulling her hips up to his as he thrust against her. She cried out as she came again. He held her in place as he lifted her slightly using the pillow for leverage as he crashed into her again and again.

Delilah whimpered and closed her eyes, overwhelmed by the rollercoaster of emotions and sensations. Her body was too sensitive, too responsive to his. He leaned over her and grabbed her back and her shoulders, holding her in place as he rammed his immense cock into her once more. She stretched for him and bit his shoulder as she came again. He grunted in pain. His hand fisted her hair tightly and he pulled her back, causing her to scrape her teeth over his salty skin. Her face reddened with passion as his embrace tightened. He shoved his tongue into her mouth, kissing her roughly. She could feel his body thicken in her; harden as he grinded into her, screwing her into the mattress. Hot liquid surged from his body into hers as he came with a loud groan. He kissed her quickly, brusquely as he flexed and pulled his cock from her, rolling onto his back. They lay panting together.

"My body feels like Jell-O," she said exhaustedly.

"I love eating Jell-O," he said seriously. She laughed and reached a hand out for his sweaty, muscular chest.

CHAPTER 11

Delilah felt her chest heave with surprise before a fit of giggles attacked her. She rolled into the bed with a peal of laughter and couldn't stop as Smith stepped close to the bed. His smile melted her insides. She was sure he knew just how absurd he looked in her baby blue robe.

"What?" he asked, playfully giving it a twirl. "Don't you like it?"

She nodded and sat up, wiping her tears of laughter from her eyes. "Looks great on you." She chuckled trying to control the fit and asked, "Why are you in my robe?"

"I have to go get my clothes from yesterday. I left them upstairs. I didn't think the staff wanted to see me naked."

"Okay." She nodded again, and watched him leave the room. She gave herself a full minute to appreciate the view before she hopped from the bed and walked into the bathroom.

Delilah stopped in front of the mirror and examined her reflection. Her upper body was patchy red, blushed with pleasure. Liquid dripping down her legs pulled her eyes south and she frowned. Smith's cum slid along her toned body and she shook her head. He was putting so much into her, it had to come out but that didn't make it something she wanted to see.

She walked to the mosaic tiled shower enclave and started it with the press of a button to warm the water then she walked to the vanity and pulled out a hair clip. She didn't want to wash her hair because she didn't want to blow-dry it. She'd rinsed it after being in the chlorinated water which was enough for now. Delilah stepped into the shower and exhaled in pleasure as the hot water ran over her body from the multiple shower heads soothing the muscles Smith was making her use. She tried to remember the last time she'd had sex like this. All-consuming, multiple times a day carnal pleasure but she couldn't remember anything that had affected her the way making love with Smith did. She thought about the last time a man had touched her body and realized how different the touches were. She couldn't fathom wanting someone else's touch after her short time with Smith. She knew every time they touched, whether rough or tender, he was always making love to her. She gingerly washed between her legs, grimacing as the folds of her sex stung from overuse. The stretching, and pulling, and pushing were doing on a number on her petite frame. She lifted her face into one of the streams of water, rinsed her mouth and spit any remnants of Smith down the drain.

"Hand me the sponge," he said, from behind her.

She lifted it over her shoulder and handed it to him without looking. He stepped close and reached around her for the bottle of body wash. He squirted some liquid onto the sponge. Delilah smirked knowing he was good at squirting liquid. A heavy hand pressed against her shoulder as his other pushed the sponge across her back. She moaned in pleasure and tipped her head back. She relaxed against his shoulder, closing her eyes as his fingers massaged her while the bubbles of the heavenly scented body wash caressed her senses.

"You're so beautiful," he said, pressing a kiss to her shoulder.

"Don't even start," she warned with a smile, leaning away before she turned and faced him. "You're going to break me if you keep it up."

"Funny," he said, passing over the sponge. His eyes fell downward. "Keep it up." Her eyes followed his, he was semi-erect again.

She groaned with worried pleasure and said, "You're a machine." Her hands found his wet body as she maneuvered the sponge over him. "You're not going to want me anymore when you've had your fill," she worried out loud.

He took her face in his hands; his eyes met hers, "Never going to happen." She smiled as he reached around her and turned off the water.

Delilah dressed in a pretty, baby-blue long sleeve shirt dress in homage of Smith's bathrobe wearing display from earlier in the evening. She tied the waistband tightly around her slim middle. He was wearing khakis and a black polo shirt, his outfit from the previous day, when she stepped out of the closet.

He sat in one of the bedroom overstuffed chairs, waiting for her. "I hung my wet clothes in the bathroom," he said as he left the chair, and stepped close.

"The housekeeper will appreciate that," she smirked as they met. She wanted him again. Liquid pleasure began to pool in her lower belly, forcing her to squeeze her thighs to keep from attacking him.

"A kiss before we leave?" he asked. She didn't even think about it as she lifted her face to meet his. His mouth covered hers gently with controlled passion as his fingertips traced the outline of her jaw. His warm, wet lips left hers. She was momentarily disappointed as he leaned away. He offered, "Your phone. It looks like its working." He smiled sheepishly, "I made sure you got yours and I got mine."

"Such a gentleman," she said sweetly.

"Pops would whack me upside the head if I wasn't." He offered his hand and she placed hers within his, their fingers entwining as they left the bedroom.

Delilah pulled her cashmere coat tighter as a chill took her although the heater in the Mercedes was on. She could feel the wave of heat on her legs but the chill ran up her spine. She shivered and tried to ignore it. She opened her handbag and found her hairbrush. She began to brush her long, dark hair as she said, "Tell me about your grandparents." She knew something of his grandparents, Lee and Irene O'Keefe from Shannon's report but wanted his words and masculine voice to comfort and warm her.

Smith took the brush from her hand and made his index finger spin gesturing for her to turn around. She'd never had anyone volunteer to brush her hair before and hesitated. Finally, after a moment of indecision she did as he silently asked. "My grandparents are good people," he said. "They lead a small town kind of life. You know church, barbeques, being friendly and gossipy at the same time," he said quietly as he ran the brush through her hair a few times. "They raised me when my parents died. I know that was hard on them, mourning and being stuck raising a teenager when they weren't expecting it."

"I know they would've done anything for you."

"How do you know?"

"Because I'd do anything for you," she blushed as she quietly admitted. Silence filled the car before she asked, "Have they always lived in Orange Beach?" She turned and took the brush from him, placing it back in the handbag.

He smiled and said, "You remembered. No, they're actually from Ireland, originally. They grew up in the same town, high school sweethearts. He got a job offer in Alabama too many years ago to count and she came with him."

"They're proof," she said absently. She leaned into him and he wrapped an arm around her shoulders.

"Proof of what?" he asked, before he pressed a kiss to her hair.

"Proof that real love exists."

He leaned close and kissed her gently. "Delilah," he said quietly then shifted so they looked into each other's eyes, "I'm going to tell you something, not as your...friend," he said hesitantly, "but as a law enforcement officer. I don't think you should give a statement tonight."

"Why not?" she asked and leaned from him. They were going to the Europol offices in the middle of the night because the detective wanted to speak with them. It hadn't been her idea to go to Europol. Her idea had been to remain in bed, wrapped in each other's arms.

"You can ID the guy. Tell them where you saw him but don't make it official. Once you do, it'll be part of the criminal investigation. In their official records. They'll be able to ask for more information, details on where you saw him. If you misrepresent any part of your statement you can get into trouble legally. I really want you to have your attorney with you, not just by phone for this statement."

His warning made her nervous. She didn't take his years of law enforcement lightly. He was offering her good advice. "Can I put off the statement?"

"I would," he said, leaning back into the soft leather seat. "Especially if Detective Vandersloot makes trouble for you and me and the phone thing from earlier." His hand traced her thigh gently.

She hesitated then said, "I leave tomorrow, after the store opening, to go back to New York." He grumbled something, and she asked, "Will you come to it?"

He pressed a quick kiss to her forehead. "I'll try."

"Try hard, for me."

The Europol building was frosted glass and steel, giving it an odd mossy green color in the spotlights that broke the darkness. Smith squeezed her hand as the Mercedes idled in front of the building.

"Remember," he said, "less is more."

"Do you really think I've managed a multi-billion dollar business by being an idiot?" she asked seriously.

"Right," he said, opening his door and exiting.

She watched him walk around the car and speak with Brody before Armstrong opened her door. She shook her head. She was perfectly capable of pulling a door handle to let herself out. After all, she wasn't a fucking idiot.

Smith placed his hand on the small of her back and directed her into the building through the stationary door. The revolving one was locked for the night. Smith flashed his badge to the agents at the nighttime security desk before they passed. The lobby lights were dimmed except for a row of fluorescents that were trained along the middle of the tall ceiling, almost like runway lights leading a path to the elevators. They stood nearly a foot apart as they waited in silence for the elevator. The quiet followed them into the elevator and Smith pressed the fourth floor button. Delilah removed her coat and slung it over arm, trying to warm up in the building's heat. She shifted her purse over her shoulder.

Delilah looked up at him nervously as Smith caught her eye. He winked and asked, "Did you know at the beginning of mankind there were twenty-five hours in the day? That's why we feel like there're never enough hours in a day."

"Huh?" she asked.

The elevator pinged and he lost his smile. As the doors opened, he motioned her forward. Delilah stepped into the brightly lit hall, and stopped. The immediate area was full of cubicles and halls ran to her left and right. She didn't know the protocol which made her nervous.

An older man with graying, ginger-blonde hair and a paunch in the middle, she gauged him to be in his late forties or early fifties walked directly to them from one of the cubicles. His mouth creased in a flat line which made his face pout like an aging Muppet.

He nodded to Smith and acknowledged him, "Special Agent." He turned to her and said, "Miss Laughlin, very nice to meet you. I'm Detective Vandersloot. I am the chief investigator for the violence unit, ah, something very similar to Special Agent Lowery's division at the FBI." Another man, much younger, tall with dark hair nearly jogged to meet them. "This is Detective Edwin. He's assisting with the case," Detective Vandersloot said, when the man stopped beside them.

"Pleased to meet you," she offered.

"This shouldn't take long. We just need some information then you'll be free to go." Vandersloot addressed to Smith, "You and I need to talk alone later." He turned abruptly and said, "Follow me." He led them into a glass wall conference room and closed the door after everyone had entered.

Smith meandered to the far side of the room, opposite of Delilah but well within her sightline. Vandersloot directed her to a leather office chair, one of many which surrounded the table. Edwin took a seat on the other side of Delilah while Vandersloot took the closest one. He pulled a manila folder across the table, shifting it closer. She felt surrounded. He pulled several out then rearranged the documents as he asked, "Would you like some coffee?"

"No, thank you," Delilah said. Her eyes fell to Smith as he leaned against the far wall. His arms were folded across his chest.

He wasn't offering much support, not that she expected him to but it would have been nice to have him act as if he cared for her welfare. Perhaps, she thought, if he had just sat next to her she'd feel better. She briefly wondered if she'd pissed him off in the car.

"Miss Laughlin," the detective said, he slide forms and a pen towards her as he continued, "these are witness statement forms. What I would like is for you to fill these out. We'll review them and then you can go." He looked up and smiled for her. "Easy."

She stiffened and put on her poker face though her stomach knotted with nerves. "I'm afraid it's not going to be easy, Detective Vandersloot. I do apologize if I've mispronounced your name," she gave him a warm, apologetic smile. "I have a difficult time with your language. I can never manage," she exaggerated and smiled brightly.

"No apology needed," he nodded to the other detective, "We both speak English, if you prefer."

"Thank you," she said. She looked briefly at the forms he had passed over. "These are in Dutch."

He looked to the younger man and spoke quickly in Dutch, "Go get the English forms." Detective Edwin got up and left the room. Vandersloot's gaze fell back to Delilah and switched to English, "Not a problem, we will get the forms in English."

She waited in silence until the young man arrived back in the conference room. Brody was following behind and she caught the ghost of a smile on Smith's face. Introductions were made and Brody took a spot on the far side of the room next to Smith. Brody leaned over and whispered something that brought a quick smile to Smith's face. Butterflies erupted in her stomach. Delilah wanted to know what Brody had said to get that kind of reaction. Edwin slid the documents to Vandersloot who reviewed them quickly and passed them to her.

She took another, brief look and said, "I'm not going to fill these out." Her eyes rose from the paperwork.

"Are you refusing to cooperate?" he asked.

"No, not at all. I don't mind answering a few questions but I'm not going to give an official statement without my attorney present. Since my attorney's in New York, my statement won't be given tonight."

Vandersloot leaned back in his chair and asked, "Then why did you come in?"

"You asked me to."

"Yes, to give your statement."

"That's not something I'm comfortable with."

"The same rules do not apply here, young lady as they do in America."

"Don't be patronizing. Call me by my name, Ms. Laughlin," she said seriously.

"I can make you give a statement."

She frowned and said, "That's not going to happen." She leaned back in her chair. She learned a long time ago there was nothing anyone could say or do that would make her do something she didn't want to. Her face remained passive. "Now, this is what's going to happen, you can ask a few questions, which I may or may not answer. Once I return to New York, I will contact my attorney and with him present, I will provide a more thorough statement. Your choice, Detective. Something or nothing."

Vandersloot rocked in his chair for a moment then asked, "Where did you meet the victim?"

"In the VIP bathroom of the Temple of Dagon club," she answered at once.

"What were the circumstances?"

"She liked my shoes."

"Your shoes?" the younger detective asked.

"Yes, she thought they were pretty."

"What else was said?" Vandersloot asked.

"She said she was having fun and that she had met a man. She thought her fun would continue with him."

"You own the club?" Vandersloot asked.

"I'm not going to answer that." She thought of the multitude of companies that owned each other which owned the club. Eventually, after a bit of legwork, they would find out that yes, she did own the club.

"You were in the VIP section?"

"Of course, I am a very important person," she said dryly. She glanced up just in time to see a glimmer of both Brody and Smith's smiles.

"Did you see them elsewhere?"

"Please clarify," she asked cautiously.

"In the club, outside of the club?"

"In the club, at the bar," she said, keeping her answer generic.

"Was she with this man?" he asked, sliding a color photo of their suspect to her.

She examined the photo. The man looked tired, hassled. She looked up from the photo, back to Vandersloot. "Yes, that's the man I saw with her." She rose and said, "That's all I have to offer at this time," then extended her hand for his.

Behind her, Edwin made a comment in Dutch. She almost frowned as he complimented her ass. She wanted to go off on him, but controlled herself since she'd given the impression she didn't understand the language. She shrugged on her coat and picked her purse up from the floor next to the chair.

Vandersloot thanked her for her time and motioned to the conference room door for them to leave. Brody and Smith stepped close as the group walked to the elevator bank. The detectives were speaking in hushed tones together, in a language they were sure none of their visitors knew, before the young man laughed.

Delilah laid her hand on Smith's forearm for balance and bent awkwardly adjusting her high heel. She gave him a squeeze as she set her foot back down getting his attention and whispered, "Don't trust them."

He looked to the men who'd stepped away and breathed, "Why?"

"They like my tits and can understand why you're fucking me. I won't even tell you what he said about my ass." She visibly shivered. Smith looked between the detectives and her as she continued, "He's going to tell you he'll give you a week to talk with your boss but he's going to call sooner." The elevator pinged signaling its arrival. She took a step away and whispered, "Come to the house later." She stepped into the elevator and turned back to face Smith. A flash of anger crossed his face then it was passive, empty of emotion. She recognized it as his poker face as the elevator doors closed.

The world cocooned her in darkness save for the light from the computer monitor as she worked her way through the night. She glanced over her shoulder quickly, and finished typing an email to her west coast VP.

"What are you still doing up?" Smith asked, as he crossed the room and stood behind her. His fingers touched her shoulders as she leaned to him, relaxing her cheek against his warm hand.

With the press of the last keystroke she answered, "I couldn't sleep knowing you were getting in trouble because of me." She hit the send button and turned for him. "What did he say?" she asked as Smith slumped onto the edge of the big bed. She stood and closed the distance between them. She embraced him, letting him lean onto her chest and he exhaled. She held him close, running her fingers through his soft hair.

"Good thing I don't work for him." He looked up into her eyes and said, "I didn't tell him specifics about our relationship, but he figured out a lot on his own from what he heard on the phone. He wants me fired." Smith exhaled heavily again and pulled her hands to his lips. He pressed soft kisses to each of her fingers. Smith looked up once more. "He said what you said he would. He'll give me a week to talk with my boss before he calls."

Her fingers traced his jawline; a day's worth of stubble was beginning to appear. She was trying to think of all the possibilities, running the gamut on all likely strategic outcomes as she asked, "What are you going to do?"

"About work? Nothing, for now. About you?" He stretched for her, and she met him with a warm, passionate kiss.

Delilah woke as she had fallen to sleep, naked and tangled with Smith. His powerful arms wrapped around her, holding her tightly, her back pressed to his chest. His hand moved across her stomach caressing her skin, arousing her with his touch. Liquid heat pooled deep within her belly as the apex of her thighs ached for him. She closed her eyes, and leaned back into him, shifting her hips to press against his early morning erection.

"Good morning," he whispered, before he placed a kiss beneath her ear. His hands glided along her body, one tugging gently on her breast while the other traveled south between her legs.

She reached behind her and took his shaft in her hand. She massaged him as he did the same for her. Her rapid breathing hitched as he shifted, pushing her leg out of the way as he moved above her. The tip of his cock entered her wet sex as he pressed strong, loving kisses to her back and shoulder.

Delilah pushed herself up on her elbows. His arms wrapped tightly around her, taking her slim chest within his grasp, pressing his chest against the smooth skin of her back. His hips began to grind against her, and she moaned in pleasure. His pace was leisurely, mimicking the early morning hour when there was no rush of their worlds to absorb and stress them. She was captivated by the sheer pleasure he was giving her as she shifted, holding herself on one elbow, leaning heavily back into him. Her hand slid between her legs, and a finger found her clit. She massaged herself as his pace accelerated. His thick, wet cock glided from her body before he shoved back over and over.

"Is this good?" he asked raggedly.

She nodded and pressed her head back against his shoulder. His hips grinded into her backside, rocking against her soft flesh as he took her again and again. He tasted her skin, touched her intimately. Her body responded to his rhythm as she felt his fat cock harden within her. She rubbed herself harder, wanting to come with him. She felt herself tighten with insane pleasure before her body climaxed and quaked causing her to moan with an exhale.

He groaned as her body squeezed his intimately, pulling everything from him as he spurted his hot liquid deep into her. He rocked his hips against her, stroking the last of his cum from his shaft before he came to a rest. His forehead leaned against her shoulder as he panted with exertion. His cock slipped from her as he pressed a kiss to her cheek. Delilah collapsed onto the mattress with a smug, satisfied grin.

Smith pulled a pillow from the pile and handed it to her, tucking her arms around it as he snuggled behind her. Her hair fell all around him. Smith kissed her neck and said, "Think of this as me." She felt him smile as she closed her eyes and relaxed. His weight shifted from her. "I've got to run." Her eyes flashed open and she watched over her shoulder as he got out of bed. He reached for his pants from the floor and stood to see her staring at him. "Don't give me that look," he warned playfully with a smile, and she melted. She flip-flopped on the bed, rolling over to watch him get dressed. The world outside the frosted windows was just beginning to brighten. "I have to go back to the hotel before I can get into the office."

"I thought they had their suspect," she said quietly.

His shirt went over his head and he knelt on the bed, reaching over her for his gun, ID and phone on the nightstand. "They let him go," he shrugged. He leaned back and slid the holster onto his belt. His ID and phone went into various pockets. "They didn't have anything on him other than he was at the club with her. They'll watch him, investigate him and see where it leads." He leaned onto the bed again and hovered over her. His chocolate eyes stared at her with love and adoration before he leaned down and covered her mouth gently with his. A moment of tenderness passed then he said, "Thank you for this morning. I love you, Delilah."

Her heart stuttered its pace at hearing his words. She instantly brightened with a smile like the sun rising outside. "I love you too, Smith."

He pressed a quick, hard kiss to her lips as he leaned away. "Sleep some more, babe."

She watched him walk out of her bedroom before she looked the clock on the nightstand. She'd slept six hours. She rolled over onto her back and hugged the pillow. She was awestruck; she'd slept six solid, uninterrupted hours. No nightmares, no ghosts from her past, no corporate demands. She laughed, breaking the silence in her bedroom. She never slept so long or so well. She felt smith was fully responsible as she sat up and walked into her bathroom to get a new day started.

CHAPTER 12

Delilah got to the store about an hour before the doors were going to officially open. She was excited, her heart racing. A year's worth of labor and hard work culminated in the modern structure in a great neighborhood containing the very best the sex industry had to offer. Her employees were trained and could handle anything. Everything was set.

She slowly walked each aisle with a discriminating eye to verify things were proper and in their place. The local and national news organizations were there already waiting outside, she saw through the huge glass windows. The cameramen were taking shots of the store façade. She was momentarily suffocated by a tsunami wave of anxiety. She took a few deep breaths trying to rid herself of the overwhelming feelings. She soothed her Henley burnt orange colored silk blouse and vanilla colored skirt then checked her Blancpain watch as another sleek black Mercedes rolled up smoothly. It parked behind hers.

Her number two, she concluded. She was glad he was there having flown in from the company's European headquarters in Berlin. Johan Ahlgren got out of the car fluidly, dressed in a flamboyantly bright pink shirt and matching tie only partially hidden by a stylishly-cut navy pinstripe suit. She had known him long enough to appreciate his fashion sense. She was sure he'd given a great deal of thought to the outfit. His spiky blonde hair was short and he had a nose which brought to bear his Viking heritage.

He reached back into the car and offered a hand to his boyfriend. Delilah smiled when she saw Stephan. The young Mr.

Rich was ten years Johan's junior which instantly brought to mind the phrase Sugar Daddy but they were good together. She thought of them as a beautiful couple, Johan's tall and lanky to Stephan's tall and sturdy. She was pleased he had brought Stephan with him. They rushed through the door, drama and chaos mingling in perfect harmony. Johan found her immediately. He kissed her on both cheeks before leaning away to observe the store. "Wonderful," he said without a hint of an accent. "Your hard work paid off."

"Yours too," she said with a smile.

He leaned over and pressed a kiss to the top of her head, not something she'd allow any of her other employees to do, before he said, "You're the math genius who found twenty million to work with." He studied her and got very serious, saying, "You look radiant."

She smiled at the compliment and gushed, "I slept last night."

Stephan rushed to them with boxes of toys in his hands. "I'm buying these!"

Delilah clapped her hands in joy and smiled brightly, "Our first customer!" It always made her happy to sell something. As if it was confirmation of her self-worth.

She pointed him in the direction of the payment center as Johan leaned close and said, "I expect he doesn't realize I can get an employee discount."

She laughed and checked her watch again. She thought of gathering her employees at the front of the store. "Would you like to say something?" she asked.

"Indeed I would," he said, before he clapped his hands loudly calling for everyone's attention, "People, please, come closer." She stood back and tried to smother her smile. She was just so damn happy. "I would like to begin," Johan said, "with a heartfelt thanks to all of you. The store's opening would not be possible without the diligent and conscientious efforts of our employees, both management and team members. It has been a dream of ours to open a store worthy of our reputation and known excellence, so thank you." His hands clasped in front of him as he offered, "A few words from our commander and chief."

Delilah stepped beside Johan and looked over the crowd of employees and guests. The anxiety quieted as she said, "In ten short years this company has brought a level of excellence to an industry which was previously only known for red lights and obscenity. I am honored to open this store with such amazing people, who strive with me on a daily basis to achieve much more, knowing it is possible to accomplish ones dreams and to make the world a better place." She checked her watch again, and lifted a smile. "Thank you for all of your help. Let's get this place open." She stepped to the doors and unlocked it with a twist of her hand. The employees and guests clapped and cheered as she pulled open one of the glass double doors welcoming the first customer. The store became instantly swarmed and she took a step back. She felt overwhelmed and mobbed for a moment before bracing herself with a smile as she walked through the crowd to join Johan and Stephan.

"You'll be here for the first week?" she asked to confirm.

"Yes," Johan said, "we'll be staying at your lovely home."

She nodded, she already knew. Later in the day when she would leave for New York City, her quarters would be locked kept private from all but housekeeping. She stepped to the back of the store and stood observing people come and go. She watched her employees assist customers with the patience and expertise she expected and demanded. She did several interviews with different newspapers, industry magazines, even a few bloggers who had come for the event. As she finished an interview, a warm hand touched the small of her lower back. Her adrenaline instantly spiked. She knew the feel of his hand against her body, and reached behind for it. She took it and turned for him with a smile, as the journalist stepped away.

"Hey there," Smith said, squeezing her hand, intertwining their fingers.

"Hey back," she said in a low husky voice that betrayed her calm exterior. She was amazed by her body's reaction to him. Clean shaven, very professional looking, Smith in a suit was yummy. It was the same navy blue one he'd met her in the other day, but with a different tie, a plain burgundy one. She was already ramped up, her desire pulsating through her based solely on his proximity. They stood intimately close before she looked around and whispered, "I want to kiss you." She squeezed his hand and dropped it.

"I want to do more than just kiss you," he said with a seductive smile.

Johan stepped close and offered his hand as he said, "Johan Ahlgren. Delilah's number two. I'm in charge of the European division."

"Special Agent Smith Lowery, FBI," he said as their hands clasped.

"Delilah," Johan looked to her in dismay, "are we under investigation? Something you didn't tell me?"

She smiled warmly. "No, we're good. I met Special Agent Lowery before my trip to Amsterdam."

"A friend then?" he smiled cagily.

"Yes," Smith answered, his fingers absently tracing Delilah's back through the smooth material of her blouse as they stood close together.

"And lover?" Johan asked with a grin. Smith's hand dropped. Johan reached over and closed Delilah's dropped jaw. "Don't worry. I think I'm the only one who noticed your ridiculous smile. Anyone who can make Delilah smile like that, well, it's good to see. Very nice to meet you, Special Agent." He stepped away, finding Stephan talking with several employees.

Delilah watched him leave then turned to Smith. "Sorry," she mumbled, "guess I need to be more discreet."

"Yeah, me too." He glanced around and said, "Show me your store."

She turned and led him along the first aisle. "Um," she said, starting around one of the row corners, "I like to think of this as the male aisle." She pointed as they walked and talked, "Various condoms. The flavored ones aren't bad."

"What's your favorite flavor?" he asked with a smile.

"You," she said, not missing a beat, gaining a smile from his perfect lips then answered, "Raspberry. Raspberry on any…thing…" she drew out the word. She saw his sculptured lips part to compensate for his sudden rushed breathing, and took great pleasure it causing it. She pointed again. "These are cock rings."

His shoulders shook with a laugh as he asked, "What do they do?"

"They help a man last longer by cutting off the blood supply." She winked and flirted, "You don't need that." She tugged a package from his hand and put it back on the shelf.

"Those look interesting," he said, pointing to another box.

"Those are plastic cock sleeves."

"God, I love when you say that."

"Cock," she said, unashamed. His grin got bigger. She warmed intensely and explained, "They're like condoms but without the ends so you don't come in them. The silicon spikes and bumps," she pointed with a manicured nail, "Those are for the partner, extra stimuli."

"Nice," he commented.

She led him away, further along another aisle and stopped in front of the vibrators where they had met the other day. "I invented this one," she offered. "It's based on the traditional idea, of course but it has two extended knobs on it."

"What are those for?" he asked, maneuvering the package in his hands to get a better look.

She smiled at his curiosity. "The shaft goes inside."

"Of course," he mocked with a smile.

"One extender is for the clit and the other is for the anus. The whole thing vibrates."

"Have you tried it?" He asked quickly, "Do you like that?"

She leaned in and whispered seductively, "I made it. What do you think?" He got that same droopy hound dog look as the other evening and she smiled brightly knowing she'd made an impression.

"Ms. Laughlin," the redhead interrupted, "there's a man who'd like to speak with you."

Delilah returned her attention to Smith. She felt like she was gushing emotions, playful and flirting in public though they were not supposed to flaunt their new, undefined relationship. "Give me a minute?"

"Sure, babe. Go work," he said charmingly. He stepped to the side as she passed, and followed the redhead. The young woman pointed at a man and walked away.

The man was tall but hunched over and wore an old green military jacket. His whole look was out of place in her new store. His dark hair was rough looking like he hadn't combed it in days while his beard was scruffy, unkempt. His dark eyes were alert and trained on her revealing his complete awareness.

She glanced over her shoulder and saw Smith talking with Brody. She turned back as she got closer and asked, "What can I help you with?"

He focused on her, turned with her, causing Delilah to step awkwardly. It forced her position to change with him. "Now, DeDe, is that any way to speak to an old friend? So cold and brisk, after everything we've been through."

His voice made the blood in her veins freeze. Her body recognized him a split second before her mind did. It was the eyes; they hadn't changed when the rest of him had. He wasn't a seventeen year old kid anymore. He'd matured, become a man when she remembered him as something else…something evil.

His hand reached out for her, pressing a pointed dirty nail to the exposed flesh of her chest. His finger dragged downward like a stick digging through the sands of time. He stopped at the scar he'd given her, tugging on the silky material. The contact made her breathing stop. "I've heard through the family grapevine you've been looking for me."

Her brain froze. Her mind refused to work.

She was seized by earsplitting screams. Her sister's shriek for her to run, cries of a violent death from her past. Delilah took an instinctive step back. Her knees broke again. She shuddered with the vicious memory of a metal bat swinging, cracking her bones and she collapsed. She gasped for breath as Armstrong grabbed the guy, pushing him away, manhandling him through the crowd and out of the store.

Smith knelt in front of her, lifting her face gently in his hand. "Shit, Delilah! You're shaking! What happened?"

Her barren gaze flashed from Smith to Brody. She could barely find her voice but managed, "Its Michael. That was Michael!"

"Get her in back," Brody ordered and rushed from the store.

Smith grabbed Delilah, pulling her to her feet then lifted her when the strength sapped from her legs. She felt his movements past others as he carried her into the quiet of the back hall. She buried her face into his chest as the sobs began. He kicked the office door closed with his foot. She felt him move across the office and take a seat on the leather couch.

Sobs racked her body as tears streamed down her face. Her nails dug into his shoulders, needing something real to hold onto. She couldn't catch her breath and started hiccupping as he tried to sooth her, "It's alright, Delilah. You're safe. Tell me who he is. Tell me why all the tears so I can fix it. I want to make it better."

She sobbed hard until she cried herself out. Her sister's screams quieted away. She pushed herself back as she sat in his lap, her legs dangling over his.

"There's my little raccoon," he said, pushing wet, tear soaked strands of hair from her face.

Delilah wiped her face with the back of her hand and looked at the black smudges. Her mascara stained his white shirt. "Shit, sorry," she sniffled. "I must look awful."

Brody and Armstrong stormed through the office door. Delilah pushed herself from Smith's lap as they stopped in the middle of the room.

"We didn't find him," Brody announced.

"You're both fucking fired," she snapped as she pulled her phone from her skirt pocket. She texted furiously then walked into the bathroom.

"Who's Michael?" Smith asked behind her.

"Sorry, man. I can't talk about it," Brody said apologetically. Armstrong made to leave but Brody shook his head at him advising silently to stay.

They stood waiting as Delilah walked back, shoving her phone into her skirt. "You take one step out of this store and you're really fucking fired," she barked. She paced back into the bathroom then out again.

"Tell me his last name," Smith ordered.

Delilah walked to her security ignoring Smith. The words spit from her mouth like venom, "You both are fucking ass wipes. The best part of you is what dripped down your mother's leg after she got fucked! You have one job in this world and you fucked it up! All these years! You're supposed to know what he fucking looks like and you let him touch me!" She turned on Armstrong. "You pushed him out of the fucking store. You had your hands on him and you let him go!"

"I can have Europol put out a bulletin on him," Smith offered. Brody looked interested in the offer as Delilah stepped close.

She turned her anger on Smith, "You have no fucking idea what you're talking about! Don't think you can fix this." Her brows narrowed and her voice pitched, "I spend a lot of fucking money to keep myself safe so I never have to go through that again and they let him touch me!" She turned from him and ran her fingers through her hair, clutching it painfully as she pulled. She wanted any relief from the emotional pain which was boiling through her, burning her alive.

Smith touched her shoulder. She spun on her heel and swung for him. He grabbed her wrist and held it away. "Don't think about hitting me, Delilah. I'll arrest your ass so fast for assaulting a federal officer. I don't care how upset you are. I'm not the one you want to hit." He looked away from her to her security and said, "Give us a minute, guys."

They nodded and left, closing the door tightly behind them. Smith shifted his hand on her wrist but didn't let go.

Tears slipped from her eyes unremittingly. She hated the pain, the anger, the loss of control she needed so desperately. The streams dripped over her puffy lips.

He looked at her wrist, examining the multiple thick white scars. His eyes sought hers, finding her in despair. "How many times did you try to kill yourself, Delilah?" he asked.

"Just once," she whispered.

Smith tugged her wrist and she fell into him. He held her tightly before she stretched to meet his lips and kissed him hard, pushing her tongue into his mouth. Her hands gripped the sides of his chest, holding him close, desperate to feel their connection. She pressed herself into him, feeling the warmth that radiated as if it were toxic. "Please don't, Smith," she begged, pushing him back a step. "Please don't love me." She looked up into the kindness of his eyes and she said, "I'm not a good person. I don't deserve you. You should be with someone who can love you. Who you can love wholly. Not someone like me, someone with evil creeping around."

"Damn it, Delilah." He reached for her and held her face in his hands as he said, "I'll love you if I want to love you." He leaned forward and pressed a passionate kiss to her lips. "I want to help," he said softly as he drew back, his hands falling to her slim shoulders. "Who is Michael?"

"He's evil," she said with a breath.

"Tell me about him," it was a gentle order.

She shook her head no.

"I can fix this. I can find him. If you want to feel safe, I can do that for you. You have to trust me, Delilah."

She shook her head again. Some memories were too painful to share. They were her burden. "I'm so sorry," she whispered and choked on the tears.

He pushed her hair from her face and kissed her again, slowly, passionately before he pulled away and nodded. "Ok, raccoon. I get it. This hurts to talk about. Maybe one day you'll tell me what you can't today."

Her hands hid her mouth as she tried to hold back another sob, but her shoulders shook with emotions. "I don't deserve you."

Smith leaned in, gently pulling her hands away, and kissed her again. Her hands fell to his chest as his lips caressed hers. His actions calmed her emotions but spurred her body. She moaned in desire as his hands clamped around her backside. He lifted her and set her onto the edge of her desk. "I'm here for you, Delilah. I need you to know that."

He licked her lips, his mouth covering hers as she shifted her skirt up to her hips. "Then fuck me as if the past were just a memory, as if it can't control me," she begged desperately.

Smith sank to his knees between her legs without hesitation and pushed her panties aside. His tongue ravaged her and she cried out with the intimate touch. Delilah felt swallowed by his strokes. He pushed two fingers gently into her folds and she leaned back absorbed by pleasure. Her hands pulled his hair, wanting him closer, frantic for him. He pushed and pulled his fingers, fucking her with his mouth and hand.

"Smith," she moaned urgently, "I want you. I want your cock in me. I need you!"

He stopped suddenly and looked up at her. His dark eyes were full of yearning, craving. He leaned to her thigh and wiped off his mouth before he stood and unzipped his pants.

She leaned back, pressing the heels of her hands onto the desk wanting a better position as she reached for his thick erection. He hovered over her as her hand massaged him. Her knees clasped to his sides. She rubbed his tip against her sex, wetting it with her arousal before he shoved forward. She cried out at the sudden fullness before he lips found hers. He steadied himself with a strong arm against the desk as his other hand fisted her hair, holding her in place.

"Fuck me," she hissed, wrapping her legs around his waist. "Harder!" He pulled her hair and she whimpered as he forced her head back and her mouth open. He met her with his tongue, delving into her warm, wet mouth as his cock slammed against her. She whimpered loudly with the pain and pleasure. She wrapped an arm around his shoulder to keep him close. She looked down and watched his huge cock ram into her body before he pulled back and did it again. It was such a turn on to see the fleshy, cherished connection between them.

"Please don't leave me," she begged in a whisper. "Please don't leave me because of my fears, because of my past." She turned her head and stretched for him, taking him with her mouth, meeting his tongue, sucking it greedily.

The kiss broke and his nose nuzzled her neck. Chills ran through her body as he murmured, "Never."

Her whole body tightened and tingled with his movements. Her lower body rippled with a sudden orgasm and she cried out. He thrust against her before he growled with an explosive release. She felt him pour into her, his cock jerking as he drained himself. She squeezed and tightened around his erection, taking everything he offered. His breath panted against her neck before he shifted, and slid his body from hers.

"Delilah," he said softly, his face racked with concern.

Her eyes met his seeing the truth of his words in his eyes. He would keep her safe.

He kissed her quickly and asked, "Feel better?" Her legs fell from his waist as he stepped back, maneuvering his spent cock back into his boxer briefs.

"Yes," she said quietly. She slipped off the edge of the desk and fixed her panties, pushing her skirt back in place.

He stepped back to her and leaned in for another kiss before he said, "I don't ever want to fight with you again." He smiled and her heart melted. "And I meant it when I said I'm here for you. I'm not going anywhere, Delilah."

She knew his promise was more than she deserved.

There was a quick knock on the door and it opened almost immediately. Johan stepped in and closed the door behind him. He surveyed them and said, "A few things. That was hot!" He beamed and said, "I heard the whole thing in the hall." He looked directly to Delilah and declared, "You are loud!" His eyes softened as he asked, "Are you alright? I saw that douchebag touch you." He opened his arms and she walked directly into them.

His biceps held her close, too closely she thought as his arms tightened around her face and shoulders. People don't get hugged around their face! She looked up and saw him mouthing something to Smith. She pushed back against him, pissed he was keeping something from her. "What?" she demanded.

Johan looked down and told her, "You look hideous." He waved a hand in front of her and said dramatically, "Like some kind of woodland creature. You're all blotchy from the sex. Go in the bathroom and make yourself fit to be seen."

She huffed at his order but walked away, and closed the bathroom door behind her. She looked in the mirror, Johan was right. She needed to get cleaned up. She took a few minutes, scrubbing her face and putting her makeup back on from the supplies she kept in the cabinets. When she thought she looked presentable as Johan wanted, as the press expected, and as Smith would like, she walked out of the bathroom and found four men waiting.

Smith stepped closer as Johan stepped back giving them some space. Delilah went immediately to Smith. He pressed a warm kiss to her forehead and wrapped his arms around her petite frame. "You're leaving," he said, pulling away. "We've all decided it's in your best interest." She opened her mouth to object but he interrupted, "You're going back to the house and get everything arranged to leave the country then I'll meet you at the airport. We'll go back together."

"Special Agent Lowery is right," Johan said warmly. "Having that man around, somewhere unknown to us is dangerous for you. We want to keep you safe."

Brody nodded in agreement, "Ma'am, I apologize for my staff and me. You're right. We've known about the threat for years and we failed to pick up on it. It won't happen again."

"Thank you," she said. Everything in her wanted to object, to stay at the opening, to enjoy the rewards of her hard work but they were all looking at her with the same determination. She knew they wouldn't let her stay. "I'll get my coat and purse."

Smith walked to the couch and picked the items up. He set her purse on the desk and turned with her coat in his hands. He shook it open and waited as she tucked herself into it. She picked up her purse and readied to go.

"We'll go out the back," Brody said, then nodded to Armstrong instructing him to get the car. Armstrong left the office as Brody remained close.

Johan stepped to Delilah and pressed a light kiss to the top of her head. "I'll text you and let you know how the party goes."

She looked up and ordered, "You better fucking enjoy it!" He grinned and walked out of the office.

"Ma'am," Brody said, getting her attention. "We're going to walk straight out the backdoor. Armstrong is pulling the car around now. We're going to walk directly to the car. No stopping for anything. You get right in and we'll get out of here. OK?" he asked.

She nodded; he'd never given her orders before. All of the social events she had attended, the meetings, different countries, he'd never been more concerned about her. It frightened her deeply.

Brody looked gravely at Smith and opened the office door. He stepped into the hall and stopped to look around. He nodded to Smith, who moved with Delilah, placing her between the two men as they walked determinedly along the hall.

Smith placed one hand on her shoulder, his other hand moved to his holster.

"He's not going to shoot me," she said quietly.

"How do you know?" Smith asked.

She glanced over her shoulder to him, her eyes wide with anxiety and fear and said seriously, "He likes things up close and personal." A chill of remembrance ran through her.

Brody pushed open the heavy metal door and held it momentarily for them to leave the building as he surveyed the area.

"I'm not going to take the chance," Smith said, assessing and scanning the area.

Armstrong was waiting with the Mercedes just as Brody said he would. Smith squeezed her shoulder as they walked straight to the car. Her high heels crunched on the gravel as she kept moving. She ducked into the open car door, and scooted out of the way, giving room for Smith. He entered almost immediately, and the door closed behind him. The moment Brody was in the car Armstrong sped off. He maneuvered the black sedan into narrow street and gunned it away from her new store.

She leaned back into the leather seat and exhaled heavily, pressing the palm of her hand to her forehead. The rush of anxiety hit her hard giving her a terrible headache. She looked over at Smith finding worry etched on his handsome face.

He leaned close and said, "You did good, babe," before pressing a kiss to her lips.

She couldn't understand it all she did was walk. She closed her eyes trying to ignore the pounding in her head and the aching in her knees.

CHAPTER 13

Delilah sat in one of the leather cabin chairs waiting. She didn't like waiting. Normally, the plane would wait on her and as soon as she arrived the plane would depart taking her to wherever she needed to go. Right now she needed to go back to New York but instead she waited. She stared out the oval jet window and watched suited security guards walking a perimeter around the plane as it sat on the tarmac near the private hangers of Schiphol airport.

After the less than fantastic afternoon, Brody had tripled the security crew with temporarily hired guns to get her from the house to the airport and while they waited for the others to gather before takeoff. They were missing people. Armstrong had been sent to retrieve Shannon from the store. Delilah glanced at her watch. They should be back any moment. She glanced again at the jet door wondering what was keeping Smith.

Shannon popped through the plane door and gave Delilah a fleeting smile as she entered. Brody stepped past Shannon from the interior of the plane with an apology as they pressed into each other in the small aisle then he jogged down the staircase. Delilah watched him walk to the security guards and Armstrong. They were talking animatedly.

She turned back to Shannon as the flight attendant took her briefcase and overnight bag. Shannon looked a little flushed. "How are things at the store?" Delilah asked.

Shannon slid into the seat across from Delilah, her back towards the open door and said, "Things are fine. Johan's taken total control," she smiled. "We'll keep track of the daily figures with the new computer system. Everything looks really good."

Smith stepped into the aircraft and Delilah exhaled with relief. She jumped from the chair and threw herself into his arms, bottlenecking the entrance as Brody and Armstrong followed him in.

"Hey," Smith said and pressed a quick kiss to her hair, "no worries. Everything's alright." She leaned back and nodded. Smith handed his bag to the attendant as she came to him and asked for it. Delilah took her seat again and Smith sat down beside her. Shannon stood and stepped further back into the craft.

Brody squatted next to them in the aisle as Armstrong maneuvered past. Brody watched Armstrong pass Shannon on his approach to a doorway that led to a second seating area before he looked back. "We'll be about two minutes before we get going," he said. "The pilot's already cleared for takeoff." He scooted to the side, a little closer as the flight attendant passed them and readied the door for their departure. He watched her for a long moment then turned back to them. "Once we're back in New York do you want to leave immediately for D.C., Special Agent?" he asked.

Delilah looked at him wanting an answer as well. Smith looked from her to Brody and said, "I'm scheduled for a flight at ten so I'll just grab a cab to the airport in the morning."

"No, you won't." Delilah looked from Smith to Brody and said, "He can take one of the jets anytime he wants. Someone can drive him." Brody nodded and stood. The flight attendant passed him and said something about taking his seat. The plane jerked forward and Brody held tightly to the seatback on the other side of the aisle.

"Delilah," Smith said, "I don't need to take your jet or your car. I can get myself back to Washington."

"Not a problem, Sir," Brody said. "We'll get it arranged. Just let me know your timeframe." He walked away and disappeared into a doorway.

"You can't stay?" Delilah asked quickly.

Smith squeezed her hand. "No, I can't. I need to get back to D.C. and find out what's going on with the senator's investigation. Try to manage my boss before Detective Vandersloot does." He glanced over his shoulder then turned back, his brows furrowed as he asked, "Where's everyone?"

She pointed to one of two doorways separated by the kitchen area. "The door on the right is to the sitting area for the staff." She pointed across to the other side of the jet. "That doorway leads along a hall to my office and my bedroom."

"You have a bedroom?"

She shrugged and explained, "I fly a lot. Mostly overseas. I need to sleep sometimes."

"I wasn't thinking of sleeping."

Her smile met his and she leaned close, asking, "Have you ever had sex in an airplane before?" He shook his head. "Good," she admitted, "neither have I." She leaned back into the seat and closed her eyes as the plane lifted from the ground. Smith tugged at her seatbelt as soon as the plane was airborne. "What are you doing?" she asked.

He pulled her up. "Taking advantage of my girlfriend's massive wealth and complete abuse of business equipment." He pointed to the door and she nodded with a delighted smile as he led her into the bedroom.

Hours later, after a good fuck, numerous orgasms, and a terrific meal with her assorted medications as a side dish Delilah sat in the dimly lit cabin staring out the oval window into the darkness of the Atlantic Ocean. She unwelcomingly felt the familiar despair as melancholy sweep over her. "How did Millie die?" she asked Smith quietly.

"Delilah," his tone was apologetic, "I can't talk with you about details." She looked at him, her stare boring into him until he gave up. "OK, OK, it was ugly," he said. "Very personal."

"Was it a gunshot or," she swallowed hard, "a knife wound?"

"Knife," he answered.

"Like the girl in the canal," she asked, horrific flashes of the young woman filled her mind.

"No, not like the girl in the canal," he said dismissingly. "The senator's death was a personal attack."

"That looked like a very personal attack to me," Delilah

argued with a quiet voice.

"The senator's happened in Washington. A whole continent away. There's nothing to connect the deaths in The Netherlands to the senator. There's no personal relationship between the women."

"You mean other than the way they died?"

"Right," he smirked.

She said quietly, "Michael was in Holland."

Smith leaned forward as he tried to explain, "That girl was one of a handful who were killed by some sadist bastard." His brows furrowed and looked at her. "Michael is your past, your problem. Was he Mildred's too?" She looked away, sure telling him would mean revealing their plan. He touched her hand, getting her attention. "You're pissing me off, Delilah. Tell me what you know."

"Senator Travis wasn't always Senator Travis. She wasn't even a Travis."

Delilah got up and stepped away from him. She sat in the seat furthest from him and tucked her legs into the seat. Her fingernail went nervously to her mouth and she bit it. Glancing at her broken nail, she realized she hadn't done that in years. She stared through the dark window at the nothingness, losing focus. Going home was supposed to make her happy, give her a sense of security but she felt like she was mourning again. Mourning for her sister, depressed for Millie's loss. She had been grieving the past, reserving the future for vengeance. Without that, she didn't know what else to hold onto.

Smith moved to a seat close by and leaned forward, bracing his elbows on his knees. "What's Michael's last name?" he persisted.

"Townsend," she said quietly.

"If you're going to have him killed," her eyes flashed to his, "would you tell me?"

"Would you still love me?"

"That's not a no."

"That's not a yes," she replied.

"Yes," he said, and her tension released. "But I'd try to talk you out of it. There are other ways."

"Like what?" she snapped.

"You can let the justice system work for you."

"It's been doing a stellar job so far," she said sarcastically. He went to say something but she interrupted him, "No," she snapped defensively. "You're talking about a system that forgot he existed, forgot to keep looking for him. If it weren't for Millie," she stopped suddenly.

"Millie what?" he demanded.

"Millie found him," she answered softly.

"Is that what you two were talking about at the bar?"

"Yes and no," she offered. "Smith, we can't talk about this. If something happens," she shrugged, "I don't want any of it coming back on you." She breathed and said, "Plausible deniability." She reached a hand for him, needing some kind of reassurance he hadn't changed his mind about her.

He yanked her out of the seat and into his lap. "You don't have to try to protect me." She curled herself around him as he tucked her in and said, "Nothing's going to change how I feel about you."

"Take me to bed," she pleaded. She lifted her face and he leaned in for a kiss. "I hate remembering the past."

CHAPTER 14

New York City

Smith woke with a jolt to the disembodied voice of the pilot making an announcement that they would be landing in thirty minutes. He rolled onto his side and watched Delilah stretch her naked body against a cream color sheet which draped gently over her exquisite shape.

"Good evening, raccoon," he said with a kiss.

She pushed his face away and groaned sleepily, "Don't call me that."

He could tell she didn't hate the endearment when she smiled. He grabbed her hand and nipped at her fingertips. He rolled on top of her, her legs spreading, accepting his weight as she wrapped her arms around his neck.

She stretched up and pressed a kiss to his lips. "Can you wait until we get back to the apartment? We only have thirty minutes."

Smith nudged the tip of his hard cock into her sex and shook his head, "Nope, can't wait another minute. And from how you feel you can't wait either." His full weight pressed her into the mattress and she groaned while he flexed his hips, grinding into her.

"A quickie then?" she panted.

"Never," he said, his cock filling her once more.

"How fast can you make me come?" she demanded.

He grunted, "A challenge?" He shifted his arms, pressing them tightly to her arms, keeping her in place. "If I hurt you…" he worried.

"I want you now," she said magically.

He smiled, gripped her shoulders and rammed into her. She cried out as he lost control inside of her body. He pounded into her, enjoying the feeling of her knees as they pulled up, her legs wrapped around his ass; her fingernails digging into him. He knew she did that when it felt good, when she wanted more, wanted him deeper. He slammed into her again and again as he felt her body quicken and tighten around his wet cock. He panted with a smile into the base of her neck as she came with a hoarse cry. Her hips arched against his, and he released considering his mission accomplished with her orgasm. His fingers dug into her shoulders as his body rushed with pleasure. He moaned and stroked his shaft up and down her wet, tight body, milking himself completely into her.

"Good?" he asked. She nodded with a silly grin on her face. "In a timely fashion?" he asked. She nodded again so he slid his cock from her tight body. She pouted as he slipped from her so he pressed a kiss and said, "My beautiful raccoon."

"Ah," she grunted and jumped up from the bed. "Don't call me that."

Smith rolled onto his back and watched her move around the small bedroom of the jet, gathering their clothes. He managed to catch his when she threw them at him. He sat up and began dressing. His boxer briefs and pants went on quickly. He shrugged on his shirt, tucking it in before he zipped his slacks. He wiped at the mascara stain on his white dress shirt wondering if it was going to come out though he was almost certain it wouldn't. He rolled his tie up and tucked it into his jacket pocket before shrugging the jacket on over his shoulders. He slipped on his dress shoes and looked up.

Delilah was buttoning her blouse and his stomach flipped. He'd been in love before but nothing to this degree. So strong and so fast it scared him. He imagined what he would do if he ever met Michael. He didn't know what the guy had done to her. He guessed at what the bastard had done to her sister. He wanted Delilah to tell him, to confide in him so he would know everything about her even the bad things. She glanced up and smiled when she caught him looking and his heart jumped a beat. Between the sex and her smile, his heart wasn't going to last long.

She stretched her hand for his and asked, "Ready?"

Their fingers intertwined as their hearts did.

He let her lead him out of the cabin to the forward area where she found her purse and a seat. They buckled in, side by side as the cabin lights increased, brightening the space. She offered him the hairbrush this time and he twirled his finger. She turned slightly with a smile and he began to brush her long, dark hair. It ran through his fingers like heavenly silk. He leaned in behind her and whispered in her ear, "I'm in love with you, Delilah."

She turned and he wished he could read her mind before she said with a smile, "I'm in love with you too, Smith," then he didn't need to read her mind.

"Please tell me you don't own the building," Smith said with a groan, taking in the view of the nighttime city and the brightly lit building they drove towards. He leaned back into the rich leather seat of another high end Mercedes sedan as they sped through traffic. It must have been her favorite type of vehicle with two on two different continents.

Delilah squeezed his hand, drawing a heart on his skin with her index finger.

The late night view was stunning. The city was encompassed by darkness but burst with inner light. The world to his right was completely dark. He knew from his years of living in the city that the darkness was the park. The driver, someone new to him was flying through the crowded streets as if the man had ESP. Smith glanced at the illuminated clock. It was just after eleven. He was glad he'd get some sleep before his next flight. They'd just flown for over eight hours and the time zones were messing with his head.

"Just the top six floors," she said sleepily.

"Six?"

"Technically I don't own it, one of my companies does. I only personally own the house out on Long Island."

"Just the one?" he asked incredulously.

"Yes," she replied, not catching his sarcasm. "I bought it a few years ago. It's my house." She nudged his shoulder and he pressed a kiss to her head as she sighed with a yawn, "I usually only get out there during the weekends."

"It's Saturday," he offered, "well, it will be soon." He could feel her smile when she didn't say anything.

The driver pulled into an underground garage and drove expertly through the concrete maze of pillars and parked cars. They entered deep into the belly of the building and vacant space surrounded them. The parking spaces were empty, save one. It contained a big black Suburban which reminded him of what the Secret Service was using these days. The driver pulled slowly to a keypad that extended slightly from the concrete wall. His window slid completely down before he stretched out and pressed a code into the machine. It was only a moment before the large elevator doors in front of the car opened. He glided the sedan into the elevator and stopped.

"Aren't we parking?" Smith asked, slightly confused.

"I own the bay," Delilah turned and pointed as the elevator doors closed behind them. "But that's just for the emergency vehicle and security. You know, in case the elevator's out or something else happens. Or visitors," she added absently.

Smith felt the elevator rise quickly, making his stomach tighten. "You have a car elevator?"

"How else would we get to the garage?" she asked.

"Your garage is upstairs?"

"Yes, it's a personal garage. For my cars and the staff's so no one is without a parking space. It's on the lowest level," she added.

He shook his head, disbelievingly. She had managed to find a way, in a city known for parking problems, to ensure space for her staff in a convenient location. The elevator halted and opened on a world Smith didn't know existed.

The driver pulled the vehicle out slowly and made a wide left turn, following a tiled path on the garage flooring. Unlike other high-rises he'd been in, the garage level was encapsulated in concrete walls with sparse, thin windows that arched across the tops. Fluorescent, motion sensing lights flicked on brightening the garage.

There were four other vehicles parked at an angle as they rounded the corner. Smith considered having his first heart attack as he surveyed the cars. A new burgundy Ferrari Berlinetta, a Maybach, another sleek new Mercedes and an empty space for the one he was in, he assumed. The cars value totaled more than his house. A new truck, very similar to his own, sat on the far side of the luxury vehicles like a redheaded step child at the family reunion.

"Who drives the truck?" he questioned.

"It belongs to the house so anyone can drive it. You know, to run errands, pick up big stuff."

"You always need a truck," he muttered.

She leaned close and pressed a kiss with her warm, soft lips. His stomach fluttered with the touch. "That's right, you always need a truck."

"Did you pick out the cars?"

"No, not really."

He didn't think so. She didn't seem like a car junkie.

"I asked Brody what he thought for security and went with his suggestions."

"Cause the Ferrari is so safe," he joked.

She smiled and melted his heart. "Yeah, I cheated on that one. I picked out the color too."

The Mercedes parked in the empty space marked with a metal embossed placard that hung on the concrete wall, titled 'Stale'. He read the other placards that called the Maybach 'Guard', the Ferrari 'Runner', the other Mercedes 'Action', and the Chevy's was named 'Workhorse'.

"Who named the cars?"

She smiled and admitted, "I did."

"Why's this one Stale?"

She shrugged and enlightened, "Day after day, things can get stale, too normal. It's a reminder not to let it happen." She tugged on his hand as her door opened. She dropped it as she left the car.

Smith exhaled heavily as nerves left him unsettled. He worried how soon the day would arrive when she'd realize he was stale too. Too normal, too much of a routine, not quite good enough for her he was sure. He could remember being this nervous only a few times in his life. The day he left his grandparents to fly North to start college. It was good jitters but still he was overwhelmed with worry and fear. When he entered the FBI Academy was another time, remembering that first day as one he thought would end him. He steeled himself as he left the car, reminding himself he'd gotten through college, through the academy. He watched her stretch her hand for his as she waited by the backside of the Mercedes. Their fingers intertwined as they walked across the garage. She led him to a set of elevators doors which sat directly beside the emergency stairs enclosure and the car elevator.

"Why the two sets?" he asked, nodding to the multiple elevator doors.

"This one," she pointed, "goes to the lobby. This one's strictly for the apartment."

"So you have to transfer elevators to get into the apartment from the lobby?" he asked.

"Yes. Watch," she said sternly, so he did. She typed in a code and he memorized it without realizing he had even tried. The elevator instantly opened and they stepped in. She pressed a button, and said, "I know it's late for a tour but I want to show you around. Is that alright?"

He smiled and said, "Sure."

They rose just one floor and she stepped into a dimly lit hall. The flooring was a natural polished wood. One wall was completely glass. He couldn't even see the seams in it as if were one giant piece. The world behind the glass was completely black. With its location he knew it was still well within the building.

They walked and she pointed opposite the glass wall, saying, "That's the exercise room. The media and rec rooms are down the hall."

He nodded to a door directly in front of them and asked, "What's in there?"

She answered, "That's storage for the gardener and biologist." She laughed as he looked confused. She led him to the end of the hall and apologized, "I can't turn on any lights in this room. Its natural lighting but when the sun comes up it's amazing. The ceiling is really high so there's a lot of light that gets to this room." She pushed open the glass door and stepped into the darkness with him in tow.

The first thing to hit him was the fragrance. It was sweet and fresh. The sound of rushing water made him turn his head as he tried to identify the source but was confused when it seemed to surround him.

"Just let your eyes adjust," she said quietly. "This is the meadow."

He did and breathed a, "Wow," when the trees and a rolling grassy knoll came into view. "What's the gurgling sound?" He craned his neck, trying to see in the darkness.

"That's the stream," she said with pleasure. "It's stocked with trout, if you want to fish, but its catch and release. There are only five of them that live here."

"You fish?" he asked incredulously.

"Yes, I like to fish. I've gotten better since I can practice here."

He wrapped her with his muscular arms, and tilted her back in an old fashioned way, pressing a kiss to her lips. "And that's all I have to say," he said, standing straight with her.

She tugged his hand and led him from the meadow. They walked back to the elevator and she pressed the call button.

Inside she pressed the third floor button and Smith asked, "We were just on five. Didn't we miss four for the tour?"

She smiled and advised, "Four's the staff level. That's their residence. I don't want to disturb them so late." She added, "Brody and Armstrong have their rooms there. Shannon has a room too but I know she has an apartment in the city as well."

"Anyone else?" he asked curiously.

"There are several other bedrooms. The housekeeper and the chef both live here." The door pinged and she breathed. He thought she looked worried. "Um, Smith," she said nervously, "This isn't my home. This is just where I stay."

He nodded but didn't understand until they stepped out of the elevator. He stopped as the doors closed behind him. Fucking amazing didn't really cover it. His hundred dollar shoes stood on striated marble flooring from a world away that cost some unimaginable astronomical sum, in the salon entryway. He immediately realized he needed some of those Tyvek booties the forensic guys wore over their shoes at crime scenes, so his cheap shoes wouldn't leave any marks.

Smith knew if he stretched he wouldn't touch the ceiling, which he figured made it at least eleven feet tall. Dark, carved mahogany doors closed off other areas of the home which created an optical illusion as they braced against the cream colored walls. It made the apartment seem magnificent and grander, adding to its already massive size. To his right, a carved sandstone staircase led up then split in either direction to another level.

"This is the main level," she said, watching him closely. She began to walk and he followed. "This is the reception room," it was minimally furnished but the art on the walls, taking into account his one semester of art history he knew those were real and real meant expensive. She continued as she moved through the apartment, "This is the living room."

The view was the first thing that made him stop walking. The ceiling was lower so it felt more comfortable but the exterior walls were glass and looked out on to the spectacular New York nighttime skyline. Even in the darkness, it amazed him. He hadn't seen it from so high in so long he'd almost forgotten the effect it could have. It was overwhelming, powerful. His eyes fell back to her; it was like her as she overwhelmed him powerfully.

She led him through the dining room, past the custom hardwood furniture, enough to sit at least twenty people he counted quickly. "Do you want anything to eat?" she asked as they entered the kitchen. It was all stainless steel, modern with two refrigerators and a center island of granite which she dragged her manicured nails along as she walked past. It was a mixture of luxury and professionalism which would make most chefs weep in ecstasy.

"No, I'm good," he said, swallowing hard. He didn't want to tell her he was getting sick to his stomach by the repeated evidence of her wealth.

They walked through the breakfast nook then past the wine cave and laundry room before she told him a closed door was the library. She led him past another closed door and said, "This is my office."

He recognized the foyer area and realized they'd walked a giant circle before she held his hand and began to slowly, awkwardly climb the stairs as if her knees hurt but she didn't complain. At the split she went left, she looked to him with the same worried look and begged, "Don't leave me because of this, Smith." He wanted to kiss her fear away. "In the city I have to keep up appearances. I have to welcome guests and make an impression."

"You've made one," he said with a half-hearted laugh.

At the top of the stairs, she stopped at the first door along the carpeted hall. "Further along are three other bedrooms and a few guest rooms." She inhaled sharply and said, "This is my room." She opened the door and stepped inside. "No one comes in here." Her palm pressed to her forehead and she corrected herself, "No, what I mean is I don't bring anyone here."

He stepped in with her and pulled her hand gently from her forehead. "Are you trying to tell me that I'm the first boy you've brought home," he asked.

"Yes," her eyes flicked down then up, "but you're not a boy."

He felt himself finally relax before she turned and tossed her purse into an overstuffed leather chair. Subtle, well-placed motion lights came on behind the crown molding brightening only the portion of the room they were in. Taupe colored roman curtains mechanically lowered over the large glass exterior walls blocking the outside world from their view as he stood watching.

"They do that automatically when its night and the lights are triggered," she said as she walked away from him towards the far side of the room.

He stopped and looked around her private area. He realized the bedroom ran the length of the building. It was massive, easily dwarfing the huge living room downstairs. The ceiling was a more manageable height, making him feel comfortable. The room was relativity open with a double-sided, floor to ceiling stone fireplace which split the sitting room from the bedroom area. He looked at the area and realized there were no personal pictures, nothing to tie her to a past.

"That's the bathroom," she said, pointing to a closed door further along. She opened a door that was on the far side, furthest from the sitting room they had just entered and disappeared inside. A bright light came on so he meandered to the entryway, and watched as she kicked off her high heels.

The walk-in closet was an immense room. Her hanging clothing was vast. There were floor to ceiling racks of shoes, heels. It struck him as odd since she was so short he wondered how she reached the top rows. There were dressers, he assumed, full of folded clothes and lingerie but it was the huge safe that seemed to stick out amongst the silks and knits. His eyes shifted upward and he exclaimed, "Holy shit! What's that?"

She looked up too and smiled before she advised, "That's the pool."

The ceiling was illuminated a dark neon blue, and was see through. He checked, "So, if you're swimming, I can see you here?"

She smiled. "Yes."

"And you swim naked?" She nodded. "All the time? Amsterdam wasn't just a onetime thing?" She smiled which answered him silently. He grinned, "Well, shit, I'll just pull up a folding lawn chair and get a beer the next time you swim."

Laughter bubbled through her and said, "I can get to it there." She pointed at a small wrap around staircase that disappeared up and around a wall.

"What's upstairs? Besides the pool?" he clarified.

She tossed her blouse to the floor and kicked off her skirt. "The terrace. It's all glass and greenery. Above that's the helicopter pad."

He agreed though he couldn't really remember what she'd said as she reached behind her back and unhooked her bra. He swallowed in knowing pleasure as her breasts shifted and lowered. His mouth watered as the memories of her soft skin flooded him. He remembered the taste of her pale pink round nipples, the feel of the hard points against his tongue as he suckled and massaged her. Her fingertips skirted the lacy edge of her panties as she hooked them then slid them off with a delicate ease.

"Do you want to shower with me?" she asked alluringly, "or just go to bed?"

Shower or bed, his mind ran the gamut, indecision seized him. He wanted both, excessively. He was sure she saw the uncertainty as she sauntered temptingly towards him. Her hands glided over his shoulders, and she frowned. He instantly hated whatever had made her unhappy. He wanted her smiling, no, he thought better of it, he wanted her beneath him with that look of searing pleasure she got when her body orgasm. His indecision left immediately as if it jumped from the terrace above. He wanted her. It didn't matter he wasn't from money or that he would never be able to buy things like what hung in her closet or what was parked in her garage.

He took her in his arms, decisively, without hesitation and kissed her away from the closet. The motion sensitive walk-in closet light went out as they left tangled in each other arms. He barely found the massive bed before he was on top of her, pushing her down, trying to get rid of his clothes. He appreciated she was trying to help so he slowed and let her take over. Her fingers were better at it anyway, he mused.

With her help, he kicked and pulled off the remainder of his clothes. She lay next to him on her stomach kissing his chest, moving slowly along his stomach. Her lips left a trail of heat and passion as she caressed him. Her fingers fell to his erection, and she stroked him to a rigid hardness that fueled him with desire. The moment her lips pressed a kiss to the crown of his erection he leaned over and pulled her above him.

She straddled him on all fours, her knees above his shoulders. He exhaled in pleasure as she lowered onto his chest, pressing the soft mounds of her breasts to his stomach. She flicked the tip of his cock with her tongue then took him wholly in her mouth.

His body stretched with a needy ache as his hands caressed the soft skin of her back. He pressed her closer as she sucked his cock. His hands massaged her back, kneaded her backside as she sucked him hard. He groaned in pleasure before he pulled open her sex and lapped the length of her with a firm tongue. She moaned against his erection, and he smiled. His tongue delved into her wet folds, and she arched against him. He eagerly ate her, licking and sucking her clit. Running his clever tongue across her sex, he pushed it into her body as far as he could reach before he swirled and flicked moist folds, swallowing the liquids of her sex.

Her body tightened, intimate muscles pulled against his firm tongue as he pushed it into her again. His hand held her backside to his face, pressing her into him as he nuzzled and his mouth slurped with a yearning hunger. His mouth ate at the tight bundle of nerves, and he massaged them with his tongue. She was panting against his cock, stilled by her own pleasure as he took her within his mouth over and over. He sucked her hard and she came with a heavy cry of pleasure. His mouth instantly moved from her clit to her folds as he lapped up her moisture, pressing his face into her sex as he sucked and kissed.

He felt her body finally relax from its orgasm as he held her close. He leaned into her thigh and pressed heavy, saturated kisses as she began to work him over. His thick cock went back into her wet mouth as she hollowed her cheeks, and sucked. He gripped her around the hips, holding her place as her head moved up and down his length. He pressed his face into the junction of her backside and thigh nibbling, as she spurred him into obsessive pleasure.

He was moaning, barely audible as he told her, "Suck it, aw, harder."

Saliva dripped onto his stomach as she bowed her head again, and again. He thickened inside of her mouth and came as she went down on him once more. He growled in pleasure, pushing his hips against her mouth as he spurted against her throat.

She kept sucking until he begged, "OK, OK, Delilah." He breathed deeply as she released him. He pulled her around and stared into her emerald eyes for a long moment. He stretched up and kissed her as she hovered above him. "You taste like me," he said quietly as their kiss ended.

She beamed and said, "I was thinking the same thing."

He pulled her close and she collapsed into his arms. He hauled her closer, reaching for the blankets and wrapped her tightly, tucking her in. His fingers ran over the blanket again as she sighed and relaxed against his side. He'd never felt anything like the material, thinking it was a fantastic mixture of silk and flannel.

He pressed a kiss to her dark hair and felt her fall asleep in his arms as they embraced. His hand ran slowly, leisurely along the length of her arm. He gently turned her wrist and stared at the white scars. He frowned remembering what she had said. She had tried to kill herself. He hated the very fact it had happened, but he looked again at her scars trying to see beyond her pain.

It was the first time he'd really had a chance to look. There was a deep, ugly, almost straight one which ran from her mid forearm to the base of her wrist. But then, there were others, scattered and painful looking. He remembered how she'd cried when he first kissed them, how she told him they still hurt. There was another scar which ran parallel to the main one. He looked closely as she slept. There were others, smaller ones that seemed as if someone had hacked at her skin. He looked to the sleeping beauty of her peaceful face, realizing someone had slashed at her, cut her apart when her sensitive skin had just started healing. He thought of her knees, her surgical scars. A small scar was visible on her chest, between her breasts as she lay against him. She had gotten her knees broken she said very specifically. She had gotten her sister, Rachel, killed.

Michael.

Anger flushed through him at the thought of Michael hurting her.

But how was Senator Travis involved? He relaxed in the darkness, and held Delilah close. She shifted her petite frame and her leg moved over his, her hip leaned against his side. He closed his eyes. She had told him Senator Travis hadn't always been a senator. What did that mean? If he took it literally, he knew Mildred hadn't been a senator her whole life. She had been a young woman, a mother, his eyes flashed open. She had been a kid too.

Who was Senator Travis before she had become a senator? She'd been a teenager. Had they been friends? Delilah acknowledged it was the senator who had tracked Michael down but why would she? Delilah had also told him she had no female friends, and he believed her. So they weren't friends. They were friendly, after all she called her Millie, not Mildred. That implied there was a something personal there. They were allies.

He tried to think of what allies had in common. He glanced at the young woman in his arms. She was young. She was a few years younger than the senator. They weren't friends but they had a common enemy, one the justice system had forgotten. That was one very unlucky bastard to have a grief-stricken billionaire and a determined senator looking for him.

But why, Smith asked himself, would a senator be looking for Michael? Smith thought of the senator, trying to fill in the gaps. She was young, just a little younger than himself. He looked at Delilah and realized they all could have gone to high school together, if they had all grown up in the same town as they were all, almost the same age.

He realized with absolute certainty Senator Travis wasn't Delilah's friend. They would never have hung out in high school together. Seniors and sophomores just didn't mingle that much, unless, his brain slowed. He took a mental step backwards, unless they had a mutual connection. He groaned, Senator Travis had been Delilah's sister's friend. Probably not just any friend, he comprehended, with the amount of time which had passed and with the amount of vengeance that had been planned. They were best friends.

He sighed, and held Delilah close against his chest as her hand glided over his body. Her arm lay draped over him.

Senator Travis had been Rachel Laughlin's best friend.

Rachel had been killed.

Delilah held herself personally responsible for it.

Her parents loved her and hated her.

She was the reason her sister had been killed but she didn't kill her.

Michael killed Rachel.

Delilah's scars…her knees, excruciating, incapacitating injuries. Delilah wouldn't have been able to walk away from that type of injury, he knew.

Delilah had been bait.

He shivered with the realization. He stared at the ceiling of her bedroom understanding why the senator and Delilah wanted revenge. Michael had killed Rachel, using Delilah as bait but after all these years her case had turned cold. They just had to find him. Find Michael, when the justice system had forgotten him, just as she said.

In the nighttime quiet his mind made a leap. Senator Travis had found her best friend's killer through whatever means were available between the two of them. Had Michael found her? Smith thought of Delilah's injuries. They were inflicted with a knife. So had the senator's been, and he was sure as shit if he checked, he'd find Rachel's injuries had been inflicted with a knife as well.

"Son of a bitch," he whispered.

Smith woke to incredible pleasure. He peeked open an eye, and found Delilah atop him. He smiled instantly as her hips rocked against his.

"Good morning to you too," he said, stretching before his hands fell to her hips and moved with her. "To what do I owe the pleasure of your company this morning?"

She panted as she rode him, "I woke up excited," she smiled, and his world refocused. She was breathtaking, her skin perfect, her long dark hair swaying before it hit back against her chest. "You had a hard-on, and I needed you."

Good answer he thought as he sat up and swung his legs over the edge of the bed. He sat far enough back to give her plenty of space for her knees. He didn't want her slipping from the bed with her movements. His hands wrapped around her backside, keeping her close as she grinded against his erection. Her breasts were at eyelevel, and he sat for a long moment admiring the view but he couldn't resist and leaned forward for a kiss. His hands traveled up the sides of her chest, stroking the beautiful curves. She wrapped her arms around the back of his neck, helping him stay close.

Smith leaned forward and licked her nipple, kneading the heavy mound as his hands massaged her. He rolled the hard point with his tongue, sucking her. She grinded against him over and over, her body clenching and letting go repeatedly spurring his rock hard erection. She pressed his head forward and he suckled her breast roughly. He sure it was causing just a little bit of pain with her pleasure.

"Ah, Smith," she purred in delight.

His mouth fell from her breasts as his hands lifted her fleshy mounds, feeling the full, heavy weight. He knew if she ever got pregnant her breasts would swell. He wondered just how large her breasts would get. The sudden image of Delilah cradling an infant to her chest flashed through his mind, and he stopped. He sat very still, staring at the small white scar between her breasts.

She stopped too and looked down. "Smith," she asked, "are you alright?"

He could tell she was suddenly worried so he lifted a hand and stroked the lovely shaped brows that had furrowed. "I just," he was lost in her bright green eyes for a long moment as his hand cupped her beautiful face. He swallowed hard. "I just realized how much I love you."

She leaned in and kissed him hard before he rolled over with her. He grasped the only child Delilah would ever cradle to her breast would be his. "I'm going to have to leave, Delilah," he said remorsefully.

"There's a difference between leaving and leaving me."

He shook his head resolutely and said, "I'm not leaving you."

"Good," she said and stretched for a kiss then fell back onto the mattress, "cause I don't want you to."

Smith stepped into the kitchen, and realized Delilah was unlike any one else he'd ever dated. She was never alone.

Fluorescent overhead lights brightened the spectacular kitchen, highlighting the grandeur she had shown him the night before. He was freshly showered from her shower room. He couldn't consider it anything less since he was sure he could throw a football around in there. He was dressed in his travel gear of jeans and a black graphic T-shirt. He extended his hand, and said, "Hi, I'm Smith Lowery."

A young woman with light brown sugar skin tones and short dark hair lowered her cleaning cloth to the counter and extended her hand to meet his with a smile. "Hi, I'm Etta Clark, Ms. Laughlin's chef."

He quickly asked, "You made the cookies?"

She smiled and asked to confirm, "Last week?" He nodded, slightly dumbfounded it had only been a week. He felt he'd known Delilah forever. Etta asked, "Did you like them?"

"Best cookies ever."

"Which ones did you like the most?"

"Ah," he smiled, "They were all great but I loved the ones with the cranberries and white chocolate."

He watched her smile with pride as she asked, "What can I make you for breakfast?"

"Nothing, I'm good."

"Well, if you're not busy with him, Etta," Brody said, walking into the kitchen, "I'd love an omelet." He grinned at Smith. "Don't hurt her feelings by not requesting something."

"That's right," Etta said as she moved fluidly through the kitchen. "My parents spent a lot of money to send me to culinary school. You'll be disappointing not only me but them as well," she teased.

"Alright," Smith held up his hands in dignified resignation. "If you're making him an omelet, can you make me one too, please?"

"Any allergies?" she asked. He shook his head no. "Any dislikes?" Another no.

Smith took the seat across the kitchen table from Brody. He watched Etta gather ingredients and equipment for a long moment before he focused on Brody.

"I need to find out," Smith began, and Brody turned to him, "what kind of security measures you have in place for her."

"You ask because of Amsterdam?"

"Yes," he thanked Etta when she handed him a cup of coffee.

Brody picked up the mug she had set in front of him, and sipped. "We always thought Michael was here in the States, not overseas. It caught me off-guard. Now we know he's in Europe. I have connections with law enforcement agencies," he glanced at Smith, "and non-law enforcement individuals. We'll see if we can track his movements."

"I think that was temporary," Smith offered.

"You mean his being in Holland?"

"Yeah, I think that was for show. His way of proving to Delilah he can get to her anywhere. What's her standard security like?"

"Me and Armstrong," Brody said.

Etta placed two plates in front of the men. Home fries and cheesy, vegetable omelets filled the plates. The aroma made Smith's mouth water. Both men thanked her and continued their conversation.

"What about days off?" Smith asked shoveling the omelet.

"Days off, well," Brody smiled and said, "There aren't many but we have a back-up crew."

"Two men, secure vehicles. The house is good from what I've seen. What about her office?"

"People have to get buzzed in by the receptionist. There aren't many, if any, walk-in appointments. Her schedule's confirmed days in advance. Why the sudden concern, Special Agent?"

"I know what Delilah and the senator were planning," he said, finishing off the eggs and moving onto the home fries.

"I don't know what you're talking about," Brody said seriously.

Smith stopped and looked at him, trying to gauge the man's honesty. "Whether you do or you don't, I don't give a flying rat's ass. I care about you keeping her safe while I'm not here."

"Done," Brody said as he pushed his plate away.

Smith wondered if he meant the food or the security. Arrogance could lead to underestimations and mistakes. Smith decided to share his hypothesis. "I think Michael killed Senator Travis," he said as Delilah entered the kitchen.

She immediately stopped adjusting the brown woven belt around her waist. She looked nice in dark brown slacks and a light blue blouse. Her eyes bore into him at the news he hadn't planned on sharing with her.

"I have to prove it," Smith said, trying to reassure her, "and we'll find him."

"Did you want anything, ma'am?" Etta asked.

"No," she said sternly, and left the room.

"Just keep a fucking eye on her," he said quickly to Brody as he stood and followed her.

Smith found her in the hall sitting quietly on a carved wooden bench. He squatted in front of her, his hands on her knees.

There were no tears as she lifted her head. "I'm sorry," she said.

"For what?"

"I didn't think Millie would get hurt. I thought I'd thought of all the possibilities. All of the scenarios. I ran the analyst, the probabilities. I just wanted to find him. I believed if we could find him then there would be some kind of justice."

"I know," he offered.

She looked at him with sad green eyes, and shook her head. "I wasn't going to kill him." She sighed, "I was going to ruin him and anyone who'd helped him over the years. Millie wanted more. She wanted him dead."

"Rachel was her best friend," he said softly. "It's understandable she wanted vengeance."

"Please don't think I'm a bad person."

"Little raccoon," he said with a charming smile, and she frowned. "I'd never think that." He pulled her close and wrapped his arms around her, feeling her relax against him. "I don't know how long I'll be gone. Don't go anywhere without your security. You know," he pulled back and looked into her bright green eyes, "more than most, that the world's a dangerous place. Don't get lost in it."

CHAPTER 15

Smith wondered how he was going to catch a taxi from the private hangers at Ronald Reagan until he stepped off of the jet staircase and found a sleek new silver Mercedes sedan waiting for him. He shook his head resignedly and got in for the ride home.

Smith loved the look of his Georgetown neighborhood with its two story red brick homes and painted white trim nestled amongst the tall trees as they drove up but parking was always a sadistic bitch. He was glad to be home; having that tired well-traveled feeling of someone who'd been gone for not quite as long as he felt. He scanned the neighborhood making sure everything was the same before he stepped away from the sidewalk. He opened the wrought iron fence which quartered off his small yard from his neighbors. The house had been a steal with the prior family as motivated sellers. When he found out the house across the street was from the *Exorcist* movie he thought it was the coolest thing but, apparently, they hadn't.

He dropped off his bag in his bedroom and thought it best to call Martinez to check in before calling the assistant director to fall on the sword. He pressed Martinez's number and waited for two rings before the man answered.

"What? You don't believe in calling?" Martinez asked humorously.

Smith sat on the edge of his bed and smiled. "Too busy, man. How's everything?"

"Senator Travis' investigation is going along. No major breaks, nothing that jumps out. We did get the test results back."

"And?" Smith asked.

"Good news, there were no drugs in her system other than the alcohol Ms. Laughlin advised in her statement. No signs of sexual trauma. Forensics has gotten some good information from the wound track. They're narrowing down the type of blade used."

"I might have something there," Smith added. He felt lost momentarily trying to decide what to tell his friend and colleague.

"Yeah? Good, share with me," Martinez said.

"There might be a connection to a cold case. I'm going to do some research on it to confirm a few things first."

"What about the dead hotties in Amsterdam? Anything there?"

"I don't know." That was the second time in two days someone had mentioned the possible connection between the murders. Smith considered it then said, "It won't hurt to officially request a copy of their investigations so we can compare the wounds, the knives used. Anything else?"

"Bad news," Martinez offered, "In the whole of fucking D.C. there were no cameras anywhere within a mile of the swamp. We have no pictures to go on."

"OK," Smith said. "There's something else," he hesitated, "I'm going to call Assistant Director Patten to tell him I fucked up."

Martinez was quiet as he asked, "How?"

"I fell in love with a beautiful woman," he said with a shrug, though Martinez couldn't see the gesture. "Did a few things that will probably get you put in charge of the investigation for good."

"Are you serious? What'd you do?" he asked, curiosity flowing through the phone.

"I'll tell you more after I talk with the A.D."

"Well, balls in gravy, man. You must have really fucked up if you won't share." There was a moment of silence before Martinez guessed, "Did you fuck a pro in the Red Light District? Oh, oh, did you get your picture taken fucking a pro?" Smith smiled as Martinez kept going, "You robbed a jewelry store in the Diamond District while fucking a pro?"

"Martinez," Smith scolded with a laugh.

"No, wait, did you get your picture taken while fucking a pro, robbing a store and got your pecker stepped on by Europol?"

"Enough," Smith laughed. "See, this is why I tell you nothing. No encouragement or reassurance." He sighed. "If I get fired, I'll let you know first. If I'm not fired, we need to meet up. Talk over the new info." Martinez agreed. The doorbell rang. "Got to go, someone's here." He hung up on his friend.

Smith was slightly confused when he opened the front door and found a very well dressed delivery man with a black garment bag draped over an arm.

"Special Agent Lowery?" the man asked.

"Yes," Smith answered cautiously. The bag wasn't his.

The man held it out. "Ms. Laughlin ordered this for you. It should fit but if not please don't hesitate to contact the number on the business card." Smith took the bag from him, and the man walked down his steps and out the gate to a waiting Mercedes SUV.

Smith kicked the door closed and dropped the phone on the couch along with the bag. Curiosity got him and he pulled the zipper. There was a small white card was tied with a black ribbon to the hanger. He pulled the card loose and read it. He was sure it was dictated since it wasn't written in her pretty handwriting. 'Don't take this as permission to call me raccoon but I owed you a new shirt. Shirts go nicely with suits. ~ D'. He looked at the three piece dark gray suit and shook his head. He reached down and pulled it from the bag. He held the hanger up and resigned himself to the fact it was probably the most expensive suit he'd ever seen, let alone been given.

The bag said Brioni, New York. He'd never heard of them but if Delilah bought him a suit from them then he was sure they were exclusive. His brows furrowed as he looked at the charcoal gray suit. Astonishment blossomed when he recognized it was tailored and hand delivered from New York. He shook his head again. The amazing suit came with a crisp white shirt and a dark silver silk tie that had an abstract pattern. He admitted it was awesome. He saw the shirt would need cufflinks. He closed his eyes to think, trying to remember if his father had any. He kept his parents jewelry upstairs. He'd have to dig later.

Smith grabbed the garment bag and picked up the phone before marching upstairs. He hung the suit and shirt in his closet before looking at the phone again. His heart raced with nerves as he pressed the assistant director's number.

It rang a few times before the man answered, "Assistant Director Patten."

"Sir," Smith said, "this is Special Agent Lowery."

"Back from the Netherlands? Or just checking in?"

"I'm back. I've already checked in with Martinez on the Travis investigation. We're going to meet up, go over the information." Smith cringed, swallowed his pride and asked, "Sir, do you have some time for me to come by?"

"Today?"

"Yes, Sir, if you have time."

Smith imagined the A.D. checking his watch or glancing at his schedule before saying, "Sure, come over now."

"Yes, Sir, give me an hour." Smith hung up and sighed. He tossed his cell on the bed and fell back onto the mattress. He stared at a speck on his white bedroom ceiling.

He felt as if he'd been working his whole life to get to this point. He'd focused on his future when his parents had gotten killed in the car crash. Sometimes accidents weren't accidents. He remembered very clearly when his grandfather had knocked on his bedroom door and told him about the crash. He'd never been so wiped out, or as angry as that moment.

It was months later when déjà vu happened and his grandfather had knocked on his bedroom door and asked, very specifically, what did he want to do with his life? Smith knew the answer immediately and without hesitation. He wanted to be law enforcement. What he didn't tell Pops was why, but Smith knew the reason. It burned deep inside him like acid in a pit. Smith wanted to prevent the kind of pain and suffering he'd been through when the law had been broken and people died. He'd suspected Pops knew why as well but they had never said it out loud. They never talked about it. Uttering words of vengeance and retribution just never felt right to either of them.

But he understood it now.

He'd done everything in his power to get himself into a good school. He'd overachieved in college to ensure his acceptance into the FBI. He'd excelled at the academy. He thought it would be a form of protection. He didn't feel very secure as he stared at his ceiling.

She's worth it, a voice whispered in his mind. He had to agree with the voice. He felt hollow without her beside him. His whole body yearned for her. In the simplest terms, he missed her. He could still feel the lingering traces of the soft pressure of her lips against his when he'd kissed her goodbye in the Guard next to the private jet. He missed her already; unsure of when he would see her again, which made things worse. He sat up and grabbed his phone. The A.D. lived in Falls Church. It'd take him an hour to get there with traffic. He grabbed his keys and found his truck where he'd left it in the garage.

Smith rang the doorbell and stood on the porch of a single family two story home with beige siding and bright white trim. It was in a neighborhood of identical homes, save the coloring of the siding, some were white, others off white or beige, like the A.D.'s house.

The door was opened by a teenage girl with soft brown skin, long dark hair and a mouth full of metal as she smiled and welcomed him into the house. She turned and screamed, "DAD! SMITH'S HERE!" She turned back and smiled again then raced up the carpeted staircase to the second floor.

"There you are," Patten said as he stepped around the corner of the hall. "Come on," he gestured. Smith walked further into the house and around the corner into the TV room. There was a game showing on a nice-sized flat screen. "God, I love football." The A.D. smiled. "Much more than my wife knows."

"I heard that," the A.D.'s wife said as she walked past.

"Well, shit," he complained lightly. "Now I'll be in trouble." He gestured to the leather couch. "Want a drink? Something to eat?" He sat in a recliner.

"No, I'm alright, thanks." Smith sat on the couch and leaned forward, bracing his elbows on his knees. His heart was racing. "Thanks for letting me come over, Sir, rather than waiting until Monday."

"Sure, what'd ya want to talk about?"

Smith clasped his hands together, almost as if in prayer. "I fucked up, Sir." He inhaled heavily and added, "In Holland."

The A.D. stopped watching the game and turned to Smith as he asked, "How so?"

Smith sat uncomfortably on the couch and struggled for words. He thought about saying he'd had sexual relations but that sounded too much like Clinton. Finally he just said, "I had sex with Delilah Laughlin."

"Our material witness to the Travis murder?"

"Yes, Sir."

The chair reclined back then forward as the man shifted and leaned forward. "I have to ask, one-time thing, right? Attraction got the best of you two when you were taking a personal day?"

"No, Sir," he answered.

"No to which part?"

"All of it."

"Clarify," the A.D. demanded.

Smith cringed. "I've fallen for her. We've," he thought of a nice choice of words, "enjoyed each other's company a lot." He cleared his throat and said, "The first time happened while we were looking for the man she'd witnessed with the victim of the Europol investigation." He thought it best to get it all out there. "Detective Vandersloot became aware of our relationship and is going to call you about it next week."

"So, you wouldn't be here if he wasn't going to call?"

"Probably not."

The A.D. shook his head and leaned back, asking, "Anything else?"

"I might have some information that ties the Travis murder to a cold case. We're also going to look into any connections there might be between our cases and the Netherland murders."

"Well, shit."

"Yeah, I thought so too."

"Anything else with Ms. Laughlin?"

"The cold case is her sister's."

"Well, fuck me dry." He rocked in his recliner for a moment then asked, "Where is she now? Ms. Laughlin?"

"She's in New York, Sir," Smith answered.

"Are you going to see her again?"

"Once the investigation is finished I plan on seeing her a lot." He couldn't help it, he smiled.

"Fucking in love, are you?"

Smith's smile grew wider. "Yes, Sir."

The A.D. shook his head and said, "OK, you've got a good record. No fuck ups on it that I remember right off. Everyone's allowed one." He leaned forward, and said gravely, "One, Special Agent Lowery, one fuck up. Don't talk to her except in an official capacity with another agent present. For God's sake don't touch her again until the investigation's complete. I'll suspend your ass. Take away that brand new job of yours, if you do. Do you think I'm serious, Special Agent?" he asked.

Smith stood and extended his hand as he answered, "Yes, Sir, I know you're serious." They shook hands. "I'll let you get back to the game. Thank you."

Sunday came and went for Smith as he spent most of the day tucked in his office on the academy grounds. He started the day by bringing himself up to date on the Travis murder. He went through pages of laboratory results. He'd read all of the witness, if he could call them that, statements. Delilah's was the only one provided any real information. She had given them the timeline. Even with minimal information others had provided, Martinez had done well. He'd followed up with the staff at the restaurant, searched the restaurant neighborhood for any videos.

Smith looked at the grainy images of Senator Travis as she walked out of the restaurant. He tipped his head to the side and grumbled. The new angle didn't help. The staffers at her office had provided copies of her schedule going back months. He made a note on a yellow sticky for Martinez to get a court order for her phone records, home, office and cell. He might be able to follow her trail as to how she found Michael when law enforcement hadn't been able.

Smith sat back in his office chair and thought of his problem, Michael. He was sure about his hypothesis. Michael had killed the senator because she'd managed to track him down after years in hiding. Delilah said she wanted to, or was ready to financially destroy anyone who had helped him. So, who would help him? Family and friends immediately came to mind. He assumed that was Senator Travis' starting point, family and friends of Michael.

He started his cold case research with Google. He knew the Laughlins had moved to Connecticut approximately thirteen years ago. He searched "Rachel Laughlin murder" and his monitor filled with results. He spent the next five hours digesting information, grisly facts that the local reporter had been able to accumulate but then after a year or so, there was nothing more on the Rachel Laughlin case. Like so many others, it simply went cold. No new information, no new leads. He checked his watch, only to confirm it was Sunday. He made a mental note to call the local PD on Monday and request a copy of the file. Maybe, if he got lucky the original detective would still be working and could give him some of his impressions from the information and evidence, straight from the person who'd collected it.

Smith found it almost unsettling that Delilah's name had not been mentioned when he knew from her injuries she had been there. It seemed as if her army of lawyers had wiped the internet of her past. He stared at his computer monitor for a long time then finally moved, typing in her name before the great seal of denial came up. He typed in the password he'd been given by the A.D. during a quick, early morning phone call. He needed permission and he was officially given it in the effort to connect the cold case to the new case.

He inhaled heavily as the great seal unlocked and two files appeared. They were simply titled *Rachel Laughlin* and *Delilah Laughlin*. He released his breath and opened Rachel's case first.

He was surprised by how closely the local reporter's investigation ran with the official police department investigation. It was all very similar to what he had already read so he closed the file and opened Delilah's.

Within the file he found the world of young Delilah, and it was surprising. There was a yearbook photo of an incredibly stunning young woman. She looked annoyed and almost frightened of having her picture taken. He knew she had been terrorized daily. He was sure she couldn't have produced a smile for the photographer if one of her tormentors was waiting in line to get their picture taken. Still, there was evidence of her beauty. Her straight, dark hair hung just above her shoulders with heavy bangs. Emerald green eyes stood out against the dark green background. He reviewed her grades. She was taking accelerated math classes at the local community college but almost flunking P.E., which made him laugh until he remembered her issues with the locker room and her bullies.

He examined a family photo someone had included in the file. Rachel stood between Mr. and Mrs. Laughlin, Delilah to the side of her mother. Rachel favored their parents, blonde, several inches taller than Delilah with deep blue eyes. She was very pretty. The parents were starting to gray, but he could see their attractiveness. He wondered which side of the family Delilah's dark hair and green eyes had come from. He knew if he'd met the Laughlin girls when he was younger he wouldn't have thought them sisters. They were almost polar opposites of each other except for their beauty which both radiated.

Delilah's statement had been taken in the hospital, two days after the murder. Smith read the hand written notes which had been scanned into the file from the original detective. The detective had made a note that the interview was performed later than he would have liked due to the witness's multiple surgeries. Both of her knees had been operated on immediately as well as her wrists when she was taken to the local hospital.

Smith clicked through the hospital and injury information. He knew what had happened, reasoned it out, but reading it hit him like a brick to his head, giving him an instant headache. The attending physician on duty in the emergency room had listed her injuries in descending order of importance: blood loss, knife wounds to both wrists, both knees fractured, removal of her previous stitches, and a small knife wound to her chest. He shook his head with regret and read the physician's statement. It was a clinical examination of a young woman who'd been assaulted. He was grateful to read there was no evidence of sexual assault.

The Laughlins had almost lost both daughters that night, Smith realized as he read. The blood loss had almost killed Delilah. The hospital emergency staff had stabilized her and rushed her into surgery to repair her wrists and her knees. She'd spent two weeks in the hospital and months in rehab.

He went back to the detective's interview. A very young Delilah Laughlin knew how to protect herself. He read that she had an attorney present during the interview as well as her father. Smith wondered why her mother wasn't with her as well.

He read her statement, and it broke his heart as the story of a teenager who suffered at the hands of a group of bullies. Who was terrorized on a daily basis, and was destroyed when they found her weakness. Love, she fell in love with the wrong boy.

The detective had written as Delilah talked. She told the detective of the fateful night. She began by advising the boy, Michael Townsend, had called shortly after the Laughlin family had finished dinner, asking her to meet him at the high school. She had begged Rachel to give her a ride to the school. She'd said she just wanted to be with him, talk with him to find out what he might have to say. She confessed to Rachel during the ride that she was excited at the possibility he might kiss her. After all, she was young and in love. Rachel had agreed but didn't like it, Delilah admitted.

On the drive to the school Rachel told Delilah that Michael had been a shit to her in their classes, reminding her he was part of the group of bullies who made her life a living hell. Rachel thought Delilah could do better, that there were other guys to spend time with who were nicer. Rachel insisted on a time limit for the rendezvous, twenty minutes. After that, Rachel was going to call her and they'd figured out if she'd pick her up, or if Michael would drive her home.

Delilah waved bye to Rachel and walked to the school doors. She gave the glass door a tug but found them locked. The interior was darkened. She glanced in each direction then walked around the edge of the building and found Michael there, waiting on a concrete patio table of the cafeteria area. He smiled when she stepped closer.

"Where's Rachel?" Michael asked as he stood to meet her. "You said she was bringing you."

"She'll pick me up soon," Delilah said with a smile.

"How long do we have?"

"About twenty minutes."

"Want to walk?" Michael asked. Delilah nodded and grinned. "Ever been to the baseball field?"

"Yeah, Rachel made me go to last week's game."

"No, the practice fields," he pointed past the school. They walked side by side in that direction. "You know you're really smart, Delilah," he said. They stepped through the tree line that separated the practice field from the high school building. Across the field was the equipment shed where the baseball gear was kept, and the assistant coach kept his office. They walked, moving closer to the center of the practice field before he stopped and kicked at the dirt with the toe of his sneaker. She turned to him. "For a smart girl you never saw this coming."

Four girls stepped out of the tree line and Delilah stepped back, her stomach sank.

"Don't go anywhere," Michael said, grabbing her slim shoulders.

Delilah struggled when they swarmed. She fell to the ground as they beat her, kicked her. Her legs pulled up and she wrapped her arms around her head as their blows pounded against her petite body. She inhaled the dirt, choked on the dust. The girls drew back creating space for Michael. Standing over her, he punched her then the world went blissfully silent and dark.

Sound and pain rushed through her body. There was laughter which echoed and moved away. Her jaw throbbed in small waves of agony as she woke with a moan. She thought it odd that she was gazing at the stars in the clear night sky before she remembered why she was on the ground. A buzzing sound pulled her attention. She glanced over to find her phone laying in the dirt yards away. She looked back at the night sky. Her view was suddenly blocked by Michael as he hovered over her.

"Don't bother screaming for help," he warned. "It's just you and me. I gave the girls what they wanted and now I'm going to take what I want. How the hell are you Rachel's sister? You're nothing like her," he spat.

Delilah told the detective that Michael Townsend was a two sport athlete. Probably even good enough to get a scholarship. When he swung the metal bat he had resting on his shoulder, she chillingly realized she never had a chance.

The metal bat cracked against her left knee first and she screamed as the bone fragmented. She immediately drew it up, pulling it close as he swung again. Screams shattered the silent night as he destroyed the other. She tried to drag herself away, her nails digging into the dirt as she pulled herself towards her cell. Holding back the waves of nausea and fear that rolled over her, she stretched for the phone but couldn't reach.

Michael only allowed her to get a few feet before he jumped on her and forced her back into the dirt. He drew a knife from his jeans pocket and opened it as he sat on her stomach. "I love to hear you scream, Delilah. It does something for me. It makes me feel good. Really good," he admitted.

Delilah confessed about trying to take her own life but the detective wrote that he already knew. He told her the whole town knew about it. She looked humiliated the detective had written in his report. He told her to keep going.

Evil. Unabashed, scorching fear ripped at her soul, tearing her apart as Michael grabbed her wrist. She struggled as he stuck the sharp blade into her. She screamed again and again as he wrenched and pulled. Her stitches were ripped as he embedded the knife into her wrist digging at them. Blood began to pour again before he released her arm and grabbed the other. He mangled her once more before he dropped her arm. She instinctively pulled her wrists up and pressed them against her chest.

She was wheezing, short painful breathes. Her voice was hoarse from screaming. She gasped, "Stop! Get offa me!" she growled and screamed. "Leave me alone," she gasped again. She whimpered and cried, "I want to live!"

Michael laughed. "You didn't want to live too much a week ago." He watched her, sitting atop her where his weight pinned her down.

"Yeah, well, a lot's happened," she grunted. She was scared, terrified by the look on his face.

Michael pushed her hands from her chest and pressed the edge of the sharp knife against her breastbone. Delilah screamed again. He dragged the knife slightly as he cut her shirt and skin open. He was so focused on her skin and the dripping blood, he never saw Rachel coming.

She rammed into him, knocking him off of Delilah. She kicked him in the stomach, and jumped back. She grabbed Delilah under her arms, yanking her a foot away, and screamed, "RUN! RUN, DeDe!"

Delilah never had the chance to tell Rachel about her knees. Michael rose awkwardly as he jumped from the ground, leaping on Rachel. They fell together. Rachel twisted before they hit the ground. She managed to get out from underneath him and punched him in the nose. Warm blood sprayed across Rachel's shirt before he jumped on top of her. They rolled in the dirt and he punched her in the chest.

Rachel stopped fighting instantly, and gasped. Her bright blue eyes went wide with horror and pain. Michael stopped suddenly, seemingly unaware the knife was still in his hand. He withdrew it slowly from her body and stood staring. Rachel grabbed her chest. Blood poured from behind her hands. Gasping, she fell forward and slowly, painfully began to crawl away.

Michael stood over them for a moment before his chest heaved with a heavy breath and he screamed at Rachel, "I LOVE YOU! You bitch! How could you do this?" He pocketed the knife, and ran from the practice field.

"RACHEL!" Delilah screamed.

She dragged herself broken and bleeding a few feet as Rachel crawled to meet her. They touched and Delilah grabbed Rachel pulling her close. She rolled onto her back, holding Rachel to her chest. She screamed and cried for help. A light came on in the school, and the janitor stepped out.

Delilah told the detective she was still screaming when he raced across the field and fell to his knees beside them. She was crying when he called nine-one-one. She knew Rachel had died before he hung up. The detective noted her father left the interview at that time.

CHAPTER 16

Rachel died in Delilah's arms on the practice field of the high school. Delilah almost died by the time the ambulance had gotten her to the hospital. Nearly bled dry and broken, she was rushed into surgery, knowing her sister's killer, her attacker had fled. Smith fully understood her terror and fear. He closed her file, and leaned back in his chair. He glanced out the windows of his office and saw the world had turned dark.

He wanted to call her, to tell her he knew what she had endured. He thought she was brave to have put up with that shit every day; to have survived what the girls and Michael had done, to have excelled in a way that afforded her intense control over her life. He powered off his computer and turned off his office lights.

Smith stopped on the way home at an ATM and got out some cash. He wanted to talk to her, to hear her voice but he wasn't allowed to. He drove to a convenience store near Georgetown and bought a disposable phone. If they were good enough for criminals then they'd be good enough for him. He paid cash for the phone and tossed it onto the passenger seat of his truck before driving the remainder of the way home.

Smith backed into his garage, which always took a bit of concentration to squeeze into the tight space. He sat in his truck until the world around him had silenced. His mind was numb. He knew violence, lived it daily. Tried to find justice for others when they couldn't find it for themselves. It always surprised him that evil could be found so easily. When the silence had settled he realized he would do anything to be with Delilah. After reading her file he knew he would do anything to protect her. If he ever saw Michael again, he might not be able to stop himself from killing the man. Justice could be served in many different forms. They didn't all come with a jury and a verdict. Smith moved efficiently through his house, upstairs into the privacy of his bedroom. He dialed her cell number on the disposable phone.

A smile overtook him as she answered with a hesitant, "Laughlin."

"Hey, raccoon."

"Oh, Smith," he could hear her relief, "I've been worried. You didn't call to tell me what happened. This isn't your number."

"No, it's a disposable phone." He told her about his conversation with the A.D. and with Martinez. "If they know we're talking, I'll get fired but I couldn't," he exhaled heavily and leaned back against the headboard, "I couldn't stop being with you. Even just talking helps." He was sure she smiled and he said, "Thank you for the suit."

"You're welcome. Do you like it?"

"It's too much. Completely over the top but it's from you so I love it." He hoped that was gracious and he was sure as shit he wouldn't let her buy him anything else unless it was his birthday or a holiday. He breathed and asked, "How was your day? What'd ya do?"

"I went through all of my emails."

"How many?" Smith asked.

"You don't want to know," she teased playfully.

"Yes, I do. I want to know everything that involves you."

"I had four hundred and seventy emails today."

"Ouch!" She laughed, and his world started to heal with the sound. "That didn't leave you much time for anything else, I'm sure."

"Nope," she chuckled. "I have a gala to go to tomorrow. If you were here I'd ask you to go with me."

"With fancy dresses?"

"Yep, very fancy."

"Fancy dresses just don't work on me. Something about my hips." She laughed again and his heart mended from the previous pains.

"I get to have my hair and makeup done. It's for a charity I donate to, for women and children."

"I'd go with you, if I could."

"I know you would. Next week's my Halloween party at the New York club. Maybe you could sneak into town in costume and come see me?"

"What are you going as?"

"Sexy Princess Leia."

He groaned imaging Delilah in the outfit. "Please say it's the sexy slave costume from *Return of the Jedi*." When she agreed he groaned again and admitted, "All of my teenage dreams have just come true. Save the costume for our next sexy time." She laughed and promised. "I'm not going to be able to call you every day, raccoon," he said, "but if you need me, call."

"I will," she promised. "I miss you."

"I miss you too," he said then added, "I love you, Delilah."

"I love you too, Smith," she said before she whispered goodnight, and hung up.

"If this guy really did kill the senator and Delilah's sister, and he has the hots for killing her, would it make sense for him to go after her in a public place?" Martinez asked as they sat in a small conference room he'd set up as the main investigation office.

Smith looked up from a document he was reading and replied, "It makes sense. In Amsterdam he went after her at the store opening. The place was crowded. Her security couldn't keep up with the number of people." Smith passed over a folder containing Rachel's investigation to Martinez.

"I'm saying, her schedule can't be that hard to find. Shit, I mean, she's on TMZ like every other day."

Smith frowned and asked, "What'd ya mean?"

"TMZ, the gossip site."

"Yeah, I know that, but why's she on there?"

"She worth a few billion dollars, she's fucking hot, and single.

Everyone wants a piece of her. They want to know who she's wearing, who she's dating, who she's banging, which," Martinez said dramatically, "Is you."

"But no one knows that," Smith said seriously.

Martinez shrugged. "They will, at some point. Part of living the good life."

Smith looked down at his documents. He hadn't considered how much of her life was spent in the public eye. Smith had thought of a plan, a timeline with Delilah and he took great comfort in it. He was sure they'd date for at least six months then as soon as the investigation was concluded he'd ask her to marry him in some sweet, romantic way he hadn't thought of yet.

He knew they'd end up together. She was everything he wanted. He couldn't get enough of her. He had his mother's engagement ring in a black velvet box on his dresser at home. It was waiting for the right woman, and Smith knew Delilah was the one. Martinez stopped talking when several other agents walked into the conference room including Jenkins.

Her blonde ponytail bounced as she walked. She gave him a big smile before taking a seat. "Welcome back, Special Agent Lowery," she said.

He nodded as Martinez rose from his chair and began to pass out folders. Smith said, "Let's get right to it. We believe we've found a suspect for the Travis murder. It seems to connect back to a cold case. What we're going to do is to compare these findings to our current case, and make connections if they're there."

Jenkins opened the file and read the first line. "Rachel Laughlin?" She looked up and asked, "Is this a relative of Delilah Laughlin?"

"Her deceased sister." Smith paused, letting everyone briefly glance at the materials. "It seems Rachel Laughlin and Senator Travis went to the same high school. They were best friends during that time. From our investigation, we've learned Senator Travis was unhappy Rachel's case had gone unresolved when the killer was known but remains a fugitive."

Martinez continued as Smith looked to him, "It appears the senator made every effort to find one, Michael Adam Townsend.

We're going to base the investigation on the belief that she did indeed find him, and in return he found her."

"Earlier today I requested a copy of video security from the Delightful Finds store in Amsterdam. We should have that soon," Smith added.

"Why do we need a copy?" Jenkins asked.

"The fugitive was spotted in the store last Friday," Martinez advised.

"Do you think he's still in Holland?" she asked.

"No," Smith answered. "But there might be some connection to the young women who have been turning up dead there. We've also requested a copy of the Europol investigation. Michael Townsend likes young women, and he likes to use a knife on them." Smith's investigative mind made a leap, and he froze with the possibility then said to Martinez, "Let's get a copy of Ms. Laughlin's schedule for the last year. If Michael was tracking her, we might tie the dates of the Amsterdam murders to her timeline."

Martinez nodded and wrote a note. "I'll get that."

"Senator Travis was old business which was creating new problems for him." Smith paused and thought of another angle and said, "If he killed Senator Travis and was in Amsterdam shortly after to pursue Ms. Laughlin then he'll have taken a flight soon afterwards. That Friday or Saturday." He pointed to Jenkins and said, "Let's get on that once we have the video feed from the store. Get with the New York and Washington airports and search their security footage. Use the facial recognition program to run it. See if we get a match for his coming back to the States. If we do that'll give us the name he's traveling under, possibly a wealth of information on how he's managed to elude capture this long."

Martinez spoke up, "I think we should get a copy of Ms. Laughlin's current schedule. He went after her once he'll do it again. She's a very public person. He'll have another opportunity at some point. I bet if we search the net we can find out where she'll be. We can use the recognition program to scan the crowds of places she's going to." Martinez shrugged and added, "If he's in the crowd we can get local agents out there."

Smith agreed, "Let's do that." He checked his watch to

confirm the time. He knew Delilah would be going to the gala tonight but he didn't know exactly what time. "This is good," he said. "I'll call her security team and find out if she's got any big events for the next two weeks." He figured talking with Brody was not talking with Delilah, and since it was in official capacity he should be fine with the A.D.'s directive. Smith stepped into his office and closed the door. He pressed Brody's number and waited a moment before the call was answered.

"Special Agent, what can I do for you?" Brody asked. "Ms. Laughlin's in a meeting."

Smith thought it was odd that he was suddenly pleased to know where Delilah was and what she was doing but he refocused and said, "I'm not calling for her. I'm calling in an official capacity."

"Sure, what's up?"

"I need to get her schedule for the next few weeks. My team's working Michael's angle for the investigation. We think he'll go after her again in a public place."

"She got the charity thing tonight." Brody groaned and complained, "Those things are fucking madhouses. There will be a press gauntlet she'll have to work before she can get into the building."

"Can you take her in through a different entrance?"

"No, she'll want to go in through the front. It'll be good press for the charity." Brody paused then asked, "Should I hire some more people?"

"Yes," Smith said without hesitation. "She's a target." He sighed, wishing he was going to be with her. "I need the location and time you'll get her there. We're going to run a live feed from the location and use the facial recognition software on the crowd. If we confirm he's there, we'll send in local agents to make the arrest."

"OK, I'll text you with it. Call me if you see him in the crowd so I can move her out."

"Absolutely," Smith said. "What's the rest of her schedule like?"

"The remainder of the week is business as normal." Brody paused then added, "Next week's the Halloween party. It's usually crazy. Lots of drunk, half-naked people trying to get into the club. It's the hot spot for the holiday in the city."

"She has to go?" Smith asked.

"Again, her club, her party. She'll go."

"OK, just stay close to her. I'll call if we see him." Smith ended the call with Brody and opened his door. The phone pinged with Brody's text. They had the location and time of her arrival. He'd get Martinez to coordinate it with the local field office. He glanced at the small flat screen which hung on the wall across from his desk. It was showing a live news feed from a helicopter in Arizona. He sighed, violence was a never ending circle. He sat at his desk and pulled out paperwork on other cases which had accumulated while he was away. He forwarded the text to Martinez and told him to get it organized. He got down to doing paperwork. An hour later he looked up. The pile had reduced in size by half. An agent walked by his open door and Smith called out, "Hey, Roberts."

The man stopped and stepped back. He was ugly in a sports-had-taken-its-toll kind of way with a smashed in nose and a missing tooth. His cropped blonde hair was so short it looked as if he didn't have any hair.

"Where's your tooth, man?" Smith asked, leaning back in his chair. "Isn't that part of your official uniform?"

Roberts smiled showing off the empty space. "You know my yellow lab, BB? She banged into my mouth the other day when we were playing. I actually swallowed the mother fucker." He smiled again, it wasn't pretty.

"That hole's big enough to be the entrance to Narnia."

"I've got an order in to replace it. It should be here today or tomorrow."

"Try to get it today. It's just scary." Smith's laughter trailed off as he pointed to the flat screen and said, "That's the second victim they've found out there. They're going to call and ask for help. Why don't you call them first, offer some assistance."

"I don't like working kid cases," Roberts said seriously.

"I know, they suck but look, if you're working it and you find the fucker you'll be saving more kids. Even one is worth the shit, right?"

Roberts grumbled.

"Get two or three other people who aren't currently working on anything else and call the fucking Sheriff. Offer assistance and get your ass to Arizona."

"Yes, Sir," Roberts said flatly.

"Give 'em remarkable service, Roberts," Smith said with a smile.

"I'll remarkable the fucker, alright," Roberts said with a gaping smile. He pushed away from the door frame and walked off.

Smith went back to his paperwork.

Martinez knocked on his doorframe. "What's up, bitch?" he asked sarcastically. Smith looked up from his last document. Martinez cleared his throat with a cough and said seriously, "Sorry, it's time, boss."

Smith stood and stretched, setting the completed paperwork aside. He glanced out the windows and saw the world had turned dark. Delilah would be primped and pampered and on her way to the event. He walked out of his office, next to Martinez and asked, "Everything set?"

"I've got the live feed going already."

"Good," Smith said as they entered the computer room.

The far wall was full of large computer monitors each showing different images. The software program was searching the crowd in front of the Jefferson building where the charity event was taking place. Several of the monitors carried the press coverage while others were dedicated to the faces in the crowd. Smith didn't like it. There were too many people. Not just in front of the building but across the street as well.

Smith's phone pinged and he checked it. It was a text from Brody advising they were almost there. He looked to his team and said, "OK, they're arriving momentarily."

Michael's pictures were stationary on a far computer monitor. Martinez had used two pictures. One from the security feed in Holland so a scruffy, filthy man looked out at them. The other was a high school picture, clean shaved and young. Smith wondered if it was too young to be helpful for the computers.

"There's your girlfriend," a young woman said with a knowing smile as she sat working the computer system. Smith looked to Martinez who shrugged. Smith shook his head and watched the Maybach roll to a smooth stop in front of the building right at the edge of an honest to God red carpet. The Suburban from the basement parking lot pulled up right behind them. Three men Smith didn't recognize got out and took positions to watch and secure the scene.

Armstrong got out of the Maybach first and jogged around the rear of the car as Brody got out the front passenger area and searched the crowd for the same face they were all looking for. Armstrong gripped the rear passenger door handle and opened it after getting a knowing, approving nod from Brody. Brody blocked Smith's view for a moment before he stepped to the side and offered Delilah a hand.

Her slender leg with a high heeled sandal extended from the car. She took Brody's offered hand and stepped out. Smith's mouth gaped open. His cock went hard. Martinez cursed beside him. The computer room fell silent.

Delilah was stunning. She was breathtaking, more than he'd imagined. She was wearing a strapless green gown, the same color as her eyes, that hugged her body in all the right ways down to her hips before a high slit in the material exposed her beautiful legs. Her hair hung loose around her face then was intricately braided and pinned together at the nape of her neck. Large chandelier diamond and emerald earrings dangled from her ears catching the flashing lights of the paparazzi. They were the only jewelry she wore save huge diamond and emerald bracelets.

Martinez spoke up as Smith was still trying to get himself together, "Let's not focus on Ms. Laughlin, people. Focus on the crowd."

Smith watched Delilah smile and wave to the crowd before

she walked assuredly to the gauntlet, stopping at the first reporter. He heard the reporter speak and pointed to the monitor. "Mute that," he ordered. He didn't want to be distracted by her answer to whatever the guy was asking her. His eyes were searching as the computer was. Smith was sure Michael was back in the States. Michael would know her schedule. He would want a very public ending to their disastrous connection.

A face caught Smith's attention, and he moved around the desk to step closer to the monitor for a better look. The computer program caught the same man. The computer formed a red circle around the moving head and body. Smith stared at the man as the percentage to the side of the monitor was increasing for a positive match. Delilah moved in front of the photo journalists. Flashes lit up the night seemingly blinding her but she remained smiling.

Smith stared at the man. He was clean shaven, well dressed, a fresh haircut. Completely different than the man he'd seen in Amsterdam. The man moved through the crowd fluidly. Smith's gut kicked him into action and he turned as the computer matched at ninety-two percent and shouted, "That's him!"

Martinez picked up the radio, immediately in contact with the local New York agents, and said, "Yes, he's there. In the crowd, maybe four deep. Moving towards the target."

Smith speed dialed Brody. He watched on the monitor as Brody answered the cell. "He's there," Smith said without waiting. "Get her inside, now!"

He watched Brody and Armstrong move to Delilah. The other security cleared the way. Smith felt they were moving too slow. He saw Delilah's confusion on her beautiful face as the team stepped close. She quickly recovered and glanced to the crowd. Her step faltered, and he knew she'd seen Michael too. Smith exhaled as he watched them move her into the safety of the building. His eyes instantly shifted as the computer followed Michael. The red circle held its target as Martinez talked through the radio directing the agents. There was a rush of bodies before Michael jumped the fence into the gauntlet. As soon as his feet hit the ground he ran. Four agents jumped the fence after him. Smith lost them as Michael ran out of the cameras sight. He turned and ordered, "Get them on another camera!"

The computer techs were typing furiously but one spoke up, "Got him! On Fifth, running towards the park."

Martinez passed along the information. Smith watched the man he wanted dead run through the crowded nighttime streets. On the monitor he saw as Michael grabbed a metal post and swung himself up and over the fencing to a subway station staircase.

"Getting the view from the station now," the woman announced.

Martinez told the pursuit agents where the suspect had run. Smith watched as the agents ran down into the subway entrance as well. The grainy video feed pulled up and Smith pointed to the monitor. "There!" he shouted, finding Michael in the crowd as the current of bodies slipped into the subway car. The agents rushed the landing as the doors closed. Smith watched it pull away, taking Michael with it. He cursed and ran a hand through his hair. He walked out of the room and called Brody. "We didn't catch him," Smith said. "He got on a subway near Central Park."

"Understood," Brody said.

"Is she alright?"

"She's good, unnerved but playing it cool. She's staying for a few hours then we'll move her to the apartment." Brody said something under his breath to someone else before he addressed Smith, "I'm keeping the guards on full time. This is bullshit."

"Agreed," he said then his tone lowered, "Tell her I'll call her later."

"Roger that," Brody said and hung up.

Smith stepped back into the computer room as Martinez was finishing up the radio call with the agents. He turned to Smith and advised, "We've got them heading to the next stop but," he shrugged. Smith nodded. "At least we know what his plan is. We know he's back in the States. We'll get him next time." Martinez turned and talked into his radio.

That was exactly what Smith was worried about, the next time.

CHAPTER 17

The next time couldn't come soon enough for Smith as he and Martinez checked into a New York City hotel. He could have been given a park bench, and he'd had been ecstatic. He took the room key with a genuine 'Thank you' to the desk clerk. Martinez had been booked into the room directly next to his.

"Shit, man, don't look so fucking happy," Martinez said as the elevator doors closed.

"Can we go over soon?" Smith asked, then his head fell in resignation. He sounded like a ten year old waiting for the family to get it together to go to the amusement park.

"No," Martinez said sternly then smiled. "We have to check in with the field office first. Once they're set for the Halloween party then we can go to the apartment." The elevator doors opened and Martinez stepped out. "Don't get me fucking fired."

Thirty minutes later they were in a generic federal sedan zipping through New York traffic to the field office. The driver parked in front of a massive building, and they were whisked to the thirtieth floor by a quick elevator.

Introductions were made before the late afternoon meeting commenced. Smith let Martinez take the lead. Martinez began with a quick overview for the Agent in Charge and the agents who were going to work the crowd for the Halloween party. The AIC stood as Martinez came to a close, "Sounds good," she said. She looked to her team. "We underestimated the suspect on our previous attempt. That's not going to happen tonight." She nodded to Smith and left the room.

"Get set tactically, people," Martinez said with a smile. "Get on your costumes. Body paint is not considered a costume." Smith and Martinez took their leave. It couldn't come fast enough for Smith. "Was that suitable timing?" Martinez asked.

Smith smiled as they waited for the elevator. "No, get me to the fucking apartment."

"Yes, Sir," Martinez said dramatically.

Smith stood nervously in the private elevator flying up to Delilah's apartment with Martinez at his side. He loosened his silver silk tie, undoing the first button on his white shirt and stood casually with the charcoal suit coat unbuttoned. He hoped she would notice the suit he was wearing. It had been her gift. He wanted to be with her, to take her in his arms but he knew he had to be cautious. More than just his career hung in the balance. He didn't want to fuck up Martinez's world too.

The elevator slowed and finally settled to a stop before the doors opened. Brody was waiting in the foyer as Smith and Martinez stepped out. Martinez stood awestruck, looking around. Smith knew that feeling. The apartment had been built to overwhelm and make an impression.

"Agent Martinez, this is Ed Brody. Ms. Laughlin's security," Smith said as an introduction.

Brody extended his hand to both men and said, "Welcome to New York Agent Martinez, Special Agent Lowery. Glad to have you here." Brody turned and they followed. "We'll be heading out towards ten-thirty." He stepped into the living room, and stepped to the side of the room.

Delilah stood with her back to them, staring out the huge glass window at the darkening skyline of the city. The lights twinkled below her. She was dressed in a long sleeve silk robe that draped her curves in the right ways. It was the palest ivory, and its silky length touched the tops of her bare feet. It was tied around her slim waist by a silk cord. Her dark hair was hanging down her back, left straight and undone. She turned, and Smith fought every instinct to go to her.

Her emerald eyes bore into him. He could see the yearning,

the aching that they shared mutually. There was almost an unreasonable amount of caution as she stepped forward and offered her hand to Martinez. "Agent Martinez, thank you for coming," she said then turned and looked at Smith.

Smith held out his hand and said softly, "Ms. Laughlin."

She took his hand in hers and held it for a long time before she broke their contact and stepped back. She wrapped her arms around her chest defensively and said to Martinez, "So, what's the plan for tonight other than me not dying?"

"That's first on our list, ma'am," Martinez said with a smile. He turned to Smith and said, "Special Agent, why don't you brief Ms. Laughlin," he exaggerated, "personally." He smiled and said, "I'll talk with her security team."

Delilah was masking her emotions like a professional poker player as Smith said, "Sure." He nodded towards the foyer. "Ms. Laughlin."

They walked side by side, and he took her hand when they reached the stairs. He held it tightly as she slowly ascended the stairs. No words passed between them as they climbed. His thumb caressed the back of her hand as they stepped to her bedroom door. She opened the door and tugged his hand. He walked in and closed the door behind him then pulled her close. He pressed his forehead to hers, taking her in, his senses recovering as he closed his eyes, finally relaxing. "Delilah," he said her name like an answered prayer.

"Shh," she said, and pressed a kiss to his lips. She stretched on her toes and pressed her body into his as her fingertips dragged over his muscular shoulders.

He exhaled in pleasure as his lips covered hers. His hands slid along the sides of her chest slowly to her hips before he grabbed her under her backside, and carried her to the bed. She laughed softly as he walked. She wrapped her arms and legs around him as he held her. He set her on the bed and she shifted to her knees, pulling at his suit to keep him close.

Delilah skimmed her hands beneath the jacket material and slid it from his shoulders. "Nice suit," she said with a sly smile.

"I thought you'd like it," he murmured and leaned in for

another kiss, whispering words of love and adoration. She smiled beneath his caresses as his clothes fell to the floor. He untied her bathrobe cord and guided the silk from her body.

"Make love to me, Smith," she whispered between his kisses.

He followed her onto the bed and pressed his weight against her body. He propped himself up on his forearms. His hips fit snuggly between her legs. The tip of his cock became wet with her arousal as he pushed forward into her sex. He touched a strand of hair, moving it from her face, before he leaned to her and kissed her gently. His hips thrust against her soft body and she gasped at the pressure. "So beautiful," he said, before he lay fully on her delightful, curvy body and made love to her slowly and sweetly.

He held her hips tightly as she orgasm rocking on top of him. He felt himself come with a powerful surge, pouring hot liquid deep into her body as she cried out. Her body tightened and quivered around his hard cock. He grabbed the sides of her chest and pulled her down so she lay on top of him. He grinded his hips into hers, milking the last of the cum from his body before he stilled and panted against her neck.

She lifted her face and smiled but her smile disappeared as she touched his jaw. "I've missed you so much. I didn't think I could stand to be without you for another day." Her eyes fell to his chest before she lifted them and said seriously, "I can't ask you to quit the FBI. That wouldn't be right but I want to. I want you to be with me, for us to be together."

"Better or worse, right?" She nodded, he lifted her and slid from her body. "This is the worst part, we get through this and we'll be okay." He pulled her close and kissed her passionately. "I love you, Delilah, believe in me."

"I do, Smith," she said worriedly then broke into a breathtaking smile. "I'm just not a patient person."

Smith was dressed and waiting for Delilah with the others in the kitchen. Martinez was keeping them all amused and Smith laughed. He felt fantastic, lighthearted from his time with Delilah. He worried that maybe she had a point. His job was keeping them apart. Even after the investigation was complete he would still be based in Washington. How often was his job going to take him away from her? He turned it around, how often was her job going to take her away from him? By her own admittance, she travelled often. Would they spend weeks apart once they were together? He sipped his bottle of water and knew he wouldn't give up on her. Traveling, times apart were just days on a calendar. It wasn't something to give up on because they wouldn't be together for a few days or a few weeks.

As she stepped into the kitchen Smith became intensely aware all conversation and laughter in the kitchen had ceased. She wasn't kidding when she said she was dressing as sexy Princess Leia. She even wore the copper bracelets to match. He remembered as a kid thinking the outfit was fucking sexy. Now, as his fantasy stood in the entryway, he got hard. From the other men reactions, he wasn't the only one thinking about her costume in erotic ways.

He stood from his bar stool and walked to her. In front of everyone he bent and kissed her on the lips. Her hands fell to his arms as she returned his kiss. "You look fantastic," he murmured and stepped aside. He noticed she was actually blushing at their display which added to her sexiness. He was surprised she hadn't had the costume modified in some way to hide the small white scar between her breasts. Perhaps she thought, correctly he decided, that no one would notice.

Martinez stood, clearing his throat with a cough then said, "Ms. Laughlin, if you're ready, we'll go." He nodded to Smith. "Special Agent Lowery will ride with you, Armstrong and Brody. I'll ride with the other security members. Once we get to the club you'll walk the press gauntlet and get you inside the building as quick as we can. Our team," he nodded to Smith, "will be searching the crowd using the same technique and software as we did with the charity event. We were able to find him. Now we just have to catch him."

Delilah smiled and said nervously, "Okay, let's go."

Smith asked as they walked side by side, "Aren't you cold? You want a jacket?"

She smiled and said, "No, I'm good."

"Your breasts are telling me differently."

She looked down at her curvy body then up and said, "I'm not cold."

Smith laughed as the elevator opened and they stepped in together.

He leaned to her while they rode in the car, catching a view of her plump, full breasts from above as he said, "Remember, I'm just the hired help tonight." He moved his eyes away from her breasts as she looked up at him. "Don't hold my hand or try to kiss me."

"Who says I want to kiss you?" she teased.

"Your breasts say so."

She looked at her breasts then back to Smith. "Maybe I'll let you fuck my breasts." When he didn't reply, she laughed.

"We're here," Armstrong said as he pulled the Mercedes sedan to the curb. All of the men fixed ear pieces and listened as the field office took control of the operation.

"7 Veils?" Smith asked, viewing the neon sign.

She shrugged and said, "Seemed appropriate."

The car came to a stop at the curb and Smith opened his door, stepping out immediately as Brody did the same. Smith walked around the back of the car and stood as Brody opened her door. He was scanning the crowd catching faces. The neon didn't help. He saw Martinez by the front door. He spotted several agents in the crowd some with face paint. Others in costumes trying to fit in with the Halloween party crowd.

Delilah stepped out and smiled for the crowd. She glanced to Smith but didn't acknowledge him as she walked the red carpet. Brody took the lead walking to the far side of the press as Delilah stopped for photographs. Smith caught her in his peripheral vision posing. It took all of his concentration not to ogle her.

"The computer's not picking up Townsend," a male voice said. "Once she moves inside we won't have a video feed."

Smith caught Brody's look. Neither liked that. Delilah moved away from the photographers. Her sexy skirt fluttered in the cold late October breeze as she walked calmly but purposefully. Martinez pulled open the club door for her and followed Smith and Brody inside. Once inside Delilah kept moving forward. She stopped at the entryway joining Shannon.

Brody tripped but caught himself quickly. Smith followed Brody's gaze and looked at Shannon. She was wearing the ever faithful sexy Bo Peep costume that all men adored. A tiny stuffed lamb was tied to her wrist. Her blonde hair was curled and left hanging just past her breasts, the top half of which Smith could see from the costume design. He looked back at Brody who was trying to recover himself. Smith smiled and stepped closer to the women.

"Sorry to interrupt." She acknowledged him with a look and a nod. Her face was grim as she said, "There was a warehouse fire at the LA location. The sprinklers came on but," she shrugged, "preliminary estimates are that we've lost half the warehouse."

"Shit," Delilah said. She closed her eyes. He could tell she was doing the calculations in her head before she opened her eyes and said, "That's over four million of inventory." She exhaled slowly and asked, "Was anyone hurt?"

"No employees but a few of the firemen were injured. Nothing serious, I heard."

"OK," Delilah said, "Make sure their medical bills are paid." Shannon went to step away but Delilah took her arm and said, "Hey, I'll fly out tomorrow." Shannon nodded and glanced at Brody. She smiled brightly and walked away. Delilah turned to Smith and said, "I have to go in the morning."

His hand settled on the small of her back and he leaned in to be heard above the loud, thumping music, "Me too."

She nodded and walked further into the club directly to the VIP section. She was separated from the mass of costumed people by a slim velvet rope. As she sat on the velvety cushioned sofa a hostess placed a mixed drink in front of her on a small glass table. She smiled a thank you before picking it up for a sip. Smith stood off to one side as Armstrong did the same, opposite him. Brody and Martinez wandered the crowd as costumed agents blended into the masses.

Smith stepped aside and withdrew slightly as a man in the VIP section came over and sat down with Delilah. She smiled when she saw him and gave him a small hug. Smith couldn't hear what they were talking about but watched them intensely. Delilah was friendly and animated. The man leaned close and asked something. She pointed to Smith. The man glanced over his shoulder to him and laughed. Smith hated him immediately. Anger simmered just beneath the calm exterior. The man leaned forward and kissed Delilah on the cheek before standing. He looked Smith up and down before walking back to the VIP bar with a wicked grin on his face. When Smith looked back at Delilah, she rolled her eyes at him and smirked. He tried and failed hide his amusement.

Time passed as she seemed the queen viewing her realm. She sat slightly elevated above the dance floor, watching those below her from her velvety throne. Only people with some type of status came and went from quick visits with her. He recognized a few celebrities and one up and coming politician as they paid their respects.

Smith noticed people on the dance floor actually moved towards her when they thought she was watching. People grinding against each other, swaying to the overly loud music under her ever watchful eyes. The booze, the sweat, the pounding music and pulsing lights added to the world she controlled. It was hers, he realized. If she wanted to leave, she would. If she wanted to turn off the music and send everyone home for no reason, she could. There was immense power in her control of others.

She stood and Armstrong stepped forward. She waved him away and stepped to Smith. Without words she took his hand and led him past the velvet rope. She held his hand tightly and pulled him into the center of the crowd as people separated, making a path. She turned and pressed herself into Smith.

His hands immediately went to her bare back as he leaned close and said, "Delilah, this isn't a good idea. The FBI's here."

"Fuck 'em," she said with a shrug. "I want to dance with you." Her manicured fingernails ran through his hair at the nape of his neck making his entire body tingle with anticipation.

"Who was that asshole?" he asked.

She viewed him warily and asked, "Which asshole, specifically?"

"The guy from the VIP section who kissed you."

She broke into laughter. "You're jealous!"

"No, I'm not," he defended. "I just don't want anyone kissing you but me."

She pressed a hand to his heart and smiled brightly. "Aww, don't be jealous. He doesn't like women. He's the owner of a brand of liquors we sell. He wanted to know who I was fucking to look so fabulous," she grinned.

"You told him about me?"

"Yes," she shrugged. "He didn't believe me."

"Why not?"

"Because I don't fuck the help." She stepped back and began to move slowly, seductively before him. She was enthralling.

He grabbed her arms and pulled her close. Her legs straddled one of his as his hands held her hips. They grinded against one another to the music like two people who knew each other's bodies thoroughly. They knew how the other moved, how they felt intimately was evident to anyone who looked. She slithered up his body bewitchingly, and he held her close as the music slowed and shifted into the next song.

He embraced her in his arms. His fingers intertwined in her ponytail. He pulled her hair back and her face lifted. His eyes expressed his yearning and desire with a scorching look. She nodded to his silent appeal, and took his hand. They moved wordlessly through the loud, vibrant mob. She stepped quickly out of the crowd, her fingers knotted with his as they moved into the barely lit hallway. They found a small, darkened office. She didn't turn on the lights as she closed the door behind him and locked it.

Delilah led him to a sofa and pushed him down. She straddled him, massaging his erection through his pants to rock hard while they kissed. Her tongue licked at his, her lips sucking and kissing him accelerating his longing. He popped the earpiece out before his hands traveled her body. She unzipped his pants, and shifted her thong away. She manhandled his heavy cock, and pushed him into her. He groaned as she immediately started to ride him.

"I want you," she panted. "I want you inside of me," she said desperately.

Smith pushed her hips downward and she moaned. He titled

his hips up to meet hers, forcing her to take him to the root as she thrust against his body. "We don't have much time," he said through her sucking his tongue.

Her arms tightened around his shoulders, and she fucked him hard. He pushed and pulled her hips, pressing himself fully into her. Her body pounded against his shaft from root to tip. His head lolled onto the sofa as he thickened and hardened inside of her, overwhelmed by the intense pleasure she was giving.

"I'm gonna come," he said, his voice husky with yearning. He growled as he spurted into her. He was still pumping liquid into her as she cried out, seized by her own orgasm.

He pressed a strong kiss to her lips and pushed the ear piece back in. He heard Martinez and Brody talking. They were wondering where he and Delilah had gone. Delilah lifted herself from him. She shifted her thong back in place. Smith leaned forward and pressed a quick kiss to her stomach before he pushed his semi-hard erection back into his boxer briefs.

"She's gone to the bathroom, guys," Smith said through the device, and nodded as Delilah repaired her appearance. She took his hand and walked out of the office. Directly across the hall were the bathrooms so she left him there and went inside. Martinez walked into the hall, and found Smith leaning against the wall. He pointed over his shoulder, and said, "She had to pee."

Martinez looked at him dubiously but didn't say anything. Brody followed Martinez into the hall. Delilah stepped out of the bathroom to find three men looking at her.

Delilah said coolly, "I want to leave. I've had enough of the party."

Brody spoke up, "I don't think he's coming tonight."

Martinez nodded and turned. He spoke the field office then back to them, "We'll get Ms. Laughlin home and call it a night."

Brody ordered Armstrong to get the car as they wandered through the club.

At the curb Delilah got into the car and slid across, making room for Smith. He closed the door and turned back for Martinez.

"I'll get her home then get myself back to the hotel."

Martinez smiled and said, "Ever the boy scout. As far as I'm concerned you were at the hotel all night and we made it to the airport at the appropriate time." He lost his smile. "I'll be on the flight. I suggest you do the same."

"Thanks, man. I will," Smith said with a smile, removing the ear piece device and handing it to Martinez. He was still smiling as he turned and got into the sedan with the others.

Delilah leaned against his shoulder after he settled into the car. Armstrong sped off into the city traffic. She murmured, "That went well." She glanced up. Her emerald eyes melting his heart and she said with a smile, "At least I didn't die."

He knew she said it to be funny, but it wasn't. Smith leaned down and pressed a hard, passionate kiss before he said, "That's my main priority."

"Help me undress," she said as Smith closed the bedroom door. He smiled subtly and she turned her back to him.

"Now, let's see how this works," he said to her back. He took both sides of the top, pushed it together, and unhooked it. Delilah sighed with relief as her breasts lowered, free of the metal top. He reached around her and massaged her breasts, kneading them with his strong hands. She exhaled heavily again with his touch.

She turned in his arms and he asked, "Are you tired? Did you want to go to bed?"

She tugged off the bracelets and dropped them to the floor. Her hands rose above her head, he was sure she did that intentionally to get his undivided attention and pulled her hair out of the ponytail band.

"Bed is good," he said. Smith raised his hands and massaged her hair, bringing a silly grin of enjoyment to her face as her hair spilled all over. His hands fell to her skirt and skimmed the edge of the material with his thumbs touching her lower belly. He leaned to her and pressed a trail of kisses starting between her breasts then along her stomach. He squatted with the kisses, and pulled off her skirt. Delilah kicked out of her sandals as Smith nuzzled her stomach, her groomed hair and finally pushed his moist tongue into her delicate skin, finding her clit. She moaned and pressed her hand to the back of his head, running her fingers through his hair as his tongue became clever.

Abruptly, she stepped away and walked into the bathroom. Smith remained kneeling on the floor and watched her leave. Confusion swamped him. She'd never walked away. He stood and took off his jacket, shoving his tie in a pocket before tossing it to a chair. He unbuttoned the vest and a few buttons of his white shirt before he sauntered to the bathroom door to find her.

She met him at the entrance with two huge white comforters. Her fingers were locked around the puffy bed things. She smiled brightly and murmured, "Carry these."

"Yes, ma'am," he said with a smile, and took the bundles from her.

She quickly grabbed her white silk robe and shrugged it on. She led him out of the bedroom and down the stairs. At the foyer, she pressed the call button for the elevator. She nudged him in playfully when the doors opened. He stepped inside and she followed.

"You know, I hear elevator sex is great," Smith said casually.

She huffed and shrugged before she said, "Does nothing for me." Her face remained placid then she broke into a laugh and a bright smile. "Anytime," she mouthed seductively.

When she chose a button, he asked, "Going to the meadow?"

She smiled and tried to wrap her arms around him and the blankets. She failed but ended up resting her hands on his sides, her head lolled against the junction of the puffy softness and the hardness of his muscular chest. She leaned back when the elevator pinged and opened. "To the meadow," she announced as they walked along the hall. "I like sleeping here sometimes." She pushed open the door and held it for him. "I think Brody'd have a frigging seizure if I tried to go really camping."

"You don't strike me as the camping type," Smith observed.

"My dad used to take Rachel and me when we lived in Germany." She moved barefoot through the tall grass. "We didn't go when we lived in Holland. He didn't even talk about it anymore by the time we got to Connecticut. But I still remember how fun it was when I was a kid." She pointed to an area where the trees sprawled and the brook ran close.

Smith spread out a comforter and tossed the other onto it. She knelt onto the fluffy whiteness and smiled up at him. Smith couldn't remember her ever looking more beautiful than that moment as the city lights twinkled behind her, and the natural beauty of the meadow enhancing her own.

"Did you ever go camping with your parents?" she asked.

He stripped off his vest and shirt, dropping them to the ground along with his pants. He sat beside her wearing only his black boxer briefs and touched her legs through the silk. "My parents weren't outdoorsy people." He looked from her legs to her beautiful eyes, "Pops was, is," he corrected. "We'd camp at the beach and make bonfires. That was helpful," he said, "at the high school parties being the one who knew how to make a proper bonfire."

"Parties on the beach?" she asked, closing the gap between them. He murmured a response as she climbed into his lap, straddling him. "I'm sure you were very popular in high school."

"And in college," he replied, pulling her closer, shifting out of his boxers so he hung ready. He untied the loose knot of her robe.

She rocked against his erection. Her hand slid up and down the length of his cock. She masturbated against his warm, rock hard skin between the slick folds of her sex and her hand. "Whore," she teased as the silk fell from her slim shoulders.

He fell back in mock disgust with a hearty laugh, taking her with him. He rolled and ended up on top of her soft body. "I'm in love you with, Delilah. Consider me a retired whore."

She smiled softly and wrapped her arms around his neck, bringing him closer. She stretched for a kiss. "I wouldn't have it any other way." He kissed her again and made love to her under the maple and evergreen trees.

"That sounded like water splashing," he said as he held her close.

"That was Ralph. He likes to jump."

"Ralph? You named the fish?"

She sighed as if naming fish was an everyday occurrence. "Yes, of course I named them. How else could I tell them apart?" She half-shrugged. "That one likes to jump. Sometimes I come down here while everyone's asleep to work and he's active. The others aren't so busy at night."

"Ralph? Terrible name," he scolded.

"You have a better name for a fish?"

"No, but I'm sure I could come up with one."

They fell into comfortable silence before she said quietly, "I'm cold."

He half-rolled over and found the other blanket. He tucked it around her and tucked her into him. Smith just couldn't bring it up and break the easy calm between them. He couldn't tell her he'd read about the assault. He felt her fall asleep against his chest. He was hopelessly in love with her. He wanted a future with her. He couldn't see any future without her. He didn't want to wait for it to arrive. He whispered, knowing she was half asleep, "If I ask you to marry me one day, what would you say?"

He felt her smile against his chest as she said, "I do."

Smith woke with a start. He swore he heard birds chirping in the trees, and opened his eyes to look for them. The sky through the tall glass windows was a soft amber hue, welcoming November. Delilah was on her side, spooning against him with her bare back to his chest. He tucked his cold arm under the blanket and pressed his hand to her flat belly. He knew she liked early morning sex and he was always happy to accommodate, besides he realized sadly, he didn't know when he'd see her again.

One hand slid over her silken skin to her breasts, and he kneaded the soft, full mound as he nuzzled her neck. His other hand moved from her lower stomach to between her legs. He gently circled her clit with his finger, and she woke with a deep, pleasurable moan. Her legs shifted open, and she pressed herself back into him with a sexy stretch. He smiled into her neck and continued kissing her.

Her hand reached behind her and she found his heavy erection. He watched her smile as she felt it, stroking him from root to tip. Her eyes flickered open, and he pushed her onto all fours. He mounted her from behind and she gasped as he filled her quickly, shoving his cock deep inside. He leaned forward on all fours, hovering over her and pressed his chest against her back, planting kisses along her shoulders. He rocked his hips against her backside, sliding his cock slowly in and out of her, creating a slick connection to their bodies. His hand traced her soft skin between her hips. He found her clit and massaged her once more with his fingers.

Her fingers found his and she pushed them away. He rose to his knees, completely enjoying the look of her in front of him. She tossed her long hair back so it fell in a dark sheet over her back as her fingers massaged herself. Smith's hands moved to her hips and he held her tightly as he slid his long, thick cock from her wetness before slamming forward. She cried out and hissed over her shoulder, "Not so fucking hard!"

He smiled an apology and swiveled his hips pushing himself further inside of her then pulled out over and over, grinding into her. She moaned again and he pulled her hips to him, creating a pleasurable rhythm. "Is this good?" he asked as she collapsed onto her forearms, pushing her ass further into the air for him to take. "Mmm, I like that," he said, his hand kneading her backside. She moaned her approval so he picked up his pace, pounding himself harder and deeper into her wet, tight body. He felt her body squeeze and tremble as she began to orgasm. Her hair fell forward as she cried out in ecstasy with the throbbing release.

He wrapped an arm around her chest and lifted her up then pressed her forward, so she laid flat on the blanket. He lay on top of her, his arms wrapped tightly around her. Her plump backside pressed softly against his hips as he spread her legs further apart. He fucked her roughly, taking every bit of her as she cried out with another orgasm. Her manicured nails dug into the blanket, her knees tried to press against the softness to lift her against his body but he held her in place. He pulled her hair back and to the side giving him access to her mouth. He kissed her roughly as he growled and came hard inside of her. He continued to caress her as the last of his cum spurted into her body.

He felt their bodies relax from the orgasms so he slid carefully from her wet folds and collapsed beside her. She lay on her stomach. Her face was splotchy as she rested against her arms. Smith caressed her breast with his thumb as it lay pressed between her body and the comforter. "I miss you already," he said quietly.

She crawled onto his chest and hovered over him, her dark hair creating a curtain to keep out the world. "We're tough people, you and me. We'll be good."

He nodded agreeing with her, "I have to go."

She leaned to him, hovering closer. "Me too." She blushed and asked, "Think of me?"

He stretched for a kiss then said, "Every minute of every day."

Smith found Martinez flirting with the gate attendant as she typed information into the computer. "She'll never get anything done, if you keep it up," he said with a smile. Martinez winked at her then stepped away with Smith.

"So glad you made it. Not that I was worried." He looked Smith over and observed, "Slept well in your hotel room?"

"Yes, very well."

"Yeah, you were snoring all night long. Kept me up," Martinez complained.

"I can be a bastard that way." Smith stopped talking at the boarding announcement then stood and said, "back to Washington."

CHAPTER 18

"Get out!" Smith shouted at Roberts. The man had fucked up badly and Smith was pissed. Roberts yanked open the office door and rushed out, knocking into Martinez on his way by.

Martinez glanced at the man then back to Smith. "Problem or big problem?" he asked. He stepped inside the office and sat down in the chair Roberts had just vacated.

Smith walked around his desk and threw himself into his chair. He was furious. "I don't understand how anyone could fuck up so badly. I sent him to Arizona to help," Smith groaned and leaned forward pressing his forehead momentarily to his desk, "and two more kids get fucking killed. Motherfucker!" He leaned back, and ran his hands through his hair. "Two kids because he didn't want to be there. He was a shit to the sheriff, even to the fucking parents then he roughs up the suspect so there will probably be some kind of civil rights investigation."

Martinez shook his head. "What are you going to do?"

Smith rocked in his chair for a moment then said, "I'm going to send formal sympathy letters to the parents." He sighed and cursed. "I'll apologize to the sheriff," he glanced at the empty doorway, "and I'm writing up that motherfucker. I really want to fire his ass." He rocked in the chair and looked at Martinez.

"That sounds like a plan. I would've invited him for a jog and beat the shit out of him in the woods."

Smith half-heartedly laughed and said, "That'll be my back-up plan."

Martinez continued, "The missus wants me to invite you to Thanksgiving dinner. Day after tomorrow, four sharp."

Smith checked his watch, and sighed, "I'm flying out tomorrow to my grandparents. Appreciate the invite." He looked out the windows and exhaled heavily.

"How long's it been?" Martinez asked seriously.

Smith's eyes fell back to his friend. He shrugged and admitted, "I haven't talked with her in weeks. Almost three weeks. What if she doesn't want me anymore?"

"God, you sound like a teenager," Martinez chastised.

Smith laughed. "Shit, I am so out of her league. I just expect her to realize it one day."

Martinez rose and said, "Do me a favor and call her from your grandparents. It's the holiday. She'll want to hear from you." He knocked on the desk and walked out.

Smith's phone rang, and he startled awake. The flat screen was still on. A nightly sports show was playing, almost soundlessly. The side lamps were dimmed but cast long shadows around his living room. He sat up and grabbed his phone, answering it on the third ring, "Special Agent Lowery."

"Hi, Special Agent. This is Shannon Young. Ms. Laughlin's personal assistant."

"Is everything okay, Shannon?" he asked, concern ringing through his voice.

"Well, no. That's why I'm calling." She sighed and continued, "Ms. Laughlin isn't aware I'm calling." There was a pause, "I'm worried about her."

"Why? How so?"

"She's off her meds. She stopped taking them, cold turkey."

"How do you know?"

"It's part of my job. I refill the pill box weekly. Make sure her prescriptions are filled, up to date. She stopped about a week ago. I asked her about it and she said she's not depressed anymore. That's she happy and doesn't need her medication."

"She takes several prescriptions," he said, remembering the pills she took in Holland. "Which ones did she stop?"

"She stopped taking the anxiety and depression meds."

"Has she seen her psychiatrist?"

"No, she doesn't want to make an appointment but I know she needs to. I found her yesterday morning lying on the living room sofa crying. I think she'd been there all night. Those aren't medications you can just pick and choose what to take and what not to take."

"What can I do?" he asked with overwhelming need to fix the situation.

"I've never seen her like this. She loves you. I know she misses you. Maybe you can tell her to take them? Maybe if you came to see her?"

"I can't go to New York."

"Even for a quick visit? I can have one of the jets come get you."

He knew they were falling apart away from each other. He missed her. Every day was more difficult than the last without her. "Shannon, this is what you're going to do." He exhaled and said, "Clear her schedule for the holiday weekend. If anyone, I mean anyone asks, tell 'em she went to visit old friends in Colorado or Idaho, if you want. Give the entire staff the holiday off, everyone. Even the security team. Close the apartment down for the long weekend. Put her on a plane and fly her to Gulf Shores Alabama in the morning. There's a small airport there." He ran his hand through his hair and said, "I'll have my grandparents pick her up. No security, not even a car to drive her around. I'll take care of her."

"Brody's not going to like that."

"Give him the holiday off, Shannon." He smiled and offered, "Why don't you two spend the holiday together? Make plans, go somewhere sunny and relax." He got serious, "But, when you pack her bag, put her fucking medication in it. I'll talk with her about it."

"Thank you. I'll get her to your grandparents. I'll text you the flight info."

She hung up, and Smith looked at his phone. He checked his

watch and called his grandparents. He let the phone ring a few times before his grandfather answered. The odd mixture of adopted Southern and born Irish tones rang through the older man's voice as he said, "The bad guys must have nothing to do, giving you time to call."

Smith smiled at hearing his grandfather's voice. "Hi, Pops." He leaned back into the couch and asked, "How's Gran?"

"She's good. She's waiting for the pie to come out of the oven before we can go to bed."

"She cooking already?" he asked, amazed.

"Of course, you're coming home. You are, aren't you? Is that why you're calling?"

"Pops, everything's fine. I just," he stopped. He'd never brought anyone home though it wasn't really as if he was bringing Delilah with him. He hadn't even told them he'd met someone. "It's just that I have a favor to ask. I've asked my girlfriend to come with me but she's going to get to town first. Can you two meet her?"

"You have a girlfriend?"

"Trust you to pick up on the finer points," Smith said with a smile. "Yes, her name's Delilah."

"Aww, beautiful."

"She is; in every way," he inhaled and tried to think of a good way to tell his grandfather to keep it all a secret. "Because of my job we're not supposed to be dating so don't go telling anyone she's coming for a visit."

"Am I allowed to tell your grandmother?"

"Yes," Smith replied with a smile. "I'll call you when I know the time she's getting in. She's flying into Gulf Shores." His flight was going into Pensacola. He didn't want them driving all over the Florida panhandle so he said, "I'll rent a car when I get there so you don't have to pick me up."

"Nonsense, we'll come get you," Pops said.

"Really, Pops, it's okay. Take Delilah home and make her comfortable. She needs a break." He sighed and admitted, "I do too. I need to be with her and y'all. It's been too long."

"That's true. OK, boy, you can text me her flight information." He paused for effect, "That's right, your Gran and I are texting now. She's much better at it than I am."

Smith laughed. "texting? Y'all are getting high tech. Thanks, pops. I'll see you tomorrow." He hung up the phone and smiled. He chuckled and turned off the flat screen and the lights. He wouldn't get much sleep now, excitement ran through his body. He decided to get the airport early; maybe he could catch an earlier flight.

CHAPTER 19

Smith pushed open the front door of his grandparents' one story, white clapboard house and stepped inside to the smell of baking bread and the sound of Delilah laughing. It instantly set his heart to racing. He dropped his overnight bag in the foyer, and called out, "Honey, I'm home."

There was a squeal of delight as he stepped quickly through the living room and rounded the kitchen entrance. He stopped and took in the sight of Delilah with his grandparents. Her hands were raised awkwardly to the side, her manicured nails covered in dough. She was wearing one of his Gran's aprons; the faded yellow one with decorative roosters that he'd bought his grandmother years ago for a birthday present.

Delilah remained in one spot but was hopping side to side, antsy as his grandmother untied the strings. She ducked under Gran's arm and out of the apron, racing around the kitchen island for him. Smith caught Delilah in his arms. Her warmth radiated through him as he held her. He felt her exhale, her whole body relaxed. She pulled back and lifted her face as he leaned for a kiss. Their lips met, their mouths sealed, igniting the passion that had been unrequited for weeks.

He kissed her again quickly and roughly before saying, "I've missed you." Her smile brightened the room.

He looked over to Pops as the old man stood from the kitchen table chair and said, "I missed you too but don't expect a kiss like that from me."

Smith clung to Delilah with one arm as he hugged Pops, then Gran with the other. Delilah leaned against his chest once more as Gran stepped back to the dough. "We're making cookies," Delilah announced. She wiggled her fingers with a devious smile. "I have dough under my nails."

He couldn't help it as he leaned down and kissed her again. He was sure he had the same ridiculous smile on his face too. "Smells great," he said, taking her by the hand. He led her to the sink and started the water, pulling her hands beneath the warm flow.

"That'd be the bread and the brownies," Gran said.

"Mmm, I love brownies," he commented, washing the dough from Delilah's hands.

"I've never made cookies from scratch," she admitted softly.

His eyes locked on her emerald ones, concern coursing through his body and asked, "How are you?"

"I'm OK." She glanced away then back and said more firmly, "I'm better now."

He shut off the water and dried her hands. "Yeah, me too." He dropped the cloth on the laminate counter and took her in his arms again. She murmured in delight as he nuzzled her neck.

"How was the flight?" Pops asked.

Smith removed himself from Delilah's neck to reply, "Fine, I managed to catch an earlier one. Flashed my badge," he flashed a smile.

"Better than flashing other things," Pops said.

"Lee O'Keeffe!" Gran exclaimed. She looked disapprovingly to her husband then shifted with a smile to Smith and Delilah. "I thought we'd have an early dinner then you two can have some quiet time to catch up."

Smith held Delilah's hand as he stepped close to his grandmother and pressed a kiss to her cheek. "How long? I didn't eat lunch."

"An hour? Maybe less," she smiled subtly. "Enough time for a walk in the neighborhood to show Delilah around."

He looked back at Delilah thinking he could spend the time with her doing other things but tugged her hand and walked back through the small house to the front door. They stepped down the wooden steps of the old house and Smith stopped. The late afternoon air had turned chilly. Not New York City temperatures but still, he didn't want to her cold. He turned to her and began to button her gray cardigan that covered a white T-shirt. It was incredibly soft to his touch, reminding him of the woman who wore it. His fingers strayed after he finished the button between her breasts. He touched the round fullness, caressing her with his thumbs before he leaned in and kissed her. He had missed her, and the feel of her body renewed his passion.

She smiled beneath his kiss and took his hands from her breasts. "We're in public," she said. "Show me around."

He took her hand and turned for the sidewalk. He went left and they walked side by side holding hands. He leaned back and whistled. "Your ass looks great in those jeans." She laughed. He felt his whole body heal from their time apart with the bubbly sound. She leaned her head against his arm for a moment before she straightened. They walked in silence for a few minutes before he said, "This is an old neighborhood." He pointed back to the right as they came to an intersection. "If you go that way it puts you out on the main drive. See those two condo buildings?" He pointed to buildings which had been constructed on the other side of the main road. She nodded. "The Gulf's on the other side. It's really grown up a lot since I was a kid. Lots of tourists, snow birds now."

"I'm sure the water's beautiful, that's why everyone comes here," she offered.

He nodded and turned in the opposite direction. "My high school's over there," he pointed off into the distance. He could make out the low, brick building and the football stands behind it. He didn't want to walk too far from the house with Gran getting the food onto the table. "I didn't live near here with my parents," he offered.

"Oh?" she asked quietly.

His face took a grim line as he remembered the accident. "We lived further north, more towards Foley. My dad was an engineer for one of the chemical plants. Mom was the prosecutor for Baldwin County. I came to live here after the accident, switched high schools."

"I know that was hard."

He shrugged and agreed, "It was." He left it hanging in the cool Southern air. "Everything changed so quickly. You know, I was told they died and then I moved, changed schools. I tried to make new friends. I didn't want to be known as the kid whose parents died." He smiled quickly. "Of course, it did help with the girls. Sympathy sex."

She shook her head and smirked disapprovingly. He laughed as they took another left, taking them round the block. "Can we head back?" she asked. "I'm not feeling great."

"Sure," he said, turning and leading them through a short cut.

"Your grandparents are very nice." He agreed. "They talked about you."

"Really?" He raised a brow as he asked, "Should I be worried?"

She teased, "Yes." She bumped his shoulder. "I'm the only woman you've brought home. You did have a serious girlfriend in college but Gran's glad you dumped her. She thought she was too," Delilah thought for a moment, "trashy for you."

He gestured to the small house as they walked in front of it. He held her hand tightly as she walked slowly up the front steps. "I'll see about getting the handrail fixed while I'm here," he said, looking at the broken railing. She threw a look and he sputtered, "Not for you, for them. I don't want them falling if they grab that thing."

She nodded with approval as he opened the door, "Good thinking."

They walked back into the kitchen and found the table full of empty plates and lots of food. Delilah breathed a 'Wow' and Smith grew instantly hungry. They sat beside each other as Pops took his usual seat on the far side of the table. Gran took hers on the opposite side.

Smith glanced at Delilah thinking she was paler than normal. Grace was said, and he filled her glass with water from the pitcher after checking to make sure it was room temperature. She dished out small amounts of the varieties. He smiled to reassure her as she passed him a serving spoon and whispered, "I'm hot."

He wanted to joke but she looked worried and her eyes flickered to her wrists. He understood and tried to reassure her, "It's alright. You can take off your sweater." Worry plagued her sweet face before she exhaled slowly and undid the buttons of her sweater. She removed it and hung it over the back of her chair before she turned back and began to eat.

Pops was just getting into his verbal groove, telling Smith everything that had happened to the locals recently when he frowned and asked nodding with his head and fork, "What happened to you, Delilah?"

She turned red and remained silent so Smith answered, "Delilah was attacked when she was a kid."

Gran said something about it being awful as Pops asked, "Why'd the guy do that?"

"Because he's a sadistic motherfucker." Delilah's eyes went wide with surprise and clamped her hand over her mouth. "Oh, shit, sorry." She hiccupped a laugh. "Sorry, I didn't mean to curse."

"It's alright. I've got you covered." Pops leaned to the side and pulled out some change. "Gran makes us put a quarter in the swear bear for each curse." He put down two quarters.

Smith explained for Delilah's benefit, "That's the glass jar on the counter that's shaped like a bear." He took out his wallet. "That's not going to be enough for the holiday, Pops." He removed a ten and set it on the table. Delilah smirked at him.

Pops started talking again, Gran correcting him at every chance, making the time pass quickly and easily amongst them.

Delilah suddenly clamped her hand to her mouth and stood. "Excuse…" she ran from the kitchen without finishing her sentence. All heads turned and watched her disappear around the corner.

Smith stood and followed to the far side of the house. He grimaced as he heard her vomiting. She'd left the hall bathroom door open so he stepped inside and squatted beside her as she retched again. He pulled her hair back and held it for a moment as her stomach heaved once more. She spit a few times and sat back. She leaned against the wall, and closed her watering eyes.

Smith stood and filled a little paper cup with water from the sink. He knelt in front of her and offered it. She looked at him with tears dripping over the edges of her heavy black lashes. She sipped and leaned forward to spit again before leaning back and grimacing in pain.

"What's the matter, Delilah? I know it's not Gran's cooking."

Her hand shook as she passed back the empty paper cup. "Can't you tell?" she snapped. "You're fucking law enforcement. I'd think you'd be more observant." She pressed a hand to stomach. Smith's heart began to race before she said, "My body's going through fucking withdrawal. From the fucking medication. I stopped taking it. I'm not an addict. My body's just used to it."

"Isn't denial the first sign?" he smiled, and immediately realized she wasn't in the mood for his jokes. He nodded and exhaled, admitting, "I know, Shannon told me." They sat staring at each other for a moment before he asked, "Why'd you stop?"

"I don't want to be on it anymore. I've been taking the meds for years. I'm not depressed anymore." She glanced up at him. Her bright green eyes were haunting.

"You should've talked with your doctor."

"I did."

He was relieved to hear it. "What'd he say?"

"He said it would fuck up my body for a few weeks as I adjust to being without the medications."

"How long have you been throwing up?"

"About a week. He told me he could prescribe something to make the transition easier but I don't want to be on any more medicines." She begged him with her eyes, "I hate the medications. I don't want to take anymore, ever! I had thought about doing this a few years ago but," she shrugged, "I got busy with work and stuff."

"You don't have to go through this alone."

"I didn't want you to think badly of me."

He touched her face gently wiping away the stream of tears. "Are you nervous about anything?" She shook her head vehemently. He said tenderly, "If you are, you can always take your anxiety meds without having to take the depression ones. It's not an all or nothing situation. Are you still taking your birth control pills?"

"Of course," she said to his answering smile. "Arugh, you're such a guy." His grin burst into a full blown smile, one that he saw made her go woozy. He was quietly pleased with her reaction.

"If you start feeling depressed, will you tell me?" She nodded so he stood and reached for her. "I'm here for you, Delilah. If you need me, nothing's going to stop me from getting to you." He refused to let her go, holding her closely in the small bathroom. He pressed a kiss to her forehead. "Feel like eating a little something?"

She groaned and asked, "Can I just sit at the table?"

He kissed her lips. "Sure, raccoon, you can do anything you want."

At the mention of her nickname she looked in the mirror and cringed. "I just keep reinforcing that pet name, don't I?" She rinsed her mouth and washed the makeup from her eyes quickly before following him out. He pulled out her chair at the table and sat beside her. She apologized to his grandparents and took a sip of water.

"Are you feeling alright, sweetie?" Gran asked.

Delilah nodded and pulled her cell phone from her jeans pocket checking a text. She replied quickly then glanced up and apologized again, "Sorry. That was work."

"What do you do for a living?" Pops asked.

Her face remained placid. "I own a business."

"What kind of business?" Gran asked curiously.

Smith hid his smile behind a hand as he chewed. He glanced at Delilah interested in what she had to say.

"I own Delightful Finds."

"The sex shops?" Pops asked.

"Adult boutiques," Delilah offered.

"You know those, dear," Gran said to Pops. "You remember when we went to New York to visit Smith a few years ago. We went to the store in Times Square." Smith groaned. He didn't want to hear this.

"We bought that thing there?" Pops asked.

Smith winced.

Gran smiled. "Yes, dear."

Pops looked at Delilah. "Thank you, young lady."

Smith laughed as Delilah said, "You're welcome."

Smith climbed naked into the full size bed sure Delilah hadn't slept in such a small bed for a long time. His feet touched the footboard as he stretched out. It felt odd being in his old bedroom with an incredibly beautiful woman crawling into bed with him. She was wearing a cream colored lace and silk floor-length nightgown. He was in awe of her.

She curled herself around him and exhaled. They lay quietly together, clinging to each other. She was trembling so he shifted the blankets and handmade patchwork quilt around her. "I'm not cold, Smith." They both knew it was the drug withdrawal her body was going through. "Please hold me," she pleaded.

His arms tightened around her and he shifted slightly to lie beside her. His hands ran over her stomach. He lingered above her, and pressed a gentle kiss to her lips. The silk on top of her curves was too much for him to take and he pushed the soft material up, exposing her delicate flesh. His fingers delved into her wet folds, massaging her, circling her. She pulled him closer, expressing all of her wants and desires in her caresses as their lips met and mingled. He settled between her legs.

"Delilah," he said her name softly. He touched her face gently. "I have nothing without you." He looked anxious and admitted, "I am nothing without you."

She stretched for him. "We're good together." Tears dripped along the sides of her temples. She shifted her hips and pulled her nightgown up and over her head, setting it aside on the small bed. She reached for him with an intensity that he replied to in kind, making love to her throughout the night before he pulled her close and they fell into an exhausted, peaceful sleep.

Smith stretched as he woke and opened his eyes. He'd slept really well in his old bed with Delilah tangled with him. The soft skin of her back pressed against his chest. The world was shut out, heavy curtains drawn but he could hear rain playing a tune on the tin roof. He felt her wake at his movement. He squeezed her a little tighter and she crossed her arms over his. "Delilah," he murmured.

"Yes, dear," she purred with a grin.

"Back in New York," he said quietly, "you said I could fuck your breasts. I want to do that sometime."

She opened her eyes fully and turned in his arms to face him. She smiled and asked, "You do?"

"Sorry," he shrugged. "You have beautiful breasts. We don't have to do that now. I know you're not feeling well."

Her fingers traced the outline of his jaw as she said, "Don't apologize. I want you to enjoy every part of my body as much as I enjoy yours." She sat up abruptly, and shrugged on his T-shirt before leaving. He heard her walk to the bathroom and back quickly, closing the door behind her. She had a little navy blue bathroom bag in her hand. It had gold embroidered in a design on each side. She settled back into the bed and set the little bag on the nightstand. He helped her pull the shirt up over her head as she twisted and snuggled her legs beneath the blankets.

She sat on the bed, her legs covered but her torso was beautifully naked as she reached into the bag and withdrew a hairband. He watched, enthralled as she braided her hair. She held the band between her lips. His eyes roamed between her lips and her breasts then upward again as she finished the braid and took the band from her mouth.

"Delilah, we don't have to," he managed.

"When you come on my chest you might get some in my hair," she shrugged and finished wrapping the band around the end of her hair. She smiled and shifted closer to him in the bed.

He reached for her as she straddled him and sat on his lap. He tucked the blankets around her hips.

"Smith," she said, hovering just close enough that her breasts were teasing his chest. "I want you in every sexual way known to mankind." He laughed and she pressed her hand against his mouth, "Shh, you'll wake your grandparents." She replaced her hand with her mouth.

His hands skimmed the sides of her chest and he asked through her kisses, "Every way?"

Her tongue slipped through his mouth before she said, "Yes, every way."

"That's a lot of ways," he murmured. His hand caressed her inner thigh. He moved a hand to her hip and grabbed his erection, stroking the thick length. He teased her with the tip of his cock, and she groaned wantonly.

"Not like that, not yet," she said decidedly, and shifted from him abruptly. Smith lay with his cock in his hand waiting for her direction. She reached for her bag and took out a small tube of lube and lay on her back. She scooted further down the bed and tapped the bed on either side of her, "Here boy."

He grinned ridiculously tossing aside the blankets and straddled her hips. His balls lay heavily on her stomach. He felt great, ecstatic for them just to play together. His hands fell to his thighs as he watched. She opened the tube and squeezed clear gel onto her chest in a line running from nipple to nipple. She reached for him, taking his shaft in her hand. She squeezed gel along the length of his hard cock. He shivered at its coolness. Her fingers massaged the gel over his entire length, and he groaned in pleasure.

Finally, her bright green eyes looked up and found his. "Come here," she ordered. The stern tone of her voice made him harder, and he leaned forward on all fours. His cock pressed against her chest and she stretched up. She licked and sucked his stomach as she pushed her breasts together, encompassing his cock. "Fuck me hard," she commanded.

He groaned as he pulled back and pushed forward. He lowered his hips, straddled her and began to pound against her chest. It was insanely good as he slammed into her breasts over and over. His balls thudded against her stomach. She squirted more lube on his cock and pressed her breasts tighter around him.

"Harder," she hissed, and slapped his ass. He gave her what she wanted, crashing against her again and again before his cock thickened and tightened. He built up a rhythm, enjoying the feel, the warmth that grew deep within his body. He growled as he climaxed and came over her chest. He powered the thick liquid up her neck. He came again onto her chest and she released her breasts.

Smith hovered over her on all fours, panting, breathless from the thrill. She smiled up at him. He leaned down and kissed her passionately. He kissed the smile from her face as the intensity swept over them. His hand touched her red, blotchy chest, and he smeared the cum down her stomach as his eyes flicked to hers. "Everywhere, Delilah?"

Her manicured nails ran through his hair, and she nodded.

His fingers were wet with thick cum as he stroked the entrance of her sex. She was soaking for him. He circled two fingers, gently massaging her. His mouth found hers as his fingers left her sex and moved to her anus. She gasped as he spread their liquid mixture of cum and her arousal against the tight hole.

"Smith," she whispered, "I haven't done that in a long time."

He nodded and slid down her body, kissing the cum smear. His mouth found her sex, drenched and impatient for him. He wrapped his arms around her legs, pressing his hands against her flat belly as he licked and sucked her with wanton need. He blew against her clit and she clawed at the bed. He smiled and delved into her wet folds. She tasted incredible. He swirled his tongue, taking long slow licks against her clit until she was begging to come. He shifted two fingers and pounded those into her wet folds while his tongue pushed her over the edge. Her back arched, her manicured nails pulled on the bed sheets as he sucked and sucked. When her back fell to the bed he wiped his mouth off on her inner thigh.

He knelt from her and flipped her over. He pulled her onto all fours and slammed his cock into her sex. She cried out as he filled her. He felt her body still quivering from the aftershocks of her orgasm. He thrust against her then slowed, pulling his cock from her in long, unhurried strokes. His fingers stroked her soaked sex as his cock continued its onslaught. His finger was slick as he pressed against her anus again. Delilah fell forward onto her forearms as his finger rimmed her. He delved the finger in just a little, and circled her. She grabbed a pillow and buried her face in it. A light layer of perspiration covered her back almost instantly.

One hand plumped her ass as his hips rhythmically pounded against her while one finger became two that he forced into her tight hole. Smith moved his fingers at the same pace with his cock, and she moaned in delight. He felt her body quivering. He knew she was on the verge of an explosive orgasm.

She bit the pillow and muffled a scream as her body came around him. She tightened around his fingers, around his cock with extraordinary ferocity. He pounded against her once more and came hard in response. He growled as he spurted into her body, forcing his cum deep inside. He felt the orgasm rush over her in waves as she came again, milking his body of everything he had to offer. He gently withdrew his fingers and pressed a kiss to her back before they collapsed onto the bed.

He leaned against her back, his hand splayed against her trim stomach as he asked, "Are you alright?" She mumbled, her face half hidden by the pillow she'd been biting. He lifted the pillow from her face. She was red, and splotchy, and beautiful with her just fucked look. She looked him over. Smith could see to the depths of her soul as she caressed him with her green eyes. "I'm in love with you," he said quietly.

"Good," she said flatly. "you better be considering what you just did to me," she said with a smile and pulled the pillow back over her face. "I'm in love with you too," she muttered from beneath the pillow. He smiled and pulled the blankets up and around them. He tucked his body into hers, holding her tightly and fell back to sleep.

CHAPTER 20

Smith sat behind Delilah, his arms wrapped around her waist as his chin rested on her shoulder staring out at the ocean. She'd found one of his old high school hoodies in the closet and wore it over a T-shirt with jeans. The late November wind blew off of the water pulling and tugging her dark hair away giving him a profile view of her pretty face.

She leaned back into him, pressing her hands against his. "Tell me something," she said.

"What would you like to know?"

"I want to know a hope, a dream." She shrugged. "How about telling me what you want to accomplish in life."

"I want," he hummed into her neck. He felt an intense need to be cautious. If he said his hope was for a big ass boat, he was sure one would show up on his doorstep in a week. "You," he said.

She leaned over her shoulder and kissed him. "Try again. You already have me."

"I want to look back at my life and know that I've made the right decisions. That I've made the world a better place by being in it." He grinned and pressed a kiss to her neck. Let her try to figure that one out. He guaranteed no boat, no expensive watch or another suit would enter his world via Delilah's generosity. "What do you want?" he asked.

"I think I've done well professionally."

"Better than most," he commented sarcastically.

She half turned and glared over her shoulder to find him smiling then said, "Maybe it's time to concentrate on the personal side." She turned and looked back at the gulf waters. "I think that's why I didn't want to wait to stop taking the medications. I want a fresh start on making me." She held his hands closer. "You and me."

He glanced at the beach and hummed his approval into her neck. He understood. He knew she had been working since she was a teenager to gain control over her life. She'd been desperate for it just as he had been but in a different way, for a similar need. He watched colorful kites fly high above the beach. Other people strolled along the sand; some hand in hand enjoying the long weekend. It was an active but peaceful place. He noticed two young men texting and walking, completely ignorant of the world around them. They glanced up and looked at him and Delilah. One nudged the other with a look of realization on his face.

Shit. Smith said quietly, "Delilah, love, turn around." He pulled her, helping her turn around to face him. She knelt between his legs, her hands comfortably on his thighs as he said, "Let's just tuck in this wild hair." He captured her hair from the wind.

"What's the matter?" she asked anxiously.

"Nothing," he said, pulling the hoodie up and over her hair.

"Something is," she said as worry crossed her face.

He glanced at the guys and one of them had their phone lifted to him and Delilah. Smith cursed and said, "Come here." He held her close, tucking her into him, his arms crossing over her shoulders and pressed his face against the hoodie. She leaned into his chest. "Just some kids with a cell phone and internet access." He wanted to protect her from their prying eyes. After Martinez's warning about Delilah on the gossip sites he knew anonymity was going to be difficult to get though they needed it desperately. He felt her shoulders shake and knew she was crying before she collapsed into him. He pulled her tighter and watched the kids move further along the beach. Smith pulled her slightly back. "They're gone." He wiped away the tracks of tears with his thumbs. "Its okay, Delilah. I don't think they got any pictures worth putting on the internet."

"Won't it be enough for them say I was here, or that they think I was here?"

He shrugged and pulled her close. He leaned into her and sighed. She was right. He was going to fuck it up. It being his profession or his relationship with her, he hadn't decided yet. He kissed her hooded head and leaned back. "Dinner should be ready. Want to head back?" She nodded so he stood and helped her up. They walked hand in hand back to his grandparents' house.

There was organized chaos in the kitchen as they stepped in. His grandmother took a look at Delilah and ordered, "Put out the plates. We want to eat while it's hot." Gran gestured to Smith and said, "Help your grandfather get the turkey out of the oven. He's too old to be lifting the bird."

"Damn it, Irene!" Pops said, hunched over the oven. "I am not!"

"I'll do it, Pops," Smith offered and forced, taking the oven mitts away from the older man.

Delilah readied the table and got drinks. Gran had Delilah hustling from the island as she prepped food into beautiful china dishes and bowls, moving them to the table. With the turkey out, Smith moved it onto a bone white platter. He lifted the dish up and over everyone's heads as he crossed the kitchen, and set it in the middle of the table.

"Smells great, Gran," he said, eyeing the food. He reached over and squeezed Delilah's hand. He wanted her relaxed and happy, more than anything else he wanted her happy to be with him and his family.

Gran swatted Smith on the arm with a colorful potholder as she passed and said, "I get better every year. It's the practice." She grinned and sat down in her traditional seat.

He pulled out Delilah's chair and she sat before he did.

Pops took his chair and leaned back declaring, "Too much work!"

"Pops complains every year but he loves the leftovers," Smith said with a smile to Delilah. He took her hand and Pops' as grace began. Delilah lifted her hand and placed it within Gran's. Smith squeezed Delilah's hand gently as Pops finished saying grace.

"Dig in folks. Don't want it getting cold!" Gran said, scooping the potatoes.

Smith was glad Delilah took more food than the previous night. She filled her plate and accepted the thick sawmill gravy when Smith offered it. Pops started eating and talking, making Delilah laugh as he told them of their adventures with a young Smith. He told her of his and Gran's childhood in Cork County. They'd grown up in a small town of Newmarket. He'd been sweet on gran since they were fifteen when she walked by him with a group of her friends going to the general store. Somehow, he'd managed to talk her into a wedding and a move to the States.

"Have you been?" Pops asked her.

"To Ireland?" Delilah asked. She shook her head. "No, I haven't." She frowned and said, "I don't know why I haven't. I've been to London and most of Europe but that's always for business."

"When was your last vacation?" Gran asked.

"Oh, I've…a real vacation?" Delilah stopped to think. "I took a week off about six years ago. I went fishing in Alaska."

"Fishing," Smith smiled with pride. "That's my woman."

"Six years ago?" Gran exclaimed with a tisk. "A businesswoman needs time off too. For family, for time to relax and rest." Smith looked at Gran incredulously when she mentioned family. She shrugged it off and continued, "Women need things, Smith. Not all of them are shiny or have a paycheck attached."

Pops piped in and announced, "Time." Everyone turned and looked at him. "There comes a time when time is most important."

"I agree," Gran said with a smile. "That's very true."

Pops shifted and ate some gravy covered turkey then asked, "What's your family doing for the holiday, Delilah?"

She shrugged and said, "I don't know. I don't talk with my parents often."

"Where do they live?" Gran asked.

"They still live in Connecticut. They wanted to stay close to my sister." Smith looked at her for an explanation so she clarified, "They wanted to remain close to her grave." She tried to explain, "They didn't handle her death well so they've chosen to stay where they have the best memories of her, of Rachel."

Smith tried to move the conversation away from Delilah's family and asked, "Are you two planning any trips back home?"

Pops smiled. "We are, next year, maybe towards the summer."

"I want to go for a month or so," Gran said. "We have family to visit, places to see before we get too old." She looked to Delilah and said, "Maybe you two can go with us." Delilah smiled brightly and Smith focused extraordinarily hard on adding some sweet potatoes to his plate. Next summer was too far away to plan anything.

"That was wonderful," Delilah said, crawling into bed. She snuggled into his arms and announced, "I didn't throw up today."

"Congratulations," he said sarcastically, holding her closer. Her body still trembled but it wasn't as noticeable. "Did you want to call your parents to visit? Wish them a happy holiday."

"No," she said quietly. "They won't want to talk with me."

"I can't imagine that," he said and kissed her forehead.

"Smith, you have no idea." She got very quiet then said, "I usually give the staff the time off and spend the holidays alone. This, today, is the closest thing I've had to family in years. I feel as if your grandparents actually like me." She rose on an elbow and looked at him. "I don't want to lose this." She pressed the palm of her hand to his heart and leaned in for a kiss.

"Never going to happen, raccoon," he said, responding to her passionate kiss. She climbed on top of him and made love to him as if her life depended on it.

Smith held Delilah's face in his hands as they stood next to the jet staircase a few days later. He didn't know what to say to reassure her. He pressed his lips to hers then held her close. The embrace broke and she turned then walked up the staircase. She turned at the top, blew him a kiss and smiled. He saw the smile and enthusiasm disappear before she turned and stepped further into the private jet.

Smith walked back to his rental car and watched the plane taxi away. His lighthearted mood left with her. He felt restless, wanting to be moving. He watched for a moment longer as the jet took off, taking her away from him and back to New York.

CHAPTER 21

It was nearly two weeks later that Smith sat in his office reading through the report which matched the weapons from Rachel's cold case to that of Senator Travis. Martinez had put together a well-organized and thorough report. Smith made a few notes including sending out notices to all of the field offices of their suspect information. He wanted Michael found and arrested.

He felt confident in their information. He could make the announcement. They had a suspect. The information could be released to the press and to the public. He'd have to make a few calls, one to Delilah to give her a heads up. He didn't want the news to upset her. The thought of hearing her voice brightened his mood. He'd also have to call the A.D. to find out if he and the Director would want to go over to Senator Travis' widower with him to give the news in person.

His office phone rang and Smith answered it without looking up. He stopped reading as the A.D. said, "Special Agent Lowery, you and I need to meet."

"Yes, Sir." Smith checked his watch, it was late. "Do you want me to come to H.Q. now?"

"No, meet me at Reagan tomorrow at ten, bring an overnight bag. Bring Martinez with you."

"Is this about a case?" Smith asked.

"It's about several cases. Ten tomorrow, Special Agent."

Smith said, "Yes, Sir," but the A.D. had already hung up. He looked at his phone for a moment then called Martinez. "You and I are going with the A.D. tomorrow at ten. Pack a bag."

"What's it about?" he asked.

"No fucking clue," Smith answered honestly.

Smith was dressed in the Brioni suit feeling the need to look his best. He stepped quickly out of his house, locking it up behind him at eight-thirty the next morning. A black Suburban idled in the street in front of his house. He climbed into the back next to Martinez and tossed his bag to his feet.

"Morning," he said as way of greeting, not knowing if it was a good one or not.

Martinez nodded. "Did you find out anything?" he asked as the driver sped off towards the airport.

Smith shook his head and muttered, "No." The possibilities ran the gamut. "Could have to do with the Travis case."

"Did he tell you where we're going?"

Again Smith shook his head and let the conversation die. There was no need to speculate. They'd be to the airport soon enough. The driver slowed for the early Friday morning traffic D.C. was famous for. They arrived with twenty minutes to spare as the driver pulled up to a private jet and stopped. He realized the A.D. was traveling with them, which meant it wouldn't be a commercial flight. He grabbed his bag and stepped out of the Suburban. He waited for Martinez then walked to the plane staircase.

Smith stepped inside and took a quick glance around. He immediately thought it wasn't as nice as Delilah's jet but hers was tailored to her needs. This was intended for at least twenty people to sit comfortably; to get from Point A to Point B as efficiently as possible. He handed his bag to a steward and took a facing forward seat. Martinez passed over his bag as well and sat beside Smith, taking the window seat.

When the steward walked by Smith said, "Hey, excuse me. Where's the destination for this flight?"

The man said, "New York," and continued on his way. Smith's stomach dropped.

They waited about ten minutes in silence before the A.D.

stepped on board with two other agents. Smith knew one to be his assistant but he didn't recognize the other man. The A.D. nodded gravely to Smith and took a seat opposite the aisle from them.

"I want to be wheels up right away," he said to the steward. The man walked to the doorway and began closing it. The plane taxied almost immediately and the A.D. looked grim.

Martinez leaned close and whispered, "We are so fucked."

Smith didn't say anything but he got that feeling too.

The A.D. looked to Smith as soon as the wheels left the ground and said, "We're going to have a very serious talk." He nodded to the other agent then looked back to Smith and Martinez. "Both of you move over here. I want you to see a few things." The other agent produced a laptop and pulled up a video as Smith and Martinez moved so they faced the other men. "If you haven't met this is Special Agent Heath from legal."

Smith leaned in and braced his elbows on his knees as he watched the video. He didn't have to look too hard to see himself in a black and white grainy imagery walking back into his hotel from the Halloween trip to New York. His stomach lurched. It was time stamped showing him arriving back at the hotel around six thirty in the morning. He left shortly after to get the airport. With a few key strokes Special Agent Heath brought up another. It was color this time, and shaky. Smith instantly recognized it. His stomach dropped. The stupid kids. He watched himself and Delilah sitting on the beach. He watched himself turn her around, protect her with the hoodie and hold her close. He could still feel her body against his, the smell of her body wash and as they flew to New York he knew he'd be going to see her.

"Turn it off," the A.D. said to the agent and looked to Martinez and asked, "Did Special Agent Lowery come back to the hotel Halloween night?"

Martinez thought for a moment and answered, "Special Agent Lowery and I didn't share a hotel room, Sir. I don't know."

It was the most honest thing Martinez could say, Smith realized. He couldn't hold it against Martinez. He didn't want his friend and colleague to get in trouble for him.

The A.D.'s intense glare fell to Smith and said, "Special

Agent, it has come to my attention that Ms. Laughlin wasn't forthcoming with the statement she gave you in Amsterdam."

Smith looked at him; his brows furrowed with confusion and asked, "How so?"

"It seems she misrepresented her relationship with Senator Travis as well as their conspiracy to find and kill Michael Townsend."

Smith swallowed hard. He knew everything the A.D. was talking about.

"This doesn't seem to surprise you, Special Agent."

"The relationship between Ms. Laughlin and Senator Travis has been revealed in the course of our investigation. It has also been confirmed through Senator Travis' information and electronic trail she was the one trying to locate Mr. Townsend."

"So you believe Ms. Laughlin's statement?" he asked.

"I do believe she was forthcoming at the time the statement was taken. And she has been helpful to the investigation whenever asked."

The A.D. looked at him and said determinedly, "I'm going to arrest her for obstruction of justice. I'm going to think about arresting her for conspiracy to commit murder."

"Sir, you've read the cold case files. You know the pain and suffering Ms. Laughlin has been through with the murder of her sister as well as her own physical assault. Shit, she was used as bait. She still hurts from the damage Michael Townsend did to her. It's only natural for a victim of a violent crime to talk about wanting the person who attacked them dead. Instead, she's risen above her desire for vengeance and wants him found. She wants justice for herself, her sister and now for Senator Travis." Smith exhaled and shut up.

"Give me your phone, Special Agent," the A.D. ordered holding out his hand.

Smith handed it over and knew there was no way for him to contact Delilah. No way to warn her of what was coming.

Smith sat in the back of another black Suburban as it moved

effortlessly through Long Island. They'd made arrangements to meet with her immediately upon their arrival. Through Shannon, they'd been informed Delilah was at her house on Long Island. Her home, she once told him.

He sat in the backseat and said nothing though he was exuding palpable energy. He wanted to fight. He wanted to protect her, to give her some kind of warning. He stared out the back window as the scenery raced by, watching but not seeing as he worried. He finally took notice of the properties. It was December and most of the lawns still looked spring green as they sat before mansions. The GPS announced they were close so he looked out Martinez's window. A tall iron fence advised the beginning of her wooded property as they drove the small two lane road. It seemed to go on forever before the driver slowed, and turned left into a small drive. The driver stopped and rolled the window down. Pressing a button, he announced their arrival and waited for a moment before the electric gate moved.

The driver waited for the gate to open fully before he moved the vehicle through. It took a few more minutes as they drove along the private road through the woods until the trees broke into an open field with the sea in the distance.

Smith smiled when he saw the house Delilah had bought for herself. It was her home. He immediately felt her warmth and adoration radiating from it. The size might have underwhelmed compared to the other mansions he'd seen on the road, but he thought it was perfect for her. It was one story with weatherworn gray cedar siding and pristine white paint on the trim and columns which stood like sentinels on a wraparound porch. The driver rounded the driveway and parked.

Smith glanced to the far side of the property as he got out and spotted a black helicopter as it rested on a concrete pad. Close by was a two story, four-car garage with the same decorative gray siding and bright white trim. He assumed that's were Brody stayed if he came to the house with her.

Smith stood at the rear entryway and watched Brody go get her. Her hair danced in the sea breeze, tossing about the long dark locks which he knew felt like strands of silk. She'd tucked herself into a little ball, small and insignificant with the sea and darkening sky as her background, staring out longingly at it.

But he knew otherwise. He knew she had suffered. She had survived. She didn't long for the vastness and obscurity of the ocean. Rather he knew she wanted closure, a chance to overcome, to pinpoint her place in the world, and call it home.

He loved her. He knew it with every ounce of his heart and soul. He needed to protect her, from what neither of them was expecting. He needed to protect her from the other men in suits who milled about waiting for her at the back of the house in the pool room. It had a skylight ceiling which gave the room natural lighting, and the same pool as they had shared in Amsterdam, yet this one seemed larger and was surrounded by four white columns that marked each corner of the pool. He glanced back into the house and could see all the way to the front door from where he stood.

Smith turned back and watched as Brody stopped beside her. She looked up, and Smith caught the profile of her beautiful face. He remembered how soft her lips were against his own. The memory of her breath against his skin stirred him. Her body against his, touching, yearning for more, for everything he had to give, shook him to the core.

He knew what Brody was saying though he couldn't hear the words. She nodded. Her mouth took a grim line. Her profile disappeared as she looked back to the stormy ocean. As if to mimic her mood lightning flashed miles out to sea and storm clouds darkened.

She pushed herself up and dusted off the sand. She looked very young, wearing blue jeans and a navy blue graphic T-shirt. Her bare feet walked the sandy path bordered by dancing sea grass which led back to the house as she untied a hoodie from her waist and shrugged into it. The long sleeves hid her scars, and he knew that's why she'd put it on. She zipped the jacket about half way before her emerald eyes caught his. The impact of her gaze was overwhelming and stole his breath. She was upset, rightly so. He wanted to take her, hold her and tell her the world would be better now that they were together again. But he couldn't, not in front of the suits.

"Special Agent Lowery," she said, her voice husky with emotion.

"Ms. Laughlin," he said, turning with her. He placed his hand on the small of her back. A simple gesture but one that conveyed his longing and weariness of the others as his fingertips dug into her back as a silent warning.

"It's very nice to see you again," she said as she stepped away from him and to her lawyer. "I trust introductions have been made. If not, this is Mr. Ellington, my attorney," she glanced at her attorney, "Mr. Ellington, these men are FBI."

The large room seemed overwhelmed with the A.D., his assistant, Special Agent Heath as well as Martinez and her security, Smith thought.

"Gentlemen," she said as her eyes fell to the men, "I'm surrounded." She smiled pleasantly and said, "My pool room isn't the place for us to speak, follow me." She turned her back on all of them and led them away from the pool to a sitting room. The back wall was a sheer glass panel with a breathtaking view of the ocean. There were two white cloth sofas with an interesting, colorful bird pattern that sat facing each other, separated by a dark wood coffee table. Directly opposite the entry way was a whitewashed brick fireplace, sitting empty and dark. He wanted to cross the room to get a better view of the collage of framed pictures on the mantel but didn't. It wasn't the right time for him to make himself familiar with her home.

Her security hovered about. Smith leaned against the entryway, crossing his arms defensively over his chest. Delilah sat on the couch that faced the glass wall while the three suits took the one across from her. Martinez found a high back chair that had a cloth design exactly the opposite of the sofa's pattern. Martinez had to decency to look awkward and ill at ease with everything going on. The suits shifted in their seats adjusting their jackets and ties as Delilah waited. Her eyes flickered to his and he shook his head with a discreet warning so she was the only one to notice the movement.

"Agents, Director, you have my time. Something that's very

precious to me. You're also in my house, something that pisses me off." Her lawyer laid a gentle hand on hers, her voice calmed, "What can I help you with?"

The A.D. leaned forward, bracing his elbows on his knees as he said, "Ms. Laughlin, we have several issues to discuss with you. As you're well aware, there's a trail of bodies following you." Smith watched her posture change. She sat straight on the couch, her back stiff. Her attorney leaned in, somewhat in front of her protectively but to the side. "We've come to understand," the A.D. continued, "that your statement to Special Agent Lowery misrepresented your relationship with Senator Travis and you were aware of certain activities she might have been involved in. These include tracking Michael Townsend for the purpose of finding and killing him."

Her attorney leaned in, speaking to her in hushed tones so no one could hear. She nodded, agreeing with him as her emerald eyes stared at Smith. He didn't break the connection until she leaned away.

Mr. Ellington spoke, "My client apologizes to the Federal Bureau of Investigations concerning any unintended errors. She thought the question was referring to hers and Senator Travis' previous relationship rather than at the time of the senator's death." They spoke again in hushed tones so no one heard the conversation before Mr. Ellington continued, "As for Ms. Laughlin being aware of Senator Travis' tracking Mr. Townsend my client was unaware of the senator's motives. This idea of planning a murder falls solely on the senator's intentions. Not my client's. Murder was never her goal. If Mr. Townsend had been found through Ms. Laughlin's resources the information, as well as his location would have been turned over to the proper authorities."

Delilah added, "Senator Travis was my sister's best friend. We weren't friends."

"So you knew her when you were younger?" Special Agent Heath asked.

"Yes, of course. She was Millie then not a senator."

"Why didn't you mention this?" he asked.

"I didn't think it was essential to the investigation," she said with a shrug.

"That's for us to decide," he scolded.

"We've connected your sister's death to the Senator's," the A.D. said.

"Can you share the details of your sister's death?" Special Agent Heath asked.

"It's not something I talk about." She looked at Smith and exhaled slowly before she looked away and said, "But I will. The night of the attack," his blood froze, "I was lured to the high school by Michael Townsend." He watched her subconsciously feel her wrists. "To the baseball practice fields, specifically. When I got there I was surrounded and beaten by a group of girls who'd bullied me all through my time in school." Her hands fell to her knees and said with her voice empty of emotion, "I was beaten unconscious. When I woke up I was alone with Michael. He broke my knees with a metal bat while I was on the ground."

Smith's stomach turned. He wanted to reach for her, take her in his arms to protect her from the past but he couldn't react. It was sheer will that kept him from her.

She looked at A.D. and said, "While I was on the ground Michael," she pressed her hand to her forehead momentarily, "No, wait, I should mention I was just getting over my suicide attempt. My stitches were fresh." She swallowed hard and stared at the men as if challenging them to say anything about the attempt. When they didn't she continued, "He cut my wrists open again, split my skin while I was hurt and helpless." She squared her shoulders, her voice more determined, "My sister came for me. She found him straddling me, cutting my shirt open," her fingers absently traced the scar between her breasts. "She fought with him but Michael stabbed her." She took a deep breath and continued, "He ran and she crawled. To me. And died in my arms, her head on my chest while I screamed for help." She continued to address the A.D., "You have no idea the amount of pain I was in. Of what my sister and I experienced." She shook her head as if to rid herself of the memories. "Millie was Rachel's best friend. I wanted to find Michael to bring him to justice. I am only learning the extent to which Millie's idea of justice and mine differ but we had the same objective, to find Michael." She shook her head. "I just never expected him to find her first."

The A.D. sighed thoughtfully and leaned back. "Ms. Laughlin, based on your clarification, I'm not going to charge you with obstruction. However, as this investigation progresses if I find evidence you and Senator Travis were conspiring to murder Michael Townsend once you found him I will be charging you." He looked at her attorney then back to Delilah. "If there's anything else that you know of which would assist us the time to say something is now."

"No, nothing I can think of," she said.

He asked directly, "When was the last time you saw Special Agent Lowery?"

"Ah," she said warily. Her eyes flickered to Smith and he nodded permission. She looked again to the A.D., "I last saw him in November."

"When exactly?"

"Um, Thanksgiving."

"Alright," he rose to leave. "thank you for your time, Ms. Laughlin."

CHAPTER 22

A.D. Patten glanced over his shoulder to Smith from the front seat. "Well," he said resignedly, "it goes without saying but I'll say it anyway, you're suspended." He turned around in his seat. "Give me your badge and your gun," he ordered. Smith passed the gun and his ID over. "What about your backup weapon?"

"I don't have it on me," Smith admitted.

"One big fuck up," A.D. snapped.

Smith looked out the window and watched Long Island fly by. He agreed with the A.D., he had fucked up and part of him was grateful it wasn't his relationship. They were in the city before he realized the greenery had given way to concrete and skyscrapers. The agent pulled into the valet parking of their hotel, and the SUV idled a moment before anyone moved or said anything. The A.D. got out with a heavy sigh and marched into the hotel, followed by his assistant and the other agent. Smith pushed open the door and stepped out as Martinez did.

Martinez walked with him and asked, "You want to get a beer? Something to eat?"

Smith looked at his friend. "No, I'm okay." He watched the other men enter the hotel and said, "He took my gun, my badge. It feels strange. Just wrong."

"I know, man," Martinez said.

They walked together into the main lobby area and waited for an elevator.

"Ah, shit," Smith said with sudden realization.

"What?"

"I'm suspended from the unit, not just the case." He hadn't realized until that moment the full scope of the suspension. His whole body ached in pain.

"You want that beer now?" Martinez asked.

Smith looked around and saw the hotel bar. "Yeah, I need one."

"Or two," Martinez offered.

Smith sat leaning against the headboard of his hotel room bed watching the flat screen and drinking a beer he'd brought up from the hotel bar. It wasn't dulling the ache in his chest like it should have since it was the third one. A knock on the door brought him momentarily out of his misery. The sound echoed through the room again so he slowly removed himself from the bed, set the beer aside and trudged to the door. He looked through the peephole and saw a young blond woman standing in the hall glancing from one side to the other. When her emerald eyes looked forward Smith cursed and threw open the door.

"What the fuck?" he grumbled, and quickly grabbed her. His hand fell right between her curvy, pushed up breasts which were tightly harnessed in a neon pink plastic bustier and pulled her inside. He looked in each direction of the hall before locking the door behind him. Delilah was smoothing the black leather miniskirt and only looked up when Smith stood in front of her and asked, "What are you doing here, Delilah?"

He could see her ice over as she snapped, "I can leave if you don't want me here."

"How'd you get here?" He'd left her sitting on a couch on Long Island.

"I flew back to the apartment, changed," she gestured to her outfit, "then took a taxi and walked a bit." He cringed at the idea of her walking the streets of New York dressed like that. Smith looked her over. Delilah as a blond was something different. Those beautiful, bright green eyes were hooded by full bangs and the style was cut into a crisp shoulder length bob. She looked completely different, no one would recognize her.

"What are you wearing?" he asked with a grin, fully appreciating her outfit.

"It's from our Halloween line. You know, the naughty nurse, the slutty secretary. I'm the sexy pro."

"That you are," Smith was immediately aroused. He stepped away from her and walked across the room. "I saw some working girls around the corner earlier," he commented. He clasped the window curtains in both hands and drew them together. He didn't want the world to see them online again. "I don't remember any of them wearing pink corsets and miniskirts. Aren't you cold? It's December."

"Not really," she said with a smirk as he walked back. "Maybe I'll do some research later and see what the ladies are wearing these days."

She leaned back against the wall as he zeroed in on her. "I've had a bad day, Delilah," he said, his voice husky as his hands touched the sides of her slim chest.

"I know," she said, laying her hands on his forearms. She looked up at him expressing her sorrow at his loss and her needs. "I heard." She said softly, "I'm so sorry."

"Where's your security?" he asked as his thumbs traced the voluminous curves of her exposed flesh. "Are you breasts bigger?"

"It's the outfit," she said with a shrug. "I didn't want to be seen so I left them behind," she explained. "If someone saw Brody or Armstrong they'd know I'm here. They're waiting at a diner around the corner."

Smith was pissed about her security being absent but was also glad of it. He didn't need any more trouble. Suspended was enough. He didn't need to get fired. "Where do you put your cell phone?" he asked, his eyes raking over her slowly. She smiled and he fell apart. He pushed her into the wall. His mouth was instantly upon hers, violently caressing her. A moan escaped her parted lips and he shoved his tongue into her warm, wet mouth. "Gawd, you taste like bubblegum," he murmured through kisses. He pressed his body into hers as she wrapped her arms tightly around his neck. His hands went beneath the black material of her skirt, caressing her backside as he lifted her and carried her to the bed. "Now, if

I'm paying," he joked through a kiss, "what will you do?"

Smith sat on the bed's edge and she straddled him. "Anything you want," she said with a hoarse voice he always found sexy.

"How much for head and a great fuck?"

She unbuttoned his white dress shirt and pushed it off of his shoulders. "Oh," she kissed him and flirted, "I think we can work something out." She licked and sucked his neck and shoulders. She stepped off of him and back. She grabbed the pillows off of his bed and looked to him. She frowned and ordered, "Pants off! Now!"

"Yes, ma'am," he said, and shuffled out of his suit pants and boxer briefs. He sat back down on the bed as she dropped the pillows between his legs. She knelt on the fluffy pillows between his legs. He was so ready for her touch after the shitty day he was having. She lifted her hands to take the wig off and he stopped her saying, "Leave it on." She eyed him warily then smiled, licked her lips and lowered her hands to his erection.

She looked up at him as her hands massaged him. "You feel so good in my hands." She tipped her head and moaned as she pushed him into her mouth. She flicked the crown with her tongue and murmured, "So good in my mouth." Her words were like heaven to him.

Smith grinned with pleasure as she bent her head over him, hollowing her cheeks to suck hard. A moan of carnal yearning left him. He ran his fingers through her blond hair and frowned. He liked her as is and lifted the wig from her. Her dark hair was tied back intricately to keep any of the length from falling beneath the wig. He tossed it aside and looked down to see the dark haired woman he loved jacking him off with her mouth. Her green eyes were on his and he caressed her face as a moan of pleasure escaped her lips. She smiled and shifted over him to take more in her mouth.

"Fuck me," he growled. "Aw, your mouth." His hips tilted to meet her greedy mouth. She gripped the root tightly, causing him to moan with yearning. His hand fell to the back of her head, helping with her rhythm before he leaned forward with a deep moan and burst into her mouth. He felt his tip touch the back of her throat and she gulped over and over as he came heavily in her mouth. She sucked him hard swallowing everything until he groaned and pulled her up from the pillows.

His mouth was instantly on hers and he pulled her onto him. She pulled the skirt to her hips and straddled his lap. "My cunt," she gasped. "Ah, Smith. I ache for you. I want you in me." Her tongue was in his mouth. A slender arm wrapped tightly around his shoulders as she pushed her lacy thong aside and shoved his cock into her wet sex. She started eagerly thrusting against him. Sliding up and down the length of his thick shaft, she rode him furiously.

Smith unzipped the corset freeing her body and dropped it. He picked her up and rolled with her. She whimpered as he thrust fiercely against her. He couldn't get enough of her as she moaned and her body responded to his. He grabbed her beneath her backside, lifting her, angling her to his liking as he pounded into her. His muscles clenched and released over and over until he felt her quicken, felt her shiver with anticipation of what he was giving her. Her legs wrapped around his flexing ass pulling him closer digging her manicured nails into his back as she came with a loud cry. He groaned and pounded into her again and again as her body squeezed his heavy cock. He came fiercely, pouring cum deep into her tight body. He hovered above her panting, feeling the aftershocks rake over her body. He waited for her to come off of her high before he gently slid his body from hers.

She lay beneath him, glistening from exertion, panting with him. In her eyes, he could see love and adoration. He leaned in for a kiss, sure he was looking at her the same way before he made love to her again.

"I can't stay," she said with a smile as she pushed herself up and from his arms.

"Just a little longer?" he asked.

"You've only paid for three hours," she teased and leaned forward for a kiss. Their lips met, soft and supple but firm and urgent with love and ecstasy.

"I haven't paid yet."

"Soon," she murmured, leaning close so her breasts tickled his chest. "Very soon."

"Delilah," Smith said, "you're killing me."

"And you love every minute of it."

He watched her turn away and slid naked from the bed. She began to dress and slipped on a black lace thong. The miniskirt was zipped up. It was the most erotic thing he'd watched in the last hour. She manipulated the neon pink plastic and zipped it up. He watched in amazement as her hands dug into the material and she shifted her breasts, one by one, to make them more comfortable.

"Can I do that? Next time?" he asked with a charming grin.

She smiled and sauntered to him. "Sweetheart, you can do anything you want to me." She leaned forward and kissed him, licking his lips with the tip of her tongue for good measure.

"I want you again," he said, grabbing her hips and pulling her further onto the bed.

She adjusted the wig, pulled it into the proper position and scooted further onto the bed beside him. She looked him over.

He felt as if she was evaluating him. "What're you thinking?" he asked, his fingers lightly touching her pushed up curves.

"Sit back against the head board," she ordered. He scooted back, propped a knee up and gracefully laid an arm across it. "I'm thinking I won't be able to walk in the morning." He smiled. "But I want to take care of you, Smith."

"Raccoon," he said, "You always do."

She crawled to him and rocked his world again.

"Now I'm leaving," she said with a satisfied smile. Smith felt he had no bones left. She'd sucked them right out of him. Her gorgeous lips were red and puffy from their contact with his hard cock. She looked spectacular. She hopped from the bed and zipped up her black high heel boots before he realized she really was leaving.

"Delilah, wait." He could hardly move. "I'll walk with you over to meet Brody."

She leaned across the bed and kissed him intensely. "Then no one will know we're together. Good idea, officer."

He frowned and she smiled again, brightening his world. She stood from the bed and walked out of his room. The sound of the door closing silenced the room. The pressure collapsed in on him and Smith realized it was stupid to let her go alone. She was dressed like a prostitute walking around the dark city. He jumped from the bed and tugged on his jeans and a T-shirt quickly. He shoved his feet into his sneakers then grabbed his wallet and cell before heading out.

He was sure he'd just missed her as he stepped into the elevator and pressed the down button. His cell rang and he answered it quickly, "Lowery."

"Did you enjoy DeDe, Special Agent?" a man asked. He knew immediately it was Michael. Smith felt trapped by the elevator. It couldn't move fast enough. "I'm certainly going to enjoy her."

"Motherfucker," Smith began as the phone clicked off. Smith growled and slammed his fist against the closed door. The longest minute of Smith's life ticked by as he waited for the elevator to arrive in the lobby unable to force it to move any faster. The doors finally opened and he scrambled out. He ran through the lobby, stopped and doubled back to the reception desk and asked, "There's a small diner around here, close by, which direction?" The uniformed man pointed to the right and Smith ran in that direction. He dialed Brody and asked in a rush, "Do you have her? Is she with you?"

"Not yet. Why? She isn't with you?"

"Michael just called me." Smith jogged the street and said, "I'm coming to you. We should meet her in the middle." He sprinted around the darkened corner and a saw patrol car sitting there. He came to a quick stop and knocked on the glass. The uniformed officer lowered it. "Special Agent Lowery, FBI." He went for his badge and realized he didn't have it.

"You don't look FBI," the officer said.

Smith glowered at him. "I'm searching for a suspect. He's wanted for at least two murders." He lifted his head at the first scream. The night burst with feminine screams. He shot in the direction and ran around another corner. He stopped and reached for his holster. He cursed when he didn't feel it or his gun. "FBI," he shouted and ran forward into the chaos.

Smith saw Delilah's slight form on the ground with a man hovering over her. He was beating her. A glint of metal in

Michael's hand flickered with the distant lights. Smith could see blood flying as black as the night splattering the concrete sidewalk. Other women surrounded them screaming. One hitting the man on the back.

"MICHAEL!" Smith shouted, and closed the distance, "STOP!"

Michael glanced over his shoulder, pushed the woman away and ran. Brody came in fast from the other direction. They violently collided. Michael bent low stretching out his hand and Brody shouted in pain, falling awkwardly to the cold, hard concrete.

Smith fell to Delilah's side as the officer stopped beside her. Smith grabbed her hand, desperate to hang onto her and looked up ordering, "Get on your radio! Get an ambulance here! The suspect ran in that direction," he pointed. "He's armed with a knife."

"A big ass knife," one of the ladies said.

"She was just talking to us," another said. "Asking about our clothes. What we liked or didn't like about her clothes."

"That asshole just walked up and punched her," another offered. "We don't take that kind of shit but he wouldn't stop."

Smith looked down the street as the cop moved to Brody. He was talking to his shoulder radio, ordering ambulances; more back up as he knelt beside Brody. He was lying on the sidewalk writhing in pain as he held his knee with both hands.

Delilah squeezed Smith's hand, drawing it to her chest.

The sudden arrival of police cars with flashing lights illuminated the street. The blond wig had been ripped off during the attack lay off to the edge of the sidewalk. Smith gently pushed bloody strands of dark hair away from her face. The left side of her beautiful face was swollen and bloody with bruises. She could only open her right eye, the other swollen shut.

As she stared at him he tried to reassure her, telling her the ambulance would come soon. Her mouth hung open slightly as she panted for air, her hand clutching his. He didn't want to touch her injuries; sure he would only cause her more pain. A gash had opened on her cheekbone trickling blood across her bruised cheek into her ear as she moved slightly. She groaned again.

"He hit her with something," he heard someone say over his shoulder.

"Who are you?" a cop demanded.

Smith heard himself say, "FBI." His focus sharpened and he said, "This is a witness in our investigation." He pointed to Brody and identified him, "That's her security. We need to get them both to a hospital now."

"Ambulances are in route. ETA two minutes. Stay with her."

Delilah squeezed his hand again and he looked back to her. His entire body ached for her. "Don't move. The ambulance's coming," he said quietly.

Her free hand moved to her forehead and she pressed her palm to her hair. Tears trickled from the corners of her swollen eye. "Let me sit up," she said softly. "I'm alright." She shifted to push herself up and Smith pressed his free hand against her shoulder, keeping her in place. The ambulances arrived almost at identical times.

Delilah and Brody were scooped up and whisked away. In the light of the ambulance Smith watched Delilah as the EMT worked on her. Smith squeezed her hand and tried to reassure her. He was torn between unadulterated rage, wanting to tear the ambulance apart and helplessness. It was the same kind of fury and powerlessness he'd felt with his parents accident.

When her hand fell limp within his he knew she'd passed out. Michael had hit her with something based on her bruising. From the chatter on the radio he confirmed what he had seen was a knife when Brody's injuries were described. Delilah had been right. Michael liked things up close and personal.

The tendons on the back of Brody's knee had been severed. He was going into surgery immediately when they got to the hospital. Smith assumed it was the same weapon for both injuries; the butt of the knife for her, the sharp edge for Brody. Smith stared at her face wondering why Michael didn't kill her. He had the opportunity but he didn't take it. Where the fuck was Armstrong? Smith was distracted from his thoughts as the EMT grabbed his radio.

Smith understood the list of tests and x-rays the EMT ordered via radio. Smith passed along her basic information, glad he was able to answer almost all of the personal questions except about her last period and her blood type. He shrugged unknowingly when the man asked.

Smith stepped out of the ambulance holding Delilah's hand. He didn't let go as they wheeled her into the emergency room, directly to a curtained off area. An older woman with stunning short gray hair gave directives in a take-no-shit kind of way. She was wearing dark green scrubs and several tags which identified her as Doctor Pierce.

Delilah moaned and shifted uncomfortably as she came too.

"Miss Laughlin," Pierce said, over the room noise. "This man says he's an FBI agent and your boyfriend, is that correct?"

Delilah looked at him, one eye fine, the other closed, her face contorted in pain and she whispered, "Yes."

"OK, Agent Lowery you need to step outside of the room."

"No, I'm not going anywhere," Smith said, taking her hand again.

"He goes, I go too," Delilah said sternly through the pain.

"Miss Laughlin," the doctor began.

"Shut up and fix me. He's not leaving."

The doctor gave him a pissed off look then returned her focus to Delilah and asked, "Can you tell me what hurts?"

"My teeth," Delilah said softly as if just the act of speaking was excruciating.

"We're going to run some tests, get some blood." She lifted her head and spoke with one of the nurses, "Let's get an x-ray of her zygomatic bone. It looks fractured."

Smith spent two hours in the exam room as they ran every test known on Delilah. He called Shannon and told her of Delilah's and Brody's injuries. He called Martinez and told him about Michael's call and about finding Delilah getting assaulted. When the rush of personnel slowed and the tests were completed they moved her to a private room a few floors up. The room was kept in shadows with only the bathroom light was on as Delilah was moved from the stretcher bed to the reclining hospital bed. When the nurse and orderlies left, Smith moved closer to help.

"Lean against me," he said as she grimaced and sat up.

Her legs hung over the edge of the bed, and she looked up at him with an incredibly sad eyes. He knelt in front of her and stripped off the black boots, setting them aside. He tried not to hurt her further as he removed the pink bustier. A scrap of paper fell to the floor so he grabbed it, and shoved it in his pocket. He tried to be gentle, knowing every move hurt. He helped her slip a cotton hospital gown and tied it loosely at her back trying not to tangle the IV wires as he pulled her hand through. Her hands gripped his biceps as he braced her back, and lowered her to the mattress that was propped up to a slight reclining position.

"Hips up," he said quietly. He took off her panties and miniskirt before pulling the soft gown down and tucking the white cotton blankets around her. She sighed and instantly fell asleep. Smith kissed her head, not wanting to hurt her by kissing her split lip then sat down in the padded chair next to the bed.

Delilah startled awake to a knock on the hospital room door, and Smith cursed. He knew she needed to rest. She grimaced from the sudden movement and raised a hand to her face. She touched her swollen skin and bruises as A.D. Patten entered the room followed by an NYPD officer. The A.D.'s assistant followed them in.

Smith groaned. He knew the A.D. would find out since he'd called Martinez but he'd hoped the men would postpone the visit.

"Gentlemen," Smith said sternly.

"Ms. Laughlin," the A.D. said, looking her over before scowling at Smith.

"I'm Detective Weldon, NYPD. I met Assistant Director Patten in the hall. I have some questions about your assault, Ms. Laughlin."

"We know who assaulted her," Smith advised. "The FBI has jurisdiction over the NYPD. It's an ongoing investigation."

"I agree with Special Agent Lowery," the A.D. said. "We'll take it from here, Detective." The detective nodded curtly and left.

The A.D. turned to his assistant and said, "Give us some privacy." The agent stepped out, leaving them alone. There was a moment of silence that lingered in the air like the second before the shockwave of a bomb hits.

"So, Ms. Laughlin, what happened tonight? I wouldn't have expected to see you in the city since we talked out at your home on Long Island."

She spoke slowly in agony, "I was beaten up by Michael Townsend."

"I can tell. How did you happen to be in that neighborhood?" he asked. She paused and looked unsure. "If you don't answer I can charge you with obstruction."

"Bullshit," Smith said defensively. "This is all on me. You're not going to frighten or intimidate her after what's happened tonight."

The A.D. looked at him. "So, why was she at the hotel?"

"She was with me."

"I thought so." He shook his head. His voice was severe and reverberated through the room, "What did I tell you, Smith? I said to stay the fuck away from her. She's a fucking witness. It's most likely her going to the hotel got her assaulted. If you two had just stayed apart, as I told you, she wouldn't have gotten hurt!" He shook his head with regret. "You know what's next. I told you very specifically." He growled, "You're fired."

Smith felt the blow of the words to his core.

The A.D. looked back at Delilah. Tears streamed along her bruised face. "I'll let you rest," he said, his voice calm. "Make arrangements to have your attorney present the next time we talk. I'll get your statement. At least I know I can keep my dick in my pants. I hope you feel better soon." He turned and walked out of the room.

CHAPTER 23

Smith sat down on the hospital bed beside Delilah. She rolled to him, laying her head on his thigh, her hand in her hair and cried. He held her, knowing she was too hurt to deal with it. He wasn't hurt; more stunned, and needed a minute to process it.

"It's okay," he said, shifting her so she lay against his chest. He tucked his arm behind her. He didn't really believe it himself as he said the words, "It's a job. I can get another." It wasn't really a job. It was his profession. His chosen career. He'd lost his security clearance too, that would make getting another job difficult.

Delilah sat up. Half of her face was unrecognizable with swelling and bruises. Her eye shut. He thought she was stunning. The most beautiful woman he'd ever seen even with the bruises. She swallowed hard, looking a bit sick to her stomach. She pointed across him. He reached over and grabbed a pink plastic tub from the stand. He stayed next to her as she vomited.

She lay back against the upright bed and mumbled, "My fucking face is killing me!" He took the tub from her and set it aside. "Ah, my teeth," she bitched and closed her eyes.

"I heard cursing helps ease pain."

"Mother fucker cock sucking fucking fucked-up bullshit." She grimaced and tried not to smile. "It didn't help."

He leaned back against the mattress with her, and she leaned onto his chest.

"It's my fault," she whispered. "I can fix this."

"It takes two to have sex," he said then frowned. "No, I guess it really doesn't."

She laughed and groaned, "Don't make me laugh."

"Hey," he said, and she looked up. "I love you, Delilah. Nothing's going to change that. He warned me and I didn't listen. This is my responsibility. It'll be OK, we'll figure it out." She nodded and stretched up for a kiss. His lips touched hers gently before he pulled back and said with a smile, "I really can call you raccoon now." She sighed.

There was a quick knock on the door and a doctor stepped in. "Ms. Laughlin, I'm Doctor Sener. Your case has been transferred to me." He stepped closer and Smith looked him over quickly. He was mid-forties, graying hair, carrying an iPad and wearing the traditional white lab coat that most doctors wore. A nurse, dressed in bubble gum pink scrubs followed him in and smiled briefly before she moved around the room. She took the tub and left.

The doctor looked at his iPad. "I want to start by saying that your friend…"

"My security," Delilah interrupted then grimaced. Smith was sure she wished she hadn't.

"He's out of surgery. The tendons on his left knee were completely severed in two. He'll be with us for a week or so then he'll need some rehab."

Smith's hand tightened on Delilah's, unsure of how she'd take the news since she'd experienced months of rehab herself. Her fingers intertwined with his.

"Um," Doctor Sener said and looked to Delilah. "Perhaps we should speak in private about a few things."

"No, its fine," she managed through the pain.

"As for yourself," he continued, "from the x-ray we determined that you have a hairline fracture of your zygomatic bone. That's your cheekbone in layman terms. No surgery's necessary. We'll just let it heal. You're going to be bruised and swollen for several weeks. Any eye problems, let me or your ophthalmologist know right away. The ER butterflied that gash on your cheek and once the swelling goes down we'll take those off. I don't think there will be a scar." He paused and looked up at her, asking, "Have you been having any nausea?"

"Yes," Smith answered. "She vomited before you came in."

"I don't think that's what he means," Delilah said. She inhaled heavily. He could see her brace herself against the pain. "Yes, I recently stopped taking some strong medications. My psychiatrist said it might make me sick." Smith was relieved she mentioned it to the new doctor since he'd mentioned it to the EMT, and the ER doctor, pretty much anyone who would listen.

"Well," the doctor said, "You're a few weeks along in your pregnancy so it should be fine."

The whole world ground to a halt.

"Say again," Smith said.

"What?" Delilah asked, almost at the same time.

"You're pregnant," the doctor clarified. "I want to ensure the health of your fetus so I've ordered an ultrasound. I've asked Doctor Walker to come by. She's a good OB and is on duty tonight. She'll come by shortly."

"Pregnant?" Delilah repeated.

"Can we have a minute?" Smith asked.

"Sure, other than those few things you're set. I've ordered you some pain meds. Right now rest is the most important thing," he turned on his heel and left them alone.

Smith waited until the door closed completely then he waited some more. Finally, he turned to Delilah. She looked dumbfounded, staring at the closed door.

"Hey," he said softly. His fingers gently took her chin as he turned her face to his. "Are you okay?"

She hiccupped and started crying. He pulled her into his arms and leaned back against the mattress. "I fucked up everything," she cried against his chest. "I'm on the pill! I don't understand!" She hiccupped again as the tears streamed.

"Technically, I think I fucked up everything. Maybe we both did." He kissed her hair and tried to reassure her, "It's not the end of the world." He pulled her away so he could look at her. "I think it's good."

She sniffled and asked, "You're not mad at me?"

He shook his head. "No, I actually love you more. I don't have the words to describe how happy you've made me." She almost smiled as the stream of tears dripped along her face.

She smacked his arm. "Well, I'm mad at you. You knocked me up."

"You love me more?" he asked lightheartedly.

"I'll think about it."

There was a knock on the door and it pushed open. Smith followed Delilah's stunned expression to find an older man standing just at the door's entrance.

"Dad?" she questioned.

Smith jumped off the bed like a teenage boy caught in a girl's bedroom. "Mr. Laughlin," Smith said and stepped forward extending his hand. "Sir, I'm," he paused having almost said his former title, "Smith Lowery."

The older man wore a dark suit but no tie and his white shirt was left open by several buttons. His gray hair was cut very close to his scalp, reminding Smith of a military haircut. Delilah's father was several inches shorter than Smith and sturdy through the middle. He walked across the room and stopped at the foot of her bed, extending his hand to Smith.

"Dad, what are you doing here?" she asked.

When they let go, he addressed Delilah, "Shannon called and said you'd been hurt. I can see that you have." He looked back to Smith. "I'm Joseph Laughlin, Delilah's father. You're her boyfriend?" he asked.

"Yes, Sir."

"Uh huh," his eyes fell back to her, "well, I'll go. I just wanted to check on you."

"Dad, you came all this way. Do you want to stay?"

Smith could see a spark of hope on her bruised face.

"No, I need to get back. You're fine. Shannon exaggerated. You're injuries aren't that severe. Goodnight," he said with a nod to Smith, and left the room.

Smith looked to Delilah and cursed silently as she started

crying again, curling to her side. He walked out of the room and spotted Mr. Laughlin further down the hall. Smith jogged to catch up. "Mr. Laughlin, Sir," he said as he stopped close by, "a minute." Smith stopped beside the older man. "It would mean a lot to her if you stay even for a little while."

"Son," Joseph said, turning to face Smith, "get away from that girl before she ruins your life too." Smith looked incredulously at the man, shocked. "She's beautiful, I understand. I get it, you love her. Just the way you look at her, I can tell but she's fucked up."

"That's your daughter," Smith defended angrily.

"So I know what I'm talking about. She brings nothing but death and destruction. In the old times she'd be considered a plague. Or stoned to death. God," he sighed, "we got her name right."

"You can't mean that."

"Take my advice, run far away from her." The elevator doors opened and Mr. Laughlin stepped in. "She's mine by blood and nothing else. Most days I regret that much of our connection."

Smith grabbed the door, preventing it from closing. "Tell me something. I read the police report. When Michael attacked her and killed Rachel, why did you leave the police interview? Why wasn't her mother there?"

"My wife was making funeral arrangements. I left because my daughter died. My favorite. Yes, I can say that after all these years. Rachel was my favorite and Delilah brought her pain, and suffering, and death." He stepped close and removed Smith's hand. "I've given you fair warning. It's your choice now." The doors closed leaving Smith standing alone in the hall.

Smith pushed open the hospital room door and found the room darkened, save the light of an ultrasound machine.

"Mr. Lowery," a pretty blond woman said with a gesture for him to enter as she smiled welcomingly. "Ms. Laughlin wouldn't let me start without you. I'm Doctor Walker. Please come."

· Delilah was laying down, a pillow tucked under her head. The hospital gown was pushed up exposing her flat stomach with the blanket draped across her hips. He took her offered hand and gave it a quick kiss. He leaned over and kissed her forehead. "I love you," he whispered and saw her visibly relax. Even if no one else loved her, he did. He always would. He knew she was worried about him, about what her father had said.

"Here we are," the doctor said. She studied the screen for a moment. "You're newly pregnant, Ms. Laughlin. It looks like you're about seven or eight weeks along."

Smith leaned in for a better look and tilted his head for a different angle. He couldn't really make anything out except for a little shadow in the screen of white static. "When will it look like a baby?" he asked.

"A few more weeks, and we'll see the little one get some more shape. It'll be a few months before we know the sex. Everything looks fine. I don't see any adverse effects from the assault. Listen." She flipped a switch, the room was filled with the sound of a fluttering, quick beat. "That's the heartbeat."

Delilah gasped and clamped her hand over her mouth. Smith felt suddenly weak. He leaned against the bed and looked to Delilah in awe and wonder. "You're having my baby," he said with a big smile. He leaned down and kissed her, causing her to gasp in pain. "Sorry," he said with the same smile.

The doctor interrupted, "You're going to need to find an OB. I'm available, if you like. I'm based out of the hospital. At your first appointment, we can narrow down how far along you are exactly and your due date. You'll need to start prenatal vitamins, eating well, taking care of the baby which means taking care of yourself." It remained unspoken that beatings were off the To Do list.

Smith stepped away to get the door for her as the doctor pushed the machine across the room. When she was gone and the room was quiet, illuminated only by the bathroom light, Smith crawled into bed with Delilah. His shoes flopped over the edge, and Delilah lifted the blanket for him. He lay beside her and she tucked herself around him, resting the unhurt side of her face against his chest.

She asked quietly, "What did my dad say?"

"He's glad you'll be okay." Smith was sure as shit not about to tell her what Joseph had actually said.

"Did you tell him about the pregnancy?"

"No, I'm still getting used to it." He felt her smile briefly against his chest.

She exhaled and said, "The day we met," she quieted, "my mother texted."

"I remember."

"It was the first time she'd contacted me in months. She texted me to tell me that she hates me, that she misses Rachel." Smith remembered how she had acted in the lecture. He was impressed she hadn't reacted or broken down at receiving a text like that. She sighed and said, "I'm not going to say I wished I had died and Rachel had lived that night, not anymore. But I lived for years thinking it. I'm happy, Smith. I'm happy with you and our baby."

"I'm happy too, Delilah." She looked up as he said, "I love you."

She laid back on him with a smile on her lips and pressed a kiss to his chest before she whispered, "I love you too."

CHAPTER 24

A gentle hand touched his shoulder, and Smith woke. Natural light of the early morning filtered through the one window of the private room. Shannon was leaning over him giving him the universal sign for don't make a sound. She had her index finger to her lips shushing him silently. She gestured for him to follow so he carefully slid out from underneath Delilah and slipped on his sneakers. He followed Shannon into the brightly lit hall and rubbed his hands against his face. She looked as tired as he felt. "How's Brody?" he asked.

Shannon looked grim and said, "He'll be fine eventually. He's pissed about Ms. Laughlin getting hurt."

"Yeah, me too."

"She looks really bad," Shannon said regretfully. Smith nodded, agreeing. "I didn't want to wake her up but I need to go over a few things."

"Sure, what's up?" he asked.

"I spoke with the attending. They're going to release her this morning. I want to find out what she needs, and what you need."

"Good," Smith said. He thought for a moment then said, "Let's get her back to the apartment without getting her on any gossip sites. She won't want pictures out there of herself with bruises. Does the hospital have an underground garage?"

"I'll check, but if not I'll talk with them about using the helipad. We can fly her back to the apartment."

"OK, that sounds good. See what you can do."

"What do you need?"

He regretted saying it but he had to, "Set up some kind of nurse to watch over her today. I need to get back to D.C. for a few hours."

"Why are you going back now? I thought you were suspended."

He frowned. "Yeah, I was. I managed to get myself fired last night. How'd you know?"

"Brody told me about the suspension, I told her," she shrugged.

He didn't want to focus on his lack of employment. "I need to go back to clear out my desk at Quantico and get some things from my house. I need to get there and back as fast as possible."

"OK, I can make it happen."

"I'll get her to the apartment then go." He agreed knowing it meant another ride in Delilah's plane. "About her work, she's going to need to take a few days."

"I've already contacted her number two in America. He's based in Los Angeles. His name's Paul Anderson. Swear to God, he looks just like a young Chuck Norris. He's a bad ass too, in the business world anyway," she smiled. "I told him about the assault. I've spent the last hour getting everything set, getting complete access transferred to his computer."

Smith glanced at his watch, it was only seven. Shannon had had a long night.

"Her organization's different than others," she went on. "Ms. Laughlin's set it up, worldwide, so everything filters upward. The areas of the world are broken into departments. She has a number two in all departments, but she's in charge of the overall worldwide business and the accounting. She's brilliant."

"I believe it."

"So, Paul's ready to take over for a few days. She won't have to worry about the business. We'll step up."

"Good, thank you. I know she'll appreciate it."

"Anything else?" she asked.

"Bring her some real clothes. I don't want her dressed in the costume to leave the hospital." He thought for a moment then said, "And throw away her remaining birth control pills." Shannon looked at him blankly so he added, "She's pregnant."

A smile grew across her face as she laughed, "Oh, shit!"

"Yeah, I know," he said with a smile and patted her shoulder. "Let's get her out of here as soon as they release her." He took a step away then turned back for her. "Shannon," she looked up at him, "one more thing. Remove her parents from her emergency contacts. Don't call them again. List me instead. I'm her family now." She nodded so he turned back.

He walked back into the shadowy room. Delilah lay curled on her side, her uninjured face lying on the pillow. She was sleeping soundly so he sat in the chair beside the bed. He studied her features and was overwhelmed by his feelings for her. He tried to remember if he'd ever loved another woman as much, but no one came to mind. Aside from the sex which had a ferocious intensity between them, there was comfortableness that made it easy to be together.

She had a bitchy reputation which he knew was a form of protection. She'd built up so many walls over the years to protect herself from others. He found it amazing she'd even let him in. Let him try for her heart. It didn't matter what her father said. He was a douche not to love his daughter. Smith was sure he'd never make that mistake.

Delilah blinked her eyes opened and grimaced. She lay very still watching him, watching her. "Have I messed up?" she asked quietly.

"I was thinking the same thing. Getting you pregnant throws off my whole timeline," he said seriously.

She scooted to the side, making room for him so he came and lay beside her. "Tell me about your timeline."

He snuggled her into him and breathed. "Well, we were going to date for a while and then we'd have to decide who was going to move. Me to New York, or you to D.C. but in the end we both know I'd be the one to move. You're so worth it. Once we got that settled then we'd get married and a few years from then we'd have five or six children."

"Five or six?" she gasped. "I know people think I'm a bitch but come on, a litter?"

He laughed. "OK, three or four?"

"How about we get through the first?"

"Sounds like a plan." He looked at her again and advised, "The swelling's gone down."

She gently touched her face. Her left eye was open but it was viciously bloodshot and black around the edges. "I want to leave."

He nodded and agreed, "I want to get you home." He shifted from her arms. "Let me see what we can do."

Smith helped Delilah dress in the clothes Shannon had picked out and brought to the hospital. The high-end travel bag enclosed a pair of heather gray wool lined slacks, a black satin blouse, her best lingerie, some black flats and a heavy black jacket. Delilah brushed her teeth in the bathroom and Smith saw blood hit the sink when she spit.

She shrugged and said, "I think I cut the inside of my mouth. At least I didn't lose any teeth." She smiled into the mirror and pointed, counting. She looked back to Smith and added, "Nope, didn't lose any."

He smiled and shook his head at her humor, surprised she could find anything funny in the aftermath of the attack. Smith watched her braid her dark hair. She left the bathroom and sat on the bed, exhausted but ready to leave as she waited for the paperwork she needed to sign to be officially released. He sat beside her, his hand pressed to her lower back.

"How are you feeling?" he asked.

"I'm fine," she said quickly. "Just tired."

"I know, you're fine. I'm surprised how well you're handling all this. You were attacked by Michael again. I thought you'd be freaking out, a little."

She leaned her head against his shoulder. "I really haven't thought about it. There's so much going on. I'm not scared. I'm pissed." She looked up. "That helps, to get angry instead of afraid." He leaned in for a gentle kiss.

The nurse pushed open the door and stepped in with the virtual discharge paperwork. Delilah signed quickly then handed the iPad and stylus back to the woman. Delilah stood from the bed and grabbed her Jackie O style sunglasses and a colorful Hermes silk scarf as Smith took her bag.

Shannon and Armstrong met them in the hall. Shannon pressed the elevator button as they came to it. Smith noticed Armstrong carrying his overnight bag he'd left at the hotel. "Did you check me out of the hotel?" he asked. Armstrong confirmed it. Smith sighed, at least he didn't have to go back to get his things.

Shannon nodded to Delilah and said, "Congratulations."

Delilah stepped into the elevator first and turned back as they joined her. "Thank you," she said with the hint of a smile.

Shannon pressed the up button and the elevator zoomed to the roof level. There was a trauma center on the level. They walked along the linoleum floor towards the helipad doors, passing the doctors and nurses who rushed about.

"So," Delilah asked, "how much did it cost me to fly out of here?"

"You're donating a hundred thousand to the children's unit."

Smith missed a step but recovered quickly.

Delilah looked at Shannon and agreed, "Fine, thank you." She put on her sunglasses to block the glare and tied the silk scarf loosely over her hair and face to obscure any pictures that might be taken from the surrounding skyscrapers before she stepped outside. Smith and Armstrong followed the ladies onto the windy roof. They walked immediately to the black helicopter he'd seen at her Long Island estate and got in. The pilot started the helicopter as soon as they were buckled.

Delilah put on her headset and leaned back, resting on the crafted beige leather seats. Smith gently squeezed her hand as she placed it within his, intertwining their fingers. The helicopter lift and they fly over the city. The view was stunning. Buildings glistening in the winter sun, cars appeared as toys far below them. He hadn't seen the New York City view like this before. The pilot was talking with one of the air traffic control units, Smith assumed. They flew a few hundred feet above the skyscrapers. He saw the park become larger as they lowered and made a direct path to her building.

The flight only took ten minutes from hospital to apartment and it cost her a hundred thousand dollars but Smith actually thought it was worth it to have completely avoided the paparazzi who would have stalked her and splashed her picture across the tabloids with crazy headlines like she'd been attacked by Big Foot or some drunken Hollywood celebrity. The helicopter powered down and they stepped out as soon as the rotors slowed. Smith hadn't been on her roof before. It was a senseless feeling to be so high with such minimal protection from the elements like the wind that blew hard against them. Shannon pressed the code into the elevator and it opened almost immediately.

It stopped and opened on the same level as Delilah's bedroom but in a hall he hadn't been in since they had always climbed the stairs. Smith took his bag from Armstrong who remained in the elevator.

"I've hired a nurse," Shannon said, following Delilah into her bedroom. Delilah pushed the silk scarf from her hair and gently untied the small knot from beneath her chin. "It's just for a few days until you feel better," Shannon advised.

Delilah nodded and sat down on the plush couch in the sitting room area. She sighed and held out her hand for Shannon to take the sunglasses and scarf from her. Shannon took them without another word then turned and left.

Smith dropped the bags near the couch, and squatted down in front of her. "What can I do?"

Delilah leaned forward and wrapped her arms around his shoulders. "I'm fucking exhausted and all I did was come home." She pressed her forehead against his shoulder and exhaled loudly. "I need a shower, badly, but I feel like I'm going to faint."

"Do you want something to eat first?" he asked. When she shook her head he said, "OK, let's get you cleaned up." He stood and scooped her up, bridal style, walking through the massive bedroom to the bathroom. The lights came on automatically as he entered and set her down on the chair in the place he considered the makeup area. The table was covered with different shades of things he didn't want to know anything about. He stepped to the shower enclave and pressed a few buttons to get the hot water going. He stopped in front of her, and stripped his shirt off up and over his head.

She looked up and tried not to smile. "My favorite thing." He looked down at her. "You." He shook his head and grinned, dropping his pants. She looked at his semi hard erection that was at eye level. She reached for him and he declined, pressing her hands back.

"Delilah, you're injured. No sex."

She groaned and complained, "Smith, you know you want me as much as I want you. 'Resistance is futile.'"

"A girl who quotes Star Trek, how did I get so lucky?" He reached for her and lifted her from the chair. He slowly removed her clothes and tossed them onto the space she'd vacated. "Of course I want you but you're going to have to wait." He kissed her forehead to take some of the sting of his declination away. "Let's get you clean."

He led her into the shower room, and helped her wash. He began with her long hair. He washed it, getting the dried blood out before adding some of the conditioner he thought smelled so good. He helped her wash it out before he took up the sponge and body wash. He began at her toes, scrubbing his way upward, leaving kisses on all of the body parts he washed. He smiled when he got to the apex of her legs, looking up with devilish intentions.

"Please feel free to," she said coolly as she held onto the wall with one hand.

Smith grinned and shifted slightly so he pressed a kiss against her lower belly. He glanced up and whispered, "It's up to you and me to take care of mommy." She caressed the back of his head. He pressed another kiss then stood straight and washed the rest of her diligently and efficiently. He washed her breasts but completely ignored the little sounds of pleasure which escaped her beautiful lips. "Turn around," he ordered, and she obeyed. He scrubbed her shoulders and her back as the water fell all over and around them.

"Can I sit down?"

"Sure," he said. He helped her sit on the teak bench which

lined one side of the enclave then knelt in front of her washing the soles of her feet as the water poured over them like rain.

"I'm clean," she said with a tone of finality to end his chore. Her face told of her exhaustion without her uttering a word of it.

"Give me just a minute," he said, standing and reaching for the body wash again. He cleaned himself in record time scrubbing through his hair and body.

"Smith," she said achingly. "You're so fucking hot. Do you have any idea what you're doing to me? You're covered in suds. It's like a fucking wet dream." She breathed as her shoulders slumped. "I'm so tired."

He rinsed quickly and put the sponge and body wash back on the wall shelf. He knelt in front of her, and squeezed her hair before lifting her from the bench.

He pressed a kiss to her lips. "I know you're tired, babe. Let me get you to bed." She smiled but looked fatigued. "And not in the good way," he finished. He pressed a button and the shower of water stopped.

He took a few towels from the warmer and fixed a towel around his waist then wrapped her in a large bath sheet, returning her to the chair. He scooted the clothes out of the way and walked out of the bathroom into the closet. He started pulling open drawers in one of the dressers, and found lingerie in a variety of styles and colors and laces. He studied them for a moment then moved onto his real mission. He dug through other drawers and found what he was looking for, warm pajamas. None of the lacy, silky stuff she'd wear for him.

He walked back into the bathroom and she was braiding her wet hair. She gaped and asked, "What're those?"

"I found them in your closet, you should know."

"They're ugly."

Smith looked at the pajamas set. "They're not ugly. They're comfortable." He shook them open. They were gray and black checkered flannel pajamas. They were new so he tore the price tag off without reading it, tossing it in the trash. He thought they were perfect for when she wasn't feeling good. They'd keep her warm while he was away. He looked at her as she began to dry her body. She was doing fine until she got to her shoulders. Her elbows had scrapes from the concrete sidewalk. Her shoulder was bruised from being knocked down. He took the towel from her and carefully dried her neck, squeezing her braid to get the excess water from it. He touched her injured face with the towel and she shuddered slightly. "OK, that's enough," he said as he took up the flannel pajamas and helped her put them on. He lifted her from the chair and helped her back into the bedroom. She immediately crawled into bed without a word of complaint.

She sank into the pillows and comforters, her eyes heavy with sleep and announced, "That's going to be part of our cohabitation agreement."

"What's that?" Smith asked.

"Sex. We have to have sex every day."

"Good to know," he said, and leaned for a kiss. He pressed his lips to hers softly. She was asleep as he pulled back. "Cohabitation agreement?" he asked her sleeping form.

Smith dressed quickly, tossing his clothes from the previous night into the laundry chute. He rummaged through his overnight bag, and put his suit back on. It felt like a hundred days had passed since he wore it last, not one. He grabbed his cell, his keys and wallet, slipping them into various pockets of his suit coat.

As he zipped up the bag there was a quiet knock on the bedroom door. He opened it to find Shannon and an older woman with salt and pepper hair accompanying her. She quickly introduced them, "This is Mrs. Nash. She's the nurse I've hired to take care of Ms. Laughlin." Shannon held a tall glass full of water.

"Good, she's sleeping. If she asks where I am when she wakes, just tell her I'll be back soon." The nurse took the water from Shannon and set it on the nightstand then moved to the around the bedroom area sliding a chair closer to the bed in case Delilah needed something.

Shannon stepped out with Smith and called the elevator. They stepped in together. "So, how am I getting there?" he asked.

The elevator moved upward as she said, "Helicopter to the airport. The jet will take you into Reagan. There will be another helicopter waiting for you. That's going to take you to Quantico. I've already gotten permission for it to land."

"I'll be there an hour, at most. I've got to go by the house."

"Take the helicopter back to Reagan. I'll get a car to take you to and from your house. The jet will be waiting to bring you back."

The elevator opened at the helipad. The helicopter sat there waiting for him. He spoke loudly, over the sound of the wind, "Don't let her worry about me. Hopefully, she'll sleep all day and I'll be back before she wakes."

Shannon nodded, the wind from the roof rushing through the elevator. "I'll make sure she's comfortable."

He nodded and jogged to the helicopter for the first leg of his trip.

CHAPTER 25

The helicopter lowered smoothly onto the concrete helipad outside of his building in the Quantico FBI complex. Smith stepped out and closed the door as the rotors slowed. He exhaled heavily, awash with feelings of failure and sorrow. He was going to miss it. He'd really enjoyed his time in charge. Maybe it wasn't all lost. He was sure he could find something else to do that he would enjoy just as much. He wanted to remain in law enforcement, perhaps just a different aspect was what he needed, he considered. He caught the door as someone left and entered without notice. Smith's first stop was the locker room. He cleared out his locker, tucking his workout clothes into the black backpack he kept in the bottom of the locker. He removed the lock, clicked it into place then tossed it in with his sneakers and clothes.

Smith slung it over his shoulder and walked down the hall to his office. He nodded to people as he passed them in the hall but didn't stop to talk. He retrieved his keys from his pants pocket and unlocked the office door. Pushing it open he walked into a world he knew he would never be part of again. He steeled himself against the emotions, and closed the door. He didn't need eyes watching evidence of his ultimate failure. He dropped his backpack at the door and crossed to the desk.

His first task was to review the existing cases. He sorted through the files. He wrote notes for Martinez; sure the man would take over for him, at least temporarily. He brought all of his notes, directives and information up to date before setting them on his desk in organized piles. He cleared out his inbox then shut down the computer with a sigh.

Smith found the box he'd used to move in at the bottom of his closet and finished the packing. He was glad he hadn't moved too much into his office, packing the leftovers in the backpack. He pulled open another drawer and found his backup service weapon. He set it on his desk and sat staring at it for a moment. It was a revolver encased in an ankle holster. He'd never had to draw it, never been outsmarted or outgunned by a suspect.

He was pissed Michael was taking opportunities to strike and run. Smith leaned back in his chair. It bothered him that Michael had done so much damage to Brody but had actually inflicted a less serious injury to Delilah when Smith knew she was the one Michael wanted. He had the opportunity to kill her, to end it but he didn't seize it. Why wouldn't he? Smith contemplated the possibilities. He didn't like the idea of Delilah getting hurt or worse but why wouldn't Michael take the opening?

Smith thought about her injuries, all facial; all the bruises that would linger. The bruises would force people to ask what happened. Force her to tell of the assault. She'd have to make a public statement, reveal her past. He shuddered at the possibility of her revealing a past she'd spent a lifetime keeping secret. She'd have to explain why she was talking with the prostitutes. Why she was wearing that sexy outfit.

He grinned at the memory of the outfit but his smile faded as he remembered picking up the scrap of paper from the hospital floor. It hadn't been in her bustier when she left the hotel. He'd watched her dress very carefully, enjoying everything she was doing. If she hadn't put a piece of paper in there then only one person could have. He'd shoved the paper in his jeans. Jeans which were now at the bottom of a laundry chute. Smith stood from the chair. He needed to get back as soon as he could. Michael had a message for him, he needed to get it.

Smith grabbed his box and slung his backpack over his shoulder. He glanced at his desk; it was organized for the next person. He took his gun and walked to the Master of Arms' office. He turned in his gun and signed it over. From there he walked back through the building to the helicopter and rode to Reagan. The helicopter settled down where it had taken off about a hundred feet from the private plane. There was a waiting Mercedes SUV. Smith jogged to the vehicle and set the box and backpack into the backseat before jumping into the front with the driver. The driver already had his home address and drove through the D.C. traffic showing off his skills.

Smith opened the passenger door and stepped out when the driver arrived at his house. He turned back after retrieving his belongings from the backseat and said, "Just park where you can. I won't be long."

The man agreed and drove off looking for a parking space along the street. Smith figured he only needed thirty minutes to get his things. He knew he'd come back. He considered this his chance to get what he needed immediately so he wouldn't have to leave Delilah for a few weeks. He unlocked the house door and stepped inside, setting his things in the foyer.

He went right to work, stepping into his dining room that he used as an office. He kept his personal copy of hers and Senator Travis' investigations in there. He packed his laptop and shoved the paper copies in with the tech. He set it by the front door and went upstairs skipping two stairs at a time. He grabbed his garment bag from the closet and managed the three remaining suits into it. He zipped it and tossed it onto the bed. He found his large black duffel bag in the hall closet and walked it back into the bedroom. He packed everything from the bedroom and bathroom he could think might be needed.

Smith went back to his closet and typed in the six digit combination to his gun safe. He opened it and pulled two black handguns from the interior. He grabbed a box of ammunition and set the weaponry on the bed. Smith shrugged off his suit coat. He stepped back to the closet and pulled his shoulder holster from a hanger and his belt holster from the shelf. He fastened the shoulder holster on as he walked back to the bed. He picked up one of the matching guns and slipped it into the holster, snapping it in place. He slipped his belt through the holster for the other. He automatically felt better carrying the weapons before he put his suit coat on again.

In his haste something caught his eye, distracting him and he walked to the dresser. There was a small wooden jewelry box on top of it. It was carved with a mosaic design and inlaid with mother of pearl and white gold. It had been his mother's. He lifted open the cover and stood staring at the jewelry.

Memories flashed through his mind: his mother's smile, his father's laughter. A surge of anger rushed him. He slammed his fist against the dresser. He was pissed they were taken from him. Pissed he'd never had the chance to tell them of their grandchild. His fist relaxed. The anger fled and he reached for a black box which sat tucked into the back. He withdrew it and sat down on the bed. He hadn't looked in it a very long time. It was last on his mother's finger. He wondered if Delilah would even want it.

He opened the box and sat staring at the ring for a long moment. It was exquisite. The diamonds shined and danced in the light from the bedroom windows. It had two bands of diamonds that captured a massive circular center diamond. It had an antique look with smaller diamonds in a flower pattern that tangled within the bands, which circled the finger. He knew Pops and Gran had had it cleaned, getting off his mother's blood from the accident. It looked pristine as if ready for a new love.

He snapped the box shut, tucked it into his suit coat pocket and took up the garment bag. He grabbed the handle of the duffel bag and headed downstairs. He checked the house one more time, making sure everything was off and locked. He pulled his bags outside and locked the front door before he glanced up at his house with one last look then walked away. He knew he'd made several mistakes but he was sure as he got back into the SUV that he was going to make them right. He just needed to find out what Michael had to say.

CHAPTER 26

New York City

Delilah's eyes fluttered open and she lay for a moment staring at the ceiling of her bedroom. With effort, she blinked her black eye open and groaned as she ached all over. The late afternoon light filtered through the heavy curtains and she knew she'd spent most of the day asleep. It wasn't normal. She couldn't even remember the last time she'd slept late. Of course, she realized, there were special circumstances. A few real reasons to sleep. She needed to rest and recuperate. She stretched and rolled to her side. She blinked at the older woman and asked, "Who are you?"

"Mrs. Nash. I'm your nurse, Ms. Laughlin."

Delilah pushed up onto her elbows and slid back onto the headboard. She was immediately woozy but said, "You can go now. I'm fine. I'm going to work tomorrow so I won't need you." She added as an afterthought, "Thank you." The nurse stood and pushed the chair back into place. She tucked a paperback book under her arm and left.

Delilah shifted her legs over the edge of the bed and sat for a moment. Her head cleared. The aches weren't terrible. She was definitely sore though. She stood and held onto the headboard getting her balance before she moved into the bathroom. She needed to brush her teeth and she felt like another shower. She moved delicately through her room into the bathroom, stripping off the flannel pajamas Smith had picked out for her. She untied her braid and let her hair fall. She stopped and looked in the full length mirror. She turned to the side and frowned, her stomach was flat. She pressed her hand to her belly. It was still a shock to think of herself as pregnant. She didn't even know if she was the maternal type. Her mother had set a terrible example. A wave of worry and doubt hit her. Negative thoughts inundated her as she left the mirror for the shower enclave. What if she wasn't maternal enough? What if she failed? She felt weighed down by her doubts and fears.

Delilah stepped into the shower and slowly washed herself as thoughts and feelings swept over her again. She'd been focused on the business for so long. She'd worked for days without a break. She balanced a budget larger than some countries. She had taken care of her employees, and was constantly trying to make everything better. Somehow she'd forgotten about herself. Of course, she'd made her life comfortable. She hired someone to cook so she could eat. Someone to clean and do the laundry so she'd have time to work and stay focused. She'd dated, she'd fucked but nothing had ever come of it. There'd never been anyone serious.

It was that first moment, Delilah realized, when they had shaken hands in the FBI building that she'd fallen in love. It felt as if she'd swallowed a thousand butterflies. She could still remember how she felt when Smith walked into the office. Boyishly charming and so self-confident, not to mention he hit all of her hot buttons. Tall and handsome. Lean with a good, muscular build. His hair was just long enough that she immediately wanted to run her fingers through it to find out if it really was as soft as it looked. She didn't understand how she knew he was the one but her gut knew and she trusted her gut feelings. Thinking of Smith, she got the same tingly feeling and rejoiced it in.

She sat down in the shower carefully and lay back on the floor to think and rest. She propped up her knees and let the warm water pour over her body. She smiled at the memory of his asking if he could join her for lunch. It was exciting and overwhelming, just having him close. She smiled and threw an arm over her head, recalling how she had tried not to stare as he shared her potato chips. She couldn't comprehend how strongly she felt about Smith in such a short time.

Delilah rested her hand on her lower belly again. She tried to remember her last period and knew it had been before their meeting at Quantico. A week or so she recalled. She figured she must have gotten pregnant almost immediately, maybe within the first two weeks of their meeting. She smiled in remembrance at all of the love they had made those first days when they were really together, when geography and circumstances hadn't separated them.

She let out a long, slow breath as the water pelted warmly against her skin. They were family now, something she really hadn't had for years, perhaps ever. She knew she could do it. She could let go of the past and look forward to the future, a future that included Smith and their child. Their child, the thought made her smile. She mentally examined her body for any hint of the child and could only decide she felt full in her lower belly.

"Delilah!" Smith shouted as he fell next to her. She jackknifed up. He grabbed her arms and asked, "Are you okay?"

Her hand fell to his bicep as she tried to slow her breathing and racing heart. He'd startled her. "I'm good," she exclaimed. "What's wrong?"

"I walk into the bathroom and find you on the floor of the shower! Shit! I thought you'd fallen or gotten hurt, or something," he said awkwardly, almost embarrassed.

She smiled and leaned to him for a kiss. He fisted her wet hair and kissed her as if the world had stopped spinning. Her hands slid under his wet suit coat and pushed it from his body. His shirt instantly soaked through as the water continued to pour. Her brows drew together as she frowned. "Guns? You have guns strapped to you."

Smith shifted his hands from her and removed the shoulder holster with a devilish grin setting it aside on floor and sliding it out of the enclave. He stripped the wet shirt off next. Delilah sat up carefully on her knees and leaned into him for a deep, rough kiss. Her fingers knotted within his wet hair. Her tongue explored his mouth, crushing his lips as he removed his pants and boxers with his belt holster and gun still attached. He shoved those out of the shower area as well, letting them skate across the marble floor.

He grabbed the back of her legs and slid her up his thighs as he knelt in front of her then took her to the shower floor in one move. She gasped as his full weight came upon her and he thrust his hard cock into her soft body. She felt her body stretch to accommodate his large build. He kissed her passionately filling her head with words of love and adoration as he rocked against her body bringing her world to another burst of insane pleasure.

Smith stood carefully from the shower floor as Delilah kept their intimate connection with her legs wrapped around his hips and her arms around his shoulders. He walked out of the bathroom, the crown of his hard cock tempting and teasing her. He found the bed waiting and set her down gently. She lay on the bed in a similar pose to the shower floor, throwing her hands over her head.

Smith looked at her and smiled, crinkling the corners of his eyes as he asked, "Do you have any idea of how beautiful you are?"

She grinned and mocked, "I'm sure the black eye helps."

"Sarcasm," he muttered, and walked around the bed to the far nightstand. He took his cell phone from it. He stepped back to her and she looked up at him. "Put your other arm over your beautiful tits, I want to take a picture."

"Smith, I don't like pictures. You know that," she complained.

He knelt near the bed so he was eye level and looked through his phone to her beautiful proportions. "We're going to take your picture every month so we can see how big the baby gets." He clicked it and smiled at the result. She'd angled her face to hide the bruises but gave him a smoldering look, her knees bent and slightly drawn up as one arm covered her breasts and the other framed her face. He save it and set his phone back on the nightstand. She rolled from him to sit up as he shouted, "Delilah Fitzgerald Laughlin!" She startled and turned for him. He grinned and pointed into the nightstand drawer, "Did I just find your sex drawer?"

She jumped to the other side of the bed and slammed the drawer closed. She batted her thick, black eyelashes and asked, "What's up? Where were you?"

"Oh, no! You don't get out of it that easily!" He pulled the drawer open and sat down beside her on the bed. He took out a few things out and she flushed. He held up a DVD and looked over the cover as if it was the most fascinating thing he'd ever found. "This looks interesting. Does Brittany really love Starla? Or does Starla love the guy on the cover?" he asked with a fiendish grin.

Delilah grabbed it from his hands and shoved it back into the nightstand drawer, slamming it shut. He pulled open the drawer immediately and pulled out one of several toys. The little toy looked like the head of a toothbrush in silicone.

He fit it onto the tip of his finger, and wiggled it at her. "Nice," he crawled over her body to the far side of the mattress.

She followed him, rolling over to lay beside him with a grim face. "I see how this is going to go," she said with a stern tone. "New toys have to be played with."

He propped up some pillows and sat leaning against the headboard. Smith reached over and pulled her close. She sat with her back to his chest and her legs spread over his. His arm reached around her as he asked, "How does this work?"

She glanced over her shoulder before shaking her head in resignation, finally answering, "It takes a little touch to start the vibration." She tapped the tip of his finger and the little toy wiggled. "Now put it somewhere desirable."

His arm crossed her breasts and he leaned to her shoulder pressing kisses as he said, "Relax, I'll take care of you."

Delilah stretched her arms up over her head and leaned back, running her manicured fingernails through his hair. She nuzzled into his neck and gasped as his fingertip found her clit. She grinded against his hand with an exhale of pleasure. He kneaded and plumped her breasts and she felt him harden against her back. He stroked her clit in little circles, concentrating on her most sensitive area. Her core tightened, liquid warmth rushed through her body and she moaned as she came hard.

She turned quickly and crawled up into his lap. She shoved her tongue into his warm, wet mouth, licking at his sculptured lips as she massaged him from root to tip. Her thumb caressed the head of his cock before she shifted and thrust him into her sex with a moan. "I need you," she said as she rode him. She grabbed the headboard for something to hold onto as her hips flexed, pushing and pulling against his thick length.

She felt his response quicken and he pressed her hips down onto his thrusting cock. She was awash in desire, yearning for every inch of him as she took him again and again. The luscious feelings of liquid warmth filled her core again and she cried out as she came once more. He rolled on top of her and pounded against her tender flesh over and over until he spurted into her with a deep growl of ecstasy.

Smith lay sleeping beneath her as she played with his wispy light chest hair. Delilah smiled to herself, sure he loved her as much as she loved him. She was certain they would be together. The sudden urge to pee overwhelmed her so she lifted herself quietly from his warm, hard body and went into the bathroom.

She washed her hands after taking care of business, and her eyes fell to his soaking wet suit that lay on the striated marble flooring of the bathroom. The guns lay where they had slid to a stop. She didn't want to touch those. He'd warned her before about touching the weapons so she decided to leave them but frowned at his wet suit. She crossed the bathroom to the closet and took out a bath sheet and spread it on the floor.

She picked up the pieces of his suit and dropped them one by one onto the towel. She wrapped them into a ball so it wouldn't drip and shrugged on her silky robe. She picked it up and snuck out of the bedroom trying not to disturb Smith. Delilah walked down the stairs and across the foyer, taking the short route to the laundry room. The door was open and Mrs. Marten, the housekeeper, was working on a load of laundry. She was an older woman with a pixie cut to her gray hair.

"Hello, Ms. Laughlin," Mrs. Marten said. "I hope you're feeling better."

"I am, thank you." Delilah looked at the bundle in her arms then back and said, "This is Mr. Lowery's suit, can you have it dry cleaned? He's gotten it really wet."

"Of course." She reached for the bundle and took it from Delilah. Delilah turned to go and Mrs. Marten said, "Ms. Laughlin." Delilah stopped and turned back as she continued, "I was checking pockets for the laundry, and I found this in Mr. Lowery's jeans. Would you mind giving it to him?" She took the small piece of folded paper from a shelf and passed it to Delilah.

Delilah smiled and left the room. She needed a drink, deciding against a glass of wine until she could talk with a doctor and walked into the kitchen. She moved efficiently through the large kitchen for the glass and the temperate water before she stopped next to her purse on the kitchen bar. She took a sip of water and set the glass down then unfolded the piece of paper.

She gasped and dropped it as if it had burned her.

Delilah stood staring at the cryptic message trying to think of what to do. She was probably the only person in the world who could read it. She was sure it was meant for her but it had been in Smith's jeans. She couldn't comprehend why or how it had gotten there. It didn't matter now. She reached into her purse and took out her cell. She called her attorney first.

"Eric," she said when he answered his cell. "I need you to set up an appointment with the FBI to come by the apartment in a few hours. I want you here as well." She breathed and continued, "Make sure Assistant Director Patten is with them. It concerns the senator's case and my sister's. I've come across some evidence."

"Of course, Ms. Laughlin," he said, "I'll text you with the time."

"Thank you," she said as her thoughts drifted back to the paper in front of her. She told Eric to work up an agreement with very specific wording. She knew she could fix the FBI's problem with Smith as she stared at the paper. She ended the call with her attorney and pressed Smith's cell number. He answered on the third ring so she knew she'd waken him up. "You better get dressed, babe, your old boss is coming."

"Why don't you come help me?" he asked seductively from the floor above.

She smiled and said, "I'll be right there." She hung up sliding the phone into her robe pocket along with the piece of paper.

CHAPTER 27

Delilah stood staring out at the New York nighttime skyline, watching lights of all varieties flicker and dance in the darkness. She saw in the glass reflection as the FBI entered the apartment living room. She was wearing a crisp white button up long sleeve shirt and a brand new pair of jeans that hugged her curves in all the right ways with mahogany woven leather riding boots. She knew the night was young and if the FBI went for it, she was going to have to leave the warmth and security of the apartment.

The men settled around the living room and Delilah turned and stepped close to Smith as Eric said, "Thank you for coming this evening. As you know, Ms. Laughlin wishes to assist the FBI in every way possible. She has just come across information that might be valuable to the investigation."

"Pass it over," the A.D. said.

"My client wishes to discuss the possibility of reinstating Mr. Lowery to his previous position with a transfer of his duty station to the New York field office."

"That's coercion," the A.D. warned.

"Delilah, what are you doing?" Smith asked in a grave tone. He stood and took her hand roughly. He pulled her into the kitchen and asked again, "What are you doing?"

"I can get your job back," she hissed, facing him as she yanked her hand free.

"I don't want or need you to get it back for me. It's my job!" He pointed towards the living room and said sternly, "You're fucking with evidence! You can get arrested. You're impeding a federal investigation!" He offered her his hand and demanded, "Give me the evidence. Right now, no arguing!"

"But," she whispered. Tears sprang to her eyes. She'd only wanted to help.

"Now, Delilah, before things get too messed up to fix." He gestured for her to give him the piece of paper.

Reluctantly, Delilah pulled the paper from her jeans pocket, and handed it to him.

"Good," Smith said. He pulled her into an embrace. His warm lips pressed to her temple, kissing her before he whispered, "I appreciate what you're trying to do. This is the right way." Smith took her hand, and they walked back into the living room. "Sorry for the interruption. Sir, here is the evidence Ms. Laughlin found."

The A.D. reached for the scrap of paper. "Just like that? No argument or request for anything, Mr. Lowery?"

Delilah stood by Smith's side. She knew he was right. He was doing the ethical thing and she loved him for it.

"No, Sir. That's evidence in the investigation. It needs to be with the right people."

"Ms. Laughlin wants you reinstated. Is that what you want too?"

"I'd love my job back," Smith admitted. "It's what I've spent my life doing but I'm not going to be away from Delilah. She's my priority now."

"I can appreciate that, Special Agent Lowery. Family is the most important thing." He looked at Smith and said, "You can work in the New York office." His smile but it didn't reach his dark eyes as he said, "I think you'd do well in the cold case division."

"I'd be happy to help in any way I can," Smith said sincerely.

Delilah nodded to her attorney. He pulled out two documents from his briefcase and said, "One is for you, Assistant Director and one is for our records. This is a document agreeing to the terms we've settled upon for Special Agent Lowery's reinstatement. Please sign."

The A.D. read the document and signed them quickly putting to rest any doubts about Smith's future.

Delilah couldn't help but smile. She had reasoned out it came to be in Smith's possession. It was only logical. "Michael left it during the assault. It was found in the laundry."

"How the hell am I supposed to read this?" the A.D. asked as he looked over the small scrap of paper. It read 12130100HTCRLE25. He looked at the other agents and said, "We'll need to get it run through the computers at Quantico. See if they can make some sense of it."

"Actually," Delilah offered, "I can read it. It's an old code from high school. We used it to pass notes without anyone being able to decipher them. The first four digits are the date, the second set references the time and the last series is where to meet."

"He must have known you'd contact us," the A.D. pondered.

"Possibly," Smith said, "Michael wants to finish this in a public arena. He wants others to see and what better audience than the FBI?"

A.D. Patten checked his watch. "OK," he looked up to Delilah to check. "So he wants to meet you at one in the morning, is that right?"

"Yes," she confirmed.

"Where's the location?"

"My sister's grave at Hill Top Cemetery. Row E, plot 25." Smith firmed his grip on her hand as he sat on the arm of the couch, their fingers interlaced as she stood beside him. "It'll take about two hours to drive there."

"Why not fly?" the A.D. asked.

"It's a small town. I don't know where you'd land," she said with a shrug.

"We'll figure it out. Let's go," he said to his agents and stood.

Smith stood as well and Delilah stepped forward. He asked, "Where are you going?"

"With you."

"You can't. You might get hurt."

"I know exactly where the grave is in the cemetery." She looked at him lovingly. "Plus, I'm the bait." She squeezed his hand and muttered, "I'm always the bait in that little fucking town." She dropped his hand and took up her heavy herringbone pea coat from the far end of the couch. Smith took it from her and held it as she slipped into it.

"We'll contact the local authorities once we're in the air," the A.D. said as they moved through the apartment. He turned back and said, "Special Agent Lowery, Ms. Laughlin, we'll meet you at the field office in twenty five." Delilah thought that'd be enough time to get to the office. "We'll get everyone assembled and get moving to the location."

Armstrong moved into the foyer with them. "I'll drive us to the field office," he advised. He glanced at Smith with a hard look and declared, "I'm going too." Smith nodded.

Delilah watched Smith intently during the flight to Connecticut. She could see him in the flashing navigation lights of the helicopter. His chiseled jaw was set, creating a hard line in the flickering shadows. He was armed with his service weapon which had been given back plus at least one from the apartment, she knew. He wore a black bullet proof vest with bright yellow letting identifying him as FBI under his standard issue jacket. He insisted on her wearing a vest as well under her winter coat though she kept telling him Michael liked knives, he wasn't going to shoot her.

"Humor me," Smith said flatly.

"Fine," she grumbled a second before he pulled the vest down over her head, tightening the Velcro around her chest. He helped her with the coat before they left the field office.

It was a surreal feeling to be back in the small town as the helicopter landed in the high school parking lot. Smith reached for her hand and she grabbed it, holding on tightly to circumvent all of the fear and panic that was rising within her. She glanced over her shoulder towards the baseball field, and Smith followed her gaze.

"Never going to happen again," he said as they walked quickly to meet the local sheriff.

The A.D. and the other agents were talking with the local authorities when Smith and Delilah walked to them. No introductions were made but the sheriff looked quizzically at Delilah and asked, "You're that Laughlin girl, aren't you?" She nodded. "Yeah, it's been a few years but I still remember you. All grown up now." She didn't know if his remembering was a good or bad thing. "Follow me," the sheriff said.

He showed them to a few vehicles that deputies drove. Smith and Delilah crawled in the back of an SUV with Armstrong. "To the graveyard," Smith told the man.

Delilah stared out the window watching the small town fly by. The little community rimmed the southern edge of a ravine with the high school on one side and the graveyard nearly on the other. The caravan of vehicles turned left at the flashing red light that hung solemnly in the lone intersection. She looked for things that had changed. Some things remained the same but others were worn down by marching time. Change wasn't always for the better.

The deputy veered right and drove up a steep hill that twisted back to the left on a single lane road which ran deep through the woods. It had been so long since she'd come back to see her sister. Delilah had always been wary of the small town, of its people who sheltered and protected the man who'd hurt her so badly in so many ways. The vehicle slowed for the gated entrance. It was a tall iron fence with the name of the cemetery intricately laced above the entrance that hung open. Hill Top, so aptly named sitting above the town. During the day, Delilah knew you could see through the woods across the ravine to the school and the practice fields. She could never understand why her parents would bury Rachel there, where she could eternally view the place of her own demise. The vehicles pulled to the side of the dirt road and parked. Smith got out first and surveyed the area. It was pitch dark, save the lights from the vehicles.

"It's over here," Delilah said, exiting the SUV behind Smith.

She began to walk with Smith at her side. She didn't need a flashlight to walk the rows of gravestones. What Michael had labeled in the note as E25 Delilah knew as her sister's grave. She walked right to it and knelt in front of the stone. It didn't matter that it was too dark to read the inscription, she knew it by heart. 'Loving daughter and sister, Rachel Laughlin, Taken from us much too young'. She pressed her fingers into the cold, carved words. Rachel had saved her, had given her life for Delilah. There was no greater love than that. Tears rimmed her eyes. She would try harder to make the sacrifice meaningful.

The darkness was suddenly illuminated by a bright orange glow. Delilah lifted her head to see the tree line burning as flashes of fire seared up through the spindly winter trees. She stood quickly as her heart raced. She might have stopped taking her anxiety meds just a little too soon.

The shadow of a man ran away from the flames. Smith pointed and shouted, "There! He's over there!" He took a step away then stopped and turned back for Delilah, asking, "Will you be safe here?"

"I'll stay with her," Armstrong said.

Smith nodded and took off running towards the other agents and the fiery shadows.

Delilah watched Smith disappear into the obscurity and smoke.

Armstrong stepped close as Delilah stood in front of her sister's grave. She reached for the grave, something to hold onto as her manicured nails scrapped the cold stone. Behind them a voice said, "I thought it appropriate she be with us one more time."

Delilah spun around to face Michael. He was clean shaven, wearing the same military jacket he'd had on in Amsterdam. She took an instinctive step back and reached into her jacket pocket for her phone.

"Not so fast," Armstrong said, gripping her upper arm. It was like a vice and she winced in pain.

"What the fuck?" she snapped at Armstrong as he forced her a step closer to Michael. "What are you doing?" she demanded of him as she pressed the redial button on her phone.

"Do you have any idea how hard it is to get her alone?" he asked Michael. "This is the hardest thing you've ever asked me to do! Twenty-two countries in two years! Multiple times! She's always on the go, constantly surrounded!"

"I think you did fine, cousin," Michael said.

Delilah's spirit deflated. At least she knew why Armstrong had betrayed her. She hoped Smith had answered the call. She was sure he was the last person she'd called. When she thought it was enough time for Smith to have answered she said loudly, over the crackle of the flames, "Michael, you and Armstrong are cousins? I don't remember him living around here."

Michael looked to Armstrong, "She was never very smart with real world things. Cousins don't always live in the same town, DeDe. Our mothers are sisters. His family's been very helpful over the years."

She pulled on her arm, testing Armstrong but he held her too tightly.

"You wanted her," Armstrong said, pushing her towards Michael, "Here she is."

"MICHAEL! ARMSTRONG!" Smith shouted, he and Martinez raced between the cemetery rows, guns drawn.

Michael grabbed the back of her coat as Armstrong tried to grab her arm again. Each man wanted to use her as a shield. Delilah could only think of one thing - limp - and dropped to the ground, pulling her body free from the coat each man tugged on. Her knees hit the cold ground, and she scrambled away on all fours.

Gunfire started and she threw herself behind a gravestone, drawing her knees up to her chest and clamping her hands over her ears. It was intensely loud. The sound vibrated through her body. She watched Armstrong fall to the ground, his chest bubbling with dark blood. It turned her stomach and she swallowed hard then gasped as a hand grabbed her hair.

Michael pulled her to her feet roughly then back towards Armstrong's body. She fought against him, struggling to get free of his grip. Michael punched her in the kidney, just beneath the vest. A wave of nausea rolled over her and her legs disappeared. Michael moved his arm around her neck, his other gripped around her waist as the blade of the knife glinted in the firelight. She heard the distant screams of the fire engines responding.

She pushed against his arm again as hard as she could. No more cuts, no more bruises, no more scars. His jacket sleeve shifted upward with their fight. She repeated the mantra over and over. She saw Martinez and Smith facing her. Their weapons aimed at her, at Michael. In the flames she saw the shadows of the other men rushing back. Her eyes went to Smith, longing for his arms, for the safety he offered. He was shouting orders to Michael but his voice sounded hollow, distant.

Michael's hand came around her again, skin exposed as he fought to keep her in place, to keep her as a shield. He was shouting over her shoulder. Words of evil and distain spewed from him. She pressed against his arm pushing it away as hard as she could, giving her just a little space before she leaned forward and bit his wrist.

Delilah tasted the sweaty salt of his skin and it sickened her. Her teeth cinched down and he screamed behind her. She felt him release the pressure of his hold for a just a second and she fell to her knees trying to make herself small. Her hands clamped to her ears as bullets flew above her.

She was panting. Her heart pounded with fear and adrenaline. She saw Smith's feet as he crossed to her. He grabbed her arm, and pulled her up and back with him as his gun trained on the two lifeless forms. "You're safe," Smith whispered, and Delilah collapsed into his arms.

Martinez stepped close to Michael and Armstrong pushing their weapons away with the toe of his shoe. He bent and checked for a pulse. He looked up and shook his head confirming neither had one. Delilah looked at the men from the safety of Smith's arms. She exhaled with relief. The worry and fear died with Michael.

CHAPTER 28

Delilah's burden shifted and she woke instantly with a groan as the baby moved again, making her uncomfortable. She glanced at the clock, three thirty-three. The room was cloaked in darkness. She could hear Smith's deep, rhythmic breathing beside her. She turned slowly onto her side and pushed herself up to sitting. She knew her time was coming soon. The baby had shifted over the last two weeks, lowering himself, pressing his tiny body against her bladder so she had to pee every few minutes. She stood and waddled to the bathroom. She had another two weeks to go. Those would be two very long weeks, she was sure.

They'd managed to accomplish a great deal. The baby's room was completed. It had been painted a soft yellow with white trim. The artist they had hired had painted farm animals like a chair rail across the walls. Even with the baby's room ready, she and Smith had prepped their bedroom for the baby to stay with them initially. She wanted Junior next to her for the first few weeks. For now, a bassinet sat empty near her side of the bed. They thought it best while there would be midnight and three am feedings.

She returned to the dark bedroom and sat on the edge of the bed. Her hands ran over her expanded belly. He was active, busy moving around inside of her. Delilah glanced at Smith. He was still sleeping, completely unaware his son was keeping her awake. She smiled, a son. Their first born. The doctor had chastised her and let the secret slip but she hadn't. Delilah had managed to keep the baby's gender from Smith. She wanted him to have a surprise.

She stood from the bed and walked ungracefully out of the

room. The apartment was quiet as everyone slept. She waddled into the kitchen barefoot, and made herself a snack. Food wasn't an issue anymore. If she wanted something to eat, she'd have it. She didn't even balk at the scale. She hadn't gained too much weight, relatively. How she took care of herself reflected how she was going to take care of the baby once he was born. She was going to do a good job, she was sure of it. Smith would be with her and together they would do a good job, be great parents. She poured herself a bowl of Fruit Loops and sat in the shadows eating.

"You doing okay?" Smith asked, walking into the kitchen.

"I'm fine. Just hungry," Delilah said as she scooped the cereal.

He found a bowl in the cabinet and sat down beside her. He poured himself some cereal as well and added milk. He ate along with her and finished first.

She smiled as a dribble of milk slipped from Smith's mouth. She leaned close and wiped it away with her thumb. "I love you," she said quietly with a smile.

Smith pulled her out of her chair and into his lap. "I love you too," he said, nuzzling into her neck. She laughed as he tickled her and she slid her hands over his shoulders. She shifted and straddled his lap. "One of the guys at work," he said, "told me sex is good for you." Delilah looked at him suspiciously. Smith laughed as his hands fell to her hips. "Not you personally but pregnant women. Apparently, semen helps to soften your," he closed his eyes and she watched him think for a moment, "cervix." He looked at her and smiled charmingly. "I'm here to help you."

She shook her head and looked him disapprovingly. "Sex fiend," she said with a seductive tone. She lifted slightly and swayed her hips against his growing erection. "I don't know if I'm coordinated enough to rock your world."

He wiggled his eyebrows. "Blow my mind?" His fingertips massaged her thighs, dragging them slowly upward beneath her silky gown. "I can help," he murmured as he leaned into her neck and pressed his lips to her skin.

A shiver ran through her. He slipped the strap of her nightgown from her shoulder and leaned down to her breast. She moaned in pleasure. His tongue rolled her nipple, hardening it into a point as he sucked on it. She felt his attention all the way to her core. She held his head closer and closed her eyes as carnal indulgence washed over her. His hand slipped between her legs and circled her clit, igniting her desires. His mouth found hers again as he shifted his boxer briefs and pushed his thick erection into her sex.

She groaned as he filled her. Her tongue filled his warm, wet mouth and she grabbed the back of his chair to steady herself as she rocked slowly, steadily against him. His hands ran across her back, massaging her soft skin as her hips pushed and pulled on his thick length. She felt her body quicken as her muscles tightened and relaxed, pushing them closer to ecstasy. Her orgasm seized her and she cried out as her body tightened around his cock. He grabbed her hips and pumped himself over and over until he growled and poured into her.

"Dear God, woman!" he exclaimed then murmured into her neck. "I don't think I'm ever going to get over you."

Delilah smiled as she sat on her husband's lap, his cock filling her sex as his child filled her belly. "Me neither," she said quietly.

"I don't want you to."

"Anything you want to do tonight?" Smith asked as they pulled up to her building.

"I think we should skydive tonight, go horseback riding or tango in the moonlight." She laughed as Smith smirked. She thought for a moment and said, "Sushi. Let's go for sushi." The more she thought about it, the better the idea became.

He frowned and reminded her, "You're not supposed to eat raw fish."

She stuck out her tongue then smiled. Brody opened her door so she leaned to Smith and kissed him passionately. "Thank you for this morning," she whispered. "Once won't hurt." There was another quick kiss. "Baby wants sushi." She turned from him, and took Brody's extended hand.

He helped her from the Mercedes and Smith called out, making her stop and look back, "Your dress is pretty, but I like your flats even more." She grimaced as he commented on her footwear. She turned back, purposely ignoring him. She walked into the building as gracefully as she could manage, letting her belly lead the way.

Delilah was answering an email from Johan concerning the Russian stores. The plans had come back from the architect and were waiting for her approval. The design was similar to the store in Amsterdam with the same materials being used in the construction. She was giving him the approval to move forward with an initial budget of twenty million, ten per store when Shannon knocked and entered with her hands full.

"If you have time I thought we could go over next week's schedule and figure out your leave schedule. How are you feeling?"

Delilah glanced to the side as Shannon set a porcelain plate on her desk and pushed it close. Delilah pressed a hand against her stomach. "I'm alright," she said, though she wasn't feeling great. She felt a little sick to her stomach.

"A working lunch," Shannon said with a smile. She set her own plate to the side then walked across the room to the refrigerator behind the bar, in the kitchen area of Delilah's office. Delilah watched her grab two soda. Shannon set them on the desk and waited a moment longer for Delilah to finish.

Delilah smelled the food and was instantly distracted. She pressed the send button on her email, giving approval and turned for the plate. "Thanks, Shannon," Delilah said as she sipped the soda and pulled the plate closer. "Tell me about next week."

Shannon shifted her iPad and balanced the plate as she swallowed a lobster ravioli.

Delilah murmured in pleasure with the taste of the raviolis. "Everything tastes so freaking good." She smiled and ate.

Shannon listed several appointments which were on the schedule and said, "HR is going to discuss the hiring freeze."

Delilah looked up. "Why?"

"They want to hire more people for a few of the US stores."

"They'll have to justify it. Make sure they run the numbers through accounting before the meeting."

"Will do. What about your leave? Did you want to take a week off before the due date?"

"Why would I do that?" Delilah asked, and pressed her hand against her stomach again. It rolled uneasily then settled. "Ah, I think that was too spicy." Maybe sushi later wasn't a good idea.

Shannon looked at her own plate then back. "Sorry, I thought it was fine." She refocused, "To finish getting ready, to rest, relax?"

Delilah considered for a moment than shook her head. "No, I think we're set."

"How long after the baby's born before you want to start working again?"

"I think I'll take a week at home then we'll see how I feel."

"Just a week?" Shannon asked skeptically. She stared at Delilah and said, "My sister took months off when she had her baby."

"I don't need months."

"You'll need more than a week. If you have a C-section, you'll have to rest for ten days. If it's a traditional birth you're still going to need time."

"Fine, take me off the schedule for two weeks then we'll revisit my timeframe to see how the baby and I are doing. I can always check in or work from home. Being the boss has its perks." She smiled and glanced at Shannon's hand. Her heart leapt. "OH MY GOD!" Delilah screamed and jumped. She crossed around her desk.

Shannon jumped from her chair as well, "What! What is it?"

Delilah grabbed her hand and stared at the chunk of white stone which was beautifully set in white gold. "When did he give you this?!?"

Shannon smiled and it warmed Delilah's heart. "Brody gave it to me last night."

"I'm so happy for you both!" Delilah said as she hugged

Shannon. "If you need anything, tell me!"

Shannon's bright smile continued. "Thank you! We're just enjoying the moment, happy being engaged."

Delilah's smile matched Shannon's and she exclaimed, "This is wonderful news. We should celebrate." Delilah thought for a moment then said, "Ice cream!"

"There are a few pints in the freezer." Delilah waddled away from Shannon. "I'll get 'em," Shannon offered.

"No, it's okay," Delilah said as she opened the freezer section of the refrigerator and took out two pints. She found two spoons in one of the drawers and waddled back towards Shannon. "I hope strawberry's okay." Delilah handed one of the pints and a spoon to Shannon. Delilah pulled the lid from her own. The strawberry melted in her mouth and she licked the spoon. Food was just so good. A gush of water splashed between her feet and Delilah jumped back a step. "Holy shit! What was that?" Delilah asked, her eyes flickering between a startled Shannon and the pool of water on the floor.

"Your fucking water!" Shannon dropped the pint of ice cream to the floor. Delilah saw the panic rise in Shannon's expression. "Your fucking water broke!" she exclaimed.

"What do I do?" Delilah asked, reflecting the panic.

"I don't know!" Shannon shouted.

"Shit! It won't stop!" The drizzle of liquid continued unmitigated from between her legs.

"Are you having contractions? Are you in pain?" Shannon asked quickly.

"No," Delilah shrugged. "I feel alright." She ignored the water and walked to her desk. She dropped the pint and spoon to the desktop. "My due date's two weeks away. This isn't supposed to be happening." She grabbed her phone and called Smith.

He answered on the second ring, "What's up, baby?"

"Exactly!" Delilah said her voice raspy, rising with panic. "The baby! My water's broken."

"Oh shit!" Smith exclaimed. "OK, OK, how far apart are you contractions?"

"I'm not having any," Delilah said just a moment before the first wave of pain rolled over her.

She bent over the desk and Shannon took the phone from her. "She's having a contraction!" Shannon shouted, fear ringing through her voice. "I'm taking her to the hospital. I'll call the doctor on the way. Get there fast. We'll meet you." She hung up before Smith could respond.

Delilah stood straight. A light layer of perspiration covered her body giving her an instant chill in the air conditioning. "I'm early. You're right. I need to go." She looked to the floor again. The water was still drizzling down her bare legs. Delilah walked away from a panicked Shannon to her private bathroom. She squatted carefully down and looked in the cabinet. She was looking for a box of pads. She didn't wear them often, preferring tampons, and it had been months since she had use of those. She found a package of pads and put one on. She couldn't walk through the lobby leaking water everywhere. Delilah left the bathroom and found Brody in her office. Shannon was standing next to him, her face agonized with worry. She held Delilah's sweater and purse in her hands. "We can go now," Delilah said as she crossed to them.

Brody took the sweater from Shannon and helped Delilah put it on. He grabbed the office door and held it open for the women.

Shannon spoke quickly to the receptionist, "We're going to the hospital. Call all remaining appointments and cancel them. I'll reschedule at a later point." Delilah watched her finally breathe as Shannon inhaled deeply and said again as if to confirm to herself, "We're going to the hospital."

Delilah stepped into the elevator as Shannon jogged in her heels to catch up. As soon as she was in the elevator Brody allowed the doors to close and it whisked them to the lobby.

"Mr. Lowery's going to meet us? Or do I need to stop and pick him up?" Brody asked as he led the way through the lobby to the waiting Mercedes.

"He's meeting us," Shannon said. She dug her phone out of her purse and called the doctor's office.

"Put it on speaker," Delilah said as she crawled across the rear seat of the sedan to make room for Shannon.

Shannon nodded and pressed the button. "Yes, I have Mrs. Lowery with me. Her water has broken."

"How long ago?" a feminine voice asked.

Shannon looked at the watch Delilah had given her and said with a shrug, "Fifteen, maybe twenty minutes ago. What do you want us to do?"

The nurse said, "OK, bring her to the hospital and get checked into the maternity ward. I'll call Doctor Walker and let her know. Don't rush, these things take time."

Shannon hung up and looked to Delilah. "Are you feeling alright? You don't look well."

Delilah hunched forward and retched. Bits of vomit splashed across her flats. She gasped, "Oh shit!" She groaned and leaned back. "I'm so sorry, Brody."

"No problem, ma'am. It'll clean."

"Shannon, I think I'm going to vomit again." Delilah wiped her mouth with the back of her hand.

Shannon dug through her purse frantically looking for anything helpful. In the front Brody calmly reached over and grabbed a plastic bag from the passenger seat floorboard. He tipped it upside down in the passenger seat and dumped out his lunch then passed it back as he drove. Delilah grabbed it from him and retched again, the bag catching the contents.

She leaned back into the seat and closed her eyes. Her throat and nose burned. Her stomach rolled but she didn't heave. Shannon took the bag from her and set it aside. Delilah pressed her hands against her belly as her eyes watered. Pain seized her and she bent over, pressing a hand to her stomach while she dug at the car window with the other. Delilah gasped for breath and screamed, "OW, FUCK! FUCK ME!"

"That's kind of what got you in this trouble," Shannon smirked.

Delilah glared at her, finding no humor. Tears streamed down her face as the car burst forward from a pocket of traffic. She could hardly catch her breath and looked to Shannon. Terror was all over her face like bad makeup, frightening Delilah.

The pain washed away leaving Delilah panting as she leaned back against the leather seat. She closed her eyes and tried to catch her breath. She couldn't believe how fast Brody was driving but it was taking forever to get to the hospital.

Her phone rang and Shannon answered it on speaker. She didn't have a chance to speak as Smith shouted, "I'm here! Where are you?"

"Sir," Shannon said, "we're not there yet. Traffic's a bitch." She looked at Brody and asked, "How long?"

"Ten minutes max," he said.

Delilah panted and wiped the tears from her face. She gulped for a big breath and exhaled slowly. She nodded to Shannon, she felt better. The pain had eased. Even the burning in her throat lessened.

"You doing alright, babe?" Smith asked through the phone.

"Yep," Delilah said as she breathed heavily. "I'm definitely in labor. This isn't a false alarm."

"I didn't think it was when you said your water broke." He inhaled loudly so she heard over the phone. "I'm going to tell the registration office you're coming. Maybe I can check you in faster. I'm at the main entrance."

"OK," Brody said over his shoulder. "Give us approximately seven minutes, Sir."

"Delilah, are you having contractions?" Smith asked.

Shannon answered, "Yes, she is." She glanced at her watch again. "They're about ten," she shrugged, "minutes apart."

"I'll tell registration. Delilah," he said.

"Yes?"

"Love you!"

She smiled as his words warmed her. "Love you too."

Brody timed the hospital trip to the minute as they arrived seven minutes later. He stopped the sedan in the valet parking waiting area and got out to open Delilah's door. Shannon jumped from the vehicle before Delilah could shift her body in the rear seat.

Brody grabbed her beneath her arms and lifted, helping her out of the car. "I've got you, ma'am. Let's just get you out of the car." He pulled her from the interior, and gave her a moment to get her feet beneath her.

Delilah smiled and said, "Thank you, Brody."

Smith rushed from the building as Delilah took a step around the car. "There you are!" he said with deep relief. He smiled crookedly and she melted. He took her face in his hands and kissed her deeply.

When he pulled back she said, "I've been throwing up."

Smith laughed and wrapped his arm around her back. "I thought you tasted different." He smiled brightly. "Let's get you inside."

Delilah sat on one of the plastic lobby couches as Smith talked with the registration nurse. He pointed at her and smiled. She could see his charming the woman. She gasped as the pain hit her again. It overwhelmed her once more and she grabbed the couch, bending over her swollen belly. She panted through the pain as Smith jogged back to her. He squatted in front of her and watched her endure the agony.

When it eased he asked, "OK?"

She nodded but was intensely worried how she would fare when the contractions would come closer together, when the pain would be more intense than what she was currently feeling as she was sure it would.

"Your wrist, please," the registration nurse said. Delilah lifted her arm and the woman hooked a few plastic wristlets around her small wrist. She looked as the woman spoke with Smith, "Go ahead and take her up to the maternity ward." She nodded to Delilah, "If you can't walk we'll get you a wheelchair." The older woman smiled briefly to reassure her.

"No, I think I can walk."

Smith lifted her under her arms from the couch and let her get her balance before they walked slowly hand in hand towards the elevator bank. Brody jogged ahead and pressed the button. It opened just a moment before Delilah arrived so she continued without stopping, waddling directly into the elevator. Smith held her hand, his thumb caressing her sensitive skin as they rode upward. The elevator pinged, and Delilah stepped out. The others followed but Shannon skipped around them and trotted to the nurse's station. Delilah watched her talk animatedly to one of the nurses, pointing to Delilah several times as they closed the distance.

The nurse nodded and smiled, welcoming Delilah and Smith. "Mr. and Mrs. Lowery, we're so happy to have you." She stepped from around the workstation and pointed to a door just down the hall. "I'm going to get you all set in our deluxe labor suite. I'll help you get comfortable. Doctor Walker will check in with you in just a little while. Please, follow me."

Delilah stopped midstride in the hall and stared at a closed door. There were muffled screams that brought shivers to her body. There was a span of silence, just long enough for a breath, before another scream filled the hall. Delilah felt faint. She knew in a few hours that would be her, screaming in agony.

Smith tugged her hand and got her walking again as he said seriously, "It'll be OK."

The small group followed the nurse into the suite. It was a large room, much larger than the one she had stayed in when she'd been shot. The traditional hospital bed was already in a raised position. The exterior wall was completely glass. Delilah could see the busy world, the New York skyline which surrounded the hospital.

"Can anyone see in?" she asked without thinking.

"No, it's reflective. Once the sun sets, I'll lower the curtains to ensure your privacy." The nurse walked and talked, "The bathroom's over there," she pointed to a door. She showed them a group of sofas and stuffed, comfortable looking chairs. "A waiting area for your friends and family, if they prefer to stay in the room during your labor. If not, there's another waiting area just along the hall." Delilah stopped in the middle of the room, not sure where to go first. The nurse pulled a cotton gown from a cabinet and said, "Your husband can help you change out of your clothes then I'll get you hooked up to the fetal monitor." Delilah nodded and stepped close to take the gown. "How far apart are your contractions?" the nurse asked.

Delilah took the gown from her and answered, "About ten minutes."

"OK, go ahead and change."

Smith led Delilah into the bathroom. Again, it was spacious with a walk-in shower enclosure. It had one glazed window which allowed the afternoon light to pour into the room but Smith flipped on the fluorescent overheads.

"Come on," he said, getting her attention. She turned back somewhat dazed and overwhelmed. He smiled. "Let's get you changed so you can pop this baby out already."

"Oh, so romantic and not funny at all," Delilah scolded with a smile, starting to feel more like herself. She stepped close and he helped her undress. Her cardigan came off first. He folded it and set it aside. "I think my clothes need to be cleaned," she said, remembering the vomiting mess she had left in the car.

"Don't worry about it. I'll have Shannon get you some fresh clothes anyway before you go home." He smiled again.

She could tell he was really excited. "You're happy, aren't you?" she asked.

He folded her into his arms and pressed a kiss to the top of her head. "I'm ecstatic." He caressed her again. "I'm so excited." He turned her around and unzipped her dress. He carefully lifted it over her head, leaving her in just her panties and bra as she turned back to him.

She kicked off her flats and said, "I don't want to see those again."

He laughed, heartily and masculine, making her feel gooey again. He frowned and asked, "Do you leave on the bra and panties?" She shrugged so he stepped to the door and opened it a crack. Spotting the nurse, he called out, "Do you want all of her clothes off?"

"Yes, Sir," Delilah heard in reply.

He closed the door and sauntered back. He took her in his

arms and nuzzled her neck. "She wants you naked but not for the same reasons I want you naked." He undid her bra as he held her close. He dropped the bra on the sweater and said, "God, you are so beautiful." He found the hospital gown. He gave it a shake and held it open as Delilah shoved her hands into each arm hole. She tied it in the front and examined herself in the mirror. She was pale, more than normal. Her eyes dropped to her bare feet.

"Ready?" Smith asked.

"Ready or not?" she replied with a hesitant smile.

Delilah had never felt so much pain. It was as if her body was tearing itself apart from the inside out. She vomited water again, which only added to the pain as her throat hurt from the acid since there was no food left on her stomach. Smith moved the plastic pink tub aside and reassured her, "You're doing great."

"It hurts," she whimpered and cried.

"Mrs. Lowery, you need to concentrate on breathing," the nurse said.

"Fuck you!" Delilah snapped. She cried out again as another contraction hit. She was sweating, tears streaming along her face. Smith tried to push her hair out of her face, off of her neck. Delilah knew she should have pulled her hair back hours ago. She couldn't remember the reason she hadn't.

"You're doing really well," he said. "I love you."

"Well, it hurts, Smith," she snapped. "It hurts a lot!" She cried again as another wave of pain rolled over her.

"Mrs. Lowery, you have to stop pushing!" the nurse said.

"I'M NOT!" Delilah screamed.

"Can we give her anything for the pain?" Smith asked.

"NO," Delilah shouted. "I don't want any meds."

"It's too late now," Doctor Walker said flatly. "She's too close."

Delilah gripped the bedrails determinedly. "I need to stand up," she declared. With one arm she pushed and with the other she pulled, trying to maneuver herself to stand. She needed to get out of the bed, sure moving around would ease the pain.

Everyone rushed Delilah at once.

"No," Smith told her. "You need to stay."

"Delilah, the baby's coming soon. Getting up isn't a good idea," Doctor Walker advised.

"I'll raise the bed some more," one of the nurses offered.

Smith tucked a few pillows behind her back, and it eased the pressure for just a moment. At that moment, when her body felt numb rather than in agonizing pain, she squeezed his hand and said, "I love you." He leaned forward and pressed a kiss to her sweaty forehead. He tried to shift her sweat-soaked cotton gown back up and over her shoulders, but it slipped again exposing her breasts. Delilah didn't care. Pain rolled over her again and she screamed, bending forward. Her stomach muscles wrung her inside out.

"Don't push yet," the doctor ordered.

"I'M NOT!" Delilah screamed. Her body was in control. It was pushing, twisting her into knots to get the child out. Her mind was playing catch-up. Her fear rose with the volume of her voice. Everything was going to change. Doubts and fears rushed her, swarming her mind like stinging wasps as she screamed again with the intense pain.

Doctor Walker pulled up a wheelie chair and sat between Delilah's spread legs. Smith grabbed her hand and pressed his other against her lower back, giving her leverage she needed. "You can do this," he said quietly beside her.

She nodded, her head lolled against his muscular chest. She could do it, she needed to. Millions, billions of women had, she could too.

"Time to push," the doctor ordered. "Big, deep breath on the next contraction."

She felt it coming like a tsunami's wave, rolling over her. She gasped, trying to breathe deeply. She held the air and pushed. She exhaled quickly and gasped for another breath as pain hit her. She pushed.

Again and again the pain hit her, torturing her with agony

before the pressure burst and the doctor said, "The head's out. Don't push yet." There was an eternal moment then, "One more good push, Delilah then the baby will be out. On the next contraction."

It hit Delilah before the doctor had finished speaking. She wasn't ready. She hadn't breathed but she gritted her teeth and pushed again. Pressure again released from her body like flood waters from a dam. There was a flurry of activity as Delilah leaned back into the pillows, gasping. The baby cried with its first breath and she sighed in relief. Doctor Walker lifted the little naked form up and over her depressed belly. She set the little thing against Delilah's chest and smiled. "Your son has arrived."

They were still attached mother and son. Delilah leaned to his patch of dark hair and whispered, "You're worth it." Smith took a picture as she looked up at him with a tired, weary smile. Smith came close and she pulled him tightly to her and the baby. "Welcome to our family," she whispered, "Aiden Fitzgerald Lowery." She looked at Aiden adoringly then back to Smith. He had seen through her cool façade. When others had failed, he understood the woman within. He loved her, encouraged her unconditionally. It was what she had always needed. What she had always wanted. They were a family. They were her family. "We've been waiting for you," she said assuredly.

MEET THE AUTHOR

Katherine McLellan

Katherine grew up in the rolling, green mountains of Vermont. She is an avid reader crediting her grandmother with giving her that first, life-altering romance novel during her teens. Life led her away from the home she holds dear to her heart, and she received a bachelor's degree in humanities from The Pennsylvania State University. As a military spouse with two young-adult children she has lived across both the United States and Europe. In addition to being well traveled, Katherine is a member of the Romance Writers of America and the Passion Ink Chapter. Her romance stories are set in fantastic locations with strong, feisty heroines and captivating heroes so get ready for some enthralling nights in bed with her stories!

Look for author information and current events on katherinemclellanromance.com

www.ingramcontent.com/pod-product-compliance
Lightning Source LLC
Chambersburg PA
CBHW031705170626
46808CB00005B/1624